Posthumous
Correspondence
(Vol. 1)

FROM THE SAME AUTHOR

The Discovery of the Austral Continent by a Flying Man
ISBN 978-1-61227-512-3

Posthumous Correspondence (3 vols.) ISBNs 978-61227-513-0; 514-7 & 515-4.

Posthumous Correspondence (Vol. 1)

by
Nicolas Restif de la Bretonne

Translated, annotated and introduced by
Brian Stableford

A Black Coat Press Book

Visit our website at www.blackcoatpress.com

ISBN 978-1-61227-513-0. First Printing. June 2016. Published by Black Coat Press, an imprint of Hollywood Comics.com, LLC, P.O. Box 17270, Encino, CA 91416. All rights reserved. Except for review purposes, no part of this book may be reproduced or transmitted in any form or by any means, electronic or mechanical, including photocopying, recording, or by any information storage and retrieval system, without permission in writing from the publisher. The stories and characters depicted in this novel are entirely fictional. Printed in the United States of America.

Introduction

Les Posthumes: Lettres reçues après la mort du mari par sa femme, qui le croit à Florence, par feu Cazotte [The Posthumous: Letters received after the death of a husband by his wife, who believes him to be in Florence, by the late Cazotte] was originally published in Paris by Duchène in 1802. It is here translated as *Posthumous Correspondence*, and attributed to its actual author, who was baptized Nicolas-Edmé Rétif (1734-1806) but styled himself, with satirical pretentiousness when he began his career as a professional writer "Restif de La Bretonne," La Bretonne being a field on a farm that his father had owned during his childhood. The joke of aping aristocratic formularization was no longer as funny when the Revolution had turned into the Terror, claiming among its victims more than one of his friends, including the writer, humorist and self-styled Illuminatus Jacques Cazotte (1719-1792), best known as the author of the fantasy novella *Le Diable amoureux* (1772; tr. as *The Devil in Love*).

The present translation is the second of four volumes, the first being a translation of *La Découverte australe par un homme-volant, ou Le Dédale français*, as *The Discovery of the Austral Continent by a Flying Man; or, The French Daedalus*, which was originally published in 1781, with a title-page claiming to have been published in Leipzig, but actually printed by "the widow Duschene," the mother of the publisher of *Les Posthumes*. That work too had not borne the author's "real" name; a pre-title page had announced it as the second in a series of the *Oeuvres posthumes de N******* [presumably Nicolas] and it posed as the work of the author ("Dulis") and editor ("T. Joly") who had allegedly been responsible for the first work in the seemingly-intended series, novel *La Malédiction paternelle, lettres sincères et véritables de N****** à ses parents, ses amis et ses maîtresses, avec les* *responses; recueilli et publié par Timothée Joly, son exécuteur testamentaire* [The Paternal Curse; Sincere and Veritable Letters by N****** to his parents, friends and mistresses, with the Responses, collected and published by Timothée Joly, the executor of his will], also allegedly published in Leipzig, but actually printed by the widow Duchesne.

No more books in that planned series were published, although the supplementary material to the text advertized several titles, two of which were ultimately written and published under Restif's usual signature. As well as the title novel, the four volumes containing *La Découverte australe* also included an assortment of non-fiction and fiction, whose nature and spirit confirmed the idea that "the posthumous works of N******" were intended to consist of the author's more eccentric and idiosyncratic items, some satirical and some merely peculiar, in contrast to the naturalistic and—at least in the author's view—moralistic works that would constitute his normal fare.

In fact, hardly anyone ever considered Restif's work, or the man himself, "normal." Although he was an amazingly prolific writer by the standards of his day, in a manner that implied obsession rather than efficient professionalism, he was always working in parallel on his long-planned masterpiece, an autobiography to be entitled or subtitled *Le Coeur humain dévoilé* [The Human Heart Laid Bare], which he advertized to himself and others as the most honest autobiography that had or ever would be written, not in the trivial sense of mere factual accuracy, but in the sense that it really would lay bear the hidden mechanisms of his own heart, and, in so doing, the mechanics of the human heart in general. In the meantime, he reprocessed its raw material into a number of other quasi-autobiographical items, with varying degrees of fictionalization and fantasization, all with the same pretention of laying bare the inner workings of the human soul. (The French word *coeur* is more ambiguous than its English equivalent.)

That was not, as it turned out, an entirely thankless task, but it did cause violent reactions from people who could not or did not want to recognize their own inner workings in Restif's often-unflattering account of human tendency. Perhaps he did generalize too much from a single instance, and imagine that some of his own idiosyncrasies were more commonplace than they were, but on the other hand, he did cut through certain layers of popular hypocrisy with surgical precision, and there really was an aspect of his uncomfortable honesty that was truer in general than the conventional literature of his day was prepared to admit.

From a distance of more than two centuries, it is not easy to see a clear dividing line between the idiosyncrasies of Restif's "normal" production and some of the works that even he considered, briefly, to be sufficiently bizarre to warrant separate classification as the "posthumous works of N******," but there was little doubt about *La Découverte australe*, a strikingly original work developed from the seeds of a daydream of his childhood, in which a young man named Victorin, who invents artificial wings in the early years of the 18th century, employs his acquired superpower to build a utopian community on an inaccessible mountain-top, in order to provide a suitable environment for the woman he loves obsessively but can never hope to obtain except by abduction, because she is too far above him in social status. Having created his mini-utopia (modeled on lines that Restif had already begun to sketch in a series of earnest reformist tracts), Victorin then moves it, in its entirety, to an island in the southern Pacific, part of an archipelago that replaces, in the imaginary geography of the story, the legendary Terra Australis for which James Cook had been sent by the British Admiralty to search, not long before it was written.

On the islands of the archipelago the winged explorer and his descendants find various legendary species, including patagons (giants), satyrs and centaurs, and many other human/animal hybrids of an allegedly similar sort, gathering them all gradually into their utopian confraternity, before the ultimate discovery of the superhuman megapatagons allow

7

them to learn the evolutionary and cosmogonic context into which the entire spectrum of strange species fits.

La Découverte australe, unlike anything Restif or anyone else had published before it, really was bizarre. It had been preceded by numerous extravagant fantasies written as satires and *contes philosophiques* inspired by the Enlightenment, which were equally or even more exotic, but none of them had ever done what Restif did in providing a theoretical account of the way the universe was structured and organized that could not only contain and explain everything known to exist, but all the novel's inventions as well. He was one of the few people fully to recognize the significance of the evolutionism and cosmogonic theory of Benoît de Maillet's *Telliamed*, the third edition of which, somewhat but not completely restored from the heavily censored first edition, had been published by the widow Duchesne's husband in 1755, and he was the only one to extrapolate its main conclusions extensively in both fiction and non-fiction.

Such an exercise can now be recognized, in a general sense, as a particularly ambitious kind of "speculative fiction" or "science fiction," but no such conceptual category existed at the time, and hindsight seems to modern readers to have disqualified *La Découverte australe* from full membership in the category, because subsequent developments in science have shown that Restif's cosmogonic and evolutionary theories are entirely false. That was not, however, obvious at the time, and however unlikely they seemed—they did, admittedly, seem very unlikely—they were nevertheless sufficiently plausible, in the absence of anything compelling rivals, to be capable of belief.

It seems that Restif, in common with many people blessed or cursed with an obsessive personality, really did talk himself into believing his theses once he had published polemical arguments in their favor. Perhaps he was reckless, and we can now say for sure that he was mistaken, but that should not deflect our attention from the recognition that *La Découverte australe* was a very considerable literary achievement, even though hardly anybody liked it at the time of its publication. The theory invented to underpin its fictitious devices really was an admirable feat of the speculative imagination, which became positively titanic as the author followed it obsessively, developing it not merely in a series of earnest essays, the earliest of which were appended to its text but, ultimately, in what was intended to be the most ambitious, fantastic and all-encompassing of all the exotic literary endeavors that had originally been intended for tongue-in-cheek representation as "the posthumous works of N******."

Les Posthumes, after a number of false starts, was eventually adapted in order to be that work, or a part of it, but the project that Restif eventually envisaged was never completed—partly because it was too difficult and partly because external circumstances defeated it—and the text as it exists is the wreckage of that defeat. In purely literary terms, the work, as published, is extremely unsatisfactory; it is rambling, prolix, frequently self-contradictory, sometimes incoherent, and riddled with errors. Quite simply, it is a mess—but within it, still strikingly visible in spite of its fragmentation and the partial loss of the relevant text, is the ultimate version of Restif's speculative cosmogony, and the graphic literary illustration of some of the consequences and corollaries of that thesis. It is also the archetypal, and by far the most extreme, example of the modern genre of superhero fiction—which must qualify, today, as an asset, although it would not always have appeared so.

The messiness of the extant text is not entirely accidental; although it developed largely by accident, the author deliberately chose to retain it and not to make the slightest attempt to correct it when he was finally able to set it in type—the fact that he is the only writer in literary history who typeset all his own works is essential to an understanding of the nature of the existing text, and of the fact that it exists at all. From the standpoint of today it might look like any other book, and the fact that very few people read the work when it was published and hardly anyone has read it since is merely par for the general course of literary history, but it would be a mistake to see *Les Posthumes* as simply four more of the hundred-and-eighty-plus volumes that Restif had already published in the attempt to make a living. He knew when he began to set the type that it would not make money, and that he was exploiting the good will of the widow Duchesne's son and the unnamed "associate" who paid for the printing because he was destitute, but he was desperate to get it into print at all costs, even in poor shape, for reasons that the text states explicitly. He knew that he was no longer capable of shaping it more elegantly and more coherently, and that if he did not publish it "posthumously" while he still had a little life left in him, nobody was going to do it for him after he was dead, so he did it, warts and all, laying bare its inner workings for anyone who cared to understand.

The introduction to the companion volume containing *The Discovery of the Austral Continent* contains an account of Restif's early life and career, as a printer and writer, up to the publication of *La Découverte australe*, which there is no point in reprinting in detail here. It is, however, worth recalling that one of his earliest exercises in converting his daydreams into literary work was a poem tentatively entitled *Les Douze mois ou Mes Douze travaux* [The Twelve Months, or My Twelve Labors], in which the protagonist, having done a favor for the king, is rewarded with a private plot of land enclosed by an unbreachable wall, containing a vast aviary and twelve beautiful young women, in which he lives as if in an Earthly Paradise—an escapist fantasy partly recapitulated in the image of the utopian enclave on the Inaccessible Mountain in *La Découverte australe*.

La Découverte australe was not a success at the time, as evidenced by the fact that Hortense, when she reads it in the course of *Les Posthumes*, remarks that it is "not as bad as it is said to be." It had, however, been directly preceded into print by Restif's most successful work to date, the short story collection *Les Contemporaines, ou Aventures des plus jolies femmes de l'Age présent* [Contemporaries: Adventures of the Prettiest Women of the Present Era] (1780), which set a pattern for many similar collections—forty-two volumes in all—although none of the later ones matched the huge sales of the first. He followed *La Découverte australe* with the last in his series of utopian tracts, which must have sold equally poorly, but then probably redeemed himself in the opinion of his publisher and his audience with the latest in the series of his quasi-autobiographical fictions, *La Dernière aventure d'un homme de quarante-cinq ans* [The Last Adventure of a Forty-five Year Old Man] (1783), which gave free rein to the erotic fantasies whose indulgence he thought of as a essential component laying the human soul bare, but which some of his readers thought mere pornography (in the pejorative sense rather than the neutral one he had intended when he had coined the word)—a mistake that did not hurt their sales at all.

La Paysanne pervertie [The Corrupted Peasant-Woman] (1784), a companion-piece to his earlier quasi-autobiographical novel *Le Paysan perverti ou Les Dangers de la ville* [The Corrupted Peasant; or, The Dangers of the City] (1775-76), was in the same vein, and was similarly successful. He did publish one more of the intended "Posthumous works of N******," albeit without that designation and without the fictitious editorial interference of Timothée Joly, as *Les Veillées du Marais, or Histoire du grand prince Oribeau, roi de Momminie, au pays d'Evinland, et de la vertueuse princesse Oribelle, de Lagenie; tirée des anciennes annales irlandaises et récemment translatée en français par Nichols Donneraill, du comté de Korke, descendant de l'auteur* [Evenings in the Marsh; or, The Story of the great Prince Oribeau of Evinland and the virtuous Princess Oribelle of Lagenie; taken from old Irish sources and recently translated into French by Nichols Donneraill of the county of Cork, a descendant of the author] (1785), and he also published the next of his quasi-autobiographical novels, *La Femme infidèle* [The Unfaithful Wife] (1786) under the pseudonym Maribert Courtenay, although that probably did not enable his estranged wife to feel any better about it if she read it.

Restif focused thereafter, at least for a while, on his potentially infinite series of short stories about the women of contemporary Paris, for which he did intensive research in soliciting anecdotes from various acquaintances, and in literary salons. It was at this time, early in 1787, that he became a regular, not to say a fixture, at one particular fashionable salon where he appears to have received an unusually warm welcome (his reputation and appearance did not endear him to many people), not only attending the weekly "open house" but also the more intimate secondary gathering—equally conventional in institutions of that sort—organized by its hostess, Fanny de Beauharnais (1737-1813).

Running true to form, Restif fell in love with Fanny, although the passion, also true to form, remained hopeless, Fanny being the mistress of the writer Claude Joseph Dorat (1734-1780), and later of Michel de Cubières (1752-1820), who sometimes signed himself Dorat-Cubières. The regular attendees when Restif joined the more select group included his friend Louis-Sébastien Mercier, the feminist actress Olympe de Gouges and the mathematician Jean-Sylvain Bailly as well as Jacques Cazotte. Fanny's nephew by marriage, Alexandre de Beauharnais, was married at the time to Joséphine Tascher de la Pagerie (1763-1814), who was later to marry Napoléon Bonaparte, in 1796, after Alexandre had been guillotined during the Terror.

Restif collected anecdotes for use in his collections in Fanny's salon, whose members were as willing to supply them as any group of hardened and well-informed gossips. He undoubtedly made his own contributions to the conversation, where ideas for stories of all kinds were, inevitably, routinely circulated, most of which came to nothing. Restif, however, more obsessive then most, began developing one of the ideas he broached: that of a husband who knows he is going to die, and who writes a series of letters to be delivered to his wife one another following his demise, in order to ease her mourning.

That idea was the seed of *Les Posthumes*, and its development can be tracked through the book as it changed direction and focus several times while Restif was writing it, probably more for his own amusement and that of the members of the salon to begin with, although he must always have had the possibility of eventual publication in mind. He wrote it, throughout 1787 and 1788, alongside two works that were intended for more immediate publication with clearly-defined professional intent: the third set of his exemplary short stories, *Les Parisiennes, ou XL caractères généraux pris sans les moeurs actuelles propre à servir à l'instruction des personnes du sexe, tirés des memoires du nouveau lycée des moeurs* [Parisian Women; or, Forty Typical Character Studies Taken from Present-Day Mores, Appropriate to Serve for the Instruction of the Female Sex, taken from the New School of Morals] (four volumes 1787); and *Les Nuits de Paris ou le Spectateur nocturne* [Parisian Nights; or, The Nocturnal Spectator] (twelve volumes 1788-89, subsequently further augmented), which became one of his most famous works.

Because it is based on raw material provided by his own nocturnal wandering after the last of his four daughters had found a place and his long-estranged wife had finally left him, some readers have been tempted to think of the latter text as non-fiction, although it is actually deeply imbued with wish-fulfillment fantasy, representing its protagonist, "the nocturnal spectator" as a kind of vigilante perpetually saving women from the kinds of sticky situations that women who go out by night in Paris are all-too-likely to encounter. The fact that the text contains lightly-disguised representations of some of Restif's friends, including "Le Chevalier Rubiscée" (an anagrammatic Michel de Cubières) encouraged some readers to see it as non-fiction, although it is really an eccentric *roman à clef.*

Both of those projects "overflowed" into the slowly-growing text of what was eventually to become *Les*

Posthumes, somewhat incongruously at times, following an increasingly marked trend by which Restif's projects tended to overlap, greatly encouraged by, if not an inevitable result of, the manner in which he drew upon his life for source material even in his most extravagant and exotic endeavors.

It is evident from the first few "letters from the tomb" that formed the first version of *Les Posthumes* that Restif's initial intention was to focus narrowly on the relationship between the letter-writer, Monsieur de Fontlhète ("font l'hète," though not, strictly speaking, French, would have been recognizable to a French speaker as an approximate equivalent of the English phrase "het up"—i.e., impassioned) and his beloved wife Hortense, analyzing its development by juxtaposing day-by-day accounts of the development of four years in their relationship, two past, one ostensibly present and one future, although the scheme is confused by the fact that the letters are "actually" being written some time ahead of their intended delivery date, thus confusing the "present" and the "future" in a manner that the author never did manage to sort out or clarify

At some point after his tentative beginning, however, the author apparently realized two things: firstly, that his initially-intended scheme was too complicated and confusing to be viable as a project; and secondly, that his format, vaguely planned in the image of the *Thousand-and-One Nights*, might benefit from a much closer resemblance, in the sense that Fontlhète, instead of devoting himself to an overcomplicated analytical remembrance of things past and anticipation of the future, could become a storyteller instead, not only possessed of a more interesting predicament that Scheherazade, but equipped with the same broad license to fantasize, in accordance with "the Galland method."

For that reason, therefore, Restif changed the direction of his self-indulgent whimsy, and began to develop the sequence of letters as a sequence of fantasies with the underlying subtext of trying to convince Hortense that death was not to be seen as a bad thing but rather an entrance into a wonderland of posthumous opportunity. Fontlhète does that by allegedly making contact with two discorporated souls who have remained closely united after death by virtue of the fact that they were accidentally slain on their wedding night at the moment of their first orgasm. The individuals in question are initially called Yfflasie and Clarendon, but at some stage in the writing process Restif decided to change the spelling of the latter name to Klarendon. He had the option, of course, when he finally typeset the work, of unifying the spelling, but he did not do that, or, at least, did not do it consistently, so both spellings persist in the original text, in an uneven pattern because the sections of the text were not written in the order in which they appear in the book. During the translation process I unified the spelling, preferring the C to the K, as translators and copy-editors routinely do when they come across such anomalies, but in this particular instance it might have been an error of judgment to do so, in that Restif's decision to leave both versions as he had originally written them must have been deliberate, and perhaps reasoned—but I shall leave further discussion of that matter until later.

The account of Yfflasie and Clarendon's adventures in the afterlife, as related mysteriously to Fontlhète, initially consist in meeting lots of famous dead people, discovering who they were in previous incarnations, and what has become of the recently-reincorporated in their new identities That formula enables a good deal of wry satire, which becomes increasingly self-indulgent as the author not only panders to his own political judgments and liking for salacious gossip but increasingly begins to give vent to his personal dislikes and hatreds, in ever-more bizarre fashion, as he develops the notion of careers in the afterlife. Their various employments permit Yfflasie and Clarendon to progress from early days as pastors of desires ultimately to become king and queen of the realm of the disembodied.

When that narrative sequence became too silly, Restif apparently had another change of heart, and abruptly, without bothering with any explanation, gave Fontlhète the wings that

Victorin had invented in *La Découverte australe*, thus enabling him to become a more active nocturnal vigilante than the *alter ego* featured in *Les Nuits de Paris*. Unlike Victorin, who used his wings almost exclusively for selfish purposes, Fontlhète makes definite moves in what was ultimately to become the typical career path of comic book superheroes, using his power of flight to oppose evil, and fight crime—not on the local scale preferred in the comic books but on the world stage, taking on evil tyrants and warmongers. That particular narrative thread, however, was soon sidelined, as Restif appears to have been struck by another idea: that of giving scope to some of his other childhood fantasies and importing other superpowers into the plot: to begin with, the power of exchanging identities by taking over other people's bodies with one's own soul.

It is possible that Restif had already developed that idea in a separate story—and, indeed, that he had written several variants of that story while trying to figure out the best way to account for the origin and development of the power in question. It appears that he simply dumped that other story into his plot, as the "Galland formula" allowed him to do and had he had presumably already done with a few of the brief anecdotes associated with the careers of the discorporate souls. Indeed, he dumped several different versions of the other story into his framework, perhaps with some vague intention of deciding later which one to settle on, or perhaps realizing that the 366-day frame with which he had saddled himself was going to require a lot more filling than he had initially imagined. At any rate, the amazing Duc Multipliandre made his entrance into the scheme, more than once, in association with conflicting accounts of his birth and the back-story of his superpower, and began narrating his adventures.

Multipliandre is a much more useful superhero than Fontlhète, for the simple reason that Fontlhète, being absolutely committed to Hortense, could not use any powers he acquired for the purpose that was, from Restif's viewpoint, the primary advantage of any superpower: the opportunity to lay women by the score, or by the thousand, even while remaining deeply committed to the moral ideal of true love. Multipliandre's adventures thus involve not only the acquisition of several more superpowers, including rejuvenating himself and others, and becoming invisible, but the recounting of a vast series of varied erotic adventures, some second-hand but many of them personal. He too finds his one true love, but she is perfectly willing to share him, and not overly worried about what his soul might be doing when he is in other bodies than the handsome one she loves.

Restif was not, however, a man to waste the more extravagant opportunities now offered to him by his framework. Multipliandre, as a superhero, was naturally going to set the world to rights as well as having a lot of super sex, but he was never going to stop there; having taken up where Fontlhète left off, he was always going to follow Victorin's example of boldly crossing the boundaries of the known would in order to discover the hypothetical world of Restif's cosmogonic and evolutionary theories. That he does—and far more extravagantly than Victorin's descendants. In doing so, he not only transformed the languidly-evolving story of the letters from the tomb, but Restif's attitude to it. It ceased to be a dilatory self-indulgent spinoff from his salon conversations, and became a kind of mission: the ultimate development of his personal vision and philosophy, far grander than anything he had been able to imagine doing before, and something exceedingly dear to the heart he had not yet laid bare in his long-gestating masterpiece, which still remained to be completed.

And then the world fell apart.

It is impossible to determine now exactly how far Restif had got in the untidy and disordered series of Fontlhète's letters when the Bastille was "stormed" on 14 July 1789, but the probability is that he had got all the way to the end of Multipliandre's adventures, as detailed in the published version, including his visions of the distant future and dealings with the "angels," and that it was a relatively straightforward continuation of the sequence, that then caused him to dream the early days of the Revolution, taking aboard some of Restif's personal experiences in much the same way that the nocturnal spectator took them aboard in later volumes of *Nuits de Paris*, as the two endeavors continued to overlap. Obviously, the last few letters, which cover the period from late 1789 to 1796 were added retrospectively, but the sequence of letters up to and including the description of the fall of the Bastille can almost certainly be regarded as a more-or-less continuous sequence written in dribs and drabs, alongside other work, between the spring of 1787 and July 1789. Then, necessarily, the endeavor came to an end, at least for a while.

Restif never stopped writing during the years of the Revolution and the Terror, even when he was on the brink of starvation, as he eventually was, nor did he stop publishing, although his productions necessarily slowed down, and were tightly focused. He published some other material, but his principal endeavors were the preparation of *Le Drame de la vie, contenant un homme tout entier* [The Drama of Life, containing an entire man] (dated 1793, when it was probably typeset, but it was not distributed for some time) and the early volumes of the work from which it was spun off, *Monsieur Nicolas, ou le Coeur human dévoilé* (1794). He also added new text to *Les Nuits de Paris* and continued his vast series of short stories with *Les Provinciales, ou Histoire des filles et femmes des provinces de France* [The Provincials; or, the Story of the Women of the French Provinces] (twelve volumes, 1795).

In 1796, when the Terror was over and the famine that had followed it began to ease, Restif went to work with more fervor than ever before. He had already put together a nonfictional account of his "physics"—his cosmogony and evolutionary theory—in the supplementary volumes of his autobiography, collectively entitled *La Philosophie de Monsieur Nicolas* (1796), and in the early months of the year he set out on another dramatization of them, taking up the plot of his early wish-fulfillment fantasy about a hero who acquires a private enclosure lavishly supplied with women in which to build his own private paradise, and enveloping it as a novel entitled *L'Enclos et les oiseaux* [The Enclosure and the Birds].

There is no way to be sure, but Restif probably intended this project to be a replacement for the disorganized mess of the manuscript containing Fontlhète's inconsequential and incoherent *Lettres du tombeau* [Letters from the Tomb], as he was then calling it. He translated many of the imaginative ideas from the manuscript into the new work, organizing them into a more coherent in an account of a superhero who indulges in the usual extensive gamut of sexual adventures before employing the secret of immortality to witness the entire future history of the Earth from the end of the eighteenth century until the death of the planet, when it is swallowed by the Sun. In an ideal world, this present translation would have been the second of three volumes, and would have been followed by *The Enclosure and the Birds*, confidently introduced as the boldest futuristic fantasy imagined prior to 1800, and probably still unrivaled in its scope and ambition. Alas, that was not to be.

Even before finishing the manuscript of *L'Enclos et les oiseaux* at the end of May 1895, Restif was evidently inspired to wonder whether, in fact, the other manuscript might not be salvageable, and publishable as one of a pair with the new work, in spite of its incoherencies—which could, in principle, be partly written off as eccentricities and perhaps partly smoothed over. A note added to the final pages of *Les Posthumes* suggests that the future histories set out in the two texts are deliberately famed to complement one another rather than duplicating information, so the final phases of *L'Enclos et les oiseaux* were probably written with that intention. After completing it, Restif then set out to prepare *Les Posthumes* for publication, but his first move in so doing was not to rewrite any of the existing text but to supplement it by adding a series of responses to Fontlhète's letters, supposedly written by Hortense, and interleaving those with the existing manuscript.

The net effect of that move, as the reader of this translation will quickly appreciate, was to add a further level of complication to a text that was already extremely muddled, especially in terms of its internal chronology, where the additions help to transform an existing confusion into complete chaos. Nor is it immediately obvious why the new text makes any substantial contribution at all to the story, although it is obvious that the author wanted to pay some tribute to the story's origins in Fanny de Beauharnais' salon by adding her (lightly disguised) and some of her guests into the weave of the narrative, and also to set up the eventual denouement.

Apart from adding the last batch of letters, it is not easy to determine exactly what alterations Restif made to the pre-existent manuscript in the 1796 version, but if appearances can be trusted, almost all of what he did consisted of dropping an additional series of paragraphs into the text at various points, whose net effect, once again, was to add a further layer of confusions and contradictions to a text that was by no means short of them.

It might have been the case that Restif made a conscious decision at that point not to try to sort out any of those contradictions, but to leave them all in place, as essential features of a text whose peculiarity had already exceeded all known bounds. On the other hand, he might simply have realized that *L'Enclos et les oiseaux* was not going to get into print any time soon, that the whole joint project was a catastrophe from the viewpoint of publication, and abandoned the revision half-done. On balance, the latter seems slightly more probable.

The reason why *L'Enclos et les oiseaux* was not going to be published imminently was that Restif could not scrape together the money to pay for its publication himself—as he had done for *La Philosophie de Monsieur Nicolas*—and could not persuade anyone else to help him. He must have realized then that if all the friends he had flattered in the new material added to *Les Posthumes* were not going to help him publish it while he was alive, they were certainly not going to do it after he was dead, and that if he could not find a way to get the two books containing his imaginative testament into print himself—however difficult that might be—they would be lost forever.

In the remainder of the 1790s, Restif only contrived to publish one new book: *L'Anti-Justine ou les délices de l'amour* [The Anti-Justine; or, The Delights of Amour] (1798), his ideological reply to the Marquis de Sade, intended to demonstrate by example that pornography did not have to be disgusting and depraved, but could be delightful and virtuous. To its publishers and most of its readers, however, it was probably just pornography, and the police certainly thought so when they seized the remaining copies in 1803 and banned it.

The economic and political corner was finally turned, for France, when Bonaparte overthrew the Directoire on 18 Brumaire (9 November) 1899 and was appointed First Consul. An appearance of stability returned, and, far more importantly, a wave of optimism unfurled. Restif was still broke, but the son of the widow Duchesne, his old publisher, was eager to get the business running at full tilt again, and part of his business plan—probably in response to Restif's persuasion—was a reissue of Restif's most successful works, supplemented by new volumes such as *Les Nouvelle contemporaines* (1802). How Restif persuaded him to add *Les Posthumes* and *L'Enclos et les oiseaux* to his program no one knows, perhaps by begging, perhaps by promising to do more commercial work in exchange, but most likely simply by finding someone willing to put in a subsidy—the "associate" to whom the supplementary material of *Les Posthumes* refers. At any rate, he set out to typeset *Les Posthumes* with a furious sense of urgency, which prevented him from making any of the changes that he might have made had he been working in better circumstances.

For whatever reason, Restif does not appear to have corrected or altered anything in the confused mess that the manuscript still was, and only dropped in a few extra notes in order to add flattering references to Bonaparte, as well as adding some supplementary material to the beginning and end of the text. It was presumably at that point in time, rather than in 1796, that he decided to credit the work to "le feu Cazotte." There is no trace within the text itself of any such imposture, save for one belatedly-added note, and although Fontlhète and Hortense inevitably refer to Restif in the third person when mentioning him or his works, no sensitive reader could possibly have been in doubt as to his involvement in the text. Even in the supplementary advertisements appended to the end of the text Restif refers to himself as "the editor," but only an exceedingly dim-witted reader would have failed to take the obvious inference from the fact that all that advertisements are for works by Restif, and that no mention at all is made of Cazotte's.

As to why Restif made that adjustment, we can only guess, but it is unlikely to have been a cynical attempt to increase the sales of the book. It might have been a simple tribute to a regretted friend whose comments in discussion might indeed have made a substantial contribution to the first draft while it was in slow progress, but it seems more probable that it relates to an anecdote circulating at the time that was due to a misinterpreted remark by Restif's arch-enemy Jean-François La Harpe, in which the later commented wryly on how amazed the guests at one of Fanny de Beauharnais's dinners would have been if the Illuminatus had told them, in 1788, where they would all be in five years' time. The comment was repeated as if it were a statement that Cazotte had indeed done that, and Restif might not have been able to resist the temptation to credit his late friend with such a "prophecy," made, like La Harpe's remark, after the fact.[1]

Could Restif have done more to repair the work when he prepared it for publication? In theory, yes; in practice, probably not. After all, the one thing of which we can be certain is that it was the last thing he ever did by way of publication; he

---

[1] La Harpe's remark was dressed up with more detail and published after his death in 1803, but Restif would undoubtedly have heard about the original observation long before then.

was not able to typeset *L'Enclos et les oiseaux*, either because he was physically incapable of doing it, or because Duchène flatly refused to publish it, perhaps because the "associate" who was going to pay for it backed out. Either way, that text was lost, forever—and whatever one might think of *Les Posthumes* as an undeniably crippled and clumsy literary work, that loss is undoubtedly a tragedy, in terms of the history of speculative and futuristic fiction.

Restif was sixty-seven in 1802, old by the standards of the day, and he had never enjoyed the best of health. What was wrong with him in his youth we do not know, and he did not know either, but there is one clue as to his later vicissitudes, in the data that he carefully refrained from laying bare in any of his published autobiographical works but let slip in the private ones that he used as raw material, some of which survive. An entry there records 11 July 1789 as the thirteenth anniversary of his catching a venereal disease from a woman named Virginie, a neighbor of his with whom his encounter, as recorded in various published works, is surely represented there far more romantically than it really was, although she was one of very few women he met who was actually willing to have sex with him. He does not specify what the venereal disease in question was, but his various rants against contemporary physicians, whom he regarded as charlatans forever issuing phantom diagnoses and incapable of curing anything, frequently mention syphilis, as an example of something they cannot diagnose or cure. There is also one reference in *Les Posthumes* to a medicament that Fontlhète is supposedly taking in the attempt to stave off the poison that is gradually and inevitable destroying him, which might be construed as a reference to mercury.

Setting all speculation aside, however, there is no doubt that when Restif typeset *Les Posthumes*, he believed that he was pressed for time, and he probably identified his own predicament much more closely than he might have wished with Fontlhète's—with the crucial exception, of course, that he had no Hortense who would miss him, having never managed to find the deep and true mutual love for which he had yearned all his life, and which he had never ceased to hold up as the one great ideal of the human heart.

It was probably not at that point that Restif inserted Fontlhète's final cry of anguish into Letter CCCXXIX—"If ever death separates us, you will have things from me sufficiently extraordinary to reread them, and thus conserve my soul, rendered present by the particles of its intelligence that I am leaving you; for thoughts are the particles of the soul, and woe betide the man who does not leave behind those that are dear to him!"—but if it was already there, he must have felt its full force as he set it in type. He was surely, by then, at the absolute end of his tether, even though he was not actually to die until February 1806.

By that time, he must, indeed, have been woestruck by the thought that *L'Enclos et les oiseaux* would never see the light of day, and probably could not take as much consolation as he would have liked to do from the knowledge that, direly imperfect as it was, bearing all the scars of its slow and uncertain genesis, *Les Posthumes* would at least conserve a few of the particles of his soul that were even dearer to him than the heart he had never quite laid entirely bare.

This translation was made from the copy of the Slatkine facsimile edition published as volumes 103 and 104 of Restif's *Oeuvres* in 1988 that is reproduced on the Bibliothèque Nationale's *gallica* website. I have unified the spelling of several names that are given in different versions in the text, adapted the eccentric spelling of numerous proper names into the form in which they are most commonly rendered today and corrected some obvious typographical errors—all normal practice for anyone in my position. Even so, I am not entirely sure that I should have done it; given that so many of the plot's contradictions, neologisms and orthographic eccentricities are intrinsic to the work, an argument could be made for sticking much closer to the letter of the original, even when it is clearly incorrect as a matter of carelessness rather than deliberate choice. I have, however, been careful to leave numerous anomalies and incoherencies in place, without making any attempt to add explanatory footnotes to the majority of them, partly in order to conserve the flavor of the text, and partly because there are too many places where I cannot make head nor tail of what the author might have meant to write had he been trying to make sense.

Brian Stableford

POSTHUMOUS CORRESPONDANCE
(VOLUME 1)

EDITOR'S NOTE

Much has been heard about Illuminati, and people talk about them every day without really knowing what they are.[2] The author of this work had written in accordance with their principles. Everything that Fontlhète says to his spouse, Cazotte really thought. They are his opinions on the state of souls after death that he explains.

What Duc Multipliandre says is also in conformity with his ideas.

If he could not put his soul in another body, he believed that others could, and that the manner of taking it therefrom was unknown to him. There are other ideas of the Illuminati

---

[2] Use of this term is inevitably confused by virtue of its general meaning, but it came to the fore during Restif's lifetime thanks to the publicity given to it by Adam Weishaupt (1748-1830) of the university of Ingolstadt, who rebelled against the Jesuits controlling that institution by claiming in 1778 to have funded a secret society of illuminati dedicated to opposing religious power in all its forms and espousing the values of the Enlightenment. The actual society probably never extended beyond Weishaupt's students, but he attracted a good deal of sympathy and support from freethinkers throughout Europe, who would gladly have joined the organization had there really been one, many of whom—including Jacques Cazotte— proudly proclaimed themselves to be Illuminati, and used the name as a symbolic aegis for their own ideas.

on physics; they will be found in the fiftieth letter and elsewhere.

This minor clarification was necessary.

PREFACE

Cazotte, the author of this work, was disposed to publish it when a sanguinary Tribunal deprived him of his life. We had known one another since 1786, and supped together twice a week for a decade at the home of the Comtesse de Beauharnais. He liked me; he liked my works; he anticipated me in everything. He sent me his work when he was afraid of being arrested. He charged me to publish it under my own name, believing that it would then have a modicum of success, and avoid persecution. Those two reasons no longer exist; my reputation has declined and Cazotte is reconciled with his judges, as with his executioners. He thanked them for allowing him to live the happy life of the discorporated—for all our souls, according to the doctrine of the Illuminati, of whom he was a zealous partisan, will exist for a century above the top of the atmosphere of the place they inhabited during their incorporation.

He must have been convinced of these verities while alive, for he did nothing to avoid arrest, and before his judges, nothing to save a life that was tedious to him; he was hungry for a better one.

As for me, his friend, I render to the author today the glory of his work.

This is the short preface that he thought it necessary to add to it:

My aim, in the composition of this extraordinary work, is the same as that of Pythagoras on his arrival in Italy, to cure humans of the vain fear of death, a fear tripled or multiplied a hundredfold by Christianity. I could have reasoned by representing death as inevitable, as an indifferent object, in the manner in which people envisage it for others, even those closest to them, but all reasoning of that kind is cold. I preferred to establish those same truths in an active and dramatic manner, in accordance with a real fact, which was recounted to me by Madame Beauharnais, the aunt by marriage of the magnanimous General Bonaparte, the savior of the French nation. It is by means of extraordinary stories, which are in the class of the possible, since the human imagination cannot go beyond Nature, that I shall aim for two goals, equally moral: human wellbeing and the conservation, by a tender spouse, of the life of a cherished companion. For true morality consists of working for the happiness of human beings.

CLARIFICATIONS

The true story that serves as an introduction to these letters heads them, it is true, but does not indicate a foundation or a base. On the contrary, it might instead induce an error, since it appears only to announce lamentations on the misfortunate of the hero. But with the exception of thirteen or fourteen letters in which he speaks about his tenderness, all the others partake of a brilliant imagination. The storiettes are singular, of an absolutely new genre, of which no one has ever thought.

The first, that of the souls Yfflasie and Clarendon, veritably pertains to the subject, from which it results absolutely. It tends, skillfully, to prepare the sensible soul of an adored wife to support more tranquilly the loss of a uniquely beloved husband.

I shall not anticipate the denouement of the work by presenting it here.

The other stories, like that of Duc Multipliandre, all have the same aim. That one, most extraordinary, although more romantically plausible than the *Thousand-and-one Nights*, fills all the rest of the work, very nearly. But it is a variety of facts, always amusing, always founded on Nature. His metamorphoses, his amour, the persecutions he experiences and the victories he wins, are all new and of a genre to please reasonable readers.

President de Fontlhète[3] terminates his letters with a prediction of the Revolution, which Yfflasie and Clarendon made him, by virtue of the power they have to penetrate the future.

---

[3] The appellation of President refers to Fontlhète's entitlement within the Magistracy to preside over tribunals. The author of the note appears to have forgotten that it is Multipliandre, not Yfflasie and Clarendon, who communicates his vision of the Revolution to Fontlhète.

Politically sound principles will be found in this work; the amusing part is well above that of a recent author, lured by Italian superstitions, who mingled the marvelous in novels where it was unnecessary.[4] Those works will never be handed down to posterity; instead of which, these, full of variety, of agreeable and not repugnant marvels, show an invalid full of intelligence, writing with the double motive of giving an illusion of life to himself as well as to his dear wife, who will read them one by one for a year, after his death, and who will believe that she is receiving them from a living man, which will cheer her up, as he wishes her to be.

That is what the reader always ought to have in mind, which will sustain the charm of the reading. The wife receives these letters from a city from which her husband has really had them sent by the French minister, and the first one is dated from the day after his death. Obliged to reply, she is cleverly deceived by counterfeit dates, and responses to unforeseen circumstances, inserted in the veritable letters of her husband.

I cannot find anything to add to this advice in order to make the objective of the letters better understood, by which a tender husband undertakes in advance to preserve from despair a wife who is dear to him and whom he adores. It is said that the estimable companion of a famous man—Madame Necker,[5] mother of the sublime Madame de Staël—did the same thing for her virtuous husband, but Madame de Beauharnais will be my witness that I did not know that until a long time after the completion of the letters to Madame de Chazu.

---

[4] The reference is probably to one of the English Gothic novels that were very popular in French translation perhaps Ann Radcliffe's Italy-set *Les Mystères de Udolphe* (1797; originally *The Mysteries of Udolpho*, 1794)

[5] "Madame Necker," the mother of Madame de Staël, was Suzanne Curchod (1737-1794); I cannot find any evidence for the truth of this assertion.

THE STORY OF THE LETTERS

A magistrate fell madly in love with a married woman. At first he was content with his undeclared love, but finally, having been unable to keep quiet about it, whereas he had been welcomed before with an affectionate confidence, he was carefully avoided.

Nevertheless, one evening, Monsieur de Fontlhète encountered Madame de Chazu in a private garden. He went along the hornbeam hedge, keeping a little in arrears, in order to enjoy the sight of her, through the little gaps in the foliage. He heard her sigh. He increased his pace, and at the end of the pathway, they found themselves face to face.

She blushed. He was troubled. He took her hand. She left him take it.

"You can see by my gaze," he said to her, that my happiness depends on you, Madame. Not that I am claiming favors. Ah! A sentiment such as...the one I experience, would suffice for my happiness..."

"I'm married. Never see me again."

She took away her hand, and withdrew precipitately.

"What, Madame, *never?*"

"*Never*," the lady repeated. And she went indoors.

The President remained motionless. Then, his imagination wandering, the thought that the sighs he had heard were for another, and that idea cast him into despair. He returned home, made all his preparations to depart, and went to shut himself in his country house seven leagues from Paris. He stayed for six weeks, in bleak dolor, cruel to himself but mild to his servants and to strangers.

He came back to Paris when the sessions resumed, fulfilled his duties, presented himself at the home of Madame de Chazu, and was not admitted. He only wrote her a brief note:

What, Madame, never?

The response was: *Never.*

The President spent the winter in Paris, seeking every opportunity to see the Marquise. He glimpsed her several times. She was beautiful and sad

One evening in the following spring, being in the same garden where he had met her on the day of her declaration, he perceived her sitting on a grassy bank facing the Champs-Élysées. She was talking to the mistress of the house, the young Marquise de Marigny.[6]

"Yes, my friend," said Madame de Chazu, "I have not been able to forbid my heart. But I shall punish it, that rebel heart. The Comte shall never know my sentiments."

At that fatal word Monsieur de Fontlhète withdrew, with death in his heart, convinced that he had a beloved rival. Oh, the unfortunate! He was a Comte too, and perhaps there was a convention between the two friends only to name him by his title when they talked about him!

During the night, he only had dreams that confirmed his unhappiness. He saw Madame de Chazu in the arms of a handsome Comte, very foppish, and she received his advances advantageously. On awakening, he uttered a cry of despair. He left thereafter for the country, seven leagues away. He consumed his dolor there.

Finally, one morning, after a dream in which he thought he saw the beauty softening, and confessing to him that she loved him, he awoke so desperate, believing that the dream was an indication that she had just given herself to his rival,

---

[6] Restif's unorthodox orthography routinely substituted *i*s for *y*s at the end of words; I have altered most of those attached to the names of real people, including this one, to the more familiar form. The Marquise de Marigny—Julie Filleul, an illegitimate daughter of Louis XV—was born in 1751, and would have been in her twenties when this scene was set, according to the initial internal chronology of the story (which shifts subsequently). Her much older husband, who died in 1781, was the brother of Madame de Pompadour and the director of the king's buildings.

that he took up a slow poison, prepared long before, the life he was leading having become unbearable.

The poison had not yet been swallowed when someone knocked—the door was closed. He hastened to drink it, and opened the door.

"Madame de Chazu," said the lackey.

She came in. She ran toward him.

"Oh my friend," she said, without giving him time to salute her. "I'm free! I've known about your dolor. It has touched me. My duty retained me; I love you; I've always loved you. I'm free. I bring you my hand, which my heart anticipated."

At these words, pronounced with caresses, the lover forfeited his unhappiness. He burst forth in a transport of joy—but from that surge of joy he fell back more profoundly into himself.

His beloved could not understand his inequalities. She complained of them tenderly.

"I shall justify myself soon," he told her. "I adore no one but you, and perhaps that sentiment will render me the life that dolor is about to take away."

While he was speaking, he took a counterpoison.

Astonished, Hortense did not know what he was doing. She thought he was mentally deranged. She only became more tender in consequence.

He married his mistress as soon as possible. It was the day after the marriage that he wrote the first letter, and wrote two more every day, with the consequence that he appeared to be writing for 366 days.

When he sensed that his end was inevitable, he obtained a temporary commission from the Ministry of Foreign Affairs, first for London, and then for Florence and Rome, where he wanted to die. He was to give his letters to friends, charged with putting them in the post one by one for his wife, retained on his estate because she was pregnant. That would not appear extraordinary, because while he was alive he wrote to his wife every day. The friend was to receive the responses and add to the letters, postmarked from London, Florence or Rome, an appropriate postscriptum.

Monsieur de Fontlhète died in Rome. He had gone there expressly to end his days, taking with him the letters that you are about to read.

"My friend," he said to the man who had accompanied him, presenting them to him, "this is the deposit I mentioned to you. Think how important it is that a cherished wife, who is pregnant, should not receive the fatal news so soon! Time, as it goes by, will soften the blow."

He expired.

The first letter, dated from London, immediately went to Paris, in an envelope stamped in Rome, from which another friend in Paris, to whom it was addressed, removed it in order to send it to the Comtesse, who received that first letter, prepared by conversations and by the last from her spouse—for he had announced to his wife the genre of all those you are about to read, and his motives for writing them in that way; motives explained more than once in the letters. That was that she should suppose them to have been written beginning the day after the terrible "Never!"

The President had said to his wife: "My love, at a certain time, you shall see all that I have thought and all that I have done since my despair. I beg you to respond with what will pass through your head until the last of the 366 letters I shall send you from London, Florence or Rome."

The Comtesse had consented to that and sworn to do so...before knowing her misfortune. She would keep her word.

After that explanation, you will sense the reason for the genre of the imaginative deviations in the following letters—reasons as delicate as the genre is extraordinary.

PART I

Letter I

From my Tomb. London. Morning, 1 February 1779.[7]

Never! That word is my death sentence. It has emerged from your mouth; it is sacred; it banishes me, and my fate is decided.

You, the charm of my life, do not know how you might be, and how you ought to be, loved. Alone in the world, I know that, and alone in the world, I love you as you ought to be loved. A profound sentiment makes me see beauty, charm and joy in you alone. You have condemned me never to hope.

I adore your decree, Hortense. But despair entered my heart at the moment when you pronounced the fatal word, *Never!*

I have no complaint against you, Hortense; you could not love me, and I could not live without being yours. It is necessary to end it! But I love you with so much attachment, such a great regret in ceasing to see you, that I don't want to end it in a moment; I want to feel myself dying, and every day, for a year, make you the sacrifice of my life, to write you a letter every day, which you will perhaps read when I am no more.

Oh, if I could flatter myself, if I could hope that my thought would pass into your hope, that your eyes would drink the tears that moisten this paper...but no. Learn, if you read

---

[7] This probably ought to be the date of the day after the pronunciation of the fateful "Never," according to the last section of the text, not the date on which the letter is supposedly sent or received, as earlier suggested, but the pretence appears to have been forgotten by the time the responses were inserted into the text.

37

this one day, that the poison is here...that it is slow...that I shall, in a moment, before finishing this letter, feel a principle of death passing through me...

Alas, that frightful idea of the annihilation of thought is much less so that the horrible word *Never!* that you have just pronounced...

It is done; I shall not live longer than a year. In a year, to the day, the most unfortunate of men, gradually consumed, will render his last sigh...

Is there a means of living after death? That is what pre-occupies me. Yes I see morals in it, at least. It is necessary to take them.

There is no more time...no more remedy. I shall cease to be at a known term. But each of my last days will be con-sumed for you. Every day, it is to you that I shall immolate myself. You, who would and could have been the charm of my life, and who are...shall I say the torment? No, I take pleasure in dying for you...pity me!

My heart hurts. Death is I my bosom. Oh, it will take too long to come. Oh, my poor heart, calm down! It's is She who has vivified you; it is She who will extinguish you. When I sense the first pain, I shall say to myself: It is the thrust of the cruel Hortense, and her *Never!* is piercing my heart...!

The unfortunate de Fontlhète.

Response to Letter I

O my dear husband, what a scene you recall to me! If your letter were not agreed, it would be frightful! But it is, on the contrary, a proof of our love, and the sentiments that you have always had for me.

By chance, it remained open on my desk while I was dressing. Madame de Marigny came in and read it. She came to me, terrified.

"Oh my friend, what has happened? This letter—I've read it!"

"Oh, it's nothing."

"So much the better, for it frightened me."

And I let her understand that it was the story of something old. She loves me, that adorable Marquise. She isn't happy. She is only sensible to the unfortunate. So beautiful, and suffers rejections! From whom? From a man who isn't worthy of her!

Your son is calling me. I quit you for yourself.

Your wife,

Hortense.

Letter II

From my tomb. London, 2 February,

A fire is alight in my veins. Oh, perhaps it will calm the one that is devouring my soul! Yes, I believe that it will calm it. Since this morning's sacrifice, a kind of peace, unknown for a long time, seems to have been introduced into my heart. In spite of you, Hortense, I have been able to establish a relationship between you and me. I am your victim...I am *yours*...

That word is perhaps not without sweetness for the man who adores you. You could not love me: Nature, perhaps reason, seemed to demand it, but honor forbade it. If, instead of the terrible *Never!* that you pronounced the day before yesterday, you had said to me: "Fontlhète, I leave it to you: ought I to imprint a stain on my life and respond to your love?" I would have replied, without hesitation or disguise, firmly: "No, you ought not to do that." And if you had added: "Well, Fontlhète, if I see you, if you live, if you love me, I sense that I shall not have the strength to resist; I shall break my oath; I shall become culpable toward social law, and I shall lose honor"—if, as I say, you had spoken to me thus, I would have fled, in order to conserve that honor, in order not to imprint the slightest stain upon that masterpiece of Nature; I would have done what I did yesterday...

Oh, flattering chimera, which comes to occupy me with your suppositions, you charm my dolor! Alas, that delightful and charming cause, which would have made me drink the cup of death avidly, is only that...of despair...frightful despair has presented itself to me, and has forced me to drink to the dregs! I am no longer in despair, since I have yielded to it: a sweet and consoling thought seems to bring balm into my blood: I shall cease to be for Her!

She is the cause; I shall be the effect.

A sentiment like mine, my dear Hortense, ought to astonish! It's necessary for you to know the story. It will be the subject matter of the two letters that follow. For two years I have adored you. Each letter will present the story of two days. O consoling idea! If ever the beautiful Hortense reads me, I shall try to get those letters to her one by one. She will bring together, in a single instant, four years, the two past, of which I shall describe every day what happened, the one in which I am writing, and the one in which she is reading. Thus I am prolonging my existence, I am quadrupling it, and I sense happiness at this moment. Do not pity me, Hortense! You have not made me unhappy. Have no regrets, nor repentance; the word *Never!* that you pronounced was for you a duty! You are just, and I am being punished for not having loved you as you merited being loved.

Until tomorrow; I shall commence the history of my sentiments. I am leaving for Florence.

Response to Letter II

18 February.

You are commencing from now on the history of your sentiments. There could not be anything more agreeable for your wife, and the mother of your son. You are always sure of interesting me by that means. Your letter has the art of making the most cruel reproaches seem sweet and flattering, after the cause has been annihilated by our marriage. The more bitter they are in the distance, the sweeter they are at the moment they are made by the husband to the tender wife, who speaks of the desperate lover and the severe, cruel mistress as if of imaginary individuals. Continue, dear husband, in the same tone. It is delightful for your wife.

I am hardly attending to any business. I always put things off. But your man of confidence is taking care of everything.

Letter III

From my tomb. London. 3 February.

It was on the third of February 1777 that I saw you for the first time at the ball given by the Venetian Ambassador. Until that moment, who had hidden you from my gaze? Why had the star of my happiness not been visible to me?

All eyes were fixed upon you. Some praised the perfection of your figure, others the regularity of your features. Some praised your dark, soft and shining eyes, others your dainty mouth. You were admired from head to foot. A woman added the eulogy: "She has more qualities and virtues than attractions!" I shuddered.

I drew nearer. The holy knot of marriage by which I knew you were bound, penetrated me with respect. It was not a profane love that I felt for you. I wanted to adore you, as the masterpiece of wisdom and reason. So I drew closer. Do you remember, Hortense, the first words I spoke to you?

You had just sat down; your gaze was wandering, without settling on anyone. It came toward me, when I opened my mouth.

"Madame..." I stopped. My ideas became blurred. It seemed to me that your gaze was dissolving my thoughts, as ardent glass dissolves metals.

You looked at me; I thought it was with a sort of interest.

I became bolder. I began again. "Madame, every heart..." But I could not finish.

You smiled; the fire of your eyes was tempered.

"Madame," I resumed, "every heart brings you the purest of tributes."

I thought I had finished a long speech. I fell silent; I admired you—but I dared not raise my dazzled eyes as far as yours.

"Sit down, Monsieur."

How sweet those words appeared to me! Alas, it was only pity. I dared not sit down. I looked at our hands, your arms. You stood up. I followed you, as Charmant follows Lucinde in *L'Oracle*.[8] You left, and I felt that you were my soul.

On the third of February the following year, there was no ball. But I wanted to see you, in order to celebrate the anniversary of what I called my happiness. I knew that you were dining with Monsieur d'Ormond.[9] I was not invited, but I could render a visit after dinner. I made certain not to fail. There was a game of Lotto—a harming game. I would never love anyone but you.

Mademoiselle de Saint-Josse, Monsieur d'Ormond's niece, invited me to sit with you. How dear she became to me! I loved her almost as much as you. We only talked about trivia, and never, never, had I ever heard trivia so witty, so melodious, and so divine! I drew 69 three times in succession.

"I love 69," you said. "It often comes up for me."

What! Love could, therefore, form of a 69, an ambe, a quaterne, a quine,[10] a discourse more tender than the elegies of Tibullus! That game did not go on long enough. I can never recall it without shivering. I bought one the next day. I played alone, as soon as I had a moment. Love occupied your place. Oh, what a pleasure I experienced when one of the numbers came up that I had had with you—69, for example.

On the third of February this year, I am writing to you, and I am penetrated by the pleasures of the two preceding years.

---

[8] *L'Oracle* is a one-act comedy fantasy by Germain de Saint-Foix (1698-1776), first produced and published in 1740, and revived many times thereafter.

[9] A Monsieur and Madame d'Ormond feature in Restif's early novel *La Fille naturelle* (1769).

[10] These terms refer to three of the numerous formations of numbers that could be claimed as winners in the game of Loto or Loterie [Lotto], the ancestor of the British pastime of Bingo.

On the third of February, in a year's time...I shall no longer be...but you will! Oh, might you read this letter, and honor it with a sigh!

Response to Letter III

That story of our meeting at the ball, dear husband, has stirred my heart prodigiously. Oh, how dear it is, everything that relates to a unique passion! You combine with that what you felt the following year, at Mademoiselle Saint-Josse's Lotto game. It seems, my love, that you read my heart, to know what interests me. That game was nothing. Its numbers were boring; but my love's tone, the quarrels he and Mademoiselle Saint-Josse had, that is what interests me, by reminding me of those times of amour and palpitations! Amour that I dared not admit to myself, and which I sensed so keenly!

(The rest is mundane.)

Letter IV

On the fourth of February, and the night that had preceded it, I thought of nothing but you. But it was a charming idea.
I don't know what vague and flattering hope brought charm
into my soul. My chain was already too strong to be broken,
but I loved caring it; I loved feeling it. I tried to see you, and
as everything favors us in the commencement of a passion, I
saw you, and I saw you smiling. That is to say how beautiful
you were. You only addressed one word to me, but it was
honest. An honest word, said to a lover, on the second day, is a
favor.

I arranged my plan in my head. It was sage, for I had to
adore you without you knowing, without disturbance, without
desire, without jealousy. It was madness; it was making arrangements to have a violent amour, without amour!

But that error did not last. Why did it not last forever?

Already, it no longer existed on the fourth of February of
the following year. I recalled the divine game of the previous
evening, the Lotto calumniated by insensitive souls. They
never played it with an adored woman!

But during that session, I had sensed your charms; a deceptive dream made you tender, touched, responsive to confessions, which I dared to form, for the first time, in the liberty
of sleep.

Who could express the enchantment of a happy dream?
O beneficent Nature, you give us, in dreams, a foretaste of the
idea of perfect happiness, of the happiness that awaits us after
the detachment of the bonds of the body. Make haste, fortunate liberty! A charming idea, which makes me summon, and
makes me desire, death. Oh, how precious you are to me! You
extend over my destruction a balsamic liniment of pleasure,
and you give me to drink, when I am destroyed, the nectar of
immortality!

On the fourth of February this year, those ideas delight me at the moment when I sense...the first thrust of the stiletto of death...

Hortense, I am not writing to you to make you sad, but to prove to you that, in dying for love, I die happy...death alone can console me for the frightful misfortune of being unable to be yours.

On the fourth of February next year...oh, beautiful Hortense, who knows? Perhaps my detached soul will be fluttering around yours. Perhaps it will be your tutelary genius. How happy I would be if I could deflect the pains, the cares and the chagrins of my celestial beloved...

Will you see me, beautiful Hortense? Surely, I will not be far away from you, in a year, at the moment when you are reading me. I shall no longer be unhappy.

Souls are not, as that fellow Homer tells us, pusillanimous individuals who regret corporeal life prosaically. They are lively, cheerful, devoid of needs, devoid of shackles. Such will be my lot. I insist today on that consoling idea. Reach out your arms to me when you read this, and I shall precipitate myself into them, invisibly. I shall think: *Hortense I adore you!*—because a pure spirit can do that without crime.

Response to Letter IV

20 February

So, my dear husband, you have hope? What has given it to you, if not the electric fluid of amour, which communicates from your soul to mine, and from mine to yours? How these delightful commentaries on a veritable distant passion become less distant. One knows what they are, but when one responds to them here, subsequently, by reflection, it is a delightful sensation. You combine, in your stories, the past, the present and the future. Agree that the idea is new, and that you are the only one who has had it. So, I do not believe that any love had ever equaled yours or mine...

The somber idea of an annihilation that is not seems romantic to me, and worthy of Young.[11]

(The rest of the letter is mundane.)

---

[11] Edward Young's *Night Thoughts on Life, Death and Immortality* (1742) was a great favorite in pre-Revolutionary Parisian salon culture.

Letter V

From my tomb. 5 February.

I had made my arrangements the day before and I was happy in my love, by virtue of the delightful sentiment I experienced. Are there, then, circumstances in which one is happy in love, independent of the beloved object?

I am writing, beautiful Hortense, in order to disguise my situation from you! But is it delicate to make you perceive it? No, I do not have the vanity...no, no, do not observe it...

But what if she does? a secret voice said to me.

No, no, she hasn't...

I was, then, happy thanks to you, but without you. And you knew it, Madame, better than anyone. Without your confession, I was proud of my choice. I said to myself: *Fontlhète, you are not a vulgar man. You love the finest of women!*

The following fifth of February...

Alas, she belongs to another, I said to myself. I saw her too late; *her hand and her heart are given.* But if I had seen her sooner, would she have preferred me? No, no, I render myself justice...what if love had not prevailed over merit...? A despairing idea. Oh, how different that year was from the first of my love, when I saw everything through a prism that embellished objects with the brightest colors! Sad, concentrated, devoured by desires, I was less innocent...I was unhappy...

On the present fifth of February...

Where are you, Hortense? You are living in the country. Content and happy, you are wandering under the shady trees of an enchanted park.

Let's go to the country...let me wander, like her, while I still can, under the bushy shade of those arbors ...which she renders charming!

Ah, I believe I can see her under the lindens, whose sweet perfume embalms the breath of the zephyrs.

Yes, let's go...

Alas, what am I thinking? I open the window; snow covers the roofs, and the trees are still leafless. Am I delirious?

Oh, Fontlhète, once happy, what has stolen all the wealth of life from you? What has deflected your reason? It's an unhappy amour! No more, no more joy. It's necessary to die...

Someone is knocking. A letter...from the Comtesse de Beauharnais

What have I just learned? You really are in the country, in the middle of winter, in the season of pleasures? What has distanced you from the capital? I breathed the same air as Hortense there; you no longer live there; I want to quit it.

The future fifth of February. I shall be less unhappy than today, for I shall no longer have a body. Are you reading me, Hortense? Adieu.

Response to Letter V

Sweet charm of the interrogation of my beloved, how you have just resounded in my heart! You ask me where I am. You seek me, and not being able to find me, you imitate me. Oh, my love, did you love me then more than today? You would not willingly have been absent so long, but your absence is forced, and that is what consoles me. You cry to yourself: *Oh, Fontlhète, once happy, what has stolen all the wealth of life from you? What has deflected your reason?* Me, me, my love, who will render you a dear wife, and a son too, whom you will love with all your heart. A happy amour will render you all the wealth that an unhappy love had stolen from you...

But the end, O my love, the future fifth—which is today—*I shall be less unhappy than today, for I shall no longer have a body*...what, no more body? *Are you reading me, Hortense?* I am reading you, dear husband—be happy! But I am not; my happiness lacks you.

Letter VI

F.m.T. 6 February.

What a frightful night! A dream...a horrible dream had just shown me Hortense weeping, in despair, asking me for help, which I could not bring her!

"O you," she said to me, "Who have offered me your heart, will you give me a shelter there against the misfortune that is pursuing me?"

I wanted to act, to get up, to fly to you...my exhausted strength did not permit it...my frozen tongue could not pronounce a word...

I awoke suffering. The seed of death is developing in my bosom. Oh, if it is combined with despair, its activity will be double...

Let us calm these mortal ideas. Let us recall what I was two years ago. It was the third day of our acquaintance. I awoke full of the idea of you. My heart was floating in a vague but delicious joy. An uncertain hope, but which the experience and example of others seemed to sustain, showed me Hortense, beautiful, adored, tender...

I remember that in getting up, I formed projects, which I thought easy of execution. Their foundations crumbled that same day. I had the good fortune to dine with you, at the home of a mutual friend, and the misfortune of losing a bold illusion. I was not afflicted by it; self-regard consoled me; other chimeras succeeded it; I was less audacious, and more tender...

A year ago...oh, I was no longer advantageous. I knew then that you had adorable principles, that you were a unique woman, that it was necessary to venerate you as Virtue itself. It was a year ago that, having gone to see an unfortunate family, of whom mention had been made to me the day before, I found them happy, consoled. I experienced a sensation of sadness and humiliation because someone had anticipated me. I made enquiries. It was you. My heart dilated, and in a surge of joy, I exclaimed: "Oh, what joy: I had the same thought as her! But she is better than me, and it is just that she should have the merit, of which I am less worthy!"

That moment was one of the happiest of my life.

I only found out today, from the good father of that family, that you were instructed that same evening of my competition, and that you were flattered by it. God! If only I had known sooner that you were flattered to have something in common with me! Yes, I believe that thought would have given me the strength to support life. Well, Hortense, it will soften the idea of death...

And in a year, when you read this letter, and you will see these three epochs in it, you will say: *From the first moment that Fontlhète saw me, he only breathed for me...*

Oh, in a year, where will I be? Where will the beautiful Hortense be? And what will she think of me then...?

P.S. I add to this letter, Madame, a postcriptum that my friend did not have time to write. You know how I have always been linked to Fontlhète. Thus, I know all his thoughts. What you mark in your latest response engages me to reply to you. Let the land at Meulant be sold, if you judge it appropriate and if you believe it to be advantageous. In consequence, your husband sends you a blank power of attorney, which you can have filled in by whoever you wish.

As for the five letters you have already received, you are right to regard them as an effervescence of the imagination. Although fundamentally true, they are only the proof of the disposition of your dear husband's agreeable intelligence. I warn you that you are not finished yet, and that the singular things that he has to write to you subsequently will provide even better evidence of the tranquil disposition in which you find him. I present to you the assurance of my respect, Madame.

President Delabrisse.

Response to Letter VI

22 February.

But my dear husband, your absence is very long and very painful. It is nearly six months since you left. Oh, my love, your letter is too tender! Oh, much too…for a cherished husband who is not coming back! I conserve our letters preciously. If our son sees them one day, he will know how much his father loved his mother, and how much his mother loved her dear Fontlhète.

I don't want him to be a magistrate. He will be a soldier, and bear the name Comte Hortense-de-Fontlhète—for I remember that what gave you so much chagrin was what I said to Madame de Marigny, that I loved that dear Comte. You mistook yourself for a rival! Oh, how could I love anyone other than you? You pleased me before my marriage, before having spoken to me. You were not a fop like your peers, and in spite of my repugnance for the judge's robe, and my taste for the title of Marquis, I would have preferred you to Monsieur de Chazu if you had asked for my hand.

Madame de Beauchamois sees your letters, as well as Madame de Marigny. You know how charming she is, the celestial Beauchamois! Her supple figure would give desire to Coldness itself. I shall tell you some of the naïve stories that she recounts to us sometimes, about her youth and the commencement of her marriage. I shall also talk to you about Madame de Marigny, to whom rather singular things have happened.

Your son is well. Maternal cares are the same, as if the Supreme Being were having you reborn, me knowing it, and I were your mother.

Until tomorrow, my love. For Adieu is a word that will never terminate one of the letters I write to you.

Entirely yours,
Your wife and your beloved,
Hortense de B.

Letter VII

F.m.T. 7 February.

On the same day two years ago the situation of my soul was very different.

I am in the country. I am better off there. My dolor is less bitter there, and more tender. I am having work done there on my last dwelling. I am quitting you. I'm interrupted, in spite of my orders, given without exception... Just Heaven, what do I hear?

It's... You!

Who could have told me, two years ago? Oh, my fate was to die for you. I shall die of joy! You are free! You are offering me your hand? You have always loved me? Duty, duty alone has made you desire and dead tender sentiments!

Suspend your course, river of voluptuousness, or your impetuosity will destroy my frail existence...

Oh, why did I not know my happiness a day earlier?

I have, therefore, regrets...heart-rending regrets. I have limited myself the course of a life destined for happiness. Reckless man, who has arrogated to yourself the rights of Nature and the Divinity, was it for you to raise a sacrilegious hand against the existence that you owe to the Being-Principle, via his two intermediaries, the father Sun and the mother Earth? Insensate! At the moment when your limited sight only saw a bottomless abyss, the eternal moral order was ready to open a long career of happiness to you!

I have violated the laws of Nature, which want every being to love its conservation, and I am punished, cruelly punished!

Hortense, I spoke to you coolly; I accepted the happiness you offered, with the appearance of tranquility. Oh, how necessary it was to hide the frightful despair of having inconsiderately destroyed my supreme felicity...

A few months of languor, that is all that my crime has left me, instead of a happiness that would have embellished my entire life.

Weep, oh, weep, my eyes! This is not a circumstance in which to have firmness, philosophy; it is necessary to display all my weakness and all my dolor...

Two years ago I saw you, brilliant, adorned. I thought: *How beautiful she is! She will preserve me from amour...*

One year ago, I saw you with dolor, and I thought: *She will never be mine. The only woman I can love, and who stole a good deed from me yesterday...*

Today, you are free; you came to find me in the country and to offer me your hand, your person. Hortense, my dear, my adorable beloved, sense all that I must be suffering in thinking that I have succumbed to my despair, at the very moment when you were at my door!

Oh, can I forgive amour? If I had not loved you more than myself, I would exist entirely. But would I be worthy of you? Would I have loved you if, in losing hope, I had been able to support life?

No, my Hortense...no, my wife, I am not a suicide. No, I have not committed an odious and cowardly crime; dolor suffocated me; I would be no more. I have prolonged my life, by the salutary and terrible remedy I have taken. I have no more than a few hours to live. That voluntary sacrifice has calmed me; the certitude of perishing slowly, of distancing instant death, which does not want any delay...

You will read this letter in a year, my spouse, and you will read it...in my absence. Let your heart soften and your tears flow; they will conserve your life. I shall live in our heart and in your memory.

Of, I shall not be veritably and entirely in the tomb, until you have ceased to animate your beautiful body...

Response to Letter VII

23 February.

Dear husband! If anything can compensate for your absence, it is your letters. You have just rendered me the most dolorous moment of my life, by reminding me of my visit to the country, my offer of me whole self and its acceptance. For a few minutes, I believed at that fortunate moment...

But what do you add, my dear husband? That expansion was succeeded by a contraction of horror, against which all my reason was scarcely enough to protect me. You compare all the epochs, you show yourself three times in a single letter...and you spread a somber shadow over a fourth, which consoles me, by showing me the address that had overladen the other two with a cloud...

However, I do not know what weight is crushing me and freezing me...

Your friend Delabrisse will talk to you about business. That of the sale of Meulant is concluded.

Letter VIII

F.m.T. Florence. 8 February.

How slow they are, these preparations accelerated by the most tender amour! When one does not have a year to live, one day is worth more than 366...

O happiness, before death, you will fill every one of those enormous days, in which will be seen Titon growing old rapidly in the arms of Aurore for a second time![12]

I suspend my dolors by means of those cold calculations; they slow down the devouring ardor of my blood.

Oh, how very differently affected I was two years ago! I adored you, but I believed that my life would go placidly by in adoring you. Do you remember how I appeared, brilliant with joy, in the house where we encountered one another? You were for me the announcement of joy, and the most fortunate of omens. Oh, that was the truth!

The past year, I went to say to you: "Madame, the day before yesterday, we had the same thought, you and I." You looked at me, without asking for an explanation—and I felt a surge of joy, that we had both, at the same moment, thought the same thing...

Today, Hortense, I have just seen you. You are in the room next to the one in which I am writing. You're preparing for our marriage. You're worried about me. You're trying to hide from yourself a melancholy that appears to you to be a consequence of my old dolors...

Oh, my beauty, my ravishing beloved, do not believe, in a year's time, when I am no longer, that that dolor, that melancholy, were caused by the certainty of the brevity of my hap-

---

[12] I have not translated Titon and Aurore to the usual English forms of Tithonus and Aurora because Fontlhète is probably remembering something he really has seen, in Jean-Joseph de Mondonville's opera *Titon et l'Aurore* (first produced 1753)

piness! Another motive forces me to moderate myself, to retain the surges of my sensibility, to hide from you the excess of my ardent tenderness!

I want, in disguising three quarters of my amour, to avert your regrets, at the fatal moment...and not reveal to you the extent to which I loved you, until the moment when my detached soul, fluttering around you, is able, I dare flatter myself, to soothe your despair.

See me, dear wife, at the moment when you read this letter, for my detached soul is hovering above you. See me considering you with a pure sensuality. And do not trouble it, when you are informed, with too sharp a dolor, which I will share, without being able either to speak or to weep. Your happiness, living, will be mine, after my discorporation.

Until tomorrow, dear wife.

Response to Letter VIII

24 February.

What language that of these letters is! But it really is your hand that has traced them. Yes, it is your handwriting...it really is. Were it not for my son, I would depart for Florence...and perhaps I shall depart, with my son. You mingle with the charm of your depictions the chiarioscuro of dolor...

Dear man! I know that you only want to give me pleasure, but I implore you, spare my sensibility in the depiction of your past dolors!

In talking to me about the preparations for our marriage, you filled me with joy and felicity...a moment afterwards, I felt the somber horror of tombs. That contrast might please in Young, but it is frightening in a letter from a cherished husband

An instant afterwards, you take me back two years. Oh, here the charm is pure. I loved you, two years ago, as you loved me, and far from the importunate thought, *what if I could love you without crime?* I surrender myself entirely to that charm, without discerning it clearly...but I want to cheer up this overly serious letter.

Madame de Beauchamois made us laugh yesterday by telling us how she spent the first night of her marriage with her husband. When he was in bed beside her he touched her bosom.

"What!" said the bride of fifteen years less two months, to the husband of forty-five. "Where have you been brought up?"[13]

---

[13] "Beauchamois" is presumably a mask for "Beauharnais," although the dates are slightly inaccurate; Françoise Mouchard de Chaban did indeed marry a naval officer, Claude de Beauharnais in 1753, but she was a few months older than fifteen at the time, and he was only thirty-six.

For his only response, the husband, who was a naval officer, put his hand...

"Oh God! What horror Maman! Maman!"

It was her grandmother for whom she was calling, at the top of her voice. The grandmother arrived, to redoubled cries.

"Madame... you thought... you were giving me... to an honest man... a worthy husband, and he's a guttersnipe... aiee! He's still doing...at this moment... in front of you... vulgar... frightful..."

"Patience, my daughter, submission!"

"But Maman, I know full well what a husband is, do I not? How many times did the question not come up at the convent, between the Demoiselles de Chamborant, de Puysegur, the Princesse de Montbarrey, Mademoiselle de Richelieu and me? A husband lies beside you, you touch one another, you love one another, he warms you, and that gives you a child..."

Further cries succeeded this discourse.

"Maman! My dear Maman! He's killing me...he's stifling me...he's..."

That was the mariner Beauchamois, who became her husband. But it's necessary to hear the story from her own mouth. There was never anything in the world more agreeable, nor more decently recounted...

During the night, she needed to blow her nose. She found something close at hand, picked it up and made use of it.

"What are you doing, Madame?"

"Oh, you're there, Monsieur—I'd forgotten...and I mistook your night-cap for my handkerchief..."

Letter IX

F.m.T. 9 February

Everything is ready; in an hour, I shall go to the altar, to become Hortense's husband. Hortense's husband! I can't remove my thought from that phrase; I can't stop writing it, except by stopping altogether!

Hortense's husband! The husband of the beautiful, the celestial Hortense! I would only have to write those two words to write my entire life, if it were not necessary to stop, in order to realize them...

Who could have told me, two years ago, while considering you like a beautiful flower in a garden with iron railings, bristling with spikes, that on the same day, after two annual revolutions, I would be Hortense's husband?

Adored wife! On the same day, at the same time, the preceding year, I had drunk my fill of dolor and despair. I open the confidant of my thoughts, the locked book of my tempestuous life, in which I deposit all my secrets, and I see these words written there, which my tears effaced; *I am odious to Hortense. My amour, which she sees, renders me insupportable. Let us die...*

What! Between despair and death, there must have been a...sublime instant?

In a year, the present happiness will be, by virtue of a delectable memory, my sole existence. You will read, my Hortense, you will read this outburst of love, and you will think: *My husband is here, detached from the bonds of his body. His thought*—for the soul is only thought—*his entire self, only exists, at this moment, in the conserved idea of the past day, a year ago.*

Hortense, I am putting down the pen in order to go toward happiness...

Response to Letter IX

25 February.

You retrace happiness for me, and a somber sentiment descends upon my soul. I do not like to think of yours without a body!

I remember what you said to me, on that very day of our happiness:

"Hortense, my dear Hortense, your celestial face is the only one that is Woman for me. All the others are inanimate beings, things and not persons. My Hortense is all soul: in her eyes is voluptuousness; pleasure is in her delightful laughter; and happiness results from all her attractions...

"There still exists an unfortunate, such as I was: a sensitive and poor man, in love, as I was, with a married woman. He adores her, and has never told her so. Oh, sometimes he suffers, because he does not speak! He will become unhappy, as I have been. Her name is Madame Filou. I wanted to see her. In order to be loved liked that, it is necessary to have your figure, your stride, your foot, your leg, your bosom, your hand, your mouth, your lips, your nose, your eyes, your eyebrows, your hair, your entire face, with that charming smile... She has all that, or, at least, of all women, she is the one most approximate to Hortense. What charm, then, do that face and that figure, between average and tall, have? Oh, it is the soul that has provided it, that had formed it, that renders that face irresistible! Woe to whoever loves, in vain, the soul clad in that face!"

And that Fontlhète, is what I think about your face! Judge whether I am pleased by the idea of seeing your soul deprived of it!

Madame de Marigny has come to see me. I asked her whether she was not the beauty that you name Madame Filou.

"No," she told me, "even though we have features similar enough sometimes to be mistaken for two sisters, it's not me."

"Is it the Comtesse de Beauchamois then?"

"No."

"But by the manner in which you reply *no*, one would think that you know my resemblance?"

"Yes, Monsieur de Fontlhète mentioned it to me once. I wanted to see her, as well as her lover. He indicated the latter's dwelling to me; he was then very unhappy, because he was poor and old. I wrote a note to him. The unfortunate fellow came to see me. We got into my carriage, and we went to the home of his beauty, the wife of a clockmaker in the Rue Honoré, to whom he had never spoken, who only knew him by sight, and then only because an indiscreet person had told her that he was one of her admirers.

"I was astonished myself by the resemblance in the smallest details, and the slightest movements. She even has the little mark on the left cheek that makes you so agreeable. 'Why, my dear Marquise,' I said to her, 'have you changed estate?'

"The beauty blushed, and in a voice exactly similar to yours she replied: 'I'm not a Marquise, my lady, and my estate is exactly what you see.'

"'That isn't possible! You're Hortense de Beauchamois, Marquise de Chazu!'[14]

"The beauty smiled, and resembled you even more. 'My name is Filète Dumas.'

---

[14] Hortense signed the letter in which she first made mention of Madame de Beauchamois "Hortense de B." but this is the first time her baptismal name has been given in full; it is never made clear exactly what her relationship is to Comtesse de Beauchamois. Fanny de Beauharnais' god-daughter, Joséphine's daughter, was named Hortense (1783-1837); she subsequently married Napoléon Bonaparte's brother Louis and was the mother of Napoléon III.

"I lavished many caresses on her," Madame de Marigny continued, and I shall seek opportunities to oblige her husband. As for the lover, a man of merit, the confrontation he had with his mistress was quite different from what I expected. He asked her the name and origin of her mother.

"She replied.

"'Do you know her writing?' he asked.

"'Perfectly.'

"'Read this letter,'

"Filète read it, then reread it, and then blushed. Returning it to him, she said: 'Oh, Monsieur...but I don't doubt it...I can't doubt it...my mother has told me the same thing. I'm no longer astonished that my husband has sacrificed me.' She turned to me. 'Madame, you have brought me my father.' She kissed his hand. He hugged her in his arms..."

That, dear husband, is the petty distraction that a tender friend has just procured for me. I shall make haste to see Filète too.

Letter X

F.m.T. 10 February.

Supreme felicity! I have just known you! Oh, to savor you, why do I not have a double existence? And mine, alas, I not entire! I have emerged from the arms of my Divinity—one is, when one dispenses happiness. Leave me, my Hortense, leave me to sweet distraction, to delicious intoxication, to the persuasive delirium that my immortality raises me to the rank of the gods. Alcides dying,[15] was no less great, the immortal Alcides—death for him was only the peeling away of a vulgar envelope...

Divine, celestial Hebe, you have reanimated me. Yes, by virtue of a fortunate crisis, I no longer feel the progressive weakness that is drawing me by slow steps toward the terminus. Can an emotion as intense as mine change nature? I hope so; I believe so, because I feel it...

I only remind you the epoch of two years in order to congratulate myself. How infatuated I was with you, two years ago! I was devoid of certain hope, but nor was I in despair...

A terrible epoch, a year ago! On the same day, for the first time, the fatal idea came to me. It was a painful dream, and I woke up...

In a year, Hortense, I shall hold you in my arms; I shall show you these letters, a monument to despair. Tears and tenderness and consolation will flow from your beautiful eyes, inundating your cheeks, all the way to your bosom, still moist from the dew of voluptuousness. No more sadness...we shall grow old together. A son, the pledge of our love...

I can hear you; I am flying to you.

---

[15] Alcide [Alcides] was the birth-name of Heracles in Greek myth.

Response to Letter X

26 February.

Sweet hope, you have just reanimated me. Oh, how consoling your letter is! It dissipates all the clouds! *In a year, Hortense, I shall hold you in my arms; we shall grow old together.* Balm of consolation, you flow in my veins, and my husband consoles me, without saying to me: I shall console you...

In my joy, I have been to see Filète, this morning at eleven o'clock, with her father. If I did not fear praising myself, I would praise her. Never was a resemblance so perfect! Madame de Marigny was with us. That visit has reconciled her, I will not say with the beauty, but with the very amiable clockmaker's wife, for the latter had thought that the Marquise de Marigny had wanted to amuse herself.

As for me, delighted, I said to Filète: "If you were unmarried we would become inseparable from now on."

"That would be a joy for me, Madame."

And as my companion had identified herself, and her name is very well-known, my amiable resemblance was delighted. I asked her husband for her, for the day. He granted her to us, with a great deal of politeness.

I only wanted to give her some clothes. We would take her to our homes; she would have my double pink dress with silver lace, brilliants in her hair, which would be like mine, etc. Most of all, we would have the same shoes, those you love. She would be a little taller, and she would have more majesty.

Since she has been here—for she has stayed, with her husband's permission—we have made her a thousand caresses, the Marquise de Marigny, the young Comtesse de Beauchamois and me.

I said to her: "My dear double, we must become friends. I cannot tell you how much I like you. Do you like me too?"

"How could I refuse to, Madame? You heap me with all flattering sentiments.

"I have a son; do you have a son too?"

"Yes, Madame."

"Oh! They shall be brought up together, and treated as brothers.

Here the young lady slid to my knees, and I saw all the sensibility of her heart in her beautiful eyes. I kissed her, and held her close to my heart.

"My friends," I said to the two ladies, "you can see that she is another me—will you love her as much as me?"

"I gave her to you!" the Marquise replied.

"I shall cherish her!" exclaimed the young Comtesse.

We decorated her. Oh, how pretty she was! She gave me vanity…and I believe, my love, that I would have been jealous, if you had been there. I owe her a moment of ease in our absence. It didn't last...

We took her to a play. All my acquaintances took her for my sister. They said so to one another, and a very young, very timid lady, who was pregnant, asked whether we were twins. Madame de Marigny said yes, which gave us a moment of amusement, because Madame Filète threw her arms around her and kissed her twice. I've never been happier than this evening, except with you.

I'll continue in another letter.

Letter XI

Has a sweet repose, then, and a complete enjoyment of myself followed despair and horror? Oh, even if I don't obtain life, as I hope, if Hortense doesn't give me immortality, I have known happiness; I have nothing for which to reproach Nature. For she cannot be unjust in our regard; she owes us felicity, if felicity is a good...unless a man ought think, by virtue of a sublime idea, that he is a portion of the Being-Principle, and that his very unhappiness is the effect of the supreme power of the whole on the part...

If I am God myself, I ought to suffer without complaint; if I am separate, he owes me happiness. One of those two alternatives must be true.

What? I'm reasoning? It's a long time since I've been able to reason.

Two years ago from this beautiful day, which follows a delightful night, I was no longer reasoning; I saw nothing but flowers, and the beautiful Hortense, their queen, blossoming like a rose.

A year ago from this beautiful day, the second of the renewal of my life, I no longer saw anything but pains, dolors, deprivation and despair. Oh, I dread not being God! I dread that the Supreme Being might have separated me from happiness, in order to be just. However, in the ineffable perfection of my felicity, I believe myself to be more than human. No, a frail and destructible being could not be as happy as I am! He could not support these torrents of voluptuousness, which intoxicate me and raise me above all the existences of Nature.

Will this supreme happiness continue? In a year, how shall I feel it? Oh, Hortense, it has been increasing for two days; if it continues, it will dissolve me.

Oh, why speak, write, when one is happy? It is necessary to enjoy...

I shall stop; I want to deliver myself to the idea that drags me away: *I possess Hortense!* For since the first moment of our union, the respiration of my soul has been the purest joy...

For such a long time, it only respired dolor!

Response to Letter XI

27 February.

Some anxieties returned to me in reading your eleventh letter. There is something...

What if my sick husband has gone away in order that I shall not see him struggling against death?

Let us chase away that despairing idea. One does not write so tenderly, so agreeably, when one is dying.

Filète consoles me. She has read all your letters. When I gave them to her I said: "Other me, you ought not to be unaware of anything."

She read them. Then she kissed me, holding me for a quarter of an hour in her beautiful arms. For she has arms and hands...*like Hortense*. You can see that the phrase is the Marquise's.

I said to Filète: "My sister, would you like to make me a promise?"

"Yes."

"Good. If I die, I would like you to represent me here, and dress in my clothes, and charm the dolor of my husband."

Her eyes, already moist, shed tears. Again she pressed me against her bosom.

She began to say "*vous*" and I stopped her, and asked her to say "*tu*" so that I could continue to do the same to her.

"You can ask anything; I shall make it a law, adorable friend, only to want what you want."

Oh, how dear she is to me. I sat her on my knees. She did not stay there. She set me on hers. There, I told her how, in such a case, to organize her conduct: how she must act, in the most delicate circumstances. Oh, it was charming, and J.-J. R's Claire d'Orbe could not have done better.[16]

---

[16] Claire d'Orbe is the eponymous heroine's "inseparable friend" in Rousseau's *Julie, ou La Nouvelle Heloïse* (1761).

There were, however, a few sighs over no longer being in the world. I saw my son growing up with hers, who would live here, and her too. Her husband, for whom great advantages would be procured, would cede me everything. Oh, what things are required to numb oneself to the absence of a husband!

This is my inclination: your wife's double ought to be adored by your double, and your double is your wife herself. I want her, by a refinement of delicacy, to resemble your wife perfectly, to be faithful, and that her heart, instead of being filled by a man, should not only be filled by a woman but solely by the one that is united with you; that she should love you, and cherish you immediately, in passing for me, in order that everything that is Hortense de Beauchamois should only breathe for you.

Letter XII

F.m.T. 12 February.

River of time, draw away with you the somber ideas of destruction and death, and only leave the happy Fontlhète the flowers that border the eternal banks! I am no longer myself; I am a different being from the one who, in the distance, two revolutions ago, was sighing after an unhoped-for happiness.

It is no longer the unfortunate being who sensed in me, that other year, such cruel pains. The one that I feel today, that I see in the mirror, is radiant with wellbeing; he has a florid complexion; all his senses, full of activity, savor the favors of Hortense. He has drunk the ambrosia of immortality.

In a year...yes, I shall be a father...Hortense will be a mother. I shall be the creator of a being formed from the two of us. She will have given him the light of day and I the spark of life. I shall be a God, since I shall have organized a living beings.

I don't want to write any more. What need do I have of a monument? I shall live: the monument will be my heart, tender, sincere, devoted and adoring. No, I shall not write any more...

But a thought occurs to me: what will transmit the excess of my happiness to posterity, if I do not confide it to paper? Oh, if I lose Hortense one day, these pages, a monument of amour, despair and happiness, these letters, will become the eternal monument of our interesting adventure...

I shall write. After having adored Hortense, pen in hand, I shall go every day, as at this instant, to realize in her arms what I have just written...and then, I shall prepare stories, such as have never been written, because no one has had the opportunity to return to the Source, as I am doing.

Response to Letter XII

28 February.

I pass from hope to dread and from dread to hope. But why, my dear husband, do you not say a word about my Filète, that amiable myself, who helps me support your absence? Oh, Fontlhète, can you be jealous? Tell me whether it is necessary for me to love her, or not to love her any longer?

Alas, the other myself will not see this letter, at least not today. I shall no longer talk about her; I shall not tell you about the continuation of our amity until I know your sentiments for her, for I only want to write agreeable things to you, which you will read entirely with pleasure. Will you respond on her subject? Do you love me entirely?

Letter XIII

F.m.T. 13 February.[17]

I shall henceforth confound all the epochs; there is no longer any but one for my heart; that is felicity. Hortense, shall I show you all my happiness, my divine Hortense? No, no...its duration is not yet sufficiently certain...

In all our conversations in writing, I shall only talk to you about the happiness that ought to follow life, and the sincere union that reigns between two souls separated in body, which are tenderly enlaced by amour. I shall compose a script, which I shall entitle *Élisée*, if I give it a title. There I shall distribute the cheerful images that sometimes present themselves to my enchanted mind.

I shall represent two English lovers, who have loved one another for a long time without hope, who had quit their homeland in order to come to Naples to be married, and were only corporeally happy on the final day of their corporeal life. Death harvested them both by means of an accident that prevented them from suffering. They were holding one another in an embrace, at the peak of the intoxication of their happiness; an earthquake, on the evening of their marriage, shook the house, a beam fell and crushed them, without them having time to utter a cry. The sentiment of dolor, mingled with that of pleasure, did not have time to affect them; they ceased to feel at the very moment when they were about to suffer. That was their death...or rather, their rebirth into a better life.

---

[17] The sequence of dates in the original skips ten days here, for no apparent reason, and skips further ahead before reverting to the orderly sequence established at the outset. I have assumed that the errors are not deliberate and have substituted the dates the letters ought to have in accordance with the stated plan, as I have done thus far for misrendered dates in the response sequence, although that subsequently loses its consistency.

Because, my dear Hortense, the soul is immortal, since it is divine; it will live; it will remember; it will love those it loves. I know a charming and philosophical lady—your relative, Madame Beauharnais—who desires it, and all that she desires must be.

Response to Letter XIII

1 March.

I am beginning to glimpse, dear husband, that it is a kind of philosophy that you have, which causes you to love to talk about souls and heir union. I recall, in fact, that in our conversations, you talked to me about that union of souls, while cherishing that of bodies—for only the latter, however beautiful the other might be could have produced my son...

Tell me sincerely, my love, with the verity that you have in your character, whether I, as a woman, who do not have your strength of mind, can abandon myself without danger to those ideas, which are, I believe, called metaphysics, because they are beyond the visible limits of Nature. Perhaps I could not follow them with a certain continuity without risk? That, at least, is the opinion of Madame de Marigny, Madame de Beauchamois and my Filète, your second wife—not that you ought to have two, but because, being my resemblance, she is another myself.

However, I like the care that you are taking to cheer up everything that you present to me. Oh, when shall I see you?

Filète has made the observation that will not have received the letter in which I talked about her as yet. That is true; I had not thought of it. But when you do, you can tell me your sentiment regarding my second.

Letter XIV

F.m.T. 14 February

Let us continue the story I commenced; it will fill my letters to my dear wife, when I have no facts that are personal.

Yfflasie and Clarendon had just expired, while embracing. Even Destiny can never separate those who die thus, in the blossoming expansion of amour and procreation; it is the greatest of joys...

"Where am I?" said Yfflasie, as if she had woken up from a profound sleep.

"I don't know what has just happened," said the tender Clarendon, "but my entire being experienced a great shock!"

She looked at Yfflasie;[18] Yfflasie looked at her. They found one another more beautiful, more svelte, and lighter. Clarendon tried to press Yfflasie against her heart, and they were united so narrowly that their existences were confounded, and they were no longer more than one. That infinitely perfect contact was delicious,

Clarendon said to herself, however—and her thought as Yfflasie's—*Shall I no longer be more than one, and, a new Narcissus, love myself? Shall we separate?*

And at the same instant, they were separated.

"Oh! we are two! We really are two!" they exclaimed, simultaneously. And they united themselves again, with an inexpressible sentiment of tenderness and wellbeing...

---

[18] The reason that the feminine pronoun is used here for both individuals is that the word *âme* [soul] is a feminine noun in French, and the author is making the point that the two individuals are now disincarnate souls. The author added a footnote of his own explaining that to the next letter, but it seems more appropriate to do it right away. The sexual politics of the afterlife are complicated, so the convention becomes very difficult to maintain, and is only patchily applied.

Tomorrow, my celestial wife, I shall continue the story of Yfflasie and Clarendon. Receive the assurance of my immortal sentiments, and above all, be persuaded that death does no harm, and that it will open the doors of happiness to us.

Response to Letter XIV

2 March.

So be it, my husband: death does no harm, I believe it, since you say so. But my Filète, tenderly enlaced in my arms, does not want to believe it.

"Why do you not believe it?" I said to her.

She did not reply. She hugged me in her arms, against her heart; her beautiful arms were moist with tears, and she ran to kiss my son. She had touched me and made me anxious at the same time.

She doesn't believe it. But it's natural that she loves life: young, pretty, having a son, a father—a man of merit, newly known—and a friend who cherishes her.

My two friends do not believe, either, that death does no harm. But I, who know that my husband has more enlighten-ment and knowledge than all other men, I shall seek instead to understand it, not to convince myself—for I am convinced, as soon as he has spoken—or to attempt to convince my two friends, the Marquise and the Comtesse, who have more intel-ligence than me, but I absolutely must convince my Filète, who has as much and no more than me, in order that all of myself should be.

You see, my love, that I am a very submissive wife.

Will you continue your Yfflasie and Clarendon for me? I should like to hear the adventures recounted that two lovers have after their death. That is new or everyone, and very inter-esting for me, on your part.

Letter XV

F.m.T. 15 February.

Yfflasie and Clarendon had sensed the first moment of their new existence at five o'clock in the evening. They experienced an inexpressible wellbeing; they were neither cold nor hot. They noticed, after a few seconds, that their seat had disappeared beneath them. It was a large cloud that had just resolved into rain. They discovered a globe on to which they wanted to descend. They did so solely by an effect of their will.

It was the Earth. They found that they were in Italy, in the same place where they had perished. Everything was visible to their incorporeal sight, but they were invisible to all corporate beings. They perceived that they could pass through houses and bodies, with much more facility than a light vapor; they penetrated them as heat can, but without remaining there, as it does.

They saw their former acquaintances without dolor. They would have liked to speak to them, but although Yfflasie could see and hear Clarendon, and Clarendon could see and hear Yfflasie, and they could see and hear other dead beings like themselves, whose host was innumerable, they could not be seen or heard by corporate beings. They finally perceived that, and knew their new state.

The sun set. They could see as clearly as before. They went to the mouth of Vesuvius, but the extreme heat of minerals in fusion was not sensible for them. Nothing material could affect them anymore. They were impassible, and could no longer sense anything but the impression of souls on their souls...

Until tomorrow, my dear Hortense. I occupy myself with these ideas with pleasure; they are necessary to the two of us.

Response to Letter XV

3 March.

Worthy husband I see what your tone is by your last letter. It is no longer with reasoning that you want to prove that death is nothing, it is with facts. I lend myself with pleasure to that idea, which tends to eternalize our happy union. I have even succeeded in making my Filète like it. As for my two friends, they have assured me that they will adopt the same opinion as me with pleasure. I am, therefore, tranquil in that regard.

I am the object of continual attention here. If anything could compensate for the presence of a husband I adore, I would have it. My Filète administers petty cares, which I return. My two friends attach me to their amusements, as much as my condition as a nurse permits.

As for business affairs, they are very well handled by your friend the president. I am, therefore, tranquil; or, if I sometimes have anxieties and uncertainties, they disappear at the sight of a letter, in which I recognize your hand and your writing. I sometimes have one weakness, however, which is comparing one letter to another, and both of them to writings that I have seen you make. That tranquilizes me.

Letter XVI

F.m.T. 16 February.

When Yfflasie and Clarendon perceived that the most ardent fire did not burn them, and that the eternal snows of Etna did not diminish in the slightest the mild temperature that surrounded them, they desired to go to the Arctic Pole, and found themselves transported there almost without perceiving the distance, although they saw the various rays on which they departed.

It was our summer. They saw the sun turning horizontally around the icy pole, without rising or falling. They saw mountains of ice separating from the horrible mass to which they adhered, and then floating, pushed by the wind caused by the dilatation of the air that was continuously occasioned by the uninterrupted presence of the sun on an atmosphere condensed for nine entire months by a cold incalculable for us.

They followed those mountains. They came as far as the demi-temperate rays at the seventieth parallel. They saw them touch there; white bears leapt on to them in order to catch fish in their fissures and disembark on to more temperate beaches, to which they brought ravage and destruction. Then, with an admirable instinct, they re-embarked, when the direction of the wind appeared to want to take the icy vectors away.

They wanted to see the other pole. A desire transported them there. They traversed the entire globe, seeing everything distinctly: in Europe, ambition and egotism rendering people unhappy; in Turkey, the double Greek and Mohammedan superstition, as foolish as one another; in Africa, a tiger-animal as big as a donkey devouring a negro; further away, a giant serpent stifling a pregnant woman in its vast coils, and then covering her with saliva in order to swallow her; in O-Taïti, a king gorging himself before his hungry subjects; in New Holland, savages killing English colonists from Botany Bay and eating them roasted...

Having arrived at the pole they no longer saw the sun; Nature, languishing because of the absence of her animator, seemed dead forever. Eternal darkness: no light, no heat, no movement. Yfflasie and Clarendon were no less agile, and were breathing an atmosphere no less mild.

They traveled the globe. They wanted to see all the continents and all the islands. What voluptuousness! They visited the Earth with more facility than a Parisian bourgeois measures his sandy little garden, planted with four lindens in a fan, a lilac and two rose-bushes. They obtained an accurate idea of all the nations.

They began with the Antarctic Pole and its islands. They saw the Friendly Isles, O-Taïti, New Caledonia, New Holland and the New Hebrides They found beings in those countries of all species, half human and half brute, such as were once seen in primitive Greece, newly emerged from the waters.

Then they went toward the equator. They visited Africa and all the black peoples, whose barbarity and misfortune astonished them. Oh, how much compassion they felt for the living, when they found them suffering, mutilated, crushed in a mortar, torn apart in butchery and sold for slavery, when they saw them chained in ships, put in the bottom of the hold, perishing of bad air and vermin. Oh, how glad they were to have been born in Europe, in a civilized nation, and to be, finally, by virtue of a fortunate death, liberated from all the pains and vicissitudes of life.

"But will our happy state last?" asked the timid Clarendon of the beautiful Yfflasie—for it is male animals that have the touching timidity that characterizes women here, after their disengagement.

"I believe so," replied the prudent Yfflasie, "but it will be necessary to consult the ancients of our new world."

This is a long letter, my beauty, my dear Hortense. May these ideas, when you read them, amuse you and distract you!

(*In another hand, which attempts to imitate the handwriting:*)

A thousand tendernesses to your beautiful Filète, and my respects to your two friends.[19]

---

[19] If Hortense's replies were supposed to be taking the same sixteen days to reach Fontlhète as his letters seem at this point to be taking to reach her, her news about Filète could not have reached him by the time he supposedly wrote this letter. This might imply that the dates on Hortense's letters do not refer to the same time-scheme as the dates on Fontlhète's.

Response to Letter XVI

4 March.

I read with interest, I devour all your letters. And what redoubles my attachment to my dear Filète, about whom you have finally spoken to me, is that she devours them as I do.

She said to me this morning: "I cannot tell you, my sister, how much that other life pleases and amuses me. But it is because our husband presents these things so gaily, with so much grace, that he communicates the desire for it. Does that state of liberty only come of its own accord, without our working for it."

"Yes," I replied, "but I believe that in order to sense all its charm, it is necessary to die young."

"Oh no," she replied, "it is necessary to die tranquil, joyful, if that is possible, or at least without chagrin—and then one is perfectly happy."

That response is very intelligent, and I sensed it. So it is me that has made it to myself...

Filète has read with delight the note regarding her. You wrote it as an afterthought, my dear husband; you reproached yourself for not having said anything about the angelic Filète.

Letter XVII

F.m.T. 17 February.

The two lovers Yfflasie and Clarendon sought to make contact with ancient shades—forgive me that term, my Hortense; it does not have the same significance here as in the Greek and Latin poets. They wanted no less than to find those of Adam, Abel, Noah, Abraham, Jacob, Moses, David and Solomon. Nothing! Jewish history had deceived them regarding the existence of those individuals.

They asked for Homer, they searched for Orpheus, one of the Hercules. Nothing! Those ancient shades no longer inhabited the country where they had once lived. They asked after Lycurgus, Solon, Socrates and Demosthenes. Mention had been heard of them, but they were only known among the souls by tradition, as on Earth.

They then fell back on asking for Virgil, Cicero, and even Caesar, and the fortunate Octavian, his adoptive son, who ought to have been even more famous among the souls. But they could not encounter them, and even less Horace and Lydia, Tibullus and Delia, Catullus and Lesbia, nor Ovid or his Julia.

Surprised and afflicted, Yfflasie and Clarendon said to one another: "Are souls mortal, then?"

They were not discouraged, however. They searched for Titus, Trajan, Epictetus, Antonius, Marcus Aurelius, Constantine, the sublime Julian and Theodosius. They spoke of Augustine and Jerome. Finally, they came to Charlemagne.

Nothing; the names of all those people were familiar, but they did not appear to have been among the souls for a long time.

"Let's come closer to the present," said Clarendon to the impatient Yfflasie. They went through the following centuries, and after having asked in vain for Louis IX, Charles VII, the Maid and Dunois, they came to Henri IV.

"What!" said Yfflasie. "I shall not see Henri the Béarnais?"

"Let's see. Let's keep looking. There are a multitude of souls."

As their agility was extreme, and as rapid as will, they were everywhere in an instant...

But I shall postpone until tomorrow the continuation of their search, beautiful Hortense. This is not a fairy tale. I am saying nothing that is not the truth.

(*In an imitative hand:*)

Thank the other half of our being for me, for the bounty she believes me to have, and tell her that I love to confound her with you. I only know her through you, but she resembles you perfectly. Oh, how lovable she must be!

Response to Letter XVII

5 March.

At present all my doubts are relieved; I surrender myself with delight to the charm of your letters. But where are you going, with all these souls that are no longer to be found? I have not yet divined your objective, by virtue of that suspension.

Filète is enchanted. I want her to write a word and the bottom of my letter and I shall stop here.

(Filète wrote, but she would not permit the editor to place here the ten or twelve lines that he saw in her hand.)

Letter XVIII

F.m.T. 18 February.

Let us take up, my beloved, the thread of the story. I have no intention of causing you to languish with preambles.

Clarendon asked the best souls, which had been the most recently liberated, whether he could not see Louis XIV.

"You're just in time," replied the soul of Montausier,[20] to whom he was speaking. "That Prince is making his preparations to return to a body."

"To a body! What—the happy state that we are in will not be eternal? It will be necessary to live again?"

Montausier looked at Clarendon severely. "Noble Portion of the Divinity," she said, "who are you to disapprove of the sublime views of he Being-Principle? But you will think very differently when you have passed into the state of a pure soul, after the hundred years that this disengaged life will last. Between now and then you will be formed. At this moment you and Yfflasie are like children, but your reason will develop. You will profit from your voyage to the planets of our universe, which you will be able to visit, in order to instruct yourself on a host of matters. For it will only be in another life, when our planet falls into the sun and our disengagement from corporeal shackles will become more perfect, that we shall be able to see all the other planetary systems. But even that life—after the dissolution of our planet in the sun—will not be eternal; nothing is eternal but God, or the Sovereign Principle.

"Our Earth will re-emerge from the general amalgam made of all the planets and all the suns of the universe in the Astral Center, dissolved within it, to recommence a new life;

---

[20] Charles de Sainte-Maure, Duc de Montausier (1610-1690), a soldier and one of the tutors of Louis XIV's son Louis, "the Great Dauphin").

and all the species, as many human as animal, will similarly recommence life in bodies, to become free and disengaged again, rolling thus, throughout eternity, from life to life, through apparent death and rebirth. Everything that has happened to us will happen again, in a new life, with the result that we shall be with a body composed of homogeneous matter, without being precisely the same as any that we have been before. That is how, without suspecting it, we shall be eternal; for, resolving us into nothing by the fraction of our organs, the Being will always be reformed anew. Receive that lesson from me—but I will take you to Louis XIV."

I shall stop. Hortense; I kiss your beautiful hands, (another handwriting) and Filète's.

Response to Letter XVIII

6 March.

Montausier's speech is very good, and I am very curious to see Louis XIV and hear what he has to say. In truth, my husband, your letters are as amusing as a novel, and all that is annoying to us is not to have the continuing sequence, so that we could read a hundred in a day. But that means that we re-read them all when I receive each one, in order better to see the whole. By that means, I shall know the early ones by heart by the end of our correspondence.

Dear spouse, the interest of a letter from you is powerful enough, without you trying to add substance that is interesting to read. I thank you for it nevertheless; I obtain no more pleasure from reading but I can give more to others, to my Filète, who complains that I put her in another class than myself, and the witty Beauchamois and the pretty Marquise.

F.m.T. 19 February.

Yesterday, my Hortense, I finished my letter by saying that Montausier took Yfflasie and Clarendon to see Louis XIV. They found that ancient monarch seated, apparently, in the midst of all his Court, on the roof of the Château de Versailles, or rather on a window-sill, where there was a small tub containing a laurel bush.

All of that numerous assembly, numbering more than ten thousand, was contained on a leaf of the little laurel. They were chatting together. Louis only distinguished other souls by means of a greater politeness, laughter and a more affectionate tone.

"My dear friends," he said to his former courtiers, "I only like to spend my life with you because I loved you all when you had bodies. I wanted nothing but your good, and when I did not achieve that, it was because I was mistaken. But what completes my joy is that today, when we are all equal, you still love me, and show me deference. I was, therefore, veritably a King!"

"Yes, you were," said Montausier, introducing Yfflasie and Clarendon to him, "since we, today your equals, love you and show marks of out attachment. And your glory is not eclipsed on Earth, in spite of the faults you committed: the revocation of the Edict of Nantes, the imprisonment of your brother with an iron mask..."

"Stop, my dear Monsieur! Those two crimes frighten me. But my brother's imprisonment was not my work. Our common father had ordered it, on certain conditions, such as: *If he wanted to know*... He wanted it. He would have doomed you all, by virtue of his resemblance to me. You know that he was the elder, but that precautions had not been taken for his birth.

"It had been resolved nevertheless to render him heir to the throne by making the Queen lie with Louis XIII. The Queen was to feign a pregnancy, if she could not have a true one. But as soon as the following night, my brother's father having succeeded in fecundating her, they waited in silence to see what that pregnancy would produce. It was me. I appeared well-conformed. There would be no dangerous deception to make...

"And, my mother having had a second son, the dangerous elder was brought up in obscurity. Our father loved him, and might, in spite of his celebrated finesse, have committed some imprudence, since at sixteen years of age, my elder brother by a year, having seen me, and already suspecting something, guessed his origin...

"Unfortunately for him, he was not sufficiently instructed, or too much. He did not know the world, and thought, in his naivety, that he would only have to prove that he was the older by a year to put himself in my place. Like me, he fell in love with Hortense Mancini, our cousin—or rather our sister, since she was the daughter and not the niece of our father, who had her by his own sister, with whom he had fallen in love before coming to France...

"The false Bourbon, who believed himself to be the son of Louis XIII, therefore wanted to make himself known, marry Hortense and crown her. He revealed that to a confidant, who betrayed him, and he was not only imprisoned but masked. That is the story, which excited the curiosity of the French so much. My brother, who still holds a slight grudge against me, has become the intimate friend of my brother d'Orleans, and they're almost always together..."

But my dear spouse, that anecdote has used up all my paper.[21] Until tomorrow.

---

[21] Although the fictitious allegation that the mysterious prisoner arrested in 1669 and kept in prison, held incommunicado, until he died in 1703, wore a iron mask is usually credited to Voltaire, the investigation of the origins of the story carried out in the nineteenth century by "P. L. Jacob the Bibliophile" (Pierre Lacroix)—a close associate of Alexandre Dumas, one of the chief promoters of the myth—acknowledges that it

Response to Letter XIX

7 March.

That, my husband, is an anecdote that I did not expect in your letters! It has given my three friends the greatest pleasure. But that poor Louis XIV, with his entire court and all his admirers, of a single laurel leaf! And that inclination for Versailles, where he reigned! What did he say, on seeing a Du Barry[22] replace La Valière here? For I won't mention La Montespan, and even less La Maintenon, whom I've never liked...nor the celestial Pompadour.

The Comtesse and the Marquise thank you. As for my Filète, I believe that she's commencing to love you as much as your wife. Fortunate amphibology, which is true in both senses!

---

might have been spawned by "a detestable novel by the Chevalier de Mouhy," issued anonymously in 1746, allegedly in The Hague, entitled *Le Masque de fer, ou les aventures admirables du père et du fils*. The novel in question is an early specimen of what later come to be known as a *roman de cape-et d'épée*—a swashbuckling tale of derring-do. It remains uncertain as to whether Mouhy got the idea from Voltaire or whether Voltaire got it from him. The story told here, explaining the mystery in terms of Louis XIV having had an illegitimate older brother, is also usually credited to Voltaire, who probably did not mean a word of it, but the hypothesis proved enormously resilient—especially when seconded by Dumas in *Le Vicomte de Bragelonne* (1847-1850)—in spite of numerous rival hypotheses and protests that the mask the prisoner wore had really been made of velvet.

[22] Jeanne Bécu, Comtesse Du Barry (1743-1793) was Louis XV's last accredited mistress; she was the target of the most scurrilous of the numerous pre-Revolutionary pamphlets directed against the Ancient Régime, and was beheaded during the Terror.

Letter XX

F.m.T. 20 February.

"But whence come these two French souls that you are introducing to me?" said Louis XIV.

"Sire, they are not natives if France; they had their natality in Italy, where they were crushed by a beam while making love, as you loved Madame La Valière.[23] Their origin is English. Their grandfather and grandmother were obliged to leave France by your revocation. Their father established himself in London, and there married one of your paternal cousins on the left-hand side—for your father had more than one mistress. At any rate they have French ancestry, and are attached to you."

"Ah yes!" cried the monad of Louis XIV. "French monads, more reasonable than those of other peoples, only see in their monarch the organizing head who directs the executive hand of the nation. No king of France has ever been a despot; he only reigns by law!"

"My friend," said Montausier, taking Louis XIV's hand—for souls that have lived see, by habitude, the limbs of monads endowed with passions, which constitute the soul, properly speaking—"these two monads, newly disengaged, have asked to see you, urgently, as the most celebrated of your contemporaries."

Clarendon advanced, holding Yfflasie's hand.

"How beautiful she is!" said Louis XIV—for it is necessary to know that the souls of beauties, like my Hortense and the one who resembles her, conserve in the eyes of other mon-

---

[23] I have retained Restif's usual spelling of the name of Louise de La Vallière (1644-1710), one of Louis XIV's mistresses in the early 1660s, although he does use the more usual spelling occasionally.

ads the appearance of the beauty their bodies had. It is for that reason that it is advantageous to die young![24]

Clarendon was about to kiss Louis XIV's hand when an exactly similar monad, who had a court of curiosity-seekers, if not admirers, all placed on a laurel leaf adjacent to that of Louis XIV stopped the young man, saying to him: "I am the true Louis XIV. The one to whom you are rendering your homage is merely a usurper, a cruel tyrant. It is scorn, and not homage, that it is necessary to render to him."

Clarendon looked at the monad who had spoken, and thought he was looking at Louis XIV.

Montausier said to him: "Imprudent monad! It was impossible to do otherwise than imprison you and mask you! You would have troubled all of France and scandalized all Europe. It was necessary to sacrifice you. In any case, would you have done such great things as your brother?"

"I would not have committed his crimes."

"Perhaps!"

The monad of the man in the iron mask, seeing that he was not supported by anyone, withdrew angrily, with his little court and his curiosity-seekers.

Louis XIV became cheerful again after his brother's departure, and occupied himself with the two new monads, whom he was delighted to see.

I shall 1stop there, my Hortense, not for lack of material, but because urgent affairs summon me, and my delightful hour with you has elapsed.

---

[24] This remark and the previous one appear to license the reversion, here and elsewhere, to the use of masculine pronouns to refer to Louis XIV, Montausier and Clarendon, the author having temporarily abandoned the affectation of referring to all souls as "elle." The practice will recur subsequently, but somewhat erratically.

Response to Letter XX

8 March.

It would have been surprising if the monad of Louis Mazarini had not conserved some resentment against Louis XIV, which your previous letter had fully justified. That is the way it is with the families of kings. One believes that a race is continuing, and in very little time, here come two interruptions! For my two friends, the Comtesse and the Marquise, are sure that the Duchesse de Bourgogne did not have Louis XV of the Duc, and that our present king is entirely of coarse Saxon blood...[25]

But what does that matter to peoples, as long as the government is good?

While we are chatting, my Filète is caressing my son and her own. Your son, my love, although scarcely formed, mistakes her for his mother, and sometimes seeks her breast.

"In truth," she said to me a little while ago, "I wish I had milk! He would love me more! But I dare not let him try, for fear that he might sense the difference between you and me, in the sole manner that the can sense it, at present."

I took her on my knees; she held the infant and I gave him milk...

Such are my amusements. They are innocent and simple. When will you render them more complicated?

---

[25] Louis XV's mother, who was Princess Marie-Adélaide de Savoie (1685-1712) before she married the Duc de Bourgogne, the eldest son of the Grand Dauphin, was involved from the outset of her marriage in a feud with Louis XIV's daughter, the Duchesse de Bourbon (1673-1743), who might well have put about the rumor of Marie-Adélaide's adultery long before it became an established myth of scurrilous anti-royalist slander.

Letter XXI

F.m.T. 21 February.

My beloved! Louis XIV had no news to request of the two monads Yfflasie and Clarendon; he knew everything that had happened.

"My children," he said to them, "is it me for whom you asked first?"

They replied to him, as I have reported in previous letters. At the name of Henri IV, Louis XIV sighed.

"My children," he said to the young Yfflasie and the handsome Clarendon, "we remain pure souls, at least for a century, in accordance with our bodily forms, before returning to animate another. We have two lives in succession, which are continuous, the most recent of our corporeal lives and our present incorporeal life. After that we lose continuity, during the corporeal life that recommences. But as you will discover, we all have the faculty, in each incorporeal life, of remembering all that we have been in a hundred previous lives, as many corporeal as incorporeal or intellectual, as is the one we are enjoying at this moment.

"Thus, I, who have seventy-six years of intellectuality,[26] will soon gradually recover the knowledge of all that I have been during my last hundred lives, and I know that one day, having fallen, with our sun, into the bosom of God Himself, we shall remember everything that has happened to us during the entirety of the preceding eternity...

"I have had the misfortune, my ear children, of not having yet seen Henri IV. If my last corporeal career had been

---

[26] Louis XIV died in September 1715, so this statement, if the figure of 76—rendered numerically in the original—is not a misprint, implies that he is speaking in 1791, some way into the future of the point at which Fontlhète is supposed to be writing, whenever that is assumed to be.

three years shorter, I would have seen him! His monad only passed into another body after 101 years of intellectuality...[27]

"I know, as we all know, what has become of him. But in addition to the fact that we have no corporeal organ with which to speak to him and make ourselves heard, what is there to say to an old man who remembers nothing? Oh, if I had the good fortune of his being deprived of his mortal envelope before I resume a new one myself, how many things we would have to say to one another!"

Seeing that Louis XIV had fallen silent, Yfflasie said to him: "Sire, permit a young soul, newly arrived here, to ask you a question. Souls can see those they left alive, but suppose that my husband Clarendon, here present, had been the only one crushed, would he still have loved me?"

"Yes, undoubtedly," Louis XIV replied, "if your soul had continued to be worthy of him."

"Oh, or my soul, I can answer...but in growing old, I...would have become ugly, and in Italy, it happens soon. He might no longer have loved me, when I was forty."

"You're strangely mistaken, my daughter! Souls have another rule than bodies. If a woman left a window young by a tender spouse, not only conserves his memory dearly, but further increases in virtue, the soul of her husband, which is waiting for her in order to reunite with her, loves her more and more. Souls do not see the changes brought to bodies by old age; one remains, for them, at the age one was at the moment of their discorporation, still pretty, and if virtues increase, charm increases."

"Oh, how unfortunate a woman is who forgets her husband!"

"Yes, she is equally forgotten. He searches for a soul also forgotten by her spouse, and they unite."

"Oh, Clarendon, would you have forgotten me?"

---

[27] Henri IV died in May 1610, so this figure implies that he was reincorporated in 1711—four years, not three, before Louis XIV died.

"No, no! Never!"

Louis XIV smiled at that interruption, and seemed to be in a very good humor.

Response to Letter XXI

9 March.

Now I am instructed as to the circumstances of corporeal life. In truth, I would have liked it to be eternal—but as you say, the Being-Principle alone is eternal, and all other beings change, in form and situation. You have almost taken away my taste for life, my dear husband, and I'm commencing to desire to have the fate of Clarendon and Yfflasie with you. My Filète would have adopted these sentiments in order to eternal-ize herself with me. But she would have regretted her son, whom she would have liked to see a father before he com-menced an incorporeal life...

I think the same for ours, and in my opinion, what Clar-endon and his Yfflasie lack is a son. But that life to recom-mence, with all its troubles...oh! Oh...

The Comtesse is asking me what kind of single whole my letters will serve to make, in combination with yours. I am replying to her that they will serve, as in music, the same pur-pose as the repetition of passages and refrains, to engrave the situation more deeply in the soul.

F.m.T. 22 February.

"You are doubtless curious," Louis XIV continued, "to know what has become of Henri IV in his present mortal life."

"Oh yes!" exclaimed Yfflasie and Clarendon simultaneously.

Louis XIV smiled. "I shall tell you," he said, "after preceding that revelation with a brief prologue.

"All disengaged souls are equal; however, those who were good in their last corporeal life have a privilege over the wicked. Those who have been sternly righteous during a bodily life have the advantage of choosing what they want to be when they return to corporeality, whereas, rogues and traitors are obliged to obey fate, which sends them to animate bodies at random.

"In spite of that advantage, which the good have, they are often deceived in their choice, in asking to enter into the body of the son or daughter of a particular man or woman. The organs and passions of the father or mother, or both, often make souls vicious, and have false perceptions, which lead them stray, because the father and mother were in a vicious disposition at the moment of conception. The good soul, then finding itself in a bad case, the organs of which second it poorly, is dishonest and wicked, but with remorse, because it is not naturally so, whereas a monad previously in a wicked body is wicked without remorse.

"Kindness and malevolence depend on organs. The monads of the good cannot divine that. They choose, in order to return to life, the body of a child whose parents are honest and have the means to give it a good education. That is all they can do.

"Henri IV chose to be the son of a virtuous laborer. He is therefore virtuous, because he father and mother were. But he has keen and violent passions, because the monad had them in its last body, and because he is healthy and vigorous. He is at present...you won't be expecting this...he is..."

Louis XIV interrupted himself at this point, celestial Hortense, in order to tell his court that you had just had a terrible dream. You had seen me, a new Alcyone, washed up dead on the beach at Marseilles, returning from Italy. Don't believe in dreams! They contain nothing of our intellectual life; they are merely the vulgar rumination of the soul, doubly weighed down by its body and by sleep. It is only almost free in wakefulness; it is double swaddled when the body is asleep.

(One senses that a friend had written that dream, which Hortense does not mention. It is possible, however, that Fontlhète might have heard talk of one of his wife's dreams.)

Response to Letter XXII

10 March.

These are strange things—but which explain to me very well how the good are recompensed in the other life and how the wicked are punished, why some people have remorse and others do not. Your letters, my good husband, are really instructive, and I feel ready to embrace your doctrine. Since you have become accustomed to entertaining me with souls. I believe in truth that I would disdain the body, if I did not have such amiable and beloved ones around me.

Your doctrine regarding dreams is also the only reasonable one. They are a veritable mental rumination, so I do not give them any credit by saying that they are true...

Filète, who is following what I write, is kissing me, and she has moist eyes.

What have I done to Heaven, to be deprived of my husband? But what have I done to Heaven, for him to be replaced by a double of myself, all of whose movements please me, who walks, talks and sings like me, whose thoughts and sentiments are always mine?

Insensate women who love a conceited or perfidious man, who have an unworthy favorite, who love a dog, a cat, a parrot, a canary or worse still...seek your Filète! She exists somewhere! And love her! You will find, in that other self, inexpressible sweetness!

Letter XXIII

F.m.T. 23 February.

I was going to tell you yesterday, my beloved, what Henri IV is today, who is aged 76.[28] I am sure that you are all the more curious to know, as he can still be seen. He is…an Ecclesiastic.

"By that word, my love, don't believe him to be the pope or a cardinal, an archbishop, a bishop or a mitered abbé. That king, the first of his branch, is a village curé, and of the poorest village in France, which has the most stubborn inhabitants and the most inclined to evil deeds.

I have seen him, my dear wife; I have admired him, but I did not know then that he was Henri IV!

Louis XIV showed him to the two lovers, Yfflasie and Clarendon. But the latter could not speak to him to question him. They slipped then into the brain of an old soldier, an inspector-general of artillery, and solicited his soul to interrogate the octogenarian curé. This is what I heard by their means, for Yfflasie and Clarendon read his thoughts.

"It is to do more good that I put myself in this estate. I had chosen to be born in mediocrity. Once I found myself

---

[28] If he had been reincorporated in 1711, as previously implied, Henri IV's new body would be eighty in the apparent "now" of the enclosed story based on Louis XIV's claim to have been discorporated for 76 years were true—and that is supported by the subsequent reference to him as an octogenarian—but he would be 76 in Hortense's "now" if the letters were being written in 1787 (as they were in Restif's time-frame): a suggestion that is subsequently repeated more than once, although it seems inconsistent with the four-year internal time-scheme of the early letters, and with other subsequent data suggesting that the "present" in question is 1788 (as it would have become at some stage in Restif's time-frame).

there, I reflected on all the good that an individual might do, and I saw, by virtue of the great harm that priests do, how urgent it was to bring the balm of a good example into the priesthood. As a village curé, I followed a direction toward good, which had been as if instructed to me by a previous life in which I had been celebrated for my virtues. I banished from my mind any cabalistic idea with regard to humans. I sensed that it was necessary to believe my religion in order to practice it, so I believe. I forgot all things that had no relationship with my estate, in order only to conserve in my heart those that rendered it useful, important and sacred. Before being a priest, I thought, it is necessary to be an honest man—and so many of my colleagues cease to be honest men in order to become priests! Some embrace the estate of curé in order to live tranquilly with a pretty housekeeper, others, even more culpable, in order to tell lewd stories to all the pretty women in the parish and devour several, others, true swine of the herd of Epicurus, in order to eat, drink and sleep without difficulty, and others in order to be important men in a little sphere. Far be those egotistical sentiments from mine! I made myself a priest in order to give a little good advice to people, to aid the unfortunate and preserve them from despair..."

I have been interrupted. Sole charm of my life, Hortense, again I can no longer occupy myself with you. Oh, when I was next to you, I was too happy to think, Now that I am far away, I think, and I write...

Response to Letter XXIII

10 March.

Courage, my dear husband! You are preaching me sermons, under the name of Henri IV, and even Louis XIV. My friends say that you are entering the novitiate, in order to be a Capuchin, and Filète adds, with the grace that never quits her: "Let's go—his two wives will be nuns facing the Louis of the Place Vendôme, for it is not appropriate that they remain in the world, having a husband avowed to great mortification..."

However, dear husband, continue to paint us the conduct of Henri become a village curé, and be sure of amusing your wife. In any case, the subject is interesting...

(The rest is mundane business matters, to which the President's secretary responded in his own name.)

Letter XXIV

F.m.T. 24 February.

It is Louis XIV who will continue the story where I left it, because, having been interrupted yesterday, I have lost the thread of it.

"Henri found himself an honest man as soon as he believed perfectly in the religion of which he was a minister. Entirely devoted to his estate, he regarded himself as the father of his flock. The wheat that formed his income was lent, during the winter, to be returned, if possible, during the summer by the borrowers. But if that could not be done—which the pastor was far from being able to verify—in order not to encourage idleness or to afflict the unfortunate, he gave it until the possibility of return, or forever.

"He visited his flock in the six days, consoling, exhorting and never scolding, not even vice. For he said: 'I am their father, and they have no other recourse but in me; if take away that recourse, they will no longer have any.' He preached a pure but mild morality; he recommended fraternal amity.

"He was not an enemy of honest diversions, and wanted them to be presided over by fathers and mothers, or either of them. When the objection was made to him that certain diversions were forbidden, because of their danger, he replied, laughing: 'If ne takes away the prohibition, one takes away the danger.'"

Louis XIV softened, and exclaimed: "Judge how touched I was to see my respectable ancestor knowing so well the spirit of a religion—false, it is true, like all the others, but for which I still have affection, and which I served with so much zeal in the last years of my life! Alas, if I had only known it as Henri knows it today!"

And tears flowed, as the tears of souls disengaged from bodies can—which is to say that Yfflasie and Clarendon saw in that one the sentiment that produces tears...

110

I shall stop here, although my letter is very short. Until tomorrow. Is it happiness that is destroying my strength? I sense that its overactivity is a devouring fire...but fortunate! Fortunate is the man who is consumed by happiness. That is what I am experiencing, in living with my Hortense.

Response to Letter XXIV

12 March.

It is certain, my friend, that kings are better in the other world than they are here, as witness Louis XIV. Madame de Beauchamois is passionate for him! She only speaks about him with transport! As for Madame de Marigny, she is more borne toward Louis XV, although she has reason to be discontented with him—for, in truth, that Du Barry is very debasing! The Marquise, however, only ever talks about the monarch, and only in very good terms. She's a charming woman, although somewhat calumniated by stupid men and women who do not know her. Her full-length portrait was at the Salon this year. It really caused a sensation. Her husband is leaning on the back of her chair. It's said that it's the best full-length portrait the painter has made.

Madame de Beauchamois would also have shone in that way, and to paint me, without talking about myself, I've heard it said that my pretty Filète has the nicknames "Pretty leg" and "Dainty foot."

Oh, this is a woman's letter! And I've certainly never written its like, not even to my friends. I shall send it, though. Perhaps it's the tender ending of yours, which marks an advantageous state of mind, that has put me in his disposition?

Filète salutes you, and my two friends kiss you. As for me, I find my Filète too reserved.

Letter XXV

F.m.T. 25 February.

Louis XIV collected himself, in order to continue.

"Henri, as a village curé, being as heroic as when he reigned, rendered himself useful to everyone, but he was more useful to the small number that he had adopted. He was a cited example of priestly conduct, more perfect than those of the first ministers of Christianity, because he had a better and more honest soul. He has earned the admiration of disengaged souls, a host of which incessantly surrounds him, in order to contemplate him. You will be able to see him, as I have seen him—and a desire will suffice to transport you to his village. I can have you guided there by one of the souls that always accompany me, and which want to obey me even though they are my equals.

"Great King," Clarendon replied, "I do not believe myself to be your equal, although I am a soul. I will honor you until the moment when the eternal decrees return you to life, which you will honor again in a new mortal body. I shall go to see Henri, but will you forgive me if, on my return, I ask to see Louis XIII?"

Yfflasie and Clarendon hastened to the village and saw there what I recounted to you in a previous letter, in which I made Louis XIV speak. They were to return n a few minutes, to recount what they had seen and heard, and then they renewed their request to see Louis XIII.

At these repeated words, Louis XIV lowered his eyes—which is still to say that Yfflasie and Clarendon saw, in their fashion, the movement of the will by which one lowers one's eyes.

"My sisters," the former monarch replied, "I have made it a rule not to disoblige anyone. Come—I will show him to you."

A movement of will sufficed to transport them to the Bois de Vincennes. They saw a soul there, which, by virtue of its whims, inconsequential thoughts and capricious desires, resembled a child on its mother's apron-strings. That monad was dominated by another, which had a severe gaze, and rebuked it incessantly. The child-monad did not dare to want anything that the haughty monad did not also want.

Louis XIV, drawing near, gazed at Richelieu with grandeur. The omnipotent Minister did not lower his gaze.

"My father," said Louis XIV, "can you not shrug off the yoke of this tyrant?"

Louis XIII shivered, and made a fearful sign to Louis XIV as he replied: "peace! Peace! She frees me from the burden of wanting and making up my mind, for...for that's very difficult."

Yfflasie dared to ask Louis XIII what he wanted to be when he returned to the world.

"Oh," he exclaimed, "a Carthusian! A Carthusian, if Monseigneur le Cardinal will permit"

"You shall soon have that satisfaction," replied Richelieu, blushing, "for your hundred years of intellectual life are finished."[29]

Louis XIII looked at him. "Shall I live again?"

"I shall see to it."

Yfflasie smiled. "And you," she said to the cardinal. "What will you be?"

"By what right do you question me?" she replied.

"Because I am your equal. Answer me: I want that."

Then Richelieu, sensing that the law required her to reply, exclaimed: "I want to be a schoolmistress, to whip, to whip, to whip... It's only then that one is a mistress without danger, without reproach, without bitterness...you're praised

---

[29] They must have been finished for some time; Louis XIII died in May 1643. Cardinal Richelieu had preceded him by a few months, dying in December 1642.

when you have punished. A schoolmistress of a very numerous, very stupid village…oh, what delights!"

After that response, Louis XIV, Yfflasie and Clarendon
quit Louis XIII and Richelieu, whom they saw for the last time
in the number of disengaged souls.

Response to Letter XXV

13 March.

I shall outbid you, good husband. I would like Richelieu to be the whipper at the Collège Louis-le-Grand, and the feeble Louis XIII to become, indeed, a Carthusian. We will go to see the former, my three friends and I, but we shall be careful not to send him our children. That is up to us!

How the disengaged monads conserve their weaknesses! What a powerful motive to acquire virtues, and to have a tenderness, between spouses, similar to that of Clarendon and Yfflasie—in brief, to be noble individuals down here, highly-placed but good. In addition to the incomparable advantage it gives, one enjoys a hundred years of very agreeable life!

We are impatient, my friends and I, to see the continuation. But as you will not receive my letter for several days, I would like your soul to be able to divine mine.

Letter XXVI

F.m.T. 26 February.

Yes, I have been keenly desirous of the moment to pick up the pen again, in order to retrace my conversations with the fortunate souls, which I can only have by disengaging myself almost completely from the bonds of the body. It is an experiment that I advise you not to attempt, my dear wife, and which is only appropriate for me for particular reasons.

Two days after the day when we had seen them, Louis XIII and Richelieu were forced to pass into new bodies, at the moment of conception. Yfflasie and Clarendon were curious to follow those two souls, merely to see where they were lodged, and to be able to find them again easily thereafter.

Richelieu entered into the seed of the body of the child of a miller, and Louis XIII into the seed of the fetus of a prostitute and a spy. Those two beings, king and minister, had not merited during their corporeal life the right to choose.

Although the events concerning those two souls happened several years later, I shall report them in order not to come back to them.

Richelieu grew tall, guided the donkeys of the mill and rained blows upon them. He was so nasty that when he passed by, all the children fled—with the result that the paternal mill lost a great many clients. His father corrected him, but the bad boy only became crueler toward men, children, women and animals. He was beaten by his father and others, which doubtless determined him to join the army.

As a soldier, however, he was even more malevolent. He pillaged, raped and ate human flesh. He was the boldest of marauders. Finally, he robbed one of his comrades. He passed under the rods, and was left for dead on the spot. He recovered, however, because a good woman took pity on him.

To thank her, when he was better, he tied her to a bed one winter night, raped her, robbed her, stabbed her and ate

117

her. He even made black pudding with her blood and lived for a week on her and the provisions she had. After having consumed her and given her bones to the wolves that were prowling in the vicinity of the isolated house, he went into a foreign land.

Now, there was a young daughter in the house who, having seen the soldier rape and kill the woman, had hidden behind a pile of faggots, and had come to the thief's kitchen by night to eat. She did not quit her hiding-place until he had departed for the last time, without closing the doors. The child escaped as soon as she could and went to tell all. The crime of the miller's son was known throughout the world. He was tried for it, and condemned, as was customary, to be broken in effigy. In a war that was then being fought he was captured by our troops and recognized. His trial was already complete. He was taken to Paris, thrown into a dungeon, and awaited his fate...

As for Louis XIII...but that is for tomorrow.

I don't know why I've followed these black ideas. I must try to forget them, and occupy myself with you, Hortense.

Response to Letter XXVI

14 March.

Oh what a cruel man that ex-Richelieu was in his second life! It appears, dear spouse, that you judge him according to the secret dispositions of your heart. My two friends are almost annoyed with you. But Filète and I—for we are but one—excuse you for the cruelties you recount. My double and I rejoice in the fact that the little girl escaped death by hiding and eating from the Mareine,[30] doubtless less than she could have: there were bread, fruits and cheeses.

We have been very glad to see him captured. But now compassion has taken possession of the Comtesse and the Marquise again, and they have said to me and my double: "Oh, he's clever, and you'll see that he'll get away!"

We shall see, for I can't suborn you for tomorrow's letter, and they can't accuse me of it.

---

[30] "Mareine" is an obsolete spelling of *Marraine* [godmother], but knowing that does not make the sentence any more comprehensible.

Letter XXVII

F.m.T. 27 February.

What a difference from the fate of the first Richelieu was that of the miller's son, whom he was in a second life!

As for Louis XIII, he came into the world at the Hôtel-Dieu, and was put with the foundlings. As the mother was dubious, he was fed from a bottle. He remained weak, languishing and rachitic. At seven or eight he was put in the Pitié, where he ended up bandy-legged with rickets. He was taught to spin wool. He spent his days there, pale and sickly, vegetating instead of living.

All the souls that knew him were touched by compassion. Aside, they said: "People would be less harsh if they knew that the same fate might await the oppressor and the oppressed. Oh, how good people would be, how philanthropic, patriotic and obliging, if they knew that the mass of evils and goods is common to us, that the fate they give to the unfortunate today might be procured for them in a future life!"

Louis XIII, known as Jeannot Piteux, died at the age of twenty-six, after having languished, without having known any of the pleasures of life. He did not know those of amour, the unfortunate, either in his second life or his first!

On the same day that he died, Georges Meulant, alias Coeur-de-fer, formerly Richelieu, was broken on the wheel, with the result that the two souls encountered one another on exiting their bodies. But Jeannot Piteux had become bold at the Pitié; she did not recognize Georges, or stood up to her, and remained independent. It was a step toward betterment, a great lesson for weak kings, who allow their ministers to do harm!

Meanwhile, Yfflasie and Clarendon returned with Louis XIV to see Henri IV the curé, whose name was Nicolas. They found him occupied, in spite of his great age, in the functions of his ministry; he was penetrated by their utility and their grandeur. And although they were neither great nor useful, the virtuous minister rendered them so by the beauty of his views and the sublimity of his conduct.

Yfflasie and Clarendon would dearly have liked to be so useful! But such is the estate of souls that they could not even chase away a fly that was buzzing around those they loved. That was also what caused Louis XIV some annoyance. She went away. Yfflasie and Clarendon followed her. She proposed to travel the terrestrial globe and see everything that was curious on its immense surface.

I shall instruct myself as to what they did, dear spouse, in order to tell you tomorrow. The estate of souls is very singular, is it not, my Hortense?

Response to Letter XXVII

15 March.

So that is the fate of their Richelieu-Coeur-de-fer decided! They are furious about it, and even more about that of poor Louis XIII, carding and spinning wool at the Pitié and dying at twenty-six! They are glad, however, to see him emancipated, by his second corporeal life.

We were all then edified by the priestly life of Henri IV, the village curé, and very afflicted that souls can do nothing for bodies.

"It's true," said Madame Beauchamois, "that that would have its inconveniences."

"Yes, yes!" replied the Marquise. "One would sometimes receive slaps from those Messieurs the husbands that would not be those of mortmain!"

I am recounting all these bagatelles to you, not having, like you, the brilliant imagination that creates events. But did you not tell me one day, good husband, that we do not create anything, and that our wildest imaginations cannot exceed Nature, in which we are enclosed? In that case, everything you recount will become more interesting! It is a kind of truth, which exists somewhere...

That idea rejoices all three-and-four of us.

Filète observes to me here that it is singular that we do not know more about who Yfflasie and Clarendon were.

Letter XXVIII

F.m.T. 28 February.

Before following Yfflasie and Clarendon, who are about go traveling, I shall give you here, dear wife, such as they have told it to me, the story of their mortal life in England and in Italy.

Clarendon was the son of a minister, a parish priest in the city of York, Yfflasie the daughter of a Duke. The minister was often in the Duke's home, and took his son, William Clarendon, there to give lessons in music to Miss Yfflasie, who was addressed as Milady.

The young lady was charming; she was twelve years old when William was sixteen. He loved her from that age, and as the lessons lasted three years, from twelve until fifteen, she loved William Clarendon with all of her innocent and naïve soul. He was modest and reserved; the master and his pupil had often been spied on, and the former had never permitted himself a single reprehensible word, gesture or blink, nor had the latter manifested the vivacity of her liking for the young man. However, they adored one another, and told one another so every day.

This is how they did it: it was William who furnished all the books for the young lady's reading. He always read them beforehand, and left different pieces of paper, or bookmarks, there to designate the most important passages to his pupil. Those pieces of paper were entirely covered with numbers without any separation. The first indicated a page, the second a line, and the third the position of a word in the line. There was, however, a dot after the third figure, to avoid confusion.

Those numbers made up a very tender letter, which the master wrote to his pupil. She went to the page, counted the lines, found the word indicated, and so on with all the others. She wrote those words on a piece of paper, added the punctuation, and thus had a letter. She made a response by rereading

123

the book, or another, of which her master had the duplicate, searched there and encrypted all the words of the letter, and gave the numbers to her teacher as he left, in a place where they could not be perceived from anywhere.

William took the numbers away, and when he arrived home, read the letter with the aid of the duplicate copy. The very difficulty of reading in that fashion became a pleasure for the two lovers.

They were at that point when a rich lord the Duke of Kingston, asked for the hand of the beautiful Yfflasie. She would rather have died than be unfaithful to William Clarendon. She wrote to him in their fashion, knowing that they were still observed, the few words: 2164.5101.15306. *We must flee.*

William replied: *I will be ready tomorrow evening, at nightfall, with a chaise, and we shall embark at Dover.*

The numbers were seen by the father and the future husband, but not understood.

The next day, Yfflasie, furnished with all her jewels, even those given by the future husband, went to the garden door, which opened to the country. The chaise was there, and immediately rolled away silently. At the first relay station, Yfflasie, who had put on masculine clothing in the chaise, appeared to be a young man. They reached Dover thus without incident. The ferry was ready to set sail; they boarded it, and arrived four hours later in Calais.

Yfflasie, who had nothing on her, on departing, but her diamonds and jewels, had given large sums of money to Clarendon at different times in the preceding days. They were well supplied. A post-chaise enabled them to traverse France, and reach Italy by embarking in Marseilles. They went to Naples. There, they hid under false names, and as they both spoke French perfectly, they passed themselves off as being from Strasbourg, a city that Clarendon knew, were imagined to be Lutherans, and made the necessary arrangements to be married.

No one in Naples made any difficulty about the documents of the two individuals, who, if they had been less delicate, could have lived together as a married couple. Before-hand, however, they declared that they wanted to settle in Na-ples, and in consequence, they went to sell all that they pos-sessed, in order to buy lands and domains. They represented themselves as merchants, and presented their diamonds and jewels at the court. They bargained, and as the difficulty was in finding cash, they reached an understanding that they could be paid in bonds. That proposition was accepted gladly; they were given the property of Jesuits, whose Order had been sup-pressed a few years previously.

Solidly established, they married under the names they had adopted for their acquisition. The marriage celebration was devoid of ostentation, but the two spouses were radiant with joy. The evening arrived; they went to bed in their house, built on a former Jesuitry... and you know the rest, their little accident.

The first excursion of the two young souls was to Prus-sia. It is necessary to know, my dear wife, that almost all souls stay in their homeland, not so much out of affection for their native soil as because of a natural and very avid curiosity to see what their corporeal successors do. What took them to Berlin was the desire to see what had become of the monad of Frederick the Great, the legislator and king who reigned by himself, who was his own Richelieu, Colbert and Louvois all rolled into one.

They asked for him as soon as they were in his country—which is to say, half a second after leaving France. His soul was shown to them. She was on a drum, surrounded by all her warriors who had did before her: generals, officers, grenadiers and soldiers. There were two or three hundred thousand of them, all distinguished—for souls, without having bodies, conserve if they wish the appearances they had before.

Frederick II had his hand over his eyes, and appeared to be plunged in a profound reverie. Voltaire—the great, the sub-lime, the incomparable Voltaire—was sitting on one of the

King's knees, attentive to all his movements.[31] Frederick was reflecting, and his thoughts could be seen floating, like the waves of a sea that is beginning to quiver as a tempest forms.

The young and pretty Yfflasie advanced toward the heroines. (For souls conserve their attractions; that is, as I said, one of the advantages of dying young; one remains pretty when one was pretty, and even ugly young women have their graces, after disengagement from the body; but people who have lived a long time have another advantage that they can appear to be any age they wish.)

"Great King," she said, in the fashion in which souls speak. "We are English, married in Italy, who have come to admire you."

Frederick looked at her, smiling, but did not reply.

Clarendon spoke in his turn. "Sublime monarch, I bring you the tribute of my admiration."

Frederick caressed her, and set her next to Voltaire.

"Well, my children, what do you think of me, since my corporeal dissolution?"

I shall pause, reluctantly.

---

[31] Voltaire and Frederick the Great exchanged letters for a long time, from 1736 onwards—enough to fill three volumes of Voltaire's correspondence in his *Oeuvres*, although their association, when Voltaire actually went to Prussia in 1753, did not last long and ended badly. Frederick was, however, heavily influenced by Voltaire's ideas.

Response to Letter XXVIII

16 March.

We do not like it, my dear, when you cut off your stories like that! It is doubtless necessary to wait until tomorrow for Clarendon's response. To punish you, I shall only respond with a few lines. Filète thinks as I do.

I shall quit you for your son.

Letter XXIX

F.m.T. Last of February, leap year.[32]

"O King," Clarendon replied, "we admire you, in England, and call you Frederick the Great."

"You see that I am not flattering you," said Voltaire. "I have never flattered you."

"My glorious friend," Frederick replied, "my generals here, all heroes as they are, do me less honor than your friendship. But let us wait for a new corporeal life; we shall see what we do with it. My dolor is profound. What a successor I have left! He has only conserved that which he could not destroy. He has demonstrated that he is what I judged him to be: arrogant, egotistical and foolish. But while I was alive, he constrained himself. Meanwhile, he only saw valets. What conduct he has adopted in Holland![33] That of an imbecilic tyrant, who does not know the true interests of his people, who is avenging, as an insensate king, a family quarrel over a woman!

"Oh, if I had been the French general! And look at the insidious conduct of the English, whom I never liked. Arrogant, proud without reason, but always insupportable! Boasting of being Romans, and being only Carthaginians; one can see their Punic faith! I always measured them well, I was never heir dupe. My friend, my friend, if, in our new estate, one still had corporeal passions, how unhappy I would be! But one no longer has them...and yet, I am distressed!

---

[32] 1779, the date given on the first letter was not a leap year, and nor was 1787, although 1780 and 1788 were; there was, however, no response dated 29 February in the sequence of Hortense's replies, which thus gain a day in their lag at this point, albeit temporarily.

[33] The reference is to the Dutch campaign of 1787 launched by Frederick the Great's successor, Frederick William II.

"My successor, ingrate toward me, and toward my broth-er Henry, is a madman, devoid of politics. I hate him!"

"Calm down," Voltaire said to him. "You still have the passions of the other life."

Frederick calmed down...by plunging back into his rev-erie. Then, suddenly waking up: "What do I see? The insen-sate Frederick William is going to doom Prussia! He's making an alliance with all the powers to crush our sole support, France! He's allying himself with the Emperor...with Spain...Spain! Portugal! Naples! Piedmont!

"Oh, he's lost his head. He hasn't done a single useful thing! He's invading part of Poland! But he's honest...he's going to his doom. If the French have any common sense...he'll be captured in Champagne, and the third King of Prussia will be a prisoner in Paris!

"Thanks to the maneuvers of the French generals, traitors to their fatherland, he'll retreat...there'll finally be peace... May eternal prudence determine that he leaves Holland alone and never allies himself with Austria!"

Response to Letter XXIX

17 March.

Clarendon's reply to the King of Prussia is noble, and would have been longer if Voltaire hadn't cut him off. The King of Prussia's speech is initially flattering to Voltaire and then crushing for his successor. You fill your letters very well, my love, and have reason to leave matters of business to your secretary.

I must tell you that my Filète has been demanded by her husband, who has become jealous of me. That little dispute has upset me. Filète has stayed, but her husband is persecuting us. I have been obliged to seek means of calming him by reasoning, but it appears that reasoning can do nothing with his motives; it's desire for his wife that has gripped him again.

I don't know what we can do, because she doesn't want to go back. I'll consult some of your friends, like President de Gourgues, President Sarron and a few others. A libertine who had abducted the pretty woman would mock the husband, and have him locked up, but honest people can't think of such odious means. However, I'm very reluctant to surrender her. It seems to me that it's me that I'd be surrendering to that man.

It's necessary for me to try to make him see reason by way of Monsieur Sarron, who has an infinite supply. But everyone says to me: "He's right! And the reasons you have to oppose him, to keep his wife, are very weak..."

Oh my dear Filète! I shall surrender you reluctantly...

Letter XXX

Frederick desired to be alone. Immediately, his former generals arranged themselves around a corner of the drum.

Voltaire stood up and took Yfflasie's hand. "Come, my beauty," he said to her, "so I can do you the honors of Prussia. You resemble Mademoiselle Dunoyer like two drops of water.[34] Would you like to see her?"

Yfflasie did want that, and as Clarendon had only one will with her, all three of them were transported in an instant to the beautiful French refugee—for in order to please Voltaire, she always maintained herself between the ages of fourteen and fifteen. As for the poet, who was thirty in the company of the King of Prussia, he was no more than twenty with the young and pretty Pimpette, with whom he had been reunited for some years.

Seeing how smitten those two souls appeared to be with one another, Clarendon took pleasure in recounting the coronation of Voltaire, which he had witnessed. Yfflasie, who was French that day, confirmed everything he said.

"What about the mongrels of the Seminary?" sad Voltaire, laughing. "Are they still preaching against me?"

"Oh, it's a fury all the more risible," said Clarendon, "that every young Seminarian is obliged to declaim against you in order to obtain a benefit. He treats you as he would treat the Antichrist, and even a little worse. As soon as he has

---

[34] When Voltaire was still in his teens and attached to the French embassy at The Hague as a secretary he fell in love with a young French refugee named Catherine Dunoyer, whom he called "Pimpette". He wanted to marry her, but his family stopped the wedding and had Voltaire returned to Paris in 1713. Some of their letters survive, and are included in the published volumes of Voltaire's correspondence

the benefit, he buys your works and settles down tranquilly to read them.

"But what is even funnier, and demonstrates how blind that mania is, is that a preacher has been seen speaking about you to peasants who wondered, on emerging from the sermon, where Voltaire was a new name that had been given to the Devil. A surgeon who had taken his courses in Paris read them your poem on Natural Religion, and they took you for a saint. Then he read them your *Zaire* one Sunday evening, and they wept, adoring you. He read them your *Mahomet* and they shuddered, *Mérope* and they kissed their children. They were read your *Pucelle*, excluding the denouement of the donkey, and they laughed like madmen. They were read your defense of Calas, and they blessed you. Finally, they were read *L'Ingénu*, and they wondered whether you were a human or an angel."

I shall stop there; I shall resume tomorrow, beautiful Hortense.

Response to Letter XXX

18 March.

Decidedly, I shall keep my Filète, who does not want to go back. Monsieur de Sarron has had that reason prevail with the husband, and only that one. I have some remorse, however. If I were Filète's husband, would I want anyone to do the same to me?

I shall pass on to your letter, my love. I like the account that Clarendon gives Voltaire of his reputation well enough, as well as the little anecdote about Pimpette, who is rejuvenating Voltaire again in the other life. The little quip about the mongrel escaped from the seminary who preaches a satire in a village in order to practice for delivering it in the city appears curious to me and illustrates everything that is said about these vile sacerdotal insects, from whom I would like to see the last sigh wrung from the last of them, without, however, being the cause of it, so I wouldn't die of pleasure therefrom.

The man of intelligence, or taste, who reestablishes Voltaire's reputation merely by reading his works has the right approach; it's the only manner of defending a great man victoriously.

Letter XXXI

F.m.T. 2 March.

Voltaire was delighted by what Clarendon said, and the latter, as well as his Yfflasie, admired the urbanity of Voltaire, his constant amour for the lovely Pimpette and the noble attitude, worthy of a great man, that he adopted toward Frederick.

They glimpsed poor Trenck, a Prussian captain taken prisoner fighting against his homeland and condemned to death.[35] His proud soul still conserved an impression of sadness. He followed Frederick everywhere, and when he saw him laugh, he presented himself. Frederick immediately became serious.

"I'm avenged," said Trenck. "I've chased the laughter from the lips of the man who made my death last fifteen entire years. Instruct yourselves, souls of kings, and when you return to animate bodies, conserve, if it is possible the impression I have given you. The soul of the oppressed will chase the smile from the soul of the oppressor!"

Yfflasie and Clarendon were saddened. *How terrible vengeance is, they thought, against those who have carried it out!*

After having seen Voltaire and Frederick, they desired to see Racine. They did not find his monad; it had re-entered a body only a few months before. They wanted to know what condition it had chosen. It had desired to enter the fetus of the

---

[35] The reference is presumably to the Prussian officer Friedrich von de Trenck (1726-1794), who published an autobiography in 1787 that was translated into French and became a significant source for litterateurs. The details included here are inaccurate, and Restif might have confused his biography with that of his cousin Franz von de Trenck (1711-1749). Friedrich was perpetually at odds with Frederick the Great, and was certainly mistreated, but not killed by him.

son of a king, that Marie-Antoinette of Austria, the wife of the dauphin who had become Louis XVI, was then carrying. They did not see him, therefore. He died again young. He was gentle and affectionate, but easy to irritate.

Yfflasie and Clarendon then desired to see La Fontaine.[36] He had been replaced in a new body several years before. They went to see him, and the good and simple La Fontaine was animating the body of a young muleteer. They heard the rustic asked a question by a beautiful traveler.

"How do you find your estate, friend?"

"Good."

"Don't you lack anything?"

"No, except..."

"Ah! What? Speak."

"A beautiful lady like you."

The lady was Italian, and one would have thought that she did not want the young muleteer's happiness to be lacking anything

"Well," said Clarendon, "Muleteer as he is, he has still encountered La Sablière!"[37]

Yfflasie blushed, as souls blush, but she watched nevertheless what was happening.

"My God!" said Clarendon, "How I'd like to see Bossuet! We must ask for him."

---

[36] La Fontaine died in 1695 and Racine in 1699, so if the hundred-year discorporation rule were being followed here, this part of Yfflasie and Clarendon's story would appear to be set in 1800; the rule in question is frequently violated hereafter, though.

[37] The reference is to Marguerite de La Sablière (1640-1693), who was La Fontaine's patron and close friend for the last twenty years of her life.

Response to Letter XXXI

19 March.

You have found, my dear husband the inferno of kings, perhaps without looking for it, and that inferno is worth as much as any other! Racine and La Fontaine are well character-ized, although only glimpsed.

I have my Filète absolutely, and without any obstacle. Her husband has decided to ask her for a separation of bodies and goods, and it has been agreed. She is keeping her son, but the husband is content with that. She must live with me, or in a convent. She will live with me, so long as I live, and if I cease to live, all who love me will love Filète.

(Details of business matters have been omitted here.)

F.m.T. Florence, 3 March.

"Yes," said Yfflasie, "let's ask for Bossuet."

The effect followed the desire. Bossuet had not yet passed back into a body.[38] They found her surrounded by seven or eight young souls, with whom she was playing marbles.

There was one beautiful monad who seemed to be sulking to one side. Yfflasie and Clarendon looked at her without knowing her—but they desired to do so very much.

That desire was perceived by one of the nearby monads, who was very learned and very serious. That was Madame de Sévigné.[39]

"You desire to know, newcomers, who the beautiful monad is who is sulking?"

"Oh, yes!" relied Yfflasie.

"It's the beautiful Ninon.[40] She's the mother of all these beautiful children you see, and Bossuet is their father. They didn't appear to be related; they never see one another in public, but she received him in secret; she adored him, and if she was guilty of any infidelities, it was him who demanded them,

---

[38] The theologian and orator Jacques-Bénigne Bossuet (1627-1704). The colorful sex-life attributed to him here is all fantasy, wildly exaggerated even by the lax standards of scurrilous late-18th century gossip.

[39] The Marquise de Sévigné, remembered for her lively letters to her daughter, had died in 1696, so it is not obvious why she is still discorporate here if Racine has been reincorporated..

[40] The legendary beauty Anne "Ninon" de l'Enclos (1620-1705) had numerous lovers during her glittering career as a courtier, but only bore one child, fathered by Louis de Mornay, Marquis de Villarceaux.

in order better to conceal their intrigue. Such was the case with the comedian Pécour,[41] whom Ninon always detested.

"She is sulking because Bossuet amuses himself more with the children than with her. In fact, during their corporeal life, Bossuet, who had a precise mind, only liked Ninon because she was a pretty mold for children, and because she was so fecund. She perceived that, and as she loved him to excess, she was almost wounded by it.

"'My wife,' Bossuet replied to her complaints—for they were married; an Irish priest had conducted the ceremony without knowing them—'it is always necessary that Nature is the basis of our tastes and our attachments. It is to your fecundity that my constancy is attached. I find you charming, undoubtedly, but I would soon weary of inseminating a sterile woman. I adore you, not as Diana or Venus but as Cybele, the productive mother.'

"Ninon sometimes became enraged with her dear husband's pedomania, but what could she do? She adored him." Thus spoke Madame de Sévigné, rapidly.

Further away...but I shall stop, and continue tomorrow.

---

[41] Louis Pécour (1653-1729) was a dancer at the Paris Opéra. It is highly unlikely that he was ever involved with Ninon de l'Enclos.

Response to letter XXXII

20 March.

My friends and I did not know that anecdote about Bossuet. It increases our esteem for him. It's not that we regard him as a great man; he only had a provincial merit, which devoted itself to a futile genre, that of funeral orations, as if that genre were of the highest importance.

That comes, according to Madame Beauchamois, from the fact that provincials who are said to be well brought up, as opposed to rustics, have an elevated idea of everything that happens in the city. "Bossuet's so-called universal history," she added. "is a pitiful and superficial work, only taking about the Jewish horde as if it were talking about all the peoples of the world."

Madame de Marigny, for her part, made a reproach to Louis XIV, that of a taste for magnificent representation. "I imagine him sometimes," she added, "as a big guttersnipe of sixteen, presiding over a children's crèche on an afternoon of Corpus Christi, dressed in a beautiful chasuble of gilded paper. He has given that taste to his bishops and his parliaments. It's a puerile taste."

Oh, my friend, how critical they are! Filète and I don't criticize anything, or anyone.

Letter XXXIII

F.m.T. 4 March.

Yesterday, I was saying that, further away, Yfflasie and Clarendon saw a tall fellow, a rather nasty individual, who was making fun of the holy bishop, the last Father of the Church.

Yfflasie wanted to interrogate Sévigné, but she was some way off, occupied in caressing Madame de Grignan, her daughter, who was pushing her away because she had published a lacerating Memoir against her, in the course of a lawsuit they were fighting.

Instead of Sévigné, Yfflasie found herself close to the Deshoulières, mother and daughter, who never quit one another and wanted to be reincorporated together in one body.[42]

(That sometimes happens, for there is an infinity of anecdotes of that genre, which will be revealed in due course.)

Yfflasie asked: "Who is that ruffian?"

"It's Sainthiacinthe," the mother replied, "the eldest son of Bossuet—who, in parentheses, is trigamous, like the patriarchs. Sevigné didn't want to tell you that, but I will. You see that monad who has something of the peasant about her? She was a fat cook whom he all married, and who gave him that son."

"I believe, Madame," said the Deshoulières daughter, "that he had three wives—for it's said that he also married a pretty young woman."

"Peace!" interjected the mother. "Let's not talk about that one. All that I can tell you is that he had for a maxim that

---

[42] Antoinette Deshoulières (c1634-1694) was one of the most notable female poets of the era; her daughter Antoinette-Thérèse (1662-1718), who never married, was also a writer; she arranged for publication of her mother's works and her own, in the same volumes

one can have as many legitimate wives as necessary, in order not to approach those who are fecundated. That is what comprises true purity and true chastity."[43]

"And he was right," said a singular monad, who had something great, noble and extremely spiritual about her.

"Who is that soul?" Yfflasie asked Deshoulières.

"That's the Regent."[44]

"Ah!" exclaimed the two lovers. "How glad we are to encounter him."

"I need to talk to him," added Clarendon.

The Regent was already some distance away.

"I'd also like to find Molière," said Yfflasie.

"He's about to be reincorporated," replied a mild and engaging monad whose had something blissful about her.

"Oh! Where is he?"

"Come and see... He's the only man I've ever truly loved, but he didn't always know it."

Until tomorrow, my only beloved Hortense. You can see that I have a good source for all these anecdotes I am reporting to you. Let your two friends not criticize them! Those *Memoirs* have not been published, and probably never will be.

---

[43] Author's note: "This moral is established, above all, in *L'Enclos et les oiseaux*, a work presently under press." The note proved optimistic, alas.

[44] Philippe d'Orléans (1674-1723) was Regent from 1715-1723, when Louis XV was considered to have come of age (at thirteen).

Response to Letter XXXIII

21 March.

That is interesting, dear husband. My two friends would like to know what these *Memoirs* are, where you are obtaining them, and who the author is. You can tell us, if you wish. But Filète has one curiosity that it's absolutely necessary to satisfy, for I have it too: who is Bossuet's third wife? My friends presume that it is Maintenon, or Henriette d'Angeleterre, the Duchesse d'Orléans,[45] or...

"A daughter of the executioner, who was charming," Madame Du Boccage[46] says, having just come in. "That's a story I heard once..."

We were petrified by that anecdote.

"Can that woman be believed?" Filète asked.

"Oh, certainly," said Madame de Beauchamois. "She's my friend; she has a morality that doesn't permit lying.

You'll decide the question, good husband, in a fortnight.

---

[45] Henrietta of England (1644-1670), the youngest daughter of the ill-fated Charles I, was forced to flee to France at the age of three, eventually marrying Louis XIV's brother Philippe (1640-1701), the father of the future Regent.

[46] Anne-Marie Du Boccage (1710-1802) was a writer praised by Fontenelle and Voltaire, among others, best known for *La Colombiade* (1756), an epic about the discovery of the New World.

Letter XXXIV

F.m.T. 5 March.

Who was it who said, speaking of Molière: "He's the on-ly man I've ever truly loved"? I'll give your friends a hundred guesses...

Madame de Maintenon—for it was her—took us to Saint Cyr,[47] where we perceived Molière, continually occupied in watching demoiselle pupils. All that annoyed him was not being able to enjoy a few turns with the prettiest...

"But Nature doesn't permit it, because it's necessary that the corporate live tranquilly. Communication between the two existences is absolutely forbidden, because the corporate, tor-mented by invisible beings, would be too unhappy. Desperate, they would no longer be able to conserve themselves, and the visible world would end—which is contrary to the decrees of Providence," said Madame de Maintenon.

Yfflasie and Clarendon saluted the Father of Comedy, and told him that Mercier had just put his character and his house on the stage.[48]

"I know," Molière replied, "and I wept with joy, on see-ing myself almost as I was in the young artist Fleury. We still hold on to that vulgar existence, which has to recommence,

---

[47] Francoise d'Aubigné (1635-1719), first allied by a marriage of convenience to the writer Paul Scarron, was given the title of Marquise de Maintenon in 1675, and was Louis XIV's closest confidante for the rest of his life; he married her secret-ly in the mid 1680s, but the marriage was never made public and she remained his mistress in the eyes of the world, alt-hough she effectively ruled his Court. She certainly never said that Molière was the only man she ever truly loved.

[48] Louis-Sébastien Mercier's comedy *La Maison de Molière* was first produced in 1788, with "Fleury" (Abraham Bénard, 1750-1822) in the leading role.

and the distance of which, or the repugnance that it ought naturally to inspire, diminishes as the moment to resume it approaches. In any case, it's tomorrow that I have to enter the first French and Parisian body that will receive the impulsion of life. Observe me, and if possible, don't lose sight of me until that moment. But what good will it do me? Perhaps I shall be one of those models of ridicule that I played?"

"No," Clarendon replied to him. "They have been destroyed all too well."

In the meantime the beautiful d'Aubigné gazed at Molière. "Alas," she said, "I shall survive you too long. What joy if I could be reborn soon enough to be your Béjart.[49] Oh, how I would love you, how happy I would be! How I would like to be pretty, charming, rich, to have a thousand talents and wit! How I would like you to have returned already, better to prove to you my tenderness and devotion."

Molière seemed touched; he kissed the hands of the beautiful window, hiding his tears.

At the same moment Nature made him hear: "Human soul whose turn has arrived, enter the career of corporeal life."

Molière disappeared.

Yfflasie, Clarendon and the beautiful d'Aubigné followed his traces. They found him in a magnificent town house, and they saw two perfectly happy spouses delivering themselves to the delights of a legitimate amour.

"Ah!" said Scarron's widow. "Molière will be happy, for he will be virtuous and handsome. I see it in the serenity of those young spouses!"

---

[49] Armande Béjart (1645-1700) married Molière in 1662, when she was seventeen and he was forty. Three of her siblings were also members of his theater company; they separated in 1665 but she remained with the company and the two were reconciled briefly before Molière's death in 1673.

Response to Letter XXXIV

22 March.

No, dear husband, I would not have guessed that it was Madame de Maintenon, but one of my two friends knew it. She told us that Madame Scarron, even while her husband was alive—who also wrote comedies, but burlesques—fell in love with Molière, and planned, on seeing her husband declining, to go to him and ask him to train her, in order to take her into his troop. When Scarron was dead, different obstacles being encountered, his widow only went to speak to Molière three days before his death.

The Father of Comedy greeted her with distraction, and said to her: "Madame, you would do more for the fortunes of my theater, by your natural talents and your beauty, than I by my plays." Things were there when Molière died, as is known. I can see, my friend, that you are drawing from good sources.

My Filète has been very sad for days. We were talking about you two days ago and I said that if I lost you, I would not survive you. She went pale. It's necessary, in order to console her, that I repeat continually that I would live, for my son and for her.

Letter XXXV

Yfflasie and Clarendon left the tender d'Aubigné with the Molière fetus. Be sure that she no longer quits him and follows all the movements of the mother—but she can do nothing, alas. The only pain of souls is that impotence over bodies, but it is sometimes cruel. They would be too fortunate if they had that power, though, and no perfect happiness exists, even for the Divinity. It can do anything, because it is everything, but since it has everything, it has both happiness and unhappiness.

There would be another inconvenience, apart from those of which I spoke yesterday, in the influence of foreign souls on those that are in bodies, which is that the latter would no longer act by themselves. They would be perpetually guided by their friends, or led astray by their enemies; and Nature and reason want corporate beings to by guided by themselves.

Yfflasie was very curious to know who Bossuet's third wife was, but she did not know who to ask. She was about to go back to Madame de Maintenon when she saw a beautiful monad, slightly sad, who seemed to be searching for someone. She asked her who it was she wanted.

"I'm looking for Louis XIV," replied the sad monad.

"And who are you, beautiful soul?"

"I was Racine."

"In truth," said Yfflasie to Clarendon, "this is a fortunate encounter."

"I have important news to announce to Louis-le-Grand," Racine continued. "Although he caused me much chagrin, I still love him. He reproaches himself sometimes for having been inconstant with regard to La Valière, but it's necessary that I reveal a mystery to him. When she became a Carmelite she loved Bossuet, who married her secretly, known only to the Superior. They maintained, by means of the latter, a de-

146

lightful commerce, which rendered both of them equally happy.

"That's what I wanted to know!" exclaimed the young Yfflasie. She thanked Racine and went in search of La Valière.

She found her—which is to say that she and Clarendon found her—in the same situation as the beautiful d'Aubigné. Bossuet had just reentered a body; the great orator was a fetus in the womb of a young fashion-model at the Toilette-de-Vénus in the Rue Saint Honoré. The young woman, who had an impudent face, was not yet married. She had deceived her mother to go and spend the night in the city, and that was in the home of her lover, a young advocate of twenty-seven, who already had a reputation, and who had a mistress while waiting to find a rich match.

La Valière was indignant to see Bossuet destined to be the bastard of a petty fashion-model and a petty advocate, but there was nothing she could do. She was very smitten, though, for she resolved to spend her corporate life following that of the young bastard. She no longer quit the fashion-model...

I shall continue this interesting story. It gives me pleasure. And if it were an illusion, without foundation, my beautiful Hortense, it would not charm the time spent far from you.

Response to Letter XXXV

23 March.

You should have seen the long face of my friend who had sustained the veracity of Madame Du Boccage. Nothing has been said, however, that could compromise yours, and that is a great moderation. So, the friend in question is mildness itself. No one has smiled, overtly or covertly. My Filète is, in that sense, unequaled in restraint. We await with impatience what will become of Bossuet and La Valière. Great God! If the corporate could read souls like you, my love, what astonishment!

(Business matters here.)

Letter XXXVI

F.m.T. 7 March.

Little Bossuet—who was named Hardouin-Monclard, from the names of the father and mother—came into the world after nine months, in the home of a midwife to which his father had taken his mother unknown to her parents. He was so pretty that the young mother loved him madly as soon as she saw him. She employed pleas and tears to persuade the advocate to find him a nurse, but the young men of our century re egotists and hard; he refused.

La Valière, a witness to everything, quivered with indignation; she threw herself upon the advocate and tried to scratch him, but her incorporeal fingernails could not make any impression. So, and a thousand times more, a gnat might hurl itself at the thick walls of the Louvre, trying to knock them down.

La Valière, who knew that she could not do anything, implored the Celestial Power to enter into a body. She hoped that hazard might enable her to encounter Bossuet, and that she might be his lover again. But events seconded her even better. She entered into the body of the son of a Duc, and instead of being a girl she was a boy...

It is necessary to finish this story, although it was only terminated a long time afterwards.

Bossuet was found a nurse, at the expense of the fashion-model, who raised him. His name was Laurent. He was only nine years old when she took him with her, as a postilion, to carry boxes. The Duchesse who was the mother of the little La Valière—named the Comte de Chinon—saw the child and wanted to have him as a domestic. The fashion-model, who was not very well off, and who no longer loved the advocate, was glad to be rid of the child. The Duchesse de Fronsac made him the postilion of her son, who was a year younger than Laurent-Bossuet.[50]

I do not know whether it was reminiscence, but Yfflasie and Clarendon observed that the young Comte loved his postilion tenderly. They grew older. Masters were given to the young Chinon. It was Laurent who profited from them. He learned with a marvelous facility. He astonished his Masters by his intelligence and penetration. The teacher, who was not maladroit, took care that Laurent suggested to young Chinon everything that he imagined of intelligence, and when the tutor went before the Duc and Duchesse, he had Laurent's ingenious replies rendered to them by their son.

Unfortunately, Laurent was vain. He boasted about his progress, and of having, by himself, the intelligence of two, or even of three. The tutor knew it, and began to hate him. The little bastard was only kept until the studies were complete, and then the teacher had him dismissed, under the pretext of words spoken, or even written, against the Duc and Duchesse.

The Comte de Chinon wept with regret over the separation. He had the postilion secretly replaced with the mother of a mistress he maintained, with the result that Bossuet became the woman's lackey, and her daughter's confidential errand-boy.

---

[50] The chronology of this section is very problematic if the Comte de Chinon to whom this passage refers is Armand Emmanuel du Plessis (1766-1822), who had that title before inheriting the title of Duc de Fronsac, along with the title of Duc de Richelieu, from his father Louis (1696-1788). The response implies that it is—and he had no children to whom the title could have been passed—but the subsequent development of his story in the present text bears no resemblance to the actual Comte's successful political career—although Restif had no way of knowing that he would end up as Prime Minister in 1815, when the monarchy was restored.

Response to Letter XXXVI

24 March.

Madame Du Boccage has returned, dear husband. She maintains her assertion that Bossuet had as a third or fourth wife the pretty daughter of the executioner of Paris, and that he had lodged her in the Rue de la Lune, where she knew him when he as old, while she was still a child.

She became thoughtful when we had read her your last letter. "Oh, that's odd! I know the Comte de Chinon and his mistress. Singularly enough, he has also lodged her in the Rue de la Lune. The postilion has been to my house twice, very thin the last time. I got him to talk. He seems to me to have intelligence. I seem to have glimpsed that the mother...lets him sleep with her, and the daughter...sometimes makes use of him by day. As he is very delicate, I gave him to understand that it was necessary to spare himself."

That was what the old Muse said to us. Filète was slightly scandalized, but the Comtesse and he Marquise multiplied questions. There are children of Bossuet and the fourth wife, among others, a daughter who is very beautiful and well-known. We wanted to know who she was, and we were told that the child, substituted by a nurse, had been Mademoiselle Poisson, then Madame d'Étiolles, and finally Madame de Pompadour...[51]

Madame Du Boccage did not want to say more about the adventures of Bossuet-postilion.

---

[51] Madame de Pompadour (1721-1764), born Jeanne-Antoinette Poisson and later Madame d'Étiolles, was Louis XV's chief official mistress from 1745 until her death.

Letter XXXVII

F.m.T. 8 March.

Yfflasie and Clarendon were quite astonished by the blindness of souls once they had reentered a body. They bemoaned it. However, they observed two things, one of which was that they unwittingly conserved some of their former inclinations, and the other that a knowledgeable and intelligent man, replaced in a well organized body, had a singular aptitude for study and the sciences.

The Comte de Chinon married. That caused him to quarrel with his mistress Attached to Laurent-Bossuet by a blind sympathy, he proposed that he should leave little Henriette in order to devote himself to the Comtesse and future Duchesse, his wife. Laurent, who loved Henriette, and foresaw a day when he might marry her, hesitated.

The Comte chanced to take him to his house; Laurent saw the young and beautiful Chinon there; he immediately quit his Henriette, although the latter, who was afterwards Madame Du Barry, had been very generous to him.

The young Chinon was very beautiful. Laurent-Bossuet, whose constitution was exceedingly erotic, fell madly in love. Nothing he could say to himself about that passion could succeed in curing it. The Comtesse was noble, virtuous and very fond of her husband. Thus, although the valet was a handsome lad, she only looked at him with disdain.

The passion fermented. Laurent was very close to the beautiful Comtesse; he could not control his desires. He therefore resolved one day…a strange thing!…to ask his master for the possession of her. He saw that he had an inclination for him, which he believed to be *à la d'Elbeuf*.[52] He offered him

---

[52] The last Duc d'Elbeuf, Charles-Eugène de Lorraine (1751-1825) had succeeded his second cousin Emmanuel-Maurice de Lorraine (1677-1763), who had died without issue (as he did),

his own person in exchange for Madame's. Chinon, formerly the tender La Valière, shivered, but did not dismiss Laurent; a blind and insurmountable attachment opposed that.

Laurent, emboldened by that indulgent weakness, resolved one evening to give his master a powerful soporific, to remove him adroitly from his bed and replace him. He carried out that culpable project. The dose of opium was apparently too strong; Chinon died of it.

However, the guilty party enjoyed the success of his criminal skill. He only withdrew much later, and tried to put the Comte back in the bed, next to his sleeping wife. He was cold. Laurent nevertheless slipped way.

In the morning, the young husband was found dead. The affair was hushed up, but the body was opened and the cause of the accident discovered. Enquiries were mad of apothecaries, and it was found that a young man who resembled Laurent had bought the opium.

He was arrested and threatened; his feet were warmed, and he confessed everything. He was secretly killed, because the young Comtesse, whose parents were the only ones to know the secret of the crime, perceived that she had become pregnant. They even put it about that the Comte had taken the opium instead of an aphrodisiac and had poisoned himself, and that Laurent, who had committed the error, had died of despair.

The two souls of Bossuet and La Valière were then reunited. Oh, what regrets the tender amorous woman had! Bossuet, for his part, had cooled greatly toward her; he only respired for the beautiful widow Chinon. Fortunately, she died in childbirth, and he had the joy of being the first to present himself to her on her exit from the body. She recognized him. He told her the double story, and she loved him.

---

but this association of their name is yet another scurrilous allegation with no reliable foundation.

Response to Letter XXXVII

25 March.

You have given a very sad life there, dear husband, to La Valière and Bossuet, on their reincorporation, and your letter, received with transport, left us in melancholy after having read it. However, I agree that the progression amuses and interests me. The Comtesse is sure that it is not the story of Chinon. The Marquise protests that it is also not the origin of Madame de Pompadour. As for Madame Du Barry, she abandons her to you. I would have liked Madame Du Boccage to have arrived...

Ah, here she is!

We have exposed our doubts to her. My two friends are desperate. The old Muse assures us that you are right, and that Madame de Pompadour and Madame Du Barry came that way. Filète smiled.

Oh yes, smile!" the Marquise said to her. "I'm sure that Madame Du Boccage is amusing herself, and is telling you, like spoiled children, that your good friend's chimeras are true."

The old lady said, dryly, that she was speaking seriously, and Madame de Beauchamois gave in. The Marquise had to give in too.

I'm giving you an account of our little altercations, husband, because they're your work. If I had your imagination, I'd write more interesting things.

Letter XXXVIII

F.m.T. 9 March.

La Valière was in despair on seeing Bossuet's infidelity. And as she had been the mistress of the sex of her last body and the one before it, she wanted to be a masculine soul again, to present herself to her wife and prevail over a postilion...but as you know, Bossuet had explained that. And he had found that in her previous corporeal life, the Comtesse de Chinon had been Madame Henriette d'Angleterre, whom Bossuet had secretly adored. Henriette had been charmed to find herself with her funeral orator and to profit from the equality of souls to love him. Thus, when Chinon-La Valière presented himself as her husband, Henriette, who, as such, was not very content with recovered marriages, only showed disdain. Chinon-La Valière was exceedingly mortified to fail in both directions, left Bossuet forever, and went to see what Louis XIV was doing.

It was some time since the former monarch had been re-incorporated. La Valière sought information. A couturier, who had had his second corporeal life before Louis XIV passed into another body, and had only lost sight of him during a very short corporeal existence, having been killed in a duel at the age of seventeen, told La Valière that the former god of the French was in the body of a fetus procreated by a fiddler of La Courtille. La Valière hastened there.

She found the fiddler's wife pregnant, and waited for the woman to become a mother. The fiddler's wife gave birth. La Valière saw a rather ugly little embryo, very paltry. She waited for him to grow, and a few years later, she found him semi-naked, playing petit-pot with three or four other urchins of his own age at the entrance to the Rue du Faubourg du Temple. She was touched by compassion on seeing that great monarch with torn trousers, who, when he bent down, resembled a Scottish highlander.

One of the players tried to cheat. Louis XIV, who was then called Pierrot, got up, irritated, and knocked him over with a sweep of his hand. The cheat had a brother in the company. They both threw themselves on Louis-Pierrot and were beginning to give him a bad beating when, pain reanimating his courage, he threw them off, pushed them over and ended up rolling them into a market-gardener's cellar. It was thus, once before, he had been ready to submerge Holland.

That's three letters without a word about my amour, my beautiful wife. Are there words to express how much I love you?

Response to Letter XXXVIII

26 March.

So there is the great Louis XIV, no better than anyone else in a second life! However, you also give an appearance of victory to one of my friends, who claimed that Henriette d'Angleterre, the grand-daughter of Henri IV, had been the third simultaneous wife of Bossuet. But Louis XIV, thrashing the cheat, gives rise to reflections. One always senses a little of what one has been. We are going to strive, my friends and I, to divine who the people were that we have been. Filète assures me that she will not make a single mistake.

(A postcriptum about business, omitted.)

Letter XXXIX

F.m.T. 10 March.

Yfflasie and Clarendon saw a host of adventures of Louis XIV-Pierrot. They found and infinite pleasure in following human catastrophes. They had died too young in their corporate life to have had any, and with regard to their intellectual life, they were still too new to be afflicted already by being unable to conserve the philosophy they acquired.

They encountered the soul of J.-J. Rousseau, who said to them: "It is inconceivable for corporeals how, in the state of the soul, one sees the most disastrous events with indifference. Alas, as soon as death is nothing, the rest becomes even less. It is poor philosophy to say that death is the greatest of evils. That is reasoning like a condemned man who is being led to the scaffold. Death is the final term of misfortune. A person who appears to desire it is not wishing for death but for the cessation of misfortune. The death ardently summoned still horrifies him. Instead of that, souls see clearly that the greatest of evils is only an advantageous change, they laugh at all the pains of life, as a dream, while agreeing that it is painful. Everything is type and image in Nature; it gives us an idea of two alternating lives that we enjoy incessantly, in the state of wakefulness and that of sleep. The state of wakefulness resembles incorporeal life, which we enjoy at present, and the state of sleep the corporeal life from which you and I have emerged."

That idea of J.-J. Rousseau's appeared luminous to the two lovers, and they thanked the great man who had given it to them. Yfflasie asked him whether it was true that he had been paradoxical in his writings.

"I do not hold much to them now," he replied, "and they will be perfectly foreign to me in my first corporeal life; perhaps I shall even be their most ardent critic—for I've heard it said here that that is a tradition, that the monad of Zoilus had been Homer, that of Lamotte, Aristotle, and that of Calvin, Saint Bernard, etc. What makes me think in that way is that I can see now how imperfect my works are. But believe that my pretended paradoxes are only in the heads of my bizarre readers."

Yfflasie and Clarendon were content with that reply.

Response to Letter XXXIX

27 March.

Dear spouse, I like the reasoning—or, rather, the confession—of J.-J. Rousseau that even death ardently desired horrifies. But he has reason for it. There is no one in the world who knows better than him, for it's claimed that he poisoned himself. He had retired to Ermenonville in order to be free, and instead of that liberty, he found slavery. Every day the Marquis de Girardin sent him his daughters. Rousseau received them, but he was inconvenienced. He no longer dared change shelter. He took it into his head, at sixty-six, to be ashamed of his variations. He wanted to leave life. So he died fully dressed, and he said, knowing full well what he was saying; "Open the window, Wife, in order that I might enjoy the sunlight once more." He preferred poison as being the most covert, the least ignoble suicide. It is, on the contrary, the one that would give me the most horror.

(Business.)

Until tomorrow, dear spouse.

Letter XL

F.m.T. 11 March.

"My love," said Clarendon, "I have had an idea that would be very amusing. I have realized that there are privileged souls that remain without bodies much longer than others. Let us seek information about that, and when we have found one, let us procure a new kind of instruction. We shall proceed after our fashion with the common souls. It's necessary to try to discover, by way of these aged souls, what our friends who are still alive were in their last mortal life, which preceded an incorporeal life.

Yfflasie was always of the same opinion as Clarendon. There is no longer ay contradiction in the incorporeal life, because all the petty springs of pride and obstinacy are uncovered, but in this case, she applauded delightedly. "Yes, yes— let's search, let's search!"

They went I search of an aged soul, and had the good fortune to find one, who had not resumed a body in 350 years. It was the monad of Jeanne d'Arc.[53]

Yfflasie and Clarendon only approached her with a profound veneration, but the Maid still had her naïve and noble attitude. "My dear friends," she said to them, in Old French, "Our Lord has done me the favor of not returning to a mortal body until there are no more Englishmen, who so cruelly tormented me. But what do you want to ask me?"

"Courageous and chaste Maid," Clarendon relied, "we would like to know who the friends we left alive were, before their last incorporeal life."

"So be it," said the Maid. "I will tell you as much as I know. Only name them for me."

---

[53] Jeanne d'Arc died in 1431, so if the figure 350 is taken literally the time-scheme seems to have shifted this part of Yfflasie and Clarendon's adventure back to the 1780s.

Yfflasie thought for a moment, and then said. "I would like to know who Madame de Genlis-Sillery-Brûlart was in a previous life?"[54]

"You can know that," Jeanne replied, "for I knew her well and followed her. She was, in the life preceding the one she is presently living, Gabrielle d'Estrées, known as the beautiful Gabrielle, so beloved by King Henri-le-Galant."

The continuation, dear spouse, in tomorrow's letter.

---

[54] Madame de Genlis (1746-1830), who had married Charles-Alexis Brûlart, Comte de Genlis (later Marquis de Sillery) at seventeen, subsequently became governess to the children of Louis Philippe II, Duc d'Orléans (1747-1793), in which capacity she developed new theories of education. Her husband was guillotined during the Terror as well as the Duc d'Orléans, but she and the children survived, and she became a prolific writer of some note, although Restif would not have known that in 1802. He loathed d'Orléans, and thus disliked Madame de Genlis by association.

Response to Letter XL

28 March.

But that is an excellent idea that your Clarendon has had, good husband. I hope that it will procure us curious anecdotes, and my friends hope to pass all their acquaintances in review. Oh, Filète would very much like to know who she has been. And me too! The desire for that knowledge is less keen in my two friends; I don't know why. The animating Monad of a body comes from anywhere, and is not subject to filiation; thus one is not revealing the secrets of male or female ancestors.

Filète has begged me to dream about who she has been. This morning, I told her what I had learned in a dream. We were two twins, daughters of the Duc d'Epernon and a clandestine spouse. We were brought up together, one of us married to Louvois, the other to Fouquet's son.[55] We always loved one another tenderly, and we each had a son and a daughter. Filète's son was Barbieux, mine was the scion of the Louvois. Neither of those two descendants was fortunate; our daughters were more so; each of them married a Duc and were widowed early. They did not remarry and each raised two children, a boy and a girl. It is into the children of those children that our souls reentered, for we died, as wives of Louvois and Belle-Isle, before the age of thirty-six. Filète's mother was a child born to a mistress of the Comte de Gisors,

That was all that I was able to extract from my imagination. But we have not said anything about it to our friends,

_____

[55] The references to François-Michel Le Tellier, Marquis de Louvois (1641-1691) and Nicolas Fouquet (1615-1680) do not contradict the supposition that the Duc d'Epernon in question would have been the first of that line, Jean-Louis de Nogaret de La Valette (1554-1642), although it might have been his son Bernard (1592-1661).

who know genealogies and might perhaps have disputed our filiation.

Until tomorrow, also, dear spouse.

Letter XLI

F.m.T. 12 March.

Yfflasie and Clarendon were astonished by the epithet of Henri-le-Galant given to Henri IV by the Maid. But they learned from Voltaire, who happened to be there, that in Jeanne's time, "gallant" meant courteous or magnanimous, from which comes today's expression "A gallant man."

They also wanted to know who Madame de Genlis had been in a corporeal life antecedent to the one in which she had been Gabrielle.

Although very modern, Jeanne d'Arc had started to laugh. "I won't give you that crumb, for you're too curious."

Voltaire, having drawn closer, however, said to her: "Gentle Maid, who conserves no bitterness regarding insults, I am Voltaire, Know, however, that I made a spicy poem on your account, that of King Charlot, Dunois the bastard, and others. What if I ask you to return good for evil, as is said in Holy Writ, and as befits the inspired devotee that you were?"[56]

The Maid replied to that: "Only speak, for those reasons, although I do not know what ridicule has been made of me— but it ought to be good, for the joker has the air!"

On that, Voltaire began to smile, and recited the verses of *La Pucelle* in which he had made a portrait of Jeanne.

"Shut up, shut up!" she said to him. "Bad lot! Hmm! It's a fine thing like to hear such things spoken! *Il n'y a plus d'Enfans!*"[57] She looked at Yfflasie. "Come here, you who are

---

[56] Voltaire's highly controversial satirical poem about Jeanne d'Arc, *La Pucelle*, first began to circulate clandestinely in the 1730s but was first published, in a somewhat bowdlerized edition, in 1762. Like many banned books of the period it was in great demand and was widely read.

[57] "There are no more children"—a common sarcastic remark in French literary works, from Molière on, but Restif would

a young woman, who seem to me to be sober in manner, and I will gladly reply to your question."

Yfflasie drew nearer, and the Maid said to her: "Before Gabrielle was herself, she was a pretty miller's wife in the Perche, and was taken by a Duc to his château, to whom she bore three sons, who were valiant bastards in my time. Their names were Poton, Saintrailles and Lahire.[58] And I have heard it said that more anciently still she had been Fredegunda. Beyond that one cannot go."

"And you, dear Jeanne, who were you before your birth in Vauxcouleurs, the land of Madame Du Barry?""

The Maid smiled.

"You would not believe who I had been, and without any intermediate life."

"Who were you, then?"

"Brunehaut, or Brunhilde, Queen of Austrasia, my land, who perished unfortunately attached to the tail of an impetuous and ferocious moving horse—hence the news of Fredegunda, who executed me."[59]

That is a great deal of news, my dear Hortense. But I have a great deal more yet.

---

have been most familiar with it as the title of a 1772 comedy by his *bête noire* Pierre Nougaret (1724-1823).

[58] The author seems to be making three people out of two, Jean Poton de Xaintrailles (c1390-1461) and "La Hire" (Étienne de Vignolles, 1390-1443) fought battles with Jeanne d'Arc and tried to rescue her after her capture.

[59] Fredegunda , wife of the Merovingian king Childeric in the 6th century, was depicted by Gregory of Tours as mercilessly cruel, thus making her legendary. She probably had nothing to do with the death of Brunhilda, wife of King Sigisbert of Austrasia, who was probably not killed by being dragged by a wild horse, but legend always prefers the more colorful story.

Response to Letter XLI

29 March.

Now we are well-instructed on the subject of Madame de Genlis, and even the Maid. I was surprised that the former was Gabrielle, but not that she was a miller's wife, except that the epithet "pretty" astonished me. I observe that she made three heroes, but as women make them, by the common route, instead of three pupils. I found it quite natural that a woman who was to become a scholar, the educator of three princes, commenced by being Fredegunda; that appears to me most appropriate for her. As for the pupils, like Genlis, they could only make beings with petty vices and petty virtues.

By the way, where is Monsieur de Laclos, whose wrote *Les Liaisons dangereuses?* Everyone thinks him a monster because he depicted a Merteuil and a Valmont, but it is an opposite consequence that one ought to draw. A melancholy man writes comedies, a sanguine man tragedies. Madame de Beauchamois thinks like me, but not the Marquise. Filète believes me, but she thought at first like Madame de Marigny.

(Business.)

Letter XLII

When Clarendon had rejoined Yfflasie and the Maid, in response to a sign, the latter asked them what else they wanted to know about the preceding corporate lives of persons of their acquaintance presently corporeal.

"I would like to know," Clarendon replied, "What Monsieur de La Harpe was previously."[60]

Jeanne started to laugh again. "I shall tell you that naïvely. The first antecedent life of that one was as a petty commissionaire at the door of Chapelain, who also ran errands for Corneille, Racine and Molière, when the opportunity arose. And sometimes he was very proud of verses he carried on their part to Seigneurs or their mistresses. When Chapelain, Brébeuf, Racine, Corneille or Molière spoke, and de La Harpe repeated the speech of one of them, he always said 'we,' as if having a hand in their work, or their merit. And part there was, for his hands to take and render, his feet to walk, his mouth to open, etc.; he was the means by people had and read the verses. So the play ran through him. Died young, that child, who was named Gillot, crushed by a finance cart. Molière did not like him, and La Fontaine never wanted to make use of him.

---

[60] As is obvious from his account of the hypothetical descendancy of his soul, Restif did not like Jean-François de La Harpe (1739-1803) at all. When Louis-Sébastien Mercier proposed putting Restif forward as a candidate for the Académie, with the support of Bernardin de Saint-Pierre, Le Harpe, then the President, dismissed the suggestion witheringly with the remark that Restif "had genius but lacked taste." The extent to which the remark rankled is evident in the present text; a backlash reveling in tastelessness was only to be expected.

"Before that, in the time of Henri III, he was a page of the Duc de Guise, and his arquebus was loaded against the Protestants. Under François I, he was a petty valet of Ronsard, whom he sometimes criticized. Then, I don't know what else he was."

"Thank you, O Maid!"

"It's my turn to ask," said Yfflasie. "I'd like to know what the actress Clairon[61] was."

"In the life preceding this one," Jeanne replied, "she was a chambermaid of the Duchesse d'Orléans, Henriette d'Angleterre; she was the one who gave her the poison that her husband had prepared for her in a *fromage glacé*. Before that she had a great fate: she was Catherine de Medicis, and before that, a prostitute in Rome, when she was impregnated by a pope because she was marvelously pretty. The said pope kept her in the Vatican, and as she bore my name indiscreetly called her Papesse Jeanne. No more on her account."

"And Gaussin?" asked Yfflasie

"Oh, Gaussin…Hortense Mancini, sister of Louis XIV, most recently; she was nevertheless bedded by him, but Mazarin-Cardinal distanced her. No more on her subject.

"And Dumesnil?"

"Was, in the life before last, Elizabeth, Queen of England, and the one before this one a whore in London, where she was nicknamed 'the Queen,' from which a Frenchman in the Ambassador's retinue brought her, disguised as a postilion. He married her, and she was a terrible hawker in the market, where she sold fish at forty-five. She was killed at forty-six in a brawl. She was reborn in 1718 under the Regent. You know the rest."

---

[61] "La Clairon" was the stage name of Claire Leris (1723-1803). She was at the Comédie-Française for more than twenty years, where she competed for leading roles with her great rival Marie Dumesnil (1713-1803). Jeanne Gaussin (1711-1767), although beloved by Voltaire, had difficulty competing with them, and did not endure for nearly as long.

"I would like to ask you now," Yfflasie continued, "what more elevated women have been—for example, the amiable and sensible Comtesse de Beauharnais."

"I will tell you, I will tell you," replied the Maid, eagerly.

Response to Letter XLII

30 March.

Good husband, what you not have been able to tell us about the manner in which Monsieur de La Harpe came into the world and his present life, we can tell you; Madame de Marigny has it from her late husband.

The monad of Gillot, as you doubtless know better than us, remained incorporeal for ninety-nine years. Finally, around 1730, it had such a strong desire to be reincorporated that it did not wait for the hundredth to elapse. At the moment of his whim, a wiper and whipper,[62] at the College Duplessis, married that day, was demonstrating his manhood to a rather pretty nurse whom he had honored with his name. He called himself de La Harpe because he had been found in that street, lying in the bottom of a clothes-mender's barrel by the woman in question, who raised him as best she could. That was Monsieur de La Harpe's father. But you know full well that the body is nothing...

The eldest son of the wiper/whipper, whom the clothes-mender had launched into society, was rather pretty of face bit small, like his friend Puget, who had such a pretty sister. His mother was widowed but she had preserved relations with the college where her husband had wiped and whipped, and obtained a bursary for little de La Harpe, who appeared to have fortunate dispositions. But he had no soul; his own was only a true monad. He succeeded nevertheless beyond his hopes. His mother put him forward by employing him in the homes of the invalids she nursed, and young de La Harpe contributed a good deal to the convalescence of some young bourgeoises with pale complexions—which ensured that when he finished

---

[62] I have translated *frotteur* [floor-polisher] as "wiper" in order to preserve the jocularity of the original's linkage with *fouetteur* [whipper].

his studies he was properly dressed. He attached himself immediately to Voltaire, to whom he made himself known by a few verses.

Meanwhile, his poor mother finding herself too old to care for the sick, became a house-cleaner; she admired her son's progress from afar, for he neglected her greatly. He moved rapidly, becoming an Academician.

In that epoch the poor woman fell ill. She did not want to embarrass her dear son and had herself taken to the Hôtel-Dieu. Sensing her end approaching, however, she wanted to see him. She sent asking for him to come in order to embrace him before dying. He refused harshly, and the good woman was unable to obtain that consolation.

"He's right, the poor child," she said to the Sister. "The air is so bad here—and I wouldn't want him to be seen here. He's so well-known. Use prudence, Mother, in informing him of my end."

She died an hour later, and was taken to the Innocents

That's another anecdote, dear husband.

Letter XLIII

F.m.T. 14 March.

"The person mentioned, in the most recent life before this, was born one morning, like a rose, as a great princess, and finished in the evening, before having bloomed—which is to say that after giving rise to the most beautiful hopes, she died before fifteen. Her mother was the Duchesse de Savoie. Before...but ought I to tell you? For you might be greatly afflicted."

"Oh, tell, tell, Maid!" cried the sensitive Yfflasie.

"Well, she was the unfortunate... very beautiful and very unfortunate...Mary Stuart."

"Mary Stuart, the Queen of Scotland, whom Elizabeth the haughty, since Dumesnil, had killed!"

"The same."

"Oh, charming woman, you were not always happy!"

"Not always. And I have followed her since, and have scarcely seen her happy, for a sensitive soul suffers more than she is joyful, because she feels everything."

"And before Mary Stuart, what was she?"

"Less, but always good; she was my friend and companion in the time of making war for King Charlot, my sovereign lord."

"Eh? Who was she?"

"I can tell you, for the name does her honor: Agnes Sorel, good, mild and although a mistress, more honest and better in conduct than the queen and legitimate wife.[63] Beyond that, no more known. But find an old man somewhere who has not lived again or died again for two thousand years. His name is Cato, the one who killed himself in a subterrain in Capua out

---

[63] Agnes Sorel (1422-1450), the officially recognized mistress of Charles VII, was used as a model for the Virgin by at least two artists; she is a leading character in Voltaire's *La Pucelle*.

of indignation against Caesar—because of which he does not want to return to Earth until there are no more emperors and kings...and the Supreme Being has granted his wish. He can tell you a good deal about who those you know about were before my time."

"We'll see him, we'll see him!" exclaimed the two lovers.

They immediately went in search of him, but they learned, with astonishment, that he had been reincorporated for some years in the person of Dr. Franklin.

"Necessary to wait a while," said the Maid. "He won't take long to return here, and he'll remember everything, only having two lives to recall."

Clarendon resumed asking questions of the Maid, to which she willingly replied, for she had always been good.

"I'd like to know what Corneille was before he was a great man, and what he is today."

"You shall know," Jeanne d'Arc replied.

I shall put off the reply until my next...

Charm of life, sweet illusion, you are not worth as much as the reality that Hortense provides, but you will replace her when I have quit her!

Response to Letter XLIII

31 March.

There has been a transport of joy here when, at the receipt of your last letter, we saw that there was question of one of my friends. Her article has given the greatest pleasure. She has been quite content herself with the roles she has played in the world, even though they have been very dolorous. But the one with which she was most content was that of Agnes Sorel. One cannot describe how flattered she was, because Agnes was beautiful and good, to a degree that is still known, and because the present Comtesse has much of her character and delicacy, with the consequence that one can see that the one really is the prolongation of the other. I don't know if we shall have Madame de Marigny. When one is writing the truth, not imagination, one is not always the master of writing what one can.

You have not yet seen, dear spouse, what de La Harpe has been. In reading the draft of my letter, Filète said to us, as she finished it, at the death of his mother: "Oh, it's true that he has no soul; it's nothing but a monad that makes him move."

(Business.)

Letter XLIV

F.m.T. 15 March.

People are surprised that our Corneille knows the politics of the Romans so well, and that he makes them speak with so much grandeur and nobility. Jeanne explained the cause of that to Yfflasie and Clarendon.

"I know Corneille well for having haunted him while he was still with us. His next-to-last corporeal life he was Admiral Châtillon, and the one before Duguesclin. Before that he was a good mariner, navigating for commerce. And before that, according to what Cato-Franklin told me, he was the great emperor Julian the Apostate, who would have saved the empire if he had lived, and before that Marcus Aurelius, and before that Titus, and before that Germanicus, and before that Fabius. Further than that one can't go. But since you ask what he is today, his name is Ducis, and he's in the Académie."

"I'd like to know," said Yfflasie, with keen interest, "what Racine is today, whom we saw when we arrived here, and who was about to tell Louis XIV that La Valière had loved Bossuet."

(Observe that time passes rapidly—it is already thirty years that Clarendon and Yfflasie have been discorporated.)

"He's Dorat," replied Jeanne.

"And what was he before?"

"Before being Racine, he was Marot, and before that he was obscure for four corporeal lives, but he was Virgil, Sophocles and Hesiod. No more is known than that, for Orpheus, who was only reincorporated sixty years ago, and who has made himself Gluck, didn't tell me any more."

"I'd like to ask you," said Yfflasie, "who a woman was who has written a few novels that I have read: *Elizabeth, Les*

Lettres du Colonel Talbert, Les Extravagances d'une jolie femme and *Agathe et Isidore*."[64]

"I know who you mean. She was a prostitute under Louis XIV, and before, under Henri III, the same in Paris."

"I suspected as much," said Yfflasie.

(In a writing perfectly imitated:)

"And a pretty woman whose full-length portrait I have seen at the Salon?" asked Clarendon, "Madame de Marigny?"

"I can tell you what she was: in the last life before this, Duchesse de Bourgogne; before that, the Marquise de Verneuil; before that, Anne de Bretagne; before that, Gabriele de Vergo. No more known than that, but I've heard it said that she was Caesonia, wife of Caligula, who had the charm above beauty that one sees today in a lovely woman who has a strange adventure and whom I only know by the name of Hortense, and a petty bourgeoise who resembles her, by the name of Filète Dumas."

In my first life, I shall tell you what you were, my Hortense.

---

[64] Françoise-Albin Benoist (1724-1808). The third title is mis-quoted, presumably deliberately; the actual title was *Les Aveux d'une jolie femme* (1761).

Response to Letter XLIV

1 April.

I am triumphant! For the end of our letter, dear spouse, is visibly a reply to some of my responses. However, Madame de Marigny has imperceptibly shaken her head... But Filète and I were enchanted by her article, and the promise of ours, which we await impatiently. Perhaps we shall receive it tomorrow. It will have for me the charm of the truth, since it will be the expression of my husband's sentiment, which is the only thing in the world that interests me. My son is marvelously well, as is my Filète. We would like it to be tomorrow!

Letter XLV

It is of you, dear spouse, that there will be question in this letter, dated "from my tomb," for whenever my end arrives, you will read it…and whenever my end arrives, my sentiments will still be the same as they are today.

I have asked you to promise to reply to me day by day, in the same manner that I am writing. In truth, we shall not understand one another as well. But an advantage compensates for that privation, which is that you are more veritably the impulsion of my soul. I have, in addition, the certainty, by virtue of your daily letters, daily received—as you have by virtue of mine—that you are thinking about me every day, immediately after the arrival of the post. So I spend that hour in meditation, rereading you letter and he draft of mine. I want, by that correspondence, always exact on my part, commenced with a sad word, to prevent you from occupying yourself too sadly, or too joyfully, with anything at all.

Yfflasie and Clarendon, who know you, asked the Maid what you were, Hortense, before being the most beautiful, the most touching and the most lovable of all women.

"I will tell you," she replied, "for I have often seen her, corporate and incorporate. She was here only twenty or twenty-one years ago, and not long before, her great friend Fanny, whom you know, was here, who was ahead of her in her recorporation, by virtue of scarcely having lived in the last corporeality. For Hortense and Fanny were souls formed together by God on the same day, and although Fanny, today, does not know that it was Hortense who was her friend, as a girl, before being the sister of the Duchesse de Bourgogne, they are friends, as if both knew that they had been. They love one another by mental reminiscence, not just the two of them, but here, including Aglaë de Marigny.

"Know, then, that Hortense was, before the last corporate life before this one, a charming little girl protected by the Duchesse de Bourgogne, who had been recommended to her by Rose, her sister, as she died..."

You were the pupil of their charity.

Response to Letter XLV

2 April.

Never perhaps, dear husband! One cannot give a more agreeable origin—which is to say, another preceding life—to a loving soul than to make her the pupil of charity of her two best friends! That is to announce in flattering terms that I have an essentially grateful soul. That ending is worthy of the kind commencement of your letter, were you linger obligingly on the effects of our daily letters. I have had the same thought, and it appears that you have divined that I have also had some relation with my friends in a previous life. I have seen with delight their joy on reading that. I have been tenderly caressed by them.

It appears that I was an abandoned orphan, very poor, but whose origin was not vicious, since two young princesses occupied themselves with her, and the second brought me to France with her. I am sure, after that, that I was the daughter of an honest woman, honorably poor.

(Business.)

Letter XLVI

F.m.T. 17 March.

You have doubtless been annoyed by what I have told you about your origin, without adding anything. But would you have desired me to deceive you? You are a young woman full of grace, attractions philosophy, etc., born...of Ninon d'Enclos and Bossuet. Your mother gave birth to you in Turin, during a secret voyage that she made here, sent by the court, to examine the future Duchesse de Boulogne. You were as lovable as your mother, so the two Princesses of Piedmont cherished you. Do not be sorry, my beauty, to have such a mother. Ninon is worth as much as any other. She was loved by the severe Maintenon, who knew the depths of conduct better than anyone.

In any case, what does it matter what we were in one of our corporate lives?

You would have had all the perfections of your mother, almost all her gallantries—you know the reason—if you had lived; you announced beauty, talent, intelligence. The Duchesse de Bourgogne destined you for the young Prince de Gonzague, newly stripped of his estates by the house of Austria for having taken the side of Louis XIV in the war of the Spanish succession, and your marriage would have returned them to him. The Duchesse de Bourgogne died; the dolor of her loss put you in the tomb, and the Prince de Gonzague obtained nothing.

Your incorporated life was short; the Author of Nature wanted you to be reborn together, the two Princesses of Piedmont and you, in order for you to be friends again, and Nature added a fourth, your sister, a daughter of Ninon like you, who had died sooner, of the shock caused by the sight of the cadaver of her brother, the same one who, having fallen in love with his mother without knowing it, blew out his brains in the garden after she had told him what bonds united them!

In your next to last life, according to what the Maid Jeanne told us, you were the virtuous Queen of France Louise de Vaudemont, wife of Henri III. I should not tell you what you were in the existence that preceded that of the queen; it was something similar to Ninon. We cannot fathom the law of destiny. You were Diane de Poitiers.

Well before that, with three or four intermediaries, you were Emma, the daughter of Charlemagne, who was in love with the secretary Eginhard, who, having been admitted to her from one night, arrived as snow was falling. Whereupon the beautiful and tender princess, for fear that a man's feet might leave footprints emerging from her bedroom, carried him over it on her white and delicate shoulders, having the dainty woman's slippers on her feet then called *crépides*. For, the chronicler says, the good and saintly Charlemagne, since canonized, loved his daughters like a lover, and was very jealous of them—so he watched every morning from his window, aw what was happening, and saw Eginhard emerge.

And at dinner time, at nine o'clock, having summoned the secretary, he said to him: "So, Eginhard, you no longer believe in being courteous to the ladies! How is it that, this morning, in the early twilight, you came to be carried by a demoiselle? Was it a wager?"

Eginhard blushed, and then the thing was known—after which he married Emma with the emperor's consent.

Don't blush, my beauty. I was Eginhard...

That, my charming spouse, is what happened to us in 787, exactly a thousand years ago today. And it was snowing, as it is today,

Let us pass on to other adventures.

Response to Letter XLVI

3 April.

You have taken a great deal of trouble to justify to me what was already justified! But I have been charmed by the explanations that you have given me, and above all of the resemblance between Filète and me. We have been sisters! That alone would render dear to me the second source of my corporeal existence in my previous life, if your reasons had not entirely persuaded me. All four of us have been delighted by what you have told us. So it is the Author of Nature himself who wanted to compensate us for our preceding misfortunes, by enabling all four of us to be reborn at the same time, within range of being friends!

We also thank you for the story of Emma, one of my antecedent selves. Three of us did not know it, and for myself, I confess that I had completely forgotten it. But you reconciled me to my little weakness very nicely by saying that you were Eginhard.

Letter XLVII

F.m.T. 18 March.

Yfflasie and Clarendon quit the Maid, very reluctantly, for it is necessary to know that the Virgin, having learned about the American Revolution, was no longer so afraid of the English, and ceded to the irresistible penchant that souls have to resume bodies after a certain time of liberty. That is because the pleasures of the senses have a corporeal, or material, verity that is infallibly tempting when it has not been savored for a long time. That is why Achilles, who was very sensible to the pleasure of the senses, preferred to be a corporate cooking-pot rather than remain another eighty years as a pure soul. But people are more delicate nowadays.

Now, the Maid having had a whim to be recorporated, all that she had to do was choose, as was her privilege, honest people to whom to be born. She entered into the fetus of a child conceived at that very instant in the chaste womb of a newlywed fourteen-year-old newlywed who had just married a protestant minister, reintegrated into their rights as citizens. That minister was a young man of thirty, full of science and health, who only married the pretty daughter of a Dutch minister, a refugee in order not to be tempted by his bothers' wives.

But let us leave the Maid, who will be reborn in her time, and only observe that one passes immediately from corporate life to incorporate life, but to return to corporate life, it requires a kind of death, an absolute torpor, to begin with, from which one only return in twelve or fifteen years, and sometimes thirty for certain individuals. Let us follow Yfflasie and Clarendon in their new excursions.

The happiness of disengaged souls does not consist of having nothing to do. New free souls are only without occupation for some fifteen of our years. After that epoch, they cease to be infants and become citizens until the age of eighty years. Then they become free again for twenty years, more or less. It

185

is necessary to observe that I am only instructed by Yfflasie and Clarendon, who only learned gradually themselves. I thus learned from them very recently that souls have two disengaged lives, the regular, which is a hundred years, and the irregular, which is as many years as they lived on Earth. They can live both of them or only one, and choose which they want to live non-corporeally. In addition, the feminine among them, is more honorable than the masculine...

Until tomorrow, my Hortense.

Response to Letter XLVII

4 April.

Your last letter, good husband, tells us nothing in particular about such and such a soul, except for the incorporation
of the Maid in the fetus forming in the womb of a minister's
wife. One of my former protectresses, Madame de
Beauchamois, claims that the young minister is Rabaut de
Saint-Étienne.[65] We have no reason to say no, and we have our
friendship and our confidence in her to say yes, so it's necessary to believe it.

Since your last letter but one Filète and I are absolutely
sisters, and now we are forever inseparable. That letter, whose
subject would be regarded as chimerical by anyone but us, has
fortified our amity more than I can say.

One thing that is indifferent to me but gives a great deal
of pleasure to my friends and the beautiful Comarieu de
Montalembert,[66] is the primacy of our sex in the incorporate
life. Madame de Beauchamois would like to have known that
while her husband was alive. She would have been patient
about many little things.

(Business.)

---

[65] The French Protestant leader, Jean-Paul Rabaut Saint-
Étienne (1743-1793) cannot possibly be the minister in question if the internal chronology of Yfflasie and Clarendon's
story makes any sense at all (although it is now losing the few
shreds of consistency it maintained for a while).

[66] Marie-Joséphine de Comarieu, Marquise de Montalembert
(1760-1832) had not yet made a name for herself as a writer
when *Les Posthumes* was published, but Restif first met her in
the early 1780s.

Letter XLVIII

F.m.T. 19 March.

The two lovers Yfflasie and Clarendon, after thirty years of discorporate life, were employed in the Republic of Souls called France, although they had been disengaged from their bodies in Italy. They had adopted the atmospheric cap that covers Paris.

But souls do not have our needs; they only occupy themselves with intellectual pleasures, and it is their mores, their aliments, their minerals, their vegetables and their animals that I shall describe to you in the letters that follow. I shall return some day to the particular lives of our friends of whom I have not talked, such as Dorat-Cubières, Arthaud de Bellevue, the officer de Belair, now a General and Governor of Mantua, Comte Potocki, young Prince Czatorinski, Prince Gonzague, Comte Arconati, known as the Great Voyager, Comte Jablonski, the Comte de Sainte-Aldegonde—once Pythagoras, in parentheses—Vicomte Toustain, Laserté, the Marquis de Lagrange, Baron de Paraza, Cazotte and a few other individuals linked with us. But it is necessary to vary. Afterwards we shall follow together, with Yfflasie and Clarendon, the mortal life of the Maid, with those of a few others about which they talk to me, which will form a very interesting collection of anecdotes.

For the present, let us get back to the two non-corporeal citizens.

Souls, as I said just now, have minerals, vegetables and animals. Their minerals are ideas, their vegetables thoughts and their animals desires—that is, as for corporeal animals, the most difficult realm to govern. The vegetables grow in the minerals, as they do down here, and the animals nourish themselves on the vegetables, or other animals. Thus, animality is divided, as it is here, into herbivores and carnivores.

The foundation of the soul consists of ideas. The thoughts grow there and nourish themselves upon it. They are the basis of the nourishment of souls, which eat them as we eat legumes and bread, with the desires, a more succulent nourishment but too warming to be eaten alone. There are as many species of desires as we have animals, and genres of thoughts as varied as the classes and species of our vegetables. I shall talk about that.

Yfflasie and Clarendon were surprised by that order of things. The first employment that was given to them was to make them shepherds of flocks of ewe-desires—which is to say, gentle ones...

I shall continue tomorrow.

Response to Letter XLVIII

5 April.

I will admit, dear and ingenious spouse, that neither my friends nor I were expecting the manner in which you are going to fill your letters. We were counting on common details of affairs or, at the most, anecdotes of the country. But we have observed, my friends and I, that the notable events of a country during a hundred years would not fill the 365 days of the year. Other resources are necessary to you, and you have procured immense ones!

The Comtesse, who always praises you a great deal, said to us a little while ago: "If these *Letters from the Tomb* were an imaginative work for the public, I would tell him that he has, in my opinion, avoided a reef on which a thousand others would be broken. In the first moments of surprise, dolor and joy, the lover of the 366 letters thinks less about his death than about his love; he speaks of the charms and the virtues of the woman he loves. Others would only have talked about tombs and funereal clarities. Monsieur de Fontlhète's move is one of genius and sentiment."

Those are her own words, dear husband. We see now that it will be easy for you to fulfill the task you have imposed on yourself, to compensate your spouse for an absence…for which you alone can compensate her. And you are so fecund that I have no doubt that you will leave your seams half-excavated, in order to follow others perhaps even richer.

Letter XLIX

F.m.T. 20 March.

I forgot, in my last letter, my beautiful love, my unique amour, to tell you how souls eat. It is necessary to repair that omission before talking to you about the flock with which Yfflasie and Clarendon were charged.

Souls, having no mouth or hands, take their nourishment in a particular manner. They absorb an idea, a thought, or a desire by the power of their will, and they identify themselves with it by occupying themselves with it. That is the whole of the mystery. Let us return now to where I was.

I told you that Yfflasie and Clarendon were shepherds of ewe-desires, which is to say, gentle ones—that was to make you understand that there are other desires. And that is necessary, since souls have the generic equivalents of all our animals. There are, in consequence, lion-desires, tiger-desires, bear-desires, wolf- and fox-desires, serpent-desires, swine-desires, billy-goat- and nanny-goat-desires, fearful and timid desires like hares and rabbits, crawling desires like slugs, furtive ones like mice, miry ones like toads and frogs, eagle- and vulture-desires, superficial, and inconstant desires like swallows, tender, cheerful and harmonious ones like skylarks, finches, nightingales, parrot-, magpie- and jay-desires, owl-desires, etc.

In the same way, among the vegetable-thoughts there are some that are cabbages, turnips, carrots, artichokes, round lettuces, chicory, raspberries, currants, cherries, plus, walnuts or chestnuts; some are poisonous, like the fruits of the manchineel-tree, or highly-appreciated, like coffee, coconut and pineapple; and some are aconite, or the terrible tree whose poison is only collected by a man condemned to death, who receives it in a shell, who is killed if he has not taken the wind or its direction has just changed. Those poison-thoughts can denature the soul that nourishes itself on them, and even kill it—which is to say, force it to enter a body immediately, to deliver itself there to crime. That is the origin of famous villains just as poor ordinary nourishment gives us weak, stupid and false people, in all the genres of laxity. Good and healthy nourishment, on the contrary, delicious fruits and succulent meats, give us honest and virtuous individuals.

There is in addition a cooking, for animal or vegetable nourishment. One makes the cooking fire with thoughts as firm and solid as oak or any other wood; the nourishment, thoughts or desires, is cooked and elaborated, becoming more digestible and more salubrious...

I did not know all that when I commenced this article, my incomparable Hortense; I am instructing myself while instructing you, as a dove commences the digestion of the nourishment of her chicks.

Response to Letter XLIX

6 April.

This time, dear husband, we are perfectly instructed, and all four of us agree that your method will be useful to us. When we have a desire, an inconsiderate urge, we shall apply to it, and for a long time, a strong thought, in order to cook the desire or the urge well, in order that it does not give us indigestion—which, I believe, among souls, according to its gravity, is called regret, repentance or remorse. Thus, you can see that your wife and her friends are taking an excellent moral from all they are told by a man, loved by all four, in the senses appropriate to them. Your letter is very ingenious. But we are looking forward to the moment when you will talk to us again about souls of our acquaintance.
(Business.)

Letter L

One might say to me that it is madness to take desires to pasture. "What does that mean?" the reasoners would cry (for it will not be my Hortense; as good and simple as she is intelligent, Hortense will find nothing impossible, because she is not obsessed with knowing exactly how far the limits of Nature's power extend). It is therefore necessary to employ this letter in responding to the reasoners.

"Messieurs, you know, or do not know, that all is substance in Nature. You can see the vulgar substance of the Earth, and that of fixed salts, and that of water, and you can glimpse that of volatile salts. You sense the air—which is to say that you perceive it through one of your senses—and the electrical fluid, the same one that ignites wood and causes it to be consumed, and you divine the magnetic fluid by its effects; you suspect the ether, which is the air or the atmosphere of suns; you sense and you see the substance of stars, which is light and heat. You divine the divine substance, which is intelligence, by that which is within you and by the beautiful order of the universe, which is its corporeal part; and you conjecture that the intellectual substance is a fluid purer than the ether, heat and solar light, and which might be called electrico-magnetico-intellectual-divine fluid. All that is in us, the Earth, or the globe has on a larger scale; the Sun has it, even more perfect and purified. Everything that is in the Suns is almost perfect, and infinite in the Sun-of-Suns, the universal center, in God.

"Now, the intellectual fluid, by means of which everything thinks and reasons, is the electrical fluid of God, which fluid imbues the beings in the universe appropriate to receive it, not directly and immediately, but via natural intermediaries, the Sun and the Cometoplanets; it passes from them to different animals; in the Sun into the solar humans and animals;

from the Sun to the Cometoplanets; from the Cometoplanets to the planetary humans and animals.

"Everything in Nature is *type and image*. If one eats corporeally on the Earth, one must eat corporeally in the Sun, and substantially in the universal center into which everything finally falls: God. If the terrestrial insect eats, the Earth must eat in its own manner; if the solar insect eats, the Sun, in its manner, must eat also. If everything eats, the universal center must devoir everything one day, absorb everything, in order to render everything after being nourished by it. God is the Serpent that devours its tail and the non-central part of its body.

"When, as Yfflasie and Clarendon described it to me, I described to you the state of the souls of terrestrial beings, I did not intend to tell you that that order of things would be eternal—nothing is eternal but God—but only that such would be the estate of terrestrial souls so long as the terraqueous globe lasts. After that necessary explanation, let us continue.

"Souls that are still terrestrial have a life almost parallel with the one they will have in God when God has absorbed everything, Earths and Suns, which God nourishes and is nourished by. They must, therefore, eat in their manner, which is different from that of bodies, but which nevertheless conserves all possible resemblances therewith, because, the soul being a substance, like the Earth-globe, like the Sun and like God, the universal center, and having movement, as a consequence of diminution, it necessarily loses it, and must repair itself."

I do not believe, my beautiful and tender spouse, that Messieurs the scholars and reasoners have anything to respond to that.

Tomorrow, another matter.

Response to Letter L

7 April.

Oh my love, how high you rise in your latest! You give us, in summary, the gradation of all Nature. My two friends say that it is high, very high philosophy, and Filète has reread your letter three times.

I have a clear enough conception of your classification of beings, from the terrestrial animal to the universal central being; better than that, I sense that it is quite natural that things should be thus. The principle that you posit, that everything in Nature is *type and image*, is admirable. For it follows from it that, in knowing humans, one knows all beings, including God.

"A man is the image of the Earth," the Comtesse said to us, "and the Earth is his type, or his model."

"Good," said Filète, swiftly. "I understand! I lost myself in that principle, so clear, but a single example explains it, and I understand."

"The Earth," the Comtesse continued, "is the image of the Sun, and the Sun is its type, or model, on which it is formed. There is, therefore, a resemblance between the man, the previous image, and the Sun. The Sun is the image of the universe center, of God, and the universal center is the type of the Sun. There is, therefore, a resemblance between the man and the Earth, the man and the Sun, and the man and God. Well, what is that resemblance? The man, like them, is an individual; like them, he lives; like them, he has ideas, thinks, wants, executes; like them, he begins, grows, diminishes and is dissolved. But is God an individual?"

"He is the only real one, since he is everything."

"But does God think?"

"You see his thoughts, his will; it's the order and the march of things."

"But does he die?"

"No, but he dissolves everything in himself, which is the same as dissolving himself, and he reproduces everything. He resembles a fabulous clock, which the same sand can cause to move perpetually."

"But since God is the sole individual, how is it that the other beings, the Sun, the Earth, and humans, exist?"

"By resemblance only. They form little finite centers, as God forms the infinite center in which they exist." She added: "I hold to this doctrine of Monsieur de Fontlhète, when it comes to me."

That's very long today, but my head is full.

Letter LI

F.m.T. 22 March.

It is said that there are no sorcerers, or spells, or magic. That is very easy to say, and I give thanks to the philosophers for having established it convincingly. However, dear spouse, I required a little magic—which is to say, supernatural power—to converse, as I do, with Yfflasie and Clarendon. Don't say anything about it, dear wife, even fifty years after my death! People will make fun of me, and perhaps of you, who will no longer be as pretty as you are at present.

The Ancients are permitted what is not permitted to the Moderns, and nonsense is no longer nonsense when sixty, a hundred or a thousand generations have repeated it.

I could cite you famous examples of that, but I won't go back any further than Saint Ignatius and Saint Francis of Assisi, who were two great sorcerers, as is clearly evident from their works. The former carried out the greatest act of sorcery ever,[67] and although the feat of the latter was less brilliant, it was even more magical, since Francis—French by origin—spoke many a time to his brothers the animals, and his sisters the frogs, and some of them replied to him while the others obeyed him.

Don't say anything about my magic, therefore. Every ancient trickster, including Moses, Joshua, Mohammed, Saint Ignatius and Saint Francis, is a saint; every modern trickster is a rogue, and thanks to our incredulous century, neither Mesmer nor Cagliostro, nor the patriarch of the Martinists, Schulembourg,[68] will be canonized. It was the same among the Greeks; Trophonius was a saint, as well as Tiresias, whereas

---

[67] Although he is not the only Saint Ignatius, this is presumably a sarcastic reference to Ignatius of Loyola, founder of the Jesuits; his great feat of magic will be described subsequently.

[68] I can find no evidence of any Martinist with this name.

Apollonius of Tyana and the petty astrologers of the time of Nero and Domitian were banished!

But to you, my excellent love, to you, who possess all my heart, I can admit in confidence that I am something of a sorcerer, for my meager pleasures. It is, therefore by magic, not that I evoke the souls of Yfflasie and Clarendon, but that, acting on mine, I force it to half-quit its mortal envelope, to protrude its upper portion out of the body like a snail, in order to converse with souls. It is a vision that has given me that appetite; I have made it a reality.

At present, now that you are well instructed, or I believe that you are—for I am incessantly recommencing my explanations—I can resume the story of the two shepherd souls.

I have told you that the agreeable employment in question, once the prerogative of children cherished by their parents, the occupation of heroes and demigods, was that of discorporate souls that had reached their adolescence. They commence by pasturing the ewes, after which they are charged with goats, then cattle, and finally donkeys, horses, camels and elephants.

After all that, souls become huntresses, destroying lion-, tiger-, bear-, hyena-, crocodile- and serpent-desires, etc. Or they become fishers, to domesticate the souls of fish-thoughts and desires taken from the intellectual sea, or mineralogists, to dig in the mine of ideas and find there what we still call today golden ideas. They also extract ideas of copper, tin, lead, mercury, zinc, etc. of which alloys are made in order to render ideas of lead or tin firmer. All of them are colored, either with minium, which is black lead, or with iron, the general colorist of Nature.

Response to Letter LI

8 April.

Those are great details, dear husband. An ordinary author would have made that his preface. You are, then, something of a sorcerer? I am delighted by that. You will be better able to avoid traps and dangers.

You had said nothing yet about intellectual mineralogy, but your golden ideas are themselves a golden idea.

What you say regarding the saints made my friends smile. For myself, I fear that the Inquisition might open your letters, and there really is the wherewithal there to subject you to an auto-de-fé. It is true that being a public minister of a foreign power, you're less at risk than another, but I wouldn't have been so confident a few centuries ago...

In any case, such letters demonstrate that you're in perfect health; that's what renders them doubly agreeable to me.

(Business. Although Fontlhète was then in his tomb, detailed instructions were not abandoned; they were sent by the friend successor to the president's business agent, who made appropriate use of them. Thus, everything went on as it had when Fontlhète was alive. No one could stick his nose into his affairs, since there was a living child, and as for their supervision, the Minister of Justice, aware of the objective, arranged everything personally.)

Letter LII

F.m.T. 23 March.

Yfflasie and Clarendon were shepherds for three years. Nothing is comparable to their happiness during that interval. Doubtless everything that is recounted to us about the happiness of ancient shepherds comes to us from the other life. I saw the charm of their conversations. But if they were useful to me, I was equally necessary to them. I reminded them of the woes of corporeal life, which they forgot, as all the other souls forget them the further they are distanced from them. I engaged them to regulate their desires, only to take excellent intellectual nourishment, and they listened to me.

I shall describe their pastoral life for you.

The ewe-desires that they supervised were all the gentler because each of them was united with the placid soul of a ewe, or a lamb; it is for that reason that a desire is a ewe-desire rather than anything else. In the morning, after taking their flock into the vast meadows of desires, it was, however, necessary for Yfflasie and Clarendon to go to some trouble keeping foreign desires away from their charges, such as goat- and swine-, and above all wolf-desires—which, as you might think, were united with the souls of discorporated wolves—but when that triage was made, they had a tranquil day. Sick desires were left in the stable, with appropriate nourishment.

Yfflasie, however, was often heartbroken, because butcher souls came to pick the plumpest individuals from her flock and take them away for slaughter. The poor sheep left its purest substance for the nourishment of human souls, and its little bleating soul in the first embryo of its species at the moment when a ram leapt upon a ewe. It wandered after its dilaniation, until that moment came. Thus, although the life of shepherds is very pleasant, it has its troubles. It seems that Nature does not want beings to be perfectly happy, except by means of their perfect reunion with God, or the Being-Principle.

One advantage that naked souls have is that, being more enlightened, they weary of the estate that they have to quit, whereas corporeal beings love life equally until he last moment. In consequence, after some time looking after the ewe-desires, Yfflasie and Clarendon passed on without regret to goat-desires. I shall talk to you about that in my next.

You see, my very beautiful, that things are beginning to fall into place. The souls of animals are attached to every desire, and modify them. The vegetative souls of plants, indestructible like those of humans and animals, are attached to every thought, and give its species: cabbage-thought, turnip-, beet- or radish-though; strawberry- or pineapple thought; aconite-, manchineel-thought, etc. Minerals follow the same rule, but their souls, although indestructible, have a coarser substance, composed of volatile and fixed salts, linked by sulfur or oil, and terrestrial sweat is their body.

The march of Nature is always uniform, for all the variety of her emanations: every life, soul, body, in its own manner, marches in step. Nothing is as simple as Nature, from God to a rock. Tenuity, activity, heat, sight, mental consciousness, materiality, weight, solidity etc. constitutes all the differences between beings. God alone has infinite penetration, activity and intelligence because he is the most refined, most tenuous and most penetrating volatile salt. Rock, by contrast, has not only unconsciousness and insensibility, but massiveness and absolute inertia.

Response to Letter LII

9 April.

We follow all these details, good husband, with scrupulous attention, and you would laugh at our gravity if you could see us reading or listening to your letters. We feel effectively that your doctrine differs from the atheism of the most rational minds, and brings them back via physics to the admission of the Divinity. That reflection, which three of us made, has enchanted my Filète, who cried involuntarily: "Oh, that dear Monsieur de Fontlhète, I never understand him... but I believe."

Take note of what my second self desires. You can love her as much as you wish, I can guarantee that I shall not be jealous

We laughed at the idea of the butcher-souls. Doubtless they are the souls of corporeal butchers, who remain so after the soul is separate from the body. But what struck us more is the souls of animals and vegetables. The idea of desires that are sometimes ewes and sometimes tigers is new and pleasant. Everything in your work is new...but my tenderness and admiration for you are not new; they are perpetual.

Letter LIII

F.m.T. 24 March.

My beautiful Hortense, I told you that the expression "a golden idea" had passed from the language of souls into that of corporeal beings. There are ideas of silver, copper, tin, lead, iron, lodestone, mercury, antimony, bismuth, zinc, arsenic, etc., and of sulfur, salt, stone, diamond, clay and mud! What proves that the quest for the philosopher's stone is a folly is that once there were crazy whisperers among the souls, some of who wanted to be able to make golden ideas out of copper ideas, silver idea, or even ideas of tin or lead, but in spite of all the sagacity that souls have, they were never able to carry it through...

They went even further; under the pretext that diamond is the product of the juice of the purest form of stone, which is siliceous earth, they wanted to make diamond ideas with stone-ideas. They were never able to succeed.

Finally, there was one who, having taken a quintessence of one book each from Fontanes, Beaussol, Palissot, Leblanc, Durosoy, Marin, Nogaret—Jean, that is—and Cousin Jacques, wanted to make half an ounce of Voltaire. It has never been possible! The operation failed. Fontanes contributed intellectual mercury, Beaussol tombac, Palissot arsenic, Leblanc zinc—which turned the copper yellow—Durosoy the antimony that hardened the head; Marin the minium; Jean Nogaret the liver of sulfur appropriate to destroy the vermin on the heads of the children of the Pitié, and Cousin Jacques the nitrous salt to cast a light as frolicsome and cold as that of the moon. They amalgamated the whole, fused it and set it on of the furnace; the matter did not volatilize the eight living pounds yielded sixteen of death-cap, or death's-head, which precipitated out black; all the heavy molecules in the surrounding area were combined being united in the single mixture, by the law of affinity. A second manipulation changed it

204

all into ocher, or gold chalk, which was obtained instead of intellectual gold, rather than the precious metal of Voltaire.

Thus, humans, even discorporate, cannot change the nature of minerals; the power that made them cannot be communicated to finite beings.

Every plant that dies has given a part of its soul to its seed, and the latter grows, by virtue of a natural centrifugal force, with the souls of animals and humans, who have given a part of their own to the stories or children they have made on the surface of our atmosphere. It is there that vegetal souls grow, as material plants grow on the surface of the Earth; they are almost immaterial vegetables, appropriate to the nourishment of discorporate animals and humans. The souls of the former graze there, just as corporate animals graze in our fields and meadows.

As soon as an ox, a sheep, a pig, a deer, a hare or a tiger is killed, their souls, to which they have given the superabundance to their propagation—unless they have been neutered—rise up to the surface of the atmosphere, and either graze the almost incorporeal grass or devour the souls of other animals there. In their turn, they serve to aliment human souls.

The nanny-goats that Yfflasie and Clarendon were now pasturing gave incorporeal milk, which restores real souls. The cap, or surface, of the atmosphere has between twenty and forty times more circumference than the terrestrial globe it surrounds, of so many leagues. That atmospheric cap has its mobile mountains and valleys, which do not hinder souls that are as agile as them in the least. It is inhabited, traveled and built up intellectually, just as the material surface of the globe is corporeally. If I have not said all that sooner, I only erred by ignorance; I did not know it.

Also, souls, which I believed to be sheltered from all peril, do not have complete security. They can be wounded, even killed, and forced by that to take on a body sooner than they desire. A human soul can be torn apart by a lion- or tiger-soul, or envenomed by a serpent-soul, in a spiritual radiance greater than that in which lions, tigers and giant serpents find themselves down here; similarly, French souls placed above our atmosphere can be torn apart by a lynx-soul, or a beast-of-Givaudan-soul.[69]

You can see by all that, my beautiful Hortense, that the corporeal world is a perfect ape of the incorporeal world; that everything here is the imitation of its higher equivalent.

I shall soon talk to you about the government of the incorporeal estates. In the meantime, I ought to observe, firstly, how just the expression "rise to Heaven" is, in speaking of the souls of the dead, and secondly, how mistaken Homer is in assuring us that the estate of souls is so miserable, and that they continually regret their bodies; that idea is immoral, destructive of virtue and courage, and contrary to the truth.

---

[69] The Beast of Givaudan, or Gévaudan, was thought to be responsible for a number of fatal attacks carried out on the Lozère and the Haute-Loire in 1764-67, attributed to a giant wolf or dog allegedly possessed of huge teeth and a long tail. A local hunter was eventually credited, at least by local legend, with having killed the beast with a silver bullet.

Response to Letter LIII

10 April.

It is necessary to admit, my friend, to seeing realized the idea of a heaven and a kind of paradise above our heads. It is necessary not to swear to anything when one is in relation with human spirit! Here is Jesus rising naturally to Heaven on the day of his ascension! Here is his blessed mother following the same route on the day of her assumption. Here is Jacob's ladder verified. Here is the pious—as I believe—monk Bruno seeing the souls of purgatory rising into the sky as masses are said for them! Oh, what fools you render sages, plausibly, in your last letter. If you did not sometimes put a little anti-Christianity into your letters, you might be canonized one day, and we would be able to invoke Saint Fontlhète in our litanies—or, at least, our children would—saying to him *ora pro nobis*!

I am really and dolorously afflicted to learn that souls have risks to run, but you have demonstrated to us that the two kinds of death are so very little that one ought not, in truth, be embarrassed by them.

Here my two friends, and especially Filète, who are reading over my shoulder, have out their arms around my neck affectionately. That little impulse surprises me, but as we love one another so tenderly...

(Business affairs, to which the friend replied, as was agreed.)

Letter LIV

F.m.T. 25 March.

Do you not think, my dear wife, that I am paying court to the great men of the world into which I shall soon enter like an adroit courtier? Be sure, my beloved, that everything I tell you about the estate of souls is true, and that I am only telling you with the motive of a more affectionate attachment. I cannot hide from you that I am occupying myself forcefully and intensely with the idea because I have succeeded in convincing myself. They spread a salutary balm in the soul of whoever believes them.

Yfflasie and Clarendon had a great deal of trouble guarding the incorporeal goats, which sometimes caused them great impatience by going astray by going astray, climbing and perching on rock-ideas that extended over precipices of snow- and ice-ideas, or by prancing on a sea of tempestuous idea rolling in horrible waves, and going from there to browse the leaves of thorn-bush- or gorse-ideas. But it was the exactitude of fulfilling these first employments well that the confidence depended that might be placed in them for more elevated employments.

The souls that had not failed in anything in the estate of shepherds, goatherds, swineherds, donkey-, horse-, camel-tenders, mahouts etc., depending on the locale, succeeded to the most important magistracies by age and merit.

Arts and métiers are also found among souls, but the métiers are more honorable there than the arts. For the rule is that the more useful a profession is, the more esteemed it is. And as useful things become routine, a great recognition is shown to individuals that restrict themselves to unamusing things. Nothing is more common among beings detached from bodies than intelligence and penetration, so generosity is preferred there to transcendence; a limited genius is a phenomenon there, because it is rare, and he willingly does the most commonplace things. Modesty is ranked above talent there, and timidity above glory. Among souls, one is never mistaken about true merit, given that they are transparent to one another.

Response to Letter LIV

11 April

Thank you, my love, for your tender sentiments. They flatter my heart. What blows you deal to my tranquility, though, without wanting to. No longer put into your letters the disquieting implications that I can't repeat. You assure me, though, that what you report about souls is true. Filète assures me of it too.

So Yfflasie and Clarendon are now goatherds! I would have liked it more if they had done something different. But since it is necessary, and they conduct themselves well in that estate, I shall rejoice in it as a means of succeeding.

I don't know whether it is a good thing that among souls, the arts are less than métiers, and the stupid above men of great intelligence. The reasons you give, dear husband, are very down to earth!

Madame de Marigny claims that if it were like that among us, everything would be turned upside down. She is sure that the arts, children of leisure and liberty, would have saved the human species from slavery if they had existed in the times of the barbarian irruptions. She cites the opinion of missionaries to China, that it is by means of their conserved arts that the Chinese submit vanquishers as ferocious as those of the Oriental tartars to their usages.

I found that reasoning very good, and you will appreciate it. Mademoiselle de Beauchamois adds the example of the Indian castes, which have debased the laborious conditions. You shall judge that.[70]

---

[70] Author's note: "These questions would soon have been settled if these letters had been written after the Revolution. Note of July 1796."

Letter LV

F.m.T. 26 March.

After what I have just told you, my dear Hortense, you ought to suspect that among souls, there are not many play-wrights, actors, tragedies, comedies, dramas, operas, operettas or vaudevilles. The third genre, drama, is the most esteemed, then opera, then tragedy, arietta, vaudeville, and comedy least of all, for there is no parody among souls.

I propose to write the subjects of a few plays, and even report an entire play to you, as soon as I have seen one per-formed, which will not be long. I shall also talk to you about the merits of actors and actresses. (Observe that here, former males play the roles of women, and former females the roles of men.) Neither are much esteemed, although they give great pleasure, and the reason is simple: it is that they are almost all the souls of apes, which are found appropriate to imitation, those of humans being too proud to lower themselves to these employments. It is a great advantage for the ape-souls to be appropriate to that occupation, for when they have been dis-tinguished actresses, the obligatory expression of passions purifies them to the point that during their recorporation they pass into human bodies.

Ordinarily, those souls become terrestrial actors and ac-tresses after their human recorporation. Yfflasie and Claren-don leaned that Citizen Contat[71] had been the she-ape of which an officer speaks who, having found a young French officer shipwrecked, helped him, fed him and became his lover by virtue of her caresses and an apish face almost as amiable as that if the hottentot of the *Vaillant*. She kept him for three years, and it was said that it was the longest constancy she had ever had in her two lives. She only kept her ape-lovers for as

---

[71] The actress Louise Contat (1760-1813).

long as the time of coitus, and in her present life, her human lovers only for one night.

Mademoiselle de Raucourt,[72] in a preceding life, had been the great Pongote[73] that a mariner—a pilot cast away on a deserted beach at the age of thirty-five—encountered while dying of need, who also nourished him, and whom he made his mistress, mistaking her for a savage woman, and by whom he had two children. But, finally having perceived that she could not talk, he saw that she was only an ape. A ship appeared, the Pongote was absent gathering provisions; the man made signs, and the launch came to find him. He was a hundred yards from the beach when the she-ape reappeared; she threw herself into the sea and swam; she was repelled with thrusts of the oars. Indignant, she returned to shore, picked up her two children and showed them to the infidel. Seeing him board the vessel, however, she became furious, tore them apart and threw them into the sea. That is why the aforementioned Raucourt plays the part of Medea so well now.

We also know that the elder Sainval[74] was a shabby and very ill-disposed she-ape, her tearful younger sister an orangutan, Clairon a frisky cercopithecus or tailed she-ape, hence her

---

[72] "Mademoiselle Raucourt" was the stage name of the actress Françoise Saucerette (1756-1815), imprisoned when the Revolution broke out for her royalist sympathies, although Restif's animosity might have had more to do with her notorious lesbianism..

[73] The Comte de Buffon, confusing reports from Africa and Indonesia, initially conflated rumors of gorillas and orangutans into a single hypothetical species in his *Histoire naturelle*, which he called the Pongo, contrasting it with the Jocko [chimpanzee]. He revised his opinion later, as evidenced by the present text's subsequent (but highly inaccurate) discrimination.

[74] Claire de Sainval of the Comédie-Française.

212

nickname of Fretillon.[75] Lekain was a blue-faced pongo with broad shoulders; Môlet a marmoset, a kind of cynocephalus, and Larive a baboon of the kind the Dutch call Smitten, which is the size of a man. The actress Hut was a mandrill, a kind of ape that willingly has commerce with humans. The aforementioned Dieviénne, in her ape life, was of the race that the negroes properly cal guenons. The amiable Mézerai had been a pretty little marmot monkey found on the back of its mother, killed by a rifle-shot in a field of sugar-cane she was uprooting, which was brought up, and became a charming animal, as the missionary Cabasson relates at length—but the marmots, which act in concert, calling and replying to one another, are suspected of being an extreme variety of humans. The soul of young Mars had once been that of a reflective macaque, which enables her to play rational roles—which are not the same as those of reasoners—very well. Her older sister had, it is said, animated a stout Barris, a kind of orangutan that the negroes accuse of not wanting to talk for fear of being made to work. The delicate Hopkins had been a kind of macaque known as a harelip monkey. The delightful cantatrice of the Théâtre Variétés-Montansier, the inimitable Caroline, was in her previous life a pretty rat- or beaver-monkey of India, otherwise known as a bugée.[76] Those are all the most agreeable species

---

[75] Mlle. Clairon was the butt of a savage satire by Pierre de la Bataille entitled *L'Histoire de la vie et des moeurs de Mademoiselle Cronel, actrice, dit Frétillon* (1739-40; subsequently extended) Unsurprisingly, she hated anyone who applied the nickname to her. The next three names were all those of actors associated with the Comédie-Française, and the rest run the entire gamut of the Parisian stage.

[76] This species is very elusive, but the reference appears to have been slightly misquoted from François de La Chesnaye-Desbois' *Dictionnaire raisonné et universel des animaux* (1759), where it refers to a species of the genus Cebus. Many of the monkey species cited in this passage might be taken

of monkeys. Dumesnil's father had been a large Anglolan cebus the color of a wolf with the head of a bear, and her mother was a wife of the local king who had surprised them in infidelity and was condemned to be prostituted to the Cebus in the menagerie after being intoxicated by palm wine.

Let us pass on to the Opéra. Vestriss père had been a handsome titi of Brazil, the most agreeable jumper of the Nicolet of souls; his so-called son was common to him and a macaque, who slept alternately with a winged monster, half-woman and half-harpy. Macaque-winged Vestriss got his lightness from his mother and his strength from his brothers. Mademoiselle Arnoult had been one of the most alert lion-monkeys in the entire apery, Beaumesnil one of the most docile, Rosalie one of the most obstinate, Duplant one of the most vigorous.

Saint-Hubert had not animated a complete monkey but a hybrid body emerged from a baboon and a Jaloffe black woman, who was beloved by the son of the King of Ardra, and was raped one day when he went hunting. But the young Prince's Manimonbanda—which is to say, his first wife—having seen it, told the King, who cut off the half-breed's head. The son of the King of Ardra, in despair, stabbed his Manimonbanda, and the king cleaved the prince in two all the way to the waist with his English steel sword.[77]

At the same moment than the three souls were discorporated, they joined together and became friends; the half-breed as chosen to be an actress among the discorporate and her two companions wanted to imitate her. Saint-Hubert was born a woman here, as was her lover; the Manimonbanda animated a boy, who espoused her husband from Guinea, a

---

from the same book, but some of them seem to have no existence outside Restif's works.

[77] The term Manimonbanda is borrowed from Denis Diderot's satire *Les Bijoux indiscrets* (1748), where the character in question, married to Mangogul, a thinly-disguised Louis XV, stands in for the latter's wife Marie-Adélaide de Savoie.

woman in this life, in her first marriage; then, having become a musician in the spiritual choir under the name of Saint-Hubert, and a widower, he married the half-breed, who had become a musicienne. When she was eventually widowed, she consoled herself in a second marriage, as all the world knows...

Gardel had been a mediocre monkey for leaping but ingenious with regard to the invention of dances. The said Gardel had been a pretty white Elaurans with a black beard, and the charming nymph who made one of the three graces a dainty black she-monkey with a white beard.

At the Italiens, all the Italian actors had been grimacing monkeys such as marmosets, tamarins, harelip monkeys, lion tamarins, etc. Those of the Ariette had been more distinguished, and for the most part quite pretty. One of the most singular was Chenard, in *Gulnare*; he was mediocre but a clown, to the taste of those who like that sort of thing. I shall not say anything about several other charming male singers who had been she-apes among the souls, and perhaps half-played the role of women in the corporeal world; I fear to annoy them. Let us pass in to Drama.

Granger had been a villainous monkey, as ugly as ill-tempered, of the race of death's-heads. The stout Dugazon had been a she-ape of the guenon species of the Côte-d'ivoire in Guinea, so recalcitrant when she as an actress among the souls that the director soul had often been obliged to make her go on with whip-lashes.

I shall not talk about Audinot, Nicolet, etc., whose actors, actresses, and especially the dancers, had been long-tailed cercopitheci of the lowest species. And that's enough to give you an idea of the origin of the actors in terrestrial theaters, and you can render reason to the malevolence or libertinage of some of the individuals who distinguish themselves there.

As for authors, a singular observation has been made, which is that almost all men and women who write while corporeal were not authors in the state of free souls. I asked the reason for that. I was given the reply that having never written what they thought, they were replaced up there by those who had thought what the false authors had written. Thus Fréron, who has only ever set down the thoughts of others, having just died when I was there, carefully refrained, and was very eager to empty the pierced chairs of Descartes, Newton and Voltaire.

With regard to the small number of men of letters who had written what they thought, they were no longer authors but magistrates, generals princes or chiefs—for the word "prince" signifies the foremost chief, *Princeps*, a Latin syncope of *Primum-caput*. Now, it is necessary to know that as many estates exist in spirituality as can be counted in corporeality. The latter are not even a consequence of intellectual decision. So, when Revolutions occur among souls, they do not take long to make themselves felt among bodies—which is why it is said of great events that they were "written in the heavens." It is literally true.

Response to Letter LV

12 April.

Oh, what news of the other world, my friend! I shall not show your letter in this one; if it reached the acquaintance of our actors, especially our actresses, the authoress Molet, the Academician Molet[78] and the imperious Contat, even more irascible, there would be a fine fuss! If ever our letters, collected subsequently, see the light of day, your last will be a proof that it is not the work of an author, for what author would dare to unveil the origin of the souls of the delightful Contat and the incomparable Molet?

There are two kinds of people of the poor author dare not speak ill: actors and printers. The former will take revenge by making the play fail, the second will refuse to print a truth against his profession. But here I am, being serious!

My friends laughed a great deal on reading your letter. And the Comtesse, one of whose comedies the last-named had caused to fail, cried abundantly: "So that's why Contat is so malevolent!"

We have also remarked the moderation with which you talk about authors. That is, however, a rich field for gleaners, as the Burgundians say.

But one thing troubled us: that Revolutions occur in the Republic of Souls! Is there no tranquil state in the universe,

---

[78] I have retained Restif's spelling of the name of the actor François-René Molé (1734-1802) because he later makes an anagram of it. He was one of the dozen actors of the Théâtre-Français imprisoned in 1793 on suspicion of harboring monarchist sympathies. His wife from 1769 until her death in 1783, was the former Hélène Pinet, who took his surname; she was not an author (although he published his memoirs), nor was he a member of the Académie.

217

then? Oh, it's because Nature does not want stagnation any-where!

Letter LVI

F.m.T. 27 March.

There are, beautiful Hortense, wars among the souls. That is a sad truth, even though those wars do no more harm than the storms of our atmosphere. It appears that everything enters into the march of Nature, with the result that that order of things is for the best.

The most courageous soldiers among the discorporate are usually the most timid and most tender women when they are corporeal. Thus, the aforementioned Sappho Beauharnais is a Napoléon among the souls. (You know that here it is women who are the first sex; Nature considers them as more essential to multiplication than men. A single man could fecundate at least a hundred women a year; it requires two years for a woman to make and nurse a single child.) The wars of the higher realm are the source of those down here, with the difference that those of souls are fought is a superior manner; instead of cannons, rifles and bayonets, one launches arguments tending to fortify reasons for aggression, and the best reasons necessarily prevail. The vanquished nation becomes dependent on the victorious one, and is obliged to submit its opinions and fashions to it for a hundred years.

One singular thing is that the wars that will take place in Europe in a few years presently exist at the antipodes, from which they echo in our homeland. That discovery gave me the desire to know what was happening at the antipodes of discorporate France—which is to say, in the great austral country called New Holland. There was a Revolution there in the heights of the atmosphere. That prognosticates for us, in a very short time, a Revolution down here, in Europe, corresponding to the one up there, above the austral lands. I asked about its causes. I was told that it was Persian souls, driven from their lands by horror of the cruelties of Thamas-kouli-kan,[79] who, after their discorporation, had risen up against that tyrant and his satellites.

But it is necessary to let Yfflasie and Clarendon pass through different employments, and return to things that I have neglected.

As the two spouses still had leisure in their estate as goatherds, I begged them not to miss any opportunity to inform themselves of what the men and women you and I knew had been in their previous life. They satisfied that request and sought information. Here are the results that were given to me.

Marie-Antoinette, in her last corporeal life, had been a fashion model, very gallant and much sought-after, and before that a pretty gypsy, telling good and bad fortunes, More remotely still she was a public dancer, and before that Queen Brunehaut or Brunehilde.

Diane de Polignac had been a prostitute in the time of Cardinal Mazarin, who employed her to represent the Queen, the wife of Louis XIII, one night when he was caught in bed with her. The prostitute, who was ready and waiting, replaced the other whore so briskly that it was Diane who was seen leaving, still warm from the cardinal's bed. More remotely, she had been Emma, Charlemagne's daughter, who lay with her father, and with the handsome Eginhard, whom she carried on her back for fear that the gallant's masculine footprints might be noticed emerging from her room.[80]

---

[79] "Thamas-Kouli-kan" features in two significant French literary works, *Histoire de Thamas Kouli-Kan, roi de Perse* (1743) by André de Clauste and a 1780 tragedy based thereon, *Nadir, ou Thamas-Kouli-kan* (1780). The reference is to Nader Shah (1688?-1747), ruler of Persia from 1736 until his death

[80] It is perhaps not surprising that Restif, who obviously added this section during the 1796 revision, did not remember that he had previously attributed Brunehaut to the soul of Jeanne d'Arc, but it is surely odd that he did not remember having attributed Emma to that of his beloved Hortense and Eginhard to Fontlhète's—and quite incredible, of course, that Hortense

220

Princesse Carignan had been a pretty hurdy-gurdy play-er, and more remotely the beautiful Milanese who loved François I.

The Duchesse d'Orléans, a laundrywoman. Much more remotely Queen Bathilde, who had been, three or four centuries before, the elder daughter of Sejan.

The Duchesse de Bourbon had been, in her previous life, the poor actress at the Opéra that the brutal Lully had caused to give birth with a kick in the behind, and, very remotely, Queen Judith, the second and lubricious wife of Louis-le-Debonnaire or le-Nigaud, whom his bishops had had whipped for his wife's gallantries. C'a.q.L.xvi f.g.p.l.h.d.l.s.[81]

Lebrun the paintress[82] was Mademoiselle de Montpensier, the same one who secretly married the Comte de Lauslin, who was imprisoned.

The last Duchesse de Mazarin had been Marion Delorme, and very remotely a Roman prostitute named Lycisca.[83]

Contrôleur de Calonne had been the Robert le Dain or le Diable who promised to conserve daylight to the husband in return for a night with the wife, and who snatched that abused wife from the bed the next day in order to show her husband to

---

makes no comment on the new attribution of that previous incarnation. The bulk of the passage slanders Marie-Antoinette's former companions at Versailles and other members of the royal family.

[81] One would need a certain inspiration to deduce from this acrostic who Louis XVI is supposed to have been in his previous life, and why Restif did not feel free to spell it out.

[82] Louise Vigiée Lebrun (1755-1842) painted more than thirty portraits of her patron, Marie-Antoinette, but escaped the Terror by fleeing France. Her other portraits included one of Charles-Alexandre de Calonne, Louis XVI's contrôleur général des finances, also slandered in the present list.

[83] Scurrilous historical slander claimed that the Roman Empress Messalina secretly worked in a brothel under the pseudonym Lycisca.

her, hanged at the very moment that le Dain had soiled her with a forced adultery. She went mad, and tried to pluck out the monster's eyes. He had her killed.

Meaupeou had been Cartouche—not that I mean that abuse entirely as an insult; on the contrary, he had some reason to lower the legal aristocracy.[84]

De Vergènnes had been Bonneau under Charles VII, and a tawdry pimp and procurer in the times of Louis XIII.

The minister Choiseul, in his last life, had been Père Joseph, a capuchin; somewhat more remotely, Guise le Balâfré.

D'Artois was Cardinal Dubois.

Monsieur, the Harlequin Dominique...[85]

I shall continue tomorrow, my dear Hortense, to tell you all that those who are today have been, however little they are worth the trouble.

---

[84] René de Mauperou (1714-1792) was a legal reformer praised by Voltaire, one of the precursors of the Revolution and one of its supporters; it might seem surprising that Restif included him on this list, but his friend Mercier had a much lower opinion of Mauperou, who was one of the targets attacked in *L'An 2440*.

[85] "Monsieur" was the courtesy title given to Louis XVI's brother, also known as the Comte de Provence. Restif had no way of knowing that he would reign after the Restoration as Louis XVIII, or that he would be succeeded by his predecessor on this list, the Comte d'Artois who became Charles X.

Response to Letter LVI

13 April.

Always more and more interesting, dear husband. In truth, the keenest impatience makes itself felt until the moment that the post arrives, and it would be a true calamity if we missed a single day.

We are desolate that there are wars among the souls. But what you say, that it is women who excite them and fight them, provoked humorous abuse directed at the Comtesse by the Marquise.

"The gentlest down here are the most malevolent up there; so, I salute you, Madame General..." And since then, she no longer calls her anything but the Bonaparte of souls; Filète and I are her adjutants.

You then pass on to corporate souls, and instruct us as to those who live today with a degree of notoriety have been. That ought not to annoy them, but they would be annoyed if they saw it. We shall maintain a prudent silence about it. I thank you in on behalf of all four for your curious anecdotes.

Until tomorrow, desired man.

Letter LVII

F.m.T. 28 March.

One of the most agreeable amusements of souls is hunting. Discorporate monads practice that amusement against all the monads of ferocious and non-domestic animals, such as lions, tigers, leopards, gluttons, hyenas, crocodiles, serpents, wolves, etc.

In order for me to see a lion hunt, a monad who had passed through all the estates, and which Yfflasie, with her Clarendon, enabled me to recognize as that of Crébillon père, offered to take me to Africa.

The two lovers wanted to undertake the voyage because it was evening here and the goat-monads were at rest. We were there in an instant.

We found negro monads assembled around a lion monad, which was showing its teeth and claws. But as human souls have a degree of finesse superior to that of lion souls, the former had to triumph. What astonished us was to see a small soul or mulatto monad, which we were told was named Miléunefolies,[86] with whom the negroes were associated because she descended originally from their nation. That dwarf monad was seen stuck to that of the little Poinsinet, nicknamed

---

[86] "Miléunefolies" is the prolific writer and publisher Pierre Nougaret (1742-1823), whose collection of short stories *Les Mille et une folies* appeared in 1771. Restif loathed him, and the feeling was mutual. His most famous work was *Lucette, or le progrès du libertinage* (1763-1766); hence Hortense's subsequent reference. Nougaret also published *La Paysanne pervertie* (1777) not long after Restif's *Le Paysan perverti* (1775)—to which Restif subsequently added companion-piece with the same title as Nougaret's rip-off.

the Invisible,[87] but deputed by the troop of huntresses to irritate the lion. The two dwarfs, who did not see any monads smaller than them except for those of babies, advanced without hesitation, and fired their little darts and the superb animal monad. They only tickled the lion-monad, which, far from getting angry, appeared to take pleasure in it.

Miléunefolies, who thought it cowardly, advanced recklessly to within range of the incorporeal paw, which seized the dwarf monad and held her pinned to the ground, without doing her any other harm than compressing her somewhat, which caused the dwarf to render a capucinade, two ainsivalemondes, two lucètes, astucesdeparis and half a hundred anecdotesdesarts that had not been digested. The entire monad trembled; she cried out, meanwhile, with all her weakness: "Help! Help! Murder!"

Could one allow to perish thus the monad of a famous man who had written miléunefolies, not to mention those that had not been? Let us leave him in that situation until tomorrow.

---

[87] The prolific but short-lived dramatist Antoine Poinsinet (1735-1769) was renowned for his naivety, and was the butt of many cruel practical jokes, including, on one occasion, persuading him that he was invisible. Nougaret published a long letter to him regarding his play *Le Cercle*, in 1764.

14 April.

We presume that the soul hunt will be amusing—but there is an inhumanity in leaving poor Miléunefolies in his inconvenient situation for twenty-for hours! It must be the case, my friend, that you do not like him. For myself, having never read anything of his, I neither like nor hate him; I only know that of the twenty or so works published under his name he only wrote one, which is always his *Lucette*, published under three different titles. Thus the dwarf, when alive, was devoid of imagination and had no more genius than the apes and the negroes with whom he has linked himself after his discorporation. The other works were given to him by imbecile authors rendered such by arrogance and irrational presumption.

Madame de Beauchamois claims that he is not an author but a petty plagiarist, and that it is true that he had printed under his name a host of works whose true authors, overly modest, delivered to his effrontery, after having soiled them nevertheless with his stupefying drivel.

It is certain that he did not often understand what he was correcting. The worthy Marchand, the censor, having become an imbecile, took it into his head, in his weakness, to give him his latest works, which he no longer understood, to Miléunefolies for printing. The latter, who did not understand either the usage or the language of the society, understood even less of them, with the result that he suppressed as faults artistic impressions and those customary in society. Miléunefolies consistently replaced those technical expressions with platitudes.[88]

---

[88] Nougaret published several books as collaborations with Jean-Henri Marchand (died 1785), including the drama Le

But he did worse still; the good Marchand, beginning to talk nonsense, wanted to criticize the genre of drama, but he no longer employed the lightness that was the merit of his ingenious *Requête du curé de Fontenoy*, which was worthy of Voltaire. He indulged in wordplay and gave his drama as a title the blandly equivocal phrase *Le Vidangeur sensible, sensible* signifying "smells very bad." Miléunefolies took that title literally, not understanding the author's joke. In accordance with that naivety he strove to render the moral of his sensible cesspool-emptier physically sensible.

His comrade Poinsinet, mystified by Palissot, was so completely so that the little imbecile mulatto mystified himself on that occasion. He changed the entire play, to render his dirty cesspool-emptier genuinely sensitive, seriously tender. Imagine the gibberish when it happened that the stump of a man, either idly or unwittingly, left entire verses by Marchand! It was unintelligible seriocomic burlesque.

One could not believe such ineptitude if the play had not also enveloped the gibes of Lesage relative to Harcourt. Someone procured a copy for Carmontelle, who lent it to me. One read in the preface that old Marchand, in his dotage, delighted by changes that only gave his work a falsely reasonable appearance to render it more stupid, had embraced Miléunefolies delightedly. That is because, by virtue of a mechanical return to his old good taste, the old man in his second childhood had thought that the little stump of a man had sensed the pitiful application of the word "sensible" and had wanted to make even the idea of it disappear.

He gave him too much credit. But the old man was senile and Miléunefolies was then living in the Rue Béthisy.

I have never written a letter so silly.

Vidangeur sensible (1777), which Nougaret also issued under his name alone.

Letter LVIII

From my Tomb. 29 March.

Miléunefolies was making horrible grimaces under the paw of the lion-monad. The invisible Poinsinet, whom they caused to laugh, drew nearer in order to see them at closer range, and *paff!*—he was gripped by the lion-monad's other paw. He was even more pressured than his comrade, and one saw presumption disgorged, mingled with credulity, stupidity and a little wit.

While they were in that awkward situation, Durosoy appeared, who had just been discorporated,[89] at the time when he was madly in love with a black woman brought from Africa by a slave-trader captain who had sold her to him for twenty-five copies of the poem *Sens* in six parts, twenty-five of *Cécile* and the entire edition of *Clairval philosophe*. He had lost his lovely black woman because of the jealousy of his little stump of a wife, Mademoiselle Dumai, who had poisoned her, and immediately after his decapitation he had hastened to Africa in order to look for the soul of that dear black woman there, imagining that she would surely have returned there.

He saw the two little monads in their ridiculous or risible situation. He filled up his cheeks like balloons and advanced toward the lion-monad, which pretended not to see the puffed-up little monad

"How did you die?" he said to Miléunefolies.

"O Martyr to Royalism," replied Progrès du Libertinage—that was still his nickname—"save me! I died of a kick in the anus, by the publisher Maisonneuve, who was kicking

---

[89] Barnabé Durosoy died in 1792, a victim of the Terror, which implies that this section must have been added, or augmented in the 1796 revision. His poem *Le Sens*, was published in 1766, his novel *Clairval philosophe, ou La Force des passions* in 1765. The references to his "wife" are enigmatic.

me out of his house because I had had the insolence to *ettem al niam rus al egrog ed as etitep Emmef*.[90] It's because my killer was an Arab and my action a trifle arabesque."

During this exchange with Progrès du Libertinage, Durosoy had innocently come within reach of the claw of the lion-monad, which, as soon as she perceived it, tried to grab him. The poet of the six Senses was still so puffed up by the residue of his self-inflation, caused by the forty performances of his bad *Henri IV* that, the paw having struck him a glancing blow, he bounced like a balloon, rebounded almost as high as at the first shock, and continued to do so ten more times, which made all the negro monads laugh until the tears flowed.

While they were laughing, another man, no less celebrated and no less advantageous than Durosoy advanced, armed with a wooden sword, with which he had been knighted by a certain epigrammatist named Masson de Morvilliers.[91] He was the disfigurer of the charming Ovid's *Metamorphoses*, who pursued the young La Reynière with the whip of ridicule. Never had anyone fled so insolently. Métamorphosimane held his head high and projected his confident gaze in all directions. His monad finally came within reach of the lion-monad, which trapped him under the same paw as Progrès de Libertinage, or Miléunesfolies. The advantageous monad, com-

---

[90] I have left this phrase, the words of which are inverted, in French rather than translating them into reversed English; the crime to which it refers is putting a hand on the wife's breast. In *La Découverte australe* it is the superior Megapatagons who speak reversed French, although Restif rendered his own name in the same fashion when signing off its frame narrative.

[91] The poet and geographer Nicolas Masson de Morvilliers (1740-1789) published an epigram about Ange-François Fariau de Saint-Ange (1747-1810), who published his version of Ovid's *Metamorphoses* in 1783-85. The anecdote about Masson sending him a wooden sword is recorded in the published correspondence of Denis Diderot and his fellow Encyclopedist Baron von Grimm.

pressed, vomited, it's said, such stinking vanity that it infected the lion-monad to the point that she sneezed three times.

Let us leave the Sologne simpleton with the others until tomorrow.

Response to Letter LVIII

15 April.

Oh, you're attacking authors, Monsieur de Fontlhète! I'll allow you Miléunefolies-Progrès-du-Libertinage-Vidangeur-sensible, who is not greatly to be feared, invisible even before he was found dead drunk in the gutter while going to Cadiz with a troupe of comedians; I'll let pass Durosoy, dead a long time before he had ceased to live and write. But daring to address the Sologne simpleton, first volume of Brunet-Montansier,[92] the profligate sousbreteuilliste of poor one-armed La Reynière is risking too much. And perhaps we shall see others too.

Be careful, and don't give yourself to the Devil to be tormented. Has not Miléunefolies set an example with his stupid lust for revenge? He held it against the Nocturnal Spectator that he had sometimes painted nudes. What do you think he did? He imagined that one of his own actions was the surest means of dishonoring the Owl, by attributing it to him. He had ceded his wife to one Patrocin, who had fallen in love with her when she was a girl. The latter dressed her, but having found her spoiled, passed her on, fully adorned, to a surveyor who sampled her; she was sound currency, but decried, and no one wanted to keep her. Miléune imagined that her vile story was more appropriate than any other to dishonor the Spectator, and attributed it to him in one of his rhapsodies.

The Spectator was astonished by that maladroit impudence, but he was not irritated by it. He contented himself with rendering, in one of the following volumes of the Spectator, the anecdote to its true owner. What did Miléune do, at that merited restitution? He ran to Vidaut-de-la-Tour, then magis-

---

[92] Marguerite Brunet (1730-1820), whose stage name was Mademoiselle Montansier, became a theater director in 1777, but her connection with Saint-Ange remains obscure.

trate of the Librairie and made a complaint against the restitution made by the Spectator. The Magistrate wrote to the latter, who, to justify himself, had only to bring forth the rhapsody and his own work. He showed the passage in the rhapsody, which he indicated, and then his response, commanded by honor, in a volume of the Nocturnal Spectator; he offered a memoir in support of the facts; he named all the actors in the session and cited witnesses. The magistrate, convinced even without the memoir, responded: "Let the plaintiff return and I'll give him a severe reprimand."

Thus, you see that, if Miléune was able to hazard that impudent act of revenge, the Sologne simpleton, even more brazen, might dare even more, and with more skill. Do you not know the modest disinterest with which he provoked the exile of poor La Reynière, for a memoir that he thought abusive? The exile is still at Blamont, or Domévre-l'Abbaye, where he is suffering from ennui, as God knows! See the letters that he wrote to the Spectator, which are all printed at the end of the fourth volume of the *Contemporaines* and the fifth of the *Drame de la vie*. Be wise and prudent in future, therefore, if you can, Monsieur de Fontlhète.

Letter LIX

30 March, F.m.T.

Metamorphosigraphe was making a sad grimace, when we saw arriving, from four different directions, Fardeau, the Chevalier Du Coudray, the Chevalier de Moüy and Eurydicographe.[93]

"My friend, my good friends," bellowed Fardeau, "the friends of our friends are in trouble under the claws of this monster! Four men of a merit equal to mine!" That was because Durosoy, after having bounced a few times because of his inflation had come to rest quite naturally beside the late Poinsinet.

At these words, articulated stentorially, Du Coudray recoiled, Moüy stumbled and Euridicographe tried to sing a few verses of *Orphée* to charm the lion-monad, which roared at him: "Sing without words!"

Meanwhile, Fardeau tried to reanimate their courage. He pushed them before him by the impulsion of his heavy incorporeal mass. Eurydicographe was swallowed without being chewed, like an oyster. Du Coudray, tougher, was masticated. Fardeau was at least ten mouthfuls, as we would put it. But Moüy, merely choked, was undevourable. Thus perished four of the heroic monads, who, stifled or devoured by the lion-monad, in a strange atmosphere, all found themselves obliged to resume bodies and to animate, alas, four embryonic bochis,

---

[93] Louis-Gabriel Fardeau (1731-1806), author of *Le Mariage à la monde* (1774); Alexandre-Jacques Du Coudray (1744-1790), author of *Le Malheureux imaginaire* (1776); Charles de Fieux de Mouhy (1701-1784), author of *Lamekis* (1735-38 available from Black Coat Press) and many other novels; the "Eurydicographe" is presumably the dramatist Pierre-Louis Moline (1739-1820), who provided the libretto for Gluck's version of *Orphée et Eurydice* (1774).

Hottentots of a sort, who only have, like apes, the ability to express in speech a dozen simple ideas in a language that does not have many more words.

As for the four retained under the two paws, they were librated by the negroes. The lion-monad, no longer being hungry, ceded the place willingly, and went to digest them in her lair. But they did not get far. A hyena screeched like a little girl, Miléunefolies came running and was caught, torn apart and swallowed; a Senegal cayman ate Poinsinet; a panther shared Durosoy with its cubs; and Metamorphisograph, having molested a pongo with his wooden sword, was slain by a blow from the great ape's stick. "Oh," he cried, sensing himself forcibly reincorporated, "that's no way for a poet to die!"

All four, therefore, obtained bodies in the vicinity; Durosoy animated the fetus of a negress, and will one day be an Abelere, or negro prostitute, avowed by a devout dying Queen to the libertinage of men. Metamorphosigraphe was a pretty Jaggasse, destined to satisfy, after a battle, all the soldiers who had distinguished themselves, even if there were a thousand of them and she were obliged to perish after the hundredth, Miléunefolies was lodged in the fetus procreated by the monstrous union of a negress with a pongo—the same one that had slain Metamorphosigraphe; the hybrid she-ape that she will be will go, one day, by inclination, to amalgamate with the race of apes, whose amour she will prefer to that of men. When one talks to her about her degradation she will reply that she is not sorry, given that she has the hope, once discorporate, of being an actress. It's necessary not to dispute tastes; Miléunefolies has always loved the theater, and we are assured that not only has he acted in Lyon but that he has written a play, represented as the work of the director's ape, in the quality of which ape, in view of his smallness, his ugliness and his swarthy complexion, he was introduced to the audience by the actor Nainville.[94] The resemblance caused the Lyonnais to

---

[94] Nainville, whose real name was Philippe Cauvy, was a clown at the Opéra Comique.

think he was an orangutan of considerable merit and intelligence.

Response to Letter LIX

16 April.

So you don't want to correct yourself, dear husband? But if Metamorphisigrahe has you exiled, you can only blame it on your own obstinacy, as Molière was sometimes advised by his maidservant. And doubtless he listened. I hope that you will listen to your wife, when you have heard her. Moreover, Fardeau, Du Coundray and de Moüy, whom we have glimpsed in the world, have amused us far more as monads that in corporeality.

You give all eight a very sad destiny in putting the first four in the embryos of Boshis. Is that not the poor species of humans of the albino genre who, it is said, have for a leg a hairy bone, as dry as a round stick, sheathed in a plank like those used to drive through mud during the thaw, for which reason the Dutchmen of the Cape call them plank-footed men? They thought, when they established themselves in the colony, that they were one of the numerous varieties of ape, but, having soon perceived that the brutes had a language composed of the infinitives of twelve or fifteen verbs, expressing as many actions or ideas, they were obliged to classify them as human. It appears that the species in question, which is a primitive one not ameliorated by mixture, and which only subsisted in one region into which our more perfect race had not yet penetrated, occupies the middle ground between ape and human. It manifests, above all, the gradation between the albinos of Africa, which Buffon described poorly, those of America, of which he does not appear to have heard mention, and the Pesserays of Cook, a kind of animal that seems only to have one cry incessantly repeated, which lives in a rude country where our unquiet, restless species has no wish to settle. The Lapps must have for human ancestors a race less imperfect than the Bôchis (as it is necessary to pronounce it in French, for the word Boshis is English in its orthography).[95]

All four of us have composed this dissertation, aided by Comte Arconati,[96] the Italian voyager, who has come to see the Comtesse in passing on his way back to Lapland, passing through the Great Indies. We have also seen Monsieur Arthaud de Bellevue,[97] who is not that Arthaud gazette-in-hand; ours is a well of science, who talks a great deal but talks well. We have made him party to our ideas. Oh, he finds them admirable! He is passionate about you, and your letters about the other world have taken possession of all the affection he had conceived for another work entitled *L'Enclos et les oiseaux*, which is as original as yours...

That, my love, is a long letter, and more of a letter than a response!

---

[95] This correction of pronunciation make it clear that the reference is to the "bushmen" of the Kalahari.

[96] There were a lot of Comtes surnamed Arconati, but this one is probably Paul (1754-1821).

[97] Arthaud de Bellevue is also a common combination of names, associated with a prolific family from Lyon; this one might be Henry Arthaud de Bellevue de la Ferrière (1732-1826).

Letter LX

31 March, F.m.T.

In truth, my dear wife, I don't know what has come over me in my recent letters, talking to you about the hideous metamorphoses of men without merit, true nullities. But since I've commenced, it's necessary to finish, for I'm not sorry to have rid society of them. I have, nevertheless, more justice to do today. You are fond enough of literature to know those vultures who go by the name of journalists. It is necessary to tell them what their fate is required to be in discorporate life.

All souls are equal on the atmospheric cap, the abode of the discorporate, men, women or beasts, including those of murderers, lions, tigers, wolves, revolutionary judges, parliamentarians, etc., who only kill the body without causing the soul to languish—but there is a terrible punishment up there for the infamous individuals who try to kill genus, who denigrate it, sadden it or consciously sully it.

Fréron,[98] at the moment of his death, instead of enjoying, like Yfflasie and Clarendon, the mild infancy of souls, was condemned to a métier whose denomination is so vile and so base that I do not think it worthy of being read by Hortense's beautiful eyes. If souls eat—and that is proven for us—they do the opposite of eating. Now, nothing is beneath their excrement, since it is vice, lies, calumny, persiflage, perfidious slander and every species of malice, which they discharge. Well, Fréron is responsible for cleaning all that up and carrying it to the river of truth, in which he is obliged to purify all the pieced chairs of the souls of Paris.

---

[98] The journalist Élie Fréron (1718-1776), notorious for his attacks on Voltaire

Labaumelle[99] is painfully devoted to cleaning up the dysenteries of bad humors that an overly bitter bile occasions Voltaire. Neither Labaumelle or Fréron has any expurgatory pot except for their mouths; the humors of souls can only be contained by an incorporeal substance. I leave it to the imagination how Fréron cleans atmospheric Paris and Labaumelle the pierced chair of the bilious Voltaire.

Clement is to succeed Labaumelle; the pedantic Aubert and Dussieux will one day replace Fréron. They will have for valets Sautreau and Peletier, and for valets' valets Thiriot, Abbé Lacroix, Geoffroy, the ex-Jesuit Royoux, Freon's brother-in-law, and other monads of that stripe.[100] As for Querlon,[101] one of the philosopher-monads assures us that she will serve as Montesquieu's donkey, and will graze every day with the jenny-ass that Mercier, according to Tebog,[102] had the naivety to admit as his astronomy mistress. Querlon is an ass, as we know by virtue of an epigram of Fardeau's, for having attacked, with stupid hypocrisy, *L'Esprit des loix*.

Querlon had for an acolyte an imbecile named Nau, whose principal work was setting La Fontaine's fables to music.[103] He had a commission to spur Montesquieu's ass to

---

[99] I have left this name as Restif renders it, although the reference is to Laurent de La Beaumelle (1726-1773), another diehard enemy of Voltaire.

[100] This list of anti-Voltaireans not yet dead includes the royal censor Jean-Louis Aubert (1731-1814) and Louis Dussieux (1744-1805); Claude-Sixte Sautreau de Marsy (1740-1815) and the politician Louis-Michel Le Peletier (1760-1793). The last-named might, however, have felt somewhat aggrieved to be appended to such company.

[101] The critic and editor Anne-Gabriel Meusnier de Querlon (1702-1780)

[102] Presumably the publisher P. P. A. Gobet, although why his name is rendered backwards is a mystery.

[103] François Nau (1715-?)

make her go forward when she would not go of her own accord.

Imbert and La Dixmerie were charged with bottling the spirituous vinegar of the four thieves of Maille, which they gave as soup to Rumfort.[104]

---

[104] Barthelemy Imbert (1747-1790) and Nicolas Bricaire de La Dixemerie (1731-1791) are evidently condemned to feed the physicist Benjamin Thompson, Count Rumford (1753-1814), whose books, including one on nutrition were published in French translation with the signature Comte Rumfort; the "thieves of Maille" might be the anti-Voltaireans who are alleged to be stealing from the theologian Josept-Auguste Maille, but that is uncertain.

Response to Letter LX

17 April.

The malevolence is taking hold. It is giving me a desire to speak ill too, in accordance with the anecdotes that my friends tell me about your characters. Fréron only criticized Voltaire having had gifts of a thousand écus from Archbishop Beaumont. After one virulent article (that was his indecent expression) against Voltaire or Marmontel, he went to dine with the Archbishop; he cornered the fellow, explained his needs and the generous refusal to allow himself to be paid by the philosophers—who had only offered him a beating. Then he asked for a "gift."

"It's to pay off a few very urgent debts."

"Go on, a thousand écus," said the calm Beaumont.

"Monseigneur," Fréron begged, "the Libraire Edmé Rapetot has credit notes for four thousand francs!"

"Well, four thousand francs, then," the prelate consented.

And the Secretary, cursing the crook, wrote four thousand livres.

As for Querlon, he was so idle that he wasted all his time reading books that only contained false ideas and old prejudices. His wife was obliged to beat him to make him work; while shaking him she shouted: "To your study, you lazy dog!" Without that insulting harangue, the bookseller Querlon left all the work to his provincial publicists and paid hangers-on, with the result that there was almost nothing left for him.

La Dixmerie went to see a printer in Paris whose wife neglected the water. It was to him and her that an exchange is attributed: "I'm damning myself in yielding to you, Monsieur!" she said, to which La Dixmerie, fleeing, replied: "And I'm saving myself." Others claim that he replied to the remark: "I'm damned!" with "I believe so, Madame; you're not built. As for me, I've saving myself." But a scurrilous allegation against him is that there was a girl of fifteen or sixteen in the

241

house afterwards, whom he found alone; without trying to seduce her he wanted to profit from her innocence to possess her. The young woman became pregnant and owed her salvation to nature. On returning to her father, she complained to him; the imbecile V*** the elder immediately went to speak to La Dixmerie, who sniggered and replied: "A fine thing to make so much noise about!"

It's said that one of those you named had married a kept woman and made use of her to make his fortune...

My Filète is scolding me for speaking ill like this.

Letter LXI

You know, my dear wife, I'm ashamed of my recent letters. In this one I shall treat a slightly more elevated matter. Yfflasie and Clarendon have permitted themselves to follow the Maid in her new incorporation.

She was born to the young wife of a protestant minster while the two lovers had passed successively from the care of goat-desires to that of donkey-desires and then to that of horse-desires, which is the *nec plus ultra* in our degree of latitude. They had been dispensed from caring for swine-desires; that employment had been given to La Dixmerie and his aquifugal lover La V***-Gissel.

In their new employment as grooms, Yfflasie and Clarendon had a good deal of free time. They employed their leisure instructing me, without neglecting the observation of newly reincorporated monads in whom they were interested. Jeanne d'Arc, especially, attracted their attention. She died soon after being born, because the young mother had injured herself by too much ardor in seeking the pleasures of marriage. Disengaged, Jeanne—who had borne the name Emilie during the three days of her incorporate rebirth—could only remain a pure soul, in accordance with the usual rule, for a time proportionate to that in which she had animated a body. That is a rigorous rule for all children born before having the use of reason.

Yfflasie and Clarendon saw her among the souls again with pleasure. They took pleasure, during that brief interval, in reminding the great soul of her ancient valor, which she had completely forgotten because of her brief incorporation; she no longer had any idea of the glory with which she had once been covered. The moment soon arrived, however, when Emilie had to resume a body. This time, fortune favored her; she animated the fetus of Madame, the only daughter of Louis XVI,[105] then monarch, since...

Yfflasie and Clarendon were delighted by that good luck, for they hoped that the princess, having a beautiful, strong and generous soul would one day do honor to the human species.

They also followed the second career of Louis XIV-Pierrot, which was happy enough. He retained the name of Louis, by a kind of instinct, and became a porter in the Rue Saint-Jacques, at the door of Saint Yves, at the corner of the Rue des Noyers. He was thickest, strong, and a handsome fellow. There was a beautiful girl in the neighborhood, a laundress and mender of fine linen and silk stockings, which was quite well-paid. She as very well-made, so attractive and neat that a mercer asked for her hand in marriage—but she had seen Louis the porter and her tender heart sighed after the homage of that handsome fellow.

---

[105] Marie-Thérèse (1778-1851), the only member of the royal family to survive the Terror. She married the Duc d'Angoulême, the son of the future Charles X

Response to Letter LXI

18 April.

Madame will doubtless have a beautiful soul if she has that of Jeanne d'Arc, which combines the most adorable naivety of a young woman with masculine strength and courage, and purity of heart.

The fate of Louis XIV, Louis-Pierrot, interested us all the more because the three of us have seen him with Saint Yves, as well as his mistress. It's you who pointed them out to the Comtesse and me. Madame de Beauchamois remembers that one day Louis has saved his coachman from an accident that had tipped him from his seat. As for Filète, she has seen him several times in the home of her sister the picture-maker, where he was employed, and it was with the greatest surprise he she saw him with a pretty and well-educated mistress. These are verses that the Comtesse has made, on which I said to her one day, which was your birthday. She gave them to me today:

Verses to Monsieur de Fontlhète, for his Birthday

I have let your birthday go by
And I am truly sorry for that
Such forgetfulness is not honest
But is pointless to be afflicted.
Between us, it would not be wise
To deliver myself to dolor
One can disregard convention
When one is guided by one's heart.

If I am coming after a week
To offer you my compliments.
It's a little late, but I'm certain
Of having fêted you in sentiment.

Custom is sad and I'm braving it
My error might well seem real,
But I shall celebrate your octave.
As one does for the Immortals.[106]

---

[106] This poem was written by Fanny de Beauharnais, addressed to Restif. It is reprinted in her collected poems.

Letter LXII

The mercer was surprised that a delicate and pretty working girl should refuse a man with a shop and well-established. The beauty often passed Saint Yves' door. Louis saluted her and Rose Neris smiled at him. Finally, they talked to one another. Louis earned six francs a day in tips, and sometimes twelve. He made love to her by talking about his income and telling her how briskly he carried heavy parcels. It was thus that he had once recounted his victories to La Valière, Fontanges, the proud Montespan and the decent d'Aubigné. Rose listened with as much admiration to the vigorous deeds of Louis the porter as the beauties of the seventeenth century did to the victories of Louis the monarch. Finally, it was agreed between them that Louis-Pierrot would put his earnings in Rose's hands until he had fifteen hundred francs, at which time they would marry.

The mercer, who saw the familiarity established between his desired future and a porter did not know what to think. He imagined that they were related, perhaps brother and sister. He asked for an explanation, Rose simply told him the truth, as glorious in her lot as if she had known that her lover had been the powerful despot who had made all his neighbors—which is to say, all Europe—tremble.

You see, my beautiful Hortense, that there are people destined to be happy, in no matter what estate they end up. Louis XIV was happy as such, and now he is happy again in the estate of a porter. He is always born coiffed, whereas others, with all the advantages of fortune and nature, drown in a rut.

19 April.

Yes, Louis XIV is as happy today as when he was king. He does not have certain great pleasures, but nor does he have great pains. That reminds me of the story of a Duc, widowed at twenty-five of a beautiful lady whom he had adored, and subsequently found nothing but amiable. He believed that it was the fault of individuals of his condition.

One day, when taking a stroll on the Île Saint-Louis, now de la Fraternité, he perceived a ravishing young woman dressed with exquisite taste. He sought information. She was the sister of the wife of a wine-dealer in the western part of the island, facing the Rue Guillaume. He went back several times, saw her again and fell madly in love. He said that he was a young commoner, the son of his steward, named Raymond, and asked for the hand of Mademoiselle Ysabelle Descourtives in marriage. It was granted to him as soon as he had declared that he was a Jansenist. He married her, with the consent of his steward, who was presumed to be giving to his pretended son a farm in Beauce with an income of six thousand francs.

The Duc found in young Ysabelle a complete beauty, with not the slightest fault; a charming character devoid of coquetry; a tender, unalterable attachment that had all the gaiety and ease of detachment. Oh, that was happiness, he was there! *If my spouse had been born in the estate of my first wife*, he thought, *we would be above fate*. He was in that delightful situation for three years.

One day, in spite of his precautions, he was seen walking around the island by a relative of his first wife. Spies watched him. Everything was discovered. Great noise occasioned in the family by the false marriage, but the fear of scandal prevented publicity. The Duc's life was poisoned, and a murder doubt-

248

less terminated that of his Ysabelle. He was in despair, and that crime was his torment for the rest of his days.

Letter LXIII

F.m.T. 3 April.

How astonished the mercer must have been at Rose's response! His remonstrated with the lovely girl, but she remained invariable in her inclination for Louis-Pierrot.

In eighteen months the fifteen hundred francs had been amassed, and even more, for the handsome porter—as the women of the Librairie called him—had another fifteen hundred francs saved in secret, as well as a thousand écus previously saved. He represented himself in ease, with a nice apartment that he cleaned himself, nice furniture well waxed, two twenty-écu mirrors, a copper fireplace, etc. Rose and he were equally happy; there never was a better husband than Louis-Pierrot.

After two years of marriage I encountered him, already the father of two children. He was going along the Rue des Noyers, holding the arm of his genteel companion, who was carrying in her own the latest pledge of their amour. I was really touched by their good union. Oh, how I congratulated myself on the acquaintance of Yfflasie and Clarendon, which enabled me to live with all these heroes and heroines of past centuries; for Rose had been Anne of Austria, the daughter of Philip III, King of Spain, who finally had her husband entirely to herself. Fate is sometimes just.

But let us leave Louis-Pierrot to enjoy a happiness that he was unable to find on the throne and cast a glance over Monseigneur his son, older than him in this new life because he had died sooner and thus had been reborn sooner, several years before. The Grand Dauphin is presently a master cooper in the Rue de Plâtre. He has married a rather pretty wife. But the ex-dauphin is such a vulgar peasant, harnessed to the cart on a daily basis, that he had long been scorned. She regarded him as a bumpkin, especially when she saw him, clad in a leather apron, lowering barrels of wine into cellars with the aid of a cable.

I took it into my head the other day to go up to that woman, who is still a coquette, and to whisper in her ear: "Madame Brion, did you know that your husband emerges from illustrious blood, at least in a manner of speaking?"

She looked at me, smiled, blushed, and told me that she was not seduced by the joke. I told her what I knew about the subject.

"Always agreeable follies, Monsieur de Fontlhète! How cheerful you are since your marriage! May you always be!"

That rendered me serious, but I added: "Would you like to know who you were?"

"Oh no—you'll tell me something droll."

"Why something droll?"

"Go on, I'm listening."

"Well, you were...Ysabelle de Bavière, wife of the Grand Dauphin, now your husband for the second time. He chose you again in this life, and you have rendered him his disdain in full. Isn't that droll?"

"No. I wish to God that it were so and I'd known it sooner...how happy I would have been!"

I believe that there is nothing in the world as powerful, in the soul of certain bourgeois beauties, as vanity.

Response to Letter LXIII

20 April.

Never has any of your letters, dear husband, given me so much pleasure as that one, because of a word found therein. The word emerged from the mouth of the cooper's wife. I know that Dame Brion; she has very ugly daughters, a son who is a handsome enough lad and a young female neighbor named Dasses, who is good. She has for a friend an execrable woman that I call Monstrine, and whose merits that horrible name. But Ysabelle de Bavière had finally quarreled with that lady, who had been the famous witch Medea. You know, good husband who I mean, you who know the *Nuits de Paris* so well.

My three friends appeared as astonished as me. "Always agreeable follies, Monsieur de Fontlhète!" Ysabelle said to you. I can't see the reason for that astonishment.

The conduct of the porter Louis XIV with Rose—or, rather, with Anne of Austria, his antecedent spouse—also tends to prove that souls conserve many of the inclinations they had in a preceding, or more distant, life. Your science is really a consolation for those who have it. They see order continually reestablished.

One thing that I would still like to know, and soon would if I had commerce with so, is who became the heroes, of both sexes, of all our romances. For I am convinced that all of them are the history either of the author or of objects of his amour and his amity, or those of people for whom he believes he ought to have compassion. It would be curious to know the names of all those individuals. One could say: "There is one who gave me pleasure, or one who caused me so much horror! Nothing would contribute as much to the knowledge of the human heart.

A word now about our business affairs...

F.m.T. 4 April.

Agree, my beautiful Hortense, that it is a very agreeable thing to be able to divine what people were in a previous life. I am repeating that exclamation because the idea always seems to me to be new. Before coming back to our friends, about whom I shall talk to you one day, and whose antecedent fates I ought to tell you, I shall put in a word here about a few individuals of the other century who reappear in this one.

You will perhaps be surprised if I talk to you about the Marquise de Brinvilliers.[107] (He could not know that Hortense had talked about that; they had come up with the same idea.)

She is one of those who excited my curiosity most, along with Madame Tiquet.[108] I therefore asked Yfflasie and Claren-

---

[107] Marie d'Aubray, Marquise de Brinvilliers (1630-1676) was convicted of three murders—those of her father and two brothers—on the strength of a confession extracted by torture, and essentially worthless. The case became famous because it launched "the affair of the poisons" which eventually led to many more charges of murder, witchcraft and poisoning, as the eager torturers extracted more confessions, each more unlikely than the last, from numerous individuals. The affair formed the basis of several literary works in the 19th and 20th centuries.

[108] Angélique Tiquet was beheaded in the Pace de Grève in 1699, accused of soliciting a servant to attempt to murder her husband—whose subsequent frantic attempts to get his hands on her fortune might awaken suspicion in skeptical minds regarding the value of the evidence he gave against her. One of her closest friends was Madame d'Aulnoy, the famous writer of *contes de fées*, who became the first of many writers to produce an account of the case and assist it to become legendary. If she was reincorporated as Cazotte in 1719 the hundred-year

don to discover those ladies for me. They have had some difficulty succeeding, because during their discorporate life, they hid, and did not frequent other souls much. However, they finally found out from the soul of an executioner of the time, who had not been reincorporated, what they had become.

Oh, what was my surprise—and here one ought to admire with a pronounced astonishment the march of Nature! Insensible to what humans call shame, glory, crime or virtue as soon as life has elapsed, Nature reestablishes equality. She punishes crime, it is true, but always during the life in which it is committed. There is another being than the culpable one, as soon as it has been subject to dissolution. But an experienced soul made the observation to us that the souls of executed criminals always pass into a fetus of the opposite sex to the one they had. Thus, Madame Tiquet had passed into an embryo that is now a virtuous man, a sensible philosopher, although a trifle singular, and finally, a writer who has celebrity. Shall I name him? Why not? It's Monsieur Cazotte, whose productions announce so much originality.

As for the Marquise de Brinvilliers, she has done even more—even worse or even better, as you please. She had also animated a male fetus, born in Picardy, who subsequently went to Rome, where it was said that he had lice, and worked miracles. She died again, her life was written and she is almost canonized. My beautiful wife, my incomparable Hortense, prostrate yourself and adore that pretended Providence, which hypocrites attest and the stupid take literally, on which prudent people never rely, and which philosophers mock: the Marquise de Brinvilliers has been Saint Labre![109] Oh, what depths there are within us!

---

rule of discorporation must have been set aside for her, as for the Marquise de Brinvilliers.

[109] Saint Benedict Joseph Labre (1748-1783) was an obscure Franciscan mendicant made posthumously famous by his confessor, who wrote a highly fanciful account of his life and the miracles supposedly worked by his intercession after his

I am not contradicting here, what I have advanced in other letters, that one always senses what one has been. On the contrary, Madame Tiquet-Cazotte detested marriage, and Brinvilliers-Saint Labre preferred to give to his brethren the poor the aliments that he had allowed to spoil in his beggar's wallet. One holds to what one was.

---

death. Restif's assumption that he would be canonized was eventually justified in 1881.

Response to Letter LXIV

20 April.[110]

Ah, you have done well, my love, to verify for yourself the accusation of contradiction. My friends were already opening their mouths. Your anecdote about Cazotte and Saint Labre closed them.

"How prompt you are to criticize," Filète said to them, laughing. "So you don't like him."

"Oh, yes, yes," the Marquise replied, "but amity doesn't preclude criticism..."

"Doesn't preclude! Faint friends! Amity divinizes faults and turns them into qualities. The mocker becomes a joker, the malevolent individual full of penetration and exquisitely refined in his taste, the dull and the idle have a likeable nonchalance, or even a delightful insouciance. The brutal man has a vivacity that animates all those around him, the reckless man is brave and full of courage, the imprudent man is bold, and only the bold succeed—and one cites three long Latin words. The deceptive man is prudent and reserved, the cheat adroit, the liar inventive, full of imagination. The calumniator is a lion that it was fatal to have irritated, one who speaks ill a truthful man who cannot flatter. The drunkard is an Anacreon, and drunkenness in him is a state of naïve gaiety. The glutton is, at table, an appetizing guest who communicates the desire to eat. The lecher is a gallant man who adores women. The languid lover is not a bore but a tender and sensitive soul. The fickle lover is a light butterfly fluttering from flower to flower, who would reproach himself or neglecting one. The gambler is made for society; he is an essential man who is received everywhere. The crook is adroit at play, like a Russian, and one

---

[110] This is the second response dated 20 April, but as the numeration continues uncorrected from the mistake I have let it stand.

takes care to smile at him agreeably in saying so, etc. That, Mesdames, is how amity speaks."

We were very surprised by the ardor that Filète put into defending you.

"How, my beauty," the Comtesse said to her, "would it be necessary to interpret a real contradiction on Monsieur de Fontlhète's part?"

"He has a likeable variety, which he sometimes takes as far as inconsequentiality. It's necessary to have a good memory with him, without which one will be surprised into denying what he really said."

"Very good, very good!" the ladies cried. "Our friend's resemblance is worthy of her in every way, intelligence and beauty, especially excellence of heart."

That, my dear husband, is what has just been said about your letter. I try, by means of these accounts, to render us present to your eyes.

Letter LXV

From my tomb. 5 April.

You said to me one day, my dear Hortense, shortly before my departure, while conversing about the same matter
that is the subject of the letters you write on a daily basis:
"Wouldn't you like to know what Mercier was in his previous
corporeal life?"

I obtained that information last night.

Would you have suspected it? I'll give you fifty guesses.

Nothing in his character today announces to me that he
was what I have just been told, except for a certain penchant
for politicking. But I would never have perceived that he had
been a warrior, much less that he was inclined to cruelty.
Well, be astonished. He was, not Colbert, not the sage
Montausier, not Letellier, and not Chamillard. He was
Mazarin![111]

That might appear to you to be a blasphemy; nevertheless, nothing is more natural. In his corporeal estate, he had
been very afflicted by the evil he had done during his ministe-
rial life. So, when the moment to be reincorporated came, he
prayed to the Supreme Being, imploring him, with tears in his
eyes, to give him an existence that might repair the evil that he
had sometimes occasioned by his acts of government during
his last corporeal life. And the Supreme Being, touched, intimate his orders to the Sun and the Earth, the immediate and
direct producers of human beings, as of all other animals, that
they should do with him what was appropriate.

They therefore placed him in the brain of a energetic
writer with a fecund imagination, not mad like that of

---

[111] If Mercier (born 1740) had been Cardinal Mazarin (1602-
1661) the hundred-year-discorporation rule has definitely been
forgotten.

Lesuire;[112] nor always obsessed with women, like that of La Bretonne; nor atrocious like that of the author of *Aline et Valcour*;[113] nor empty of true philosophy like those who have presided over the translations of Delille and Fariot and never understood or wanted to render that of their authors, as witness the description of spring in the *Georgics* and the history of the Cerastes and the winged women of Thessaly in the *Metamorphoses*;[114] nor like that of Lalande,[115] always numbed or only dreaming of figures and numbers; nor like that of Simon Laplace,[116] who sees nothing but stars and the eternal heavens, although Nature, Reason and experience announce that everything finishes, etc. The plastic forms of Mercier were to render him a philanthropic, enlightened writer desirous of being useful, indefatigable in his literary activity, imperturbable in the choice of means, serving humanity in the theater, in the study, in society.

It is thus that the author Mercier, until the present day, April 1788, has repaired the evil that his soul did when it animated the body of Cardinal Mazarin, father of kings.

There is a certain man who has not made a great noise, of whom nothing has yet been seen in the theater, who has nevertheless written several plays that remain unknown, and several works calumniated by purists and petty authors. He has scarcely shown himself. His name, I believe, is Salokin, and he is said to be a former soldier. Mention had been made of him to me without me seeking further information It was Yfflasie who asked me whether I knew him and what was

---

[112] Robert-Martin Lesuire (1737-1815).

[113] The Marquis de Sade; the utopian *Aline et Valcour* (1795) was the first book that appeared under his real name.

[114] Jacques Delille (1738-1813) published his translation of Virgil's *Georgics* in 1769. "Fariot" is presumably Fariau Saint-Ange.

[115] The astronomer Jérôme Lalande (1732-1807).

[116] The astronomer and mathematician Pierre-Simon Laplace (1749-1827).

known about him. Clarendon did not think of it, Salokin only occupying himself in his works with the happiness of women. That was Clarendon's observation on the rather sharp reproach that Yfflasie made him regarding his ignorance—for wives are husbands among the discorporate; it is them, as I have already told you, who have science, strength of mind and authority.

I had difficulty replying to Yfflasie's question. Salokin was then plunged in profound darkness. He is one of those people that one cannot disinter, who love to hide, to live obscurely, unknown, or only to appear in public with the aid of a production, which, by virtue of its utility, draws them out of obscurity. I shall talk to you about him tomorrow, even though the man cannot be of any interest to you, given his ignobility.

Response to Letter LXV

21 April.

I recall, my dear husband, having read in Voltaire that Mazarin, while still young, did not conduct himself, like so many ministers and generals, who made a barbaric game of allowing twenty or thirty thousand men to be scythed down. He had a peace treaty in his pocket. Two armies fall upon one another, lightning is less terrible; Mazarin throws himself between them and cries: "Peace, peace! Here is the treaty! O my Brothers, men like me, don't slaughter one another!" The great Voltaire regards that trait and as worth an entire life, and it is worthy of Mercier, in whose head it has caused more than one reminiscence.

My friends have not suggested that to me; Filète and I have found it in our reading.

I do not know who the man is whom you mention to me by the name of Salokin. It's not Salaun, I hope, for he is dead; he was only a poor sub-Fréronist whose master let him die of starvation—Salaun, it's said, along with many others, was a crawling caterpillar who corroded the productions of others.[117]

---

[117] Hortense is correct about the mysterious "Salokin"; he cannot be Nicolas-Charles Salaun (1747-?). He must be someone else with the same first name spelled backwards (approximately)—i.e. Restif himself. The elaborate "ancestry" quoted in the next letter, traced back via Louis XII ("The Father of the People") and Charlemagne to Paris and Apollo is an exercise in flippant self-aggrandizement.

Letter LXVI

F.m.T. 6 April.

I testified some surprise to the beautiful Yfflasie that she should persist in speaking to me about an unknown.

"I'm sure that you would like him," she replied, "when you know what that obscure, ignored man has been, of whom almost nothing has yet been seen, but who will merit being handed down to posterity.

"Go on, then," I replied, bending my shoulders, "entertain me with your Monsieur Salokin, if it's necessary to listen to you."

"He was a hero," she said. "He was Turenne."

"Turenne!" I exclaimed. "Monsieur Salokin, Turenne! If one conserved the memory of one corporate life in another, how astonished his soul would be! It would doubtless regret not animating the hero of Italy, Egypt and France..."

"Salokin was Turenne; all the souls here know it. As for the hero you have jut mentioned, I can tell you what he was in three or four anterior lives. Bonaparte was Saint Vincent de Paul, more remotely Dunois, before that Pépin, father of Charlemagne; be for that he had the name Marcus Aurelius Antoninus; before that Cato of Utica; before that Fabius and finally Romulus, after having had the body of Achilles at the siege of Troy."

"Salokin was Turenne!" I repeated. "I know him slightly, and you astonish me greatly. Oh, it's necessary to admit that that surprises me as much as the Marquise de Brinvilliers having become Saint Labre."

"You're going to be even more amazed, for I can reveal to you what he was before."

"Well, then, who was he?"

"Louis XII."

"Louis XII! O profundity!"

262

"And before that, the Grandmaster of the Templars burned on the Île Adam, And before that, the Emperor Charlemagne, before whom he had been Pertinax, Titus, then the feeble Claudius, and Octavian-Augustus, and Tiberius-Gracchus, and Coriolanus, and Paris. We'll leave it there, for you'd laugh if I added that Salokin was Apollo in the time of the giants, who were merely men of the great race that preceded ours in holding the scepter of animality."

I didn't want to know any more, but the following morning, I went to see the human Salokin. I talked to him. I listened to him. He appeared to me to possess a profound knowledge of all of nature. I compared him with Louis XII, and I saw that he had all the faults of that great king.

Come on, I said to myself, *there are, however, a few appearances in his favor.*

The name of Turenne came up, and Salokin went in to such a great fury at the fact that the great man had carried out the devastation of the Palatinate ordered by the ferocious Louvois that I had doubt that Turenne had acted against his own wishes. I steered the conversation to Mazarin. He softened, and while criticizing him where he was blameworthy, he did his best to excuse him. I learned that he was acting thus for Mercier, and was the most ardent partisan of his dramas. I believe that all that conduct is an effect of secret reminiscence. That is what we are! Louis XII-Turenne, now Salokin! Through what strange vicissitudes the souls of great men pass, by virtue of the hazards of reincorporation!

I shall place here another discovery regarding an incorporate, Monsieur Arthaud de Bellevue, a man of intelligence whom you must have met in the home of the Comtesse. He has a host of acquaintances. He's a friend of Montgolfier and his balloons. It was him who made, in part, the Abbé Miollan's unfortunate balloon,[118] which only failed because

---

[118] The Abbé Miollan's heavily-advertised Montgolfier was ripped to shreds by an angry mob, whose members had paid

the others did not want to follow all his experience and advice—for he had already guided several. Under Louis XIV he was Labruyère, under François I, Ronsard, in the time of Philippi-le-Bel, Clement V, and previously Clovis, King of France.

Yfflasie and Clarendon saw at that moment in the Earth another of our friends; he was a French officer who had served in Holland under the Comte de Maillebois, who made several works on fortifications, etc. He has since shown great merit. He was Catinat in his last-but-one life, and previously William of Orange, King of England; more remotely he had been Belizaire, and before that Ginseric, King of the Vandals. To-day he is a placid corporate employing every instant of his life making useful discoveries in his art, which is that of war, and finding easy means of doubling or tripling the production of out lands by culture and, especially, insemination. That useful soldier is called Juliene Belair; he was named governor of Mantua before Latour-Foissac, but illness and insurmountable obstacles unfortunately retained him in Paris for three months.

Until tomorrow, my amiable love.

---

six livres for admission to the Jardin du Luxembourg to see it go up in July 1784, when it failed to get off the ground.

Response to Letter LXVI

22 April.

My friends and I know your obscure man. The Comtesse has received him in her home. The man you call Arthaud de Bellevue, otherwise Arthaud of Lyon, is an esteemed man, a trifle singular but with much intelligence. He has a taste for the arts and for the sciences; in brief, he is a man who is not a servile copy but has an original character. He brought with him a young woman, of whom he has care, who has a character so bizarre that if I were able to see souls, I would like to know what she has been before.

As for Juliene Belair, he is a man of rare merit. Although well-known, he is not yet sufficiently, with the result that he cannot, or is not allowed to, do all the good that he could. The Marquise has consented that he exploit one of her farms following his methods, and the success has been prodigious. He had quadrupled the ordinary produce, and has had the advantage of occupying all the children in the vicinity during the sowing. He will occupy them again in the spring with scrapers, to break up the earth between the wheat-stalks and open it to the influence of the atmosphere. In addition, they will sow in spring as they have sown in autumn. He takes great care, while sowing in furrows, that the clods that the germinating plant cannot pierce are broken, etc. I shall use his method, if you approve, as I think you will, for our farms in Beauce.

Letter LXVII

F.m.T. 7 April.

Yesterday, I forgot to tell you, while taking about the philosopher Arthaud, that he takes care of a young woman whose extraordinary intelligence excited my curiosity at one time. I have taken my two loving souls to see her and asked them to obtain information about her. They have done so.

Alexandrine Felicité-Payen is the natural daughter of an advocate and a lace-merchant. She has a baroque character, having been bizarrely raised, first by the family of her father and then by her mother, who had reasons for hiding her from her neighbors and relatives, keeping her locked up on her own in an isolated loft, passing hr nourishment through a cat-flap.

The woman in question had a singular mania; she had been deceived by Alexandrine's father, who refused to legitimate his child; she wanted to preserve her daughter from that misfortune by rendering conception impossible for her, and imagined a terrible means, which was to burn the sexual part in such a way that it would be permanently deformed and painful to touch. The exact and prompt execution of that project gives the measure of the character of Alexandrine's mother—who since then has believed herself justified in believing that her torturer was not her mother. She was, however, as I am sure, having seen her myself in the Petite Rue Tarante.

So, Alexandrine fled from her home as soon as she could walk. As she did not know what to become she gave herself to an old charlatan, who, seeing her English face, thought that by passing her off as a foreigner, he might make more of her. He was not mistaken. He put her in a little red hood, and in that bizarre accoutrement, with the little savage's unusual language, the emphatic expressions of her master and the ridiculous tales he told, he attracted crowds in the Boulevard du Temple. That encouraged him.

When Alexandrine was between eighteen and twenty he resolved to take her to try her fortune in England, where he represented her as a wild girl found at twelve in a wood in Somerset. He succeeded at first, but, a lord having fallen in love with his pupil, he wanted to make an immediate fortune and sold her. He did not know about the frightful burn. Milord did not look at first, but during a painful childbirth all was revealed; the sight horrified the midwife and the lover, who left her.

But who had that Alexandrine, so disdained, been? Queen Anne. Be proud, kings, queens, princes, princesses, ducs and duchesses—you do not know what awaits you in another corporate life" I have seen Louis XIV as a porter at Saint-Yves' door; Alexandrine's mother naked and begging, died of poverty in a hovel in the Petite Rue Tarante. Have I not seen Marie-Antoinette, Queen, daughter and sister of Emperors, dragged to execution in a tumbrel?[119] Let us be good, gentle, humane; we shall have need one day, in a posterior life, that someone will be so to us.

You have met, in the home of the Comtesse, the virtuous Comte de Sainte-Aldegonde,[120] who, as ugly as Socrates, has, like him, triumphed over Nature and forced her to be good. You know that he has divided his land into small parcels, which he has farmed disadvantageously by different individuals whom he pays badly and does not correct. Tell him that Yfflasie and Clarendon, who like him, have told me that he was Pythagoras, Numa, Brutus, Fabius, one of the Gracchi, Pertinax, Paul l'Hermite, and finally, in 1640, Vincent de Paul, who was made a saint, which is always something, especially when the Capuchins give illuminated images of one to children.

A caprice of Yfflasie's, who heard a soother of pains and a hawker of pleasure singing the praises their merchandise in a manner that did not mark a very healthy mind, desired to

---

[119] No, he hasn't—not yet, although the author has.

[120] Presumably François de Sainte-Aldegonde (1733-1808)

know what they had been in their last corporate life. How surprised she was to discover the herbalist and the whore Madame and Mademoiselle Deshoulières. Oh, my beautiful Hortense, that desolates me slightly...for in sum, we might one day be, in a subsequent corporeal life, you a laundress with a boat or, even worse, a tub, and me a driftwood-collector! But no sinister conjectures; we might also be something else entirely.

I have had an example; one seeing pass by this morning, in Florence, the young and brilliant wife of the Grand Duc, I wanted to know what she had been in her last corporate life. O God! The monad had animated a poor little negro slave of fifteen, whom a lustful and cruel rogue, who had just read *Justine*, stabbed while possessing her! Remembering then the lovely Du-Té, whom I saw shine in Paris, I wondered what her last corporeal existence had been. The bandy-legged, red-haired caliborgon and bleary-eyed maidservant of the shrewish wife of a bookseller, who only gave her scraps from her plate and half-gnawed bones to eat. That consoled me.

Add that by behaving well, one has a right to choose—which is an encouragement to virtue.

Response to Letter LXVII

23 April.

You have divined me, dear husband—unless Yfflasie and Clarendon, having seen me writing my response, immediately revealed it to you. You must tell me. That would have been a fine prodigy!

Yes, knew Sainte-Aldegonde well, a virtuous but eccentric man, obstinate, like the Bania, in not wanting to eat anything that had been alive, and not being any healthier for it— but he is the best soul that has ever existed.

Your soother and herbalist have put blackness into my imagination. I am glad that you have cleared it away by means of the Grand Duchesse and Mademoiselle Du-Té. However, I do not think that we ought to affect ourselves greatly with all these things; the foundation is always the same; it is only a matter of knowing it; and that we know. It is from that point of view that your letters, superficial in appearance, have the most profound moral. But this is the unfortunate thing: the present world and the future will not believe in an Yfflasie and a Clarendon; it will be thought ridiculous that their story begins on the day of their death. No one will have an implicit faith in the story of souls and their life on the roof of our atmosphere.

I have always observed, however, that it is incredulity that dooms human beings. If they believed everything with confidence, even if they were mistaken, they would be happy. But they do not want to hear. Pretended cleverdicks come to say to them: "What! You believe that! Ha ha ha!" And there are my people who no longer believe anything, and are unhappy! Oh, my love, let us have faith and let us move mountains.

Letter LXVIII

F.m.T. 8 April.

You have seen in the manner in which I almost finished my last letter that I had fears regarding what we might be one day, for we know what we have been. Last night, I had nothing more pressing, when I saw Yfflasie and Clarendon, than to ask whether it is possible to know the future fate of souls presently corporeal after the discorporate life they must lead.

The first response was that it was quite unforeseeable, since souls are not mistresses of the choice of a body and that at the instant of reincorporation they leap and fall at hazard into the first fetus read to receive them, or the nearest one to them. It is ordinarily in their own country that they are reincorporated, because old discorporate souls do not take pleasure in places that they have not had before their eyes, and also because a perpendicular fall is more natural to them than a horizontal one. However, as they travel very easily, it can often happen that their instant of reincorporation arrives when they are above a foreign country, and they are this forced to change location.

In spite of that response, we consulted Orpheus, who no longer likes Greece, any more than Cato likes modern Rome, both of them being in France. The former never leaves the Tuileries, being unable to suffer the sight of ignorant barbarians having become the tyrants of his former homeland; the later blushes at the Monsignori of his own.

Orpheus thought for a moment. Then, recalling having seen the souls of five people I had mentioned to him—you, Hortense, Comtesse Fanny Beauharnais,[121] the Marquise

---

[121] The confusion in this letter and the next of the Comtesse de Beauharnais and the Comtesse de Beauchamois might suggest that in an earlier draft of the story the latter character was, in fact, Fanny de Beauharnais, or might simply be a slip of the

Montalembert, Madame de Marigny and your Filète—he gave us a second response: "They are all five virtuous; they will have, at the end of the discorporate life that will follow, the liberty of choosing their body, and Fontlhète will have it too."

I was transported by joy to have that news and to give it to you, for although I knew that virtuous souls have that prerogative, I did not know that it was specifically reserved for you. I shall therefore give your horoscope in the following letter. I wanted to make sure that Orpheus was not joking. I have taken all precautions to have no doubt of it, and I can therefore flatter myself that I am announcing the truth to you, regarding yourself, our friends, and me.

---

pen in which Restif substituted the model's name for that of the character.

Response to Letter LXVIII

24 April.

All five of those you name will certainly be charmed, good husband, to know not only what fate we have had, but that which we shall have. We have consulted one another, and as my Letter cannot influence what you will write in yours, which is already en route, I am risking nothing in expressing our wishes, or our pretentions, as you might call them.

The Marquise de Marigny, if she were mistress of it, and able to know what the embryo she chooses to animate will become, would enter into a female body destined one day to be the favorite of a great King of France. It would not be for the pleasures, the riches or the honors; she would devote all her attention and felicity to rendering the people happy and making her lover undertake great and beautiful things. She believes that to be the most glorious destiny here.

Madame de Montalembert would like to animate the embryo of an author destined to replace the Voltaire of 1800 to 1878, proposing to be a better naturalist and less the slave of prejudices.

The Comtesse would make her arrangements to be Queen of Poland. Her dominant taste is for that nation. She would employ her credit in making the wellbeing of a people she loves.

Filète would enter the body of a woman; she has no other ambition but to be beautiful, tender and happy, for the wellbeing of her lover.

I, dear husband would follow your soul; I would be born a woman, five, eight or ten years after you and I would be. for the body in which your soul lodges, attentive and provocative, and once loved, tender—very tender—for the unique object of my choice.

Those are our wishes. Filète's and mine are not very prominent, but I think them more reasonable Madame de

Marigny sustains that hers is the most philosophical. It has every appearance of it. You may decide that, if you think it appropriate.

Letter LXIX

F.m.T. 9 April.

It is therefore certain that when we are souls after our present life we shall have the liberty of choice to be reborn of particular parents in a particular country. It is to be presumed that, enlightened by experience, endowed with the perspicacity of disengaged souls, we will chose well. But it will be necessary to take our precautions, and choose our grade appropriately, in order not to be retarded by an ordinariness that might fail o reach the desired existence. We must be sure of our sex, because it is the soul entering at the moment of conception that gives it to the fetus.

Given the character of the soul of Hortense, her fashion of thinking, the nobility of her ideas, her natural rectitude, her way of life, which ought to succeed the present ate of those things, she will want to be born the daughter of the most virtuous man and woman, wealthy, and the most beautiful there are in our country. I will choose the same conditions; I should like to be born in the same city; you will be as beautiful as you are; I shall be better than I am, without being a fop; we will love one another, and we shall be united by all conventions.

(*On the reverse, in imitated handwriting*: Filète will have chosen the same country as you and the same condition; she will be as beautiful as she is, for I remember now having seen her; I shall have a brother, whom I shall have marry her; you will be sisters.)

As for Fanny Beauchamois, she will have the desire to be born of the Dauphin, in order to have a cherished grandmother; she will want to be born male; she or he will be in tutelage for a long time because of the long life of the father. Finally, she will succeed to the throne under the name of François III, but only to descend therefrom immediately, to establish consuls and a well-ordered Republic. There being no daughter of age, or beautiful enough in Spain, Austria, Piedmont or Saxony, she will take the daughter of the King of Poland, having a taste for her and her nation. She will govern the Republic she has created brilliantly and justly, by her excellent laws and useful establishments, and the improvement of agriculture, which will double the productivity of the French territory and increase its extent.

She will reanimate commerce, capture India from the English, but to render the Hindus happy; that beautiful country will become almost French. There will be great cities in that nation, while the villages will belong entirely to the natives of all castes, the most useful of which will be favored without wounding the rights or prejudices of others. She will give the French the idea of and a taste for veritable glory, by rendering them the means of national wellbeing.

She will love Hortense, Églé, Isabelle and Filète, but by reason of their superior qualities, and their husbands will become ministers. Smitten with her justice and her grandeur, the proud English, among whom the Brunswick race will have ended, will come to offer her their throne. She will accept, and spend eight months in Paris, at the Louvre, and four months in London, at St. James's Palace. The shores of the Channel will only be inhabited henceforth by brothers...etc.

That is what Orpheus made us see in a kind of magical tableau. May his prophecy be realized, and especially that Hortense and I shall be united...

Oh, how necessary it is to be virtuous, in order that we can choose our bodies in a subsequent incorporation!

Response to Letter LXIX

25 April.

What beautiful things! But what I admire is the surety of our judgment, dear husband! Always, in a sense, you grasp the truth—which is to say, what the people themselves have desired; for the Comtesse has agreed that you have seen the depths of her soul better than she has herself.

Is all your ambition, then, limited to being my husband? That is very flattering, and I thank you sincerely for such a delicate sentiment. Madame de Marigny likes your way of seeing, to render her a favorite, better than her own. The Marquise de Montalembert will try to be reborn herself and to divine the body that will be a new Edmond, in order to love him like another Madame Parangon.[122]

If you were here, Filète would give you, she says, a thousand thanks for having rendered her my sister-in-law, and from now on we shall give one another that name. Thus your letters are for me and for my friends a source of amusements.

---

[122] Madame Parangon is a key character in several of Restif's autobiographical and quasi-autobiographical writings. Edmond is her pupil in *Le Paysan perverti*, standing in for Restif.

10 April.

You will have laughed wholeheartedly, my beautiful Hortense, to see Fanny become the future King François III— although "become the future" has never been said of such an occasion! To see Fanny, widowed of the Polish princess, taking a mistress! That isn't ridiculous, you might say. Pardon me, but it's quite ridiculous, since she was formerly a man…but what man?

Oh, it's only fair to tell you what he had been in previous existences. We asked the ancient and worthy Orpheus, who replied to us with a great deal of interest: "The one about whom you are enquiring was once Anacreon, one of my successors. After having lost sight of him for a long time, I discovered him very recently as a lively French poet; I rediscovered him as Dorat. My astonishment was extreme. I read his works. They appear to me to be inferior to those of Anacreon, with the exception of *La Feinte par amour*. I went some time without seeing him again; finally, the desire took hold of me; I asked after him. I was shown an entirely different person named Dorat-Cubières. I had never seen him before. I read his works, and found that he did indeed have many aspects of Dorat. I had him interrogated by the old Musée[123] who still had the privilege of talking to the incorporated, and of being heard by them. This is what I understood of that conversation:

Musée: Who were you before you were Dorat-Cubières?

Dorat-Cubières: I no longer remember.

M.: Who would you like to have been?

D.-C.: Scarrron.

---

[123] Presumably the legendary polymath Musaeus of Athens rather than one of his namesakes.

M.: What, Scarron! That miserable travestier! That distasteful comedian, in the view of your Jeannot—you could hold him in honor?

D.-C.: I would like to have been him.

M.: So much the better for you, for you were! I feared humiliating you by revealing it, but you're wiser than I would have imagined.

D.-C.: Listen to me, old Musée; I ask of you, once again, to hear Dorat-Cubières speak for himself. What? The man who has celebrated *Themire* in such tender and delicate verses; the man whose *Fugitive Poesies* recall so well those of Dorat, whose friend he was, those of Gresset, Chaulieu, Bernard, Desmahis, and Voltaire himself; the man who has given us a *Théâtre Moral*, in which respire simultaneously the love of virtue and the hatred of all harmful prejudices; the man who has made such ingenious eulogies to Voltaire, Fontenelle, Dorat and Conardeau; the man whose soul is so loving, so modest that he praised and praises everyone incessantly, even the advantageous La Harpe, even though that vain individual abuses everything that is not his; Dorat-Cubières, in sum, whose name alone, rival of that of Ovid, recalls the idea of the Graces, intelligence and poetic society, had, in a preceding corporate life, inhabited a deformed, counterfeit body that had rendered his monad malevolent? Scarron doubtless had some originality in his manner, but that manner is proscribed by good taste. His comedies are all farces, conducted by implausible means; the situations therein are forced and the characters grotesquely exaggerated.

I shall stop there, my beauty, observing that Dorat-Cubières, in thus appreciating himself, takes revenge on the unjust detractors of all classes who tear him apart relentlessly.

Response to Letter LXX

26 April.

Our friend is a trifle mortified, not because, being king, and widowed, she has taken a mistress, but because you seem to be taking her to task, good husband, for lending a man she esteems the ridicule of vanity. Anyway, we shall see what the denouement will be, how you will adjust that man whom Orpheus has seen doubled. I know that a host of people do not like Dorat-Cubières, but I am not one of them. At any rate, if your critique were known, it would please certain persons.

The Comtesse sighed on rereading you letter: "Oh, he once spoke in another tone, and if he were here, I would make him retract...but it's no longer possible."

Dorat-Cubières, or Rubiscée,[124] has come to see us. He asked, insistently, to see your letter. We were obliged to show it to him.

---

[124] Rubiscée is the anagrammatic pseudonym given to Michel de Cubières in Restif's *Nuits de Paris*.

Letter LXXI

F.m.T. 11 April.

We were at the judgment the Dorat-Cubières was rendering of Scarron. He continued to speak:

"As for his style, everyone knows that burlesque is the least of all. But Scarron has the glory, if it is one, of degrading beautiful things and debasing the finest conceptions of the human mind, of having introduced the burlesque in France. He is, in a way, the father of the flat and stupid persiflage of certain journalists, who soil every work that they encounter with it.

"The best work of that writer of genius, whom I was, is the *Roman Comique*, and that production does honor to our most celebrated authors. The title, above all, has a striking double justice: the *roman comique* is appropriate for extraction, and it is the history of comedians by profession, who are its very pleasant heroes. But Dorat-Cubières has published a work of that kind which loses nothing by comparison with that of the antecedent corporate life. That work, entitle *Misogynes, or les Femmes comme elles font*, will please both sexes equally. The *Roman comique* broadens the mouths of readers immeasurably by the laughter that it excites, whereas the *Misogynes* causes a slight even philosophical smile to bloom on the lips of a beauty. Wisdom shows itself there adorned with the graces of pleasantry, whereas my Scarronic gaiety bears no fruit; I was only comical by means of words, whereas, having become Dorat-Cubières, or Rubiscée, I am by means of things.

"The good companion will always like the works of Dorat-Cubières, and those of Scarron already seem only to be made for the antechamber. It is the fault of the century, and it is ours that has improved the foundation as well as the manner of my works."

That was what Dorat-Cubières said to us.

To get back to our friend, she found a pretty girl, born in the Argenson family, who seemed very changeable. But she was pretty, and that caused her caprices to be overlooked. One day she was light and witty, another—always alternately—she seemed heavy and dull. It was on a good day that Fanny, as a man, saw her for the first time. He was exceedingly smitten. But afterwards, surprised by the inequality of her character, and the different alternations of her spirit, he wanted to know the cause. Now, as he had been in our society, he had notions regarding the nature of souls. He therefore procured a conversation with that of Pamela Genlis, still discorporate, and it was because of her that the two souls of Dorat-Cubières both inhabited the body of Rubiscée-Argenson and ruled it by turns. Then he was no longer surprised by his imperious liking for the pretty Argenson-Rubiscée, and loved her more for it. And you, my love, will no longer be astonished by her inequalities.

What I learned from Yfflasie and Clarendon, who had it from Orpheus, rendered Dorat-Cubières more interesting to me. I wanted to know what he had been before being Scarron. It was found that he was Rabelais, then Laureat, author of the *Roman de la Rose*,[125] then Alcuin the chronicler, and in antiquity, Aristophanes.

---

[125] This identification is slightly odd. The authors of the 13th century poem *Roman de la Rose* were Guillaume de Lorris and Jean de Meun; the reference is presumably to the former.

Response to Letter LXXI

27 April.

Well, the Comtesse is slightly comforted. It's quite enough to have had successively four men of merit. How many women who are very proud today have never had any but obscure individuals?

We observe that you rarely respond to us. If our correspondence were a commerce of ordinary letters, I would testify our extreme curiosity to know what Beaumarchais was. Either I am much mistaken, or that man has been someone extraordinary.

For myself, who have no commerce with souls except with yours, I sometimes conjecture, for example, that J.-J. Rousseau was Lycurgus and then Epictetus; that Diderot was Pyrrho; the Fontenelle was Epicurus; that Duclos was Xenophanes; that the Abbé de Saint Pierre was Plato, then Thomas More; that the Baron d'Holbach was Socrates, instructed regarding the soul by his own experience, but that he had not, like that ancient Athenian, vanquished all the malevolence of his character; that Ninon had been Aspasia; Madame de Maintenon, Livia, the last wife of the lustful Octavian; that Marion Delorme was Phryné; Madame Du Barry Agrippina, the wife of Claudius and mother of Nero.

The Comtesse has recently made the acquaintance of a young and charming person named Mademoiselle Vigiée;[126] she announces the finest talent for painting. She is more interesting for having a very amiable little brother, already an excellent reader. We would very much like to know what they

---

[126] Louise Vigiée married Jean LeBrun in 1776, so this reference seems anachronistic. Her brother Étienne, born in 1758, would have been reading for a long time when this letter was written.

have been. My first idea was Biblis and Caunus. You can rectify my conjecture.

We still have many other estimable acquaintances whose antecedent lot excites our curiosity. The first is Monsieur de Montmorency, then Messieurs Cambacérès the Archdeacon; Servan, formerly a minister, now a general and he brother of the celebrated magistrate; Cailhava, the comic poet: Decherny the music-lover; Genève the musician; Gournan the poet; Villars the bishop; Lecomte, an estimable young man, and many others about whom you might obtain information.

Letter LXXII

F.m.T. 12 April.

While Orpheus was about to receive another soul, who had asked for him while coming in, we heard a sort of rumor similar to that made in the Inferno at the reception of Grisbourdin.[127] But the comparison is worthless since it is comparing fable with truth. Yfflasie and Clarendon wanted to see what it was. Wanting and doing are the same thing for souls.

It was the monad of the celebrated Beaumarchais, who had arrived on the surface of the atmosphere—the surface that as once known as the Empyrean.[128] All the monads were curious to see him, some because they had known him, others because they had liked his plays, all of them because they had heard talk of him. As for me, who had known him, I was also very glad to see him.

His monad had a very ordinary appearance, and the majority of monads who had not known him personally denied that it was him—but I assured them via Yfflasie and Clarendon that it really was Beaumarchais, and, in support of that opinion, I showed them a curious book, totally unknown, because it had never been put on sale, entitled *Le Drame de la*

---

[127] Grisbourdin is a lascivious Franciscan featured in Voltaire's *La Pucelle*.

[128] Pierre Beaumarchais did not die until 1799, so this passage seems anachronistic at first glance, although the text subsequently negates the assumption that he has been discorporated after his death; the reference to Christoph Gluck being newly arrived—having died in 1787—implies a markedly different time-scheme. The references in this and the next letter to Multipliandre, whom Fontlhète has not yet mentioned, compound the confusion, presumably resulting from belated insertions.

vie, by poor Restif de La Bretonne, a work in which the bonhomie of Beaumarchais is certified. I also showed them *Le Coeur human devoilé*, another singular work by the same author, in nineteen volumes, only eleven of which have appeared from Bonneville, the others being in the home the insouciant Author, who does not dare publish them. It is in the latter production that the bonhomie of the author of *Eugénie* is celebrated by a friend as true as Gadin was. I convinced them.

There had not yet been talk, however, of the decease of the father of Figaro. At any rate, I saw him, either because he too had the secret of emerging from his body as he wished— as, it will be see subsequently, Duc Multipliandre is able to do—or because he had been expelled therefrom temporarily by that Duc.

In the meantime, Orpheus came back, bringing us a newly discorporate soul holding an immortal lyre, from which she extracted harmonious sounds in the manner of souls.

Orpheus had exclaimed: "It's him! It's my friend, it's Amphion!"

"Who do I hear there?" asked the new arrival, faintly. "Didn't you want to take me to Orpheus, then?"

"It's me, who was looking for you, my friend, my dear Amphion."

At that exclamation Gluck shivered, and, moved by the most urgent desire, he united himself with Orpheus, to the point that one would have thought that there as only a single monad. All the souls uttered a cry of joy, for they had no doubt that they would soon have the most harmonious concerts, since the gods of harmony had been returned to them.

Lully, who had been Timothée, and Rameau, who had been Marsyas before being Pindar, complimented the newly disengaged monad. Mouret and Campra were even seen advancing timidly, while Sacchini, Paesiello, Pergolese, Cimarosa and Haydn threw themselves into the hero's arms. Piccinni, not yet discorporate but excorporated by Multipliandre, took Haydn by the hand; they both agreed that neither souls nor the corporeal had ever heard anything so delightful.

Tomorrow, my beautiful Hortense, I shall finish what concerns Beaumarchais, whose definite discorporation is still dubious.

Response to Letter LXXII

28 April.

No, it is not definitive, dear husband, although his testament is made; he wants to be buried in his garden at the Bastion Antoine. But what you tell us has excited our curiosity. We have sought information and have learned that Beaumarchais has been working for some time on an opera in the prologue of which he introduces discorporate souls as characters, who are to appear corporate in the opera.[129] We are assured that, in order not to put anything but the true therein, he has employed all the secrets of the chemical art, in order to extract his soul from his body and cause it to rise up to the abode of discorporate souls, while able to be reincorporated. That is why he has traced the subject of his prologue I accordance with the Illuminatus Boehme, from whom he had take lessons. He has been able to realize the hypothetical verity. That is a trait of genius.

We are annoyed by the apotheosis of luck made by Orpheus...but many people here put him above all the great musicians you mention afterwards. Some of them regard Gretry as his rival in another genre. In fact, Gretry has charming melodies, and their quantity is prodigious. Floquet is certainly not comparable to him, except in his unique opera of *L'Union de l'amour et des arts*.

We are looking forward, therefore, to the conclusion of Beaumarchais, very sorry that you cannot tell Yfflasie and Clarendon what we have learned.

---

[129] The opera in question is *Tarare*, by Antonio Salieri, premièred on 8 June 1787.

13 April.

I hastened to interrogate Yfflasie and Clarendon regarding the anterior existences of Beaumarchais. I obtained more than I requested.

The famous man had succeeded in bringing up an only daughter. It was a matter of marrying the mother. He knew Duc Multipliandre, went to see him, and asked him to extract his soul from his Beaumarchais body and replacing it with his own or another, whose body he would keep enclosed for the two hours that the emigration would last, and to procure him an ascension to the abode of souls. His objective was to discover who Madame de Villiers, the mother of the girl had been, of possible what she had done in the marriage. He obtained what he requested; Duc Multipliandre thought he owed such a distinction to the famous man. This is the story.

Beaumarchais was content with what Madame de Villiers, now his spouse, had been; I shall only cite one existence, the last before this one. She was the Comtesse de La Suze.

I sought information then as to who the husband had been. In his last corporeal existence he was Fouquet, the superintendent; before that, the Contrôleur-General that the Duchesse d'Angoulême had allowed to perish by refusing him the receipts for sums she had taken from the royal treasury; before that, Maire du Palais under the first family, the one that preceded Charles Martel; far more remotely, Sejanus; more anciently still, in the time of Scipio, the dramatist Terence, and immediately before that Menander. He was originally Greek; it was impossible to go further back than that. Perhaps he would not have liked him being Sejanus, but it is necessary not to believe all the calumnies of Suetonius of Rome against the favorite of Tiberius, when he was unfortunate, any more than those spoken in France against Beaumarchais himself.[130]

(*Postcriptum erased so as not to be legible in the letter received by Hortense.*)

Alas, my beautiful love, what will become of us? I have spent a terrible night, by virtue of the afflictions of a cruel malady, and my torment is not to be able, not to dare to think...I am not so ill at this moment, since I am writing. Oh my love, my so beloved wife, without the doctrine of which I am convinced, and which I am making it my task to inculcate in you, how unhappy I would be! But the imagination suspends real ills, if it cannot cure them... I shall write tomorrow's letter, which will contain other features.

---

[130] Author's note: "Monsieur de Fontlhète could have said many other things when he wrote these letters. *Figaro* had been performed at the Français and *Tarare* at the Opéra, but it is necessary not to forget that this collection was only put in order between 1786 and 1790."

Response to Letter LXIII

29 April.

Beaumarchais might have a double motive: one that has been told to us and the one you have exposed to us. In fact, he is married, and a beautiful letter has been found written to his wife, in which he speaks nobly about the rank to which they will both be elevated by the marriage.

We were reading your letter, and did not pause on seeing the Marquis de La Grange come in.[131] He smiled when we had finished and said: "I'm surprised that Monsieur de Fontlhète could not go back any further than Menander. I don't have his imagination, but I could have gone back as far as the grandfather or great-grandfather of Ulysses."

Madame de Beauchamois took him to task, and we perceived that she was scolding him roundly. We only understood the reason after the departure of the Marquis. I didn't think him malevolent.

---

[131] Probably François-Joseph Le Lièvre, Marquis de La Grange (1726-1808), given the seeming maturity of his frequently-expressed opinions, although possibly his eldest son, born 1766.

F.m.T. 14 April.

In finishing my last letter, dear wife, I promised you things of a new genre, but I can't tell you about them as yet. That's because last night I dreamed that I saw the good Vicomte de Toustain-Richebourg[132] and his virtuous wife. You know how estimable those two individuals are, in their tender philanthropy and their humanity. The Vicomte often devotes entire days to solicitations in order to render service to people he scarcely knows. Ingratitude does not discourage him; he is a Sainte-Aldegonde of another genre.

I asked Cato what they had been in their previous lives. He reflected momentarily.

"The husband," he replied, "is of Saxon origin. In the time when we Romans were conquering the world, the good Toustain's ancestors were ferocious Sarmates. There were very courageous, very stubborn, and every time they under-took some hazardous enterprise they were seen to march at the head of their nation. They came to France with the Normans who ravaged it in the reign of Charles the Simple, and the head of the family Toustain, or Toustein—which is equivalent to Tor-pierre or Tor-de-pierre—was one of the companions of Duc Rollon, father of William the Conqueror of England. The family remained in Normandy, which deprived it of the graces of the Court.

"In a subsequent life, the Toustein who was the chief of the branch served with distinction under the name of Raoul, but as the Normans then belonged to England they are not celebrated in our Annals. The present Vicomte was

---

[132] Charles-Gaspard Toustain, Seigneur de Richebourg (1746-1836) married Angélique du Bot de la Grignonnays in 1769; he did Restif a few favors by licensing his books when he was a royal censor, and fed him anecdotes for his short stories.

Duguesclin, because souls do not always enter into bodies of the same race, although that can happen sometimes. He was also the Duc d'Epernon under Louis XIII. In his last life he was an archivist.

"As for his wife, she has been Anne de Bretagne, and in her last life, under Louis XIV, Louise de Gonzague."

Having been asked to know something about the future of their existence, Cato summoned Erythraea, the Sibyl of Cumea, who concentrated briefly.

"What do I see!" she exclaimed. "Toustein imprisoned, ready for the scaffold! He is consoling his comrades in prison; for he is an angel of peace. But what is this other scene? His wife, her heart constricted, believing she can see her husband in the fatal tumbrel...dying of grief...it is after that that Toustein emerges, and no longer finds his wife..."

(*In a perfectly imitated handwriting*:)

Your conjectures regarded the brother and sister Vigiée are true; the latter was briefly famous under the name Lebrun; I have discovered that she had been the daughter of Dibutades, inventor of the portrait; she drew her lover's shadow on the wall on the eve of a long voyage...

As for the brother, he was Petronius in Rome, and later Marot.

As for Montmorency, he was Robert-le-Fort, then the Duc of his name beheaded in Toulouse.

Cambacérès was Gregory of Tours, after having been Plutarch more remotely and then Abbé Sugér; more recently he has been Abbé de Fleury.

Servan was Stilicon, then Henri VIII, and finally, most recently Catinat.

Cailhava was well divined by you, but most recently he was Lachaussée.

Descherny was Lully.

Genève was the author of *Ut queant laxis*.

Gournan was Lucretius, then Apuleius, and in his last incorporation, astonishingly, Cardinal de Polignac.

Villars was Boisrobert, and in his last incorporation Saint François de Sales.

Lecomte was Julian, called the Apostate by fanatics, the Philosopher by reasonable people; then he was Belisarius, then Bayard, and finally Vendôme under Louis XIV.

Domergue, the grammarian, has just been Cardinal de Janson, and the astronomer Lalande, Catherine de Medicis and then Boindin.

I have seen others, but that is enough.

Response to Letter LXXIV

30 April.

It must be admitted that I was not expecting, my ingenious love, to receive from you an oracle from the Cumaean Sibyl, whose monad you caused to appear only to predict the greatest misfortunes for the unfortunate Toustain. You must have had darkness in your soul in writing that letter. It is necessary only to predict such things when one is very sure of them, and the Comtesse will refrain carefully from mentioning them to one of her most esteemed friends. Her daughter, who is being brought up at Saint Cyr, has come out because of an indisposition. She is well, but she will one day have a considerable resemblance to Madame de Mirabeau mère.

There is a great agitation in minds here. I don't know what will come of it. I don't foresee anything good, and without being the Cumaean Sibyl, I dare to predict that the storm that is in preparation will be terrible. It is to the imprudent despotism of Sartine, Lenoir and the weakness of de Crosne that that disposition of the French is owed. As for the Parliaments, of which you are a member, you have always regarded them as the enemies of all benefit that is not personal to them.

(Business.)

Letter LXXV

F.m.T. 15 April.

Yfflasie and Clarendon have just entered into the magistracy. It was, as is only reasonable, Yfflasie who went to the Palais, and Clarendon, while calling himself Monsieur le Président, fulfils functions very similar to our Presidents.

The Law is very singular among the discorporate souls: their trials, their quibbles, their judgments, the edicts of their parliaments. One finds there, as here, prosecutors, advocates, clerks, judges and ushers; there are parliaments, bailiffs' hearings, presidential hearings, seneschals' hearings, financial courts and courts of assistance, a constabulary, and even arbitrators of points of honor. But what is curious is to see how all that is composed. Those who have been recorders or ushers are, in the Empyrean, Presidents of the High Court, the prosecutors are counselors, the advocates are courtroom guards and the presidents are, up there, clerks and jailers. The supreme court judges are interrogators and executioners. It is the souls of the broken and the hanged who are the presidents, etc.

I saw one case pleaded that amused me. It was that of a supreme court judge whose soul had become a highway robber, as one can be among the souls The accused had stolen a fine invention for making children beautiful, intelligent and virtuous which was a single secret. In order to hide his larceny he had killed the inventrice by constraining her to enter an embryo. I saw him in the dock before Cartouche, then Presidente de la Tournelle. The former rogue, whose elevated destiny is perhaps soon to animate the embryo of a monarch, was gravely seated, wrapped in ermine, whereas the poor former president, who had often sold unjust verdicts, covered in intellectual rags, responded with confusion to Monseigneur in the feminine.

The prisoner was convicted of having stolen the secret by trickery, and having thus caused such chagrin to the poor

295

monad that she had had lost her taste for the life of a pure soul and had been precipitated by the prisoner's deed into the inextricable abysms of corporate life.

"For reparation for the said crime," the sentence read, "the convicted accused is condemned to be broken alive above the Place de Grève at the moment when someone is caused a corporeal culpable to suffer the same horrible torture, in order that he will experience all its anguish. Signed P. Cartouche. P.d.T."

She was thus broken, and suffered until the moment when the broken corporate expired. But what a stroke of Fate! The two souls, that of the broken intellectual going sadly to animate a body and that of the broken corporate coming gladly to the rotunda of the atmosphere in order to be an infant soul there and become, being cleansed of the dirt of vice, a beautiful intellectual diamond, encountered one another and embraced. That brief delay caused the soul of the former Presidente de la Tournelle condemned by Dominique-Cartouche (who, in parentheses, had once been Saint Dominique) to fall precisely so as to lodge in the germ of the daughter of a prince! One day, that beauty—for the mother is beautiful and she will doubtless be—that touching beauty, will have no suspicion that she was Presidente de la Tournelle, criminal, and then, and that a monad malefactrice, broken by the sentence of Saint Dominique, become Cartouche, and then Presidente de la Tournelle in the Empyrean! O vanity of vanities, all is vanity!

Afterwards I saw a civil suit. One monad had taken the qualities of another and had appropriated them. She was condemned to make restitution. For that, she was forbidden, after a scrupulous examination, all thoughts of which she was not capable herself, and which she could only have obtained from another. She was identified as a plagiarist, and all the souls closed themselves when she approached them. That lost suit ruined the idea-plagiarizing monad, and she was very unhappy. How many people in our world would be in the same situation!

Response to Letter LXXV

1 May.

You have established a singular inversion for us there, excellent husband. That letter is more interesting than those preceding it, and I see that you are no more sparing of your body than other corporations. But I shall leave that matter to talk to you about the little Beaumarchais who has married her father and mother. She is a charming child, only eight years old, but plays the harpsichord accurately. She can play more than sixty different melodies. Her father is crazy about her. I believe that she will have a great deal of merit, and that the soul of her father will electrify hers.

A woman said to him one day: "The soul of a young woman under twenty, unless it has been corrupted by someone, is the masterpiece of the Divinity. Everything is transformed in her heart into virtue. If she has emerged from an intelligent but sinful father and mother, she usually has their intelligence but not their wickedness; everything in her is good and naïve. If, afterwards, after twenty, she becomes sinful, it is for foreign causes."

Oh, can the youth of that sex not be persuaded, to conserve that adorable bounty, which renders it so lovable, and set aside forever the malice, the cunning and the hypocrisy that enders Woman a detestable monster! It would be easy only to preach virtue by egotism, and to persuade everyone, if one were able to do it properly, that the surest means to be obliged is to oblige others. A touching scene is related in *Le Coeur humain devoilé* of the punishment of Eugénie Beaumarchais, whose heart was formed from infancy, by knowledgeable means, for philanthropy...

Letter LXXVI

F.m.T. 16 April.

It seems that these days, I only have black ideas. They occupied me last night, as they had the previous one. That is what made me desire to see the souls of a few kings, queens, ministers and noblemen, whose names I do not have the courage to write...

O Heaven! What an upheaval among the souls! Those men, proud during their corporate life, are not classed, in accordance with their ideas of their real value, in the incorporate government! One great princess was...I dare not say it...but it was a masculine name that ended in *reau*, while her feminized husband has a name that ended in *tain*,[133] with the result that the Princess was the p**p of the Prince, metamorphosed into a w***e.

It is not, dear Hortense, that liberated souls are punished for sins that they have committed while they were corporate, but a bad corporate life, crapulous, superstitious, brutal, etc. causes certain souls to contract a numbness, a non-rectitude, a falsity of views, which renders them capable of disorder, even after they are discorporate. The only difference between disengaged souls and incorporated souls is that the former are gradually corrected as they advance in their career, while the latter conserve the same character in the envelope of organic materials.

---

[133] Although one cannot be certain, it seems probable that the words that Fontlhète has in mind are *maquereau* [pimp] and *putain* [whore], and there is less ambiguity about the words that he subsequently does not spell out in full, which provide the clue to the synonymy. It is not obvious why he is so coy here, as he is explicit enough elsewhere in the text, unless he is pretending to be afraid of the inference that might be taken as to the former identities of the indicated royal couple.

I then saw a king and queen of the north. The queen was a fortune-teller and the king a barker at the door of a spectacle. They knew one another. The queen, who had been very discontented with her husband, sought to punish him. She tempted him with bait; she put within his reach a fine morsel of swine-desire, which the barker stole. The Carogne, who was watching him, had him caught in the act, and he was condemned to the galleys, as monads are condemned by attaching them to a terrestrial convict, whom they always see, and all whose moral pains they share. His former spouse went to see him pass by when she departed his chains; she heaped him with abuse in the fashion of fishwives and laughed loudly at his humiliation.

Another king and another queen, fickle, inconstant and inconsiderate, who had perished as a result of a series of imprudences, having become wise after their discorporation, attached themselves to one another, cherished one another, took for their models Yfflasie and Clarendon, and were honored like them; they succeeded to the highest dignities of the Empyrean.

Oh, my beautiful Hortense, what a beautiful gift is that of seeing what exists after death!

Response to Letter LXXVI

2 May.

These ideas of the inversion of conditions among the souls, dear husband, are philosophical, but they only teach that people only see in corporate life what is in that life. We have not divined the great princess changed into a man who follows such a vile métier; the name of the husband has not been any clearer to us. Unless it was...but she is not dead. As for the king and queen of the north, we have divined them, but we shall not name them any more than you have.

The Brunswick family, which reigns in England and Germany, gives us a very different example. It is happy and virtuous. But perhaps the king of England is only good because he is a pleasant fellow. In that case, a malevolent minister, whose maxims are Machiavellian, could do him a great deal of harm. I laugh sometimes on seeing that good king repeat like a schoolboy the lesson that his ministers have given him. It is his Pitt, above all, who makes me laugh. That child of twenty-three composes the theme of the bearded king, who recites it in parliament, after having visibly studied it while pacing back and forth in his bedroom a fortnight before. Oh, how I fear that young Pitt! These near-beardless Catos always cause great woes!

(Business.)

Letter LXXVII

F.m.T. 17 April.

It is not at all singular, my beautiful Hortense, that the souls in the Empyrean exercise the same employments as down here. It is even among the souls that all that is real; that is the veritable life: the soul is unsheathed, it acts freely. Here, on the contrary, it has touch as one has when gloves cover our hands; our universal tactility is more obtuse, within a body, than that of a shaggy bear or an armored rhinoceros. So, my love, if you have doubts about all that I am telling you, those doubts are merely childish...

I shall continue, therefore, to narrate what Yfflasie and Clarendon enabled me to see last night, while instructing as to the fate of a few important individuals who have just died among us—which is to say, really revived.

One soul that I had a great deal of pleasure in seeing was that of Piron. She did not want to tend ewe-desires; she asked for the soul of Vadé, which was found in charge of a drinking den called the Ropée, or the Frog-Pond. Piron, or Pirone, immediately took her place behind the same counter, and as Vadé as a woman greatly resembled her sister, the pretty jeweler of the Rue de l'Ambre Sec, they made love.[134]

I then saw Crébillon fils, whose father had just been re-incorporated by a condemnation to death for having in a tragedy in the Empyrean, made his character Thyestes drink soul-blood. He had entered the womb of the widow of Prince Lambale at the critical moment, but the poor Crébillon soul perceived that it had made mistake and that there were two women. Finding himself within range, he entered the womb of Madame d'Orléans, where he animated the soul of the future Duc de Valois.

---

[134] The references are to the poet Alexis Piron (1689-1773) and his friend Jean-Joseph Vade (1720-1757),

Crébillon fils' soul had a very effeminate appearance. It moved limply and played the beauty. I said to her: "Well, then Zulice, a more decent countenance!"

While I was occupied with her, I saw an exceedingly coquettish young soul arrive. I asked who the young princess was who had just discorporated.

They laughed in my face.

"It's a man...a musketeer," Yfflasie told me, emphasizing the quality. "It's Dorat, whom a malady of the chest has just delivered from a languishing life, which Fanier would have abridged if he had had the heart, but another possessed it entirely..."

Dorate was installed as a shepherdess of sheep-desires for the entire time of her *amable* youth (I am obliged to introduce that word, the idea of which does not exist among us; before my discovery the expression could not be in the language; it signifies the youth of the soul.) Dorate had no shepherd; instead of a companion, she only has a portrait, which she considers incessantly. She talks to it and kisses it. "Oh, how I loved her! How I esteemed her! I adored her!" That is all she says. Sometimes, Dorate sings a pretty song. The she sighs. "It's her that has one it. She is my love, my companion; for I'm a woman like Fanny..."

I did not understand at first why the beautiful Dorate had an Englishwoman for a companion. But Yfflasie, who saw my embarrassment, said to me, smiling: "It must be admitted that you're very distracted. It's your friend, and your wife's!"

Those two words put me in the picture. "If you see her tomorrow," the lively Yfflasie added, "kiss her beautiful hands for me, and talk to her about Dorate." But we dare not talk to her about Dorate, for her eyes would immediately turn into two fountains of tears, as those of Biblis once did.

I am quite content with that vision, my beauty.

3 May.

My three companions, dear husband, one of whom is so honorably treated in your letter, have been deeply moved. For myself, I thank you for it, privately. I would have liked you to give us the cantilena that Dorate sang in honor of Fanny! We have asked her whether she can imagine what song it might be. She cannot recall it. She has only told us that one evening, when Dorat arrived and remained in the drawing-room, without entering her study, she sang a verse of an old cantilena herself:

> *Once, when a little distracted*
> *Without responding to his speech,*
> *I listened to Timarete singing,*
> *Sighing for his tender amours.*
> *That amusement was displeasing*
> *To the tenderest of shepherds;*
> *Why did he become angry,*
> *And take four kisses from me*
> *For such a slight fault?*

(That song is more than a century old.)
The verse is effectively naïve and delicate, but it is not the one sung by Fanny's devotee Dorate, is it?

Letter LXXVIII

F.m.T. 18 April.

The following night, I dreamed about Fanny, since I could not see her. Scarcely was I in bed, scarcely had a cream of slumber (forgive the expression, but it seems to me that one falls asleep as cream flocculates on a liqueur) closed my eyes than I found myself in Fanny's house. She had a great many visitors. I sat at her feet without knowing why, because that hasn't been good form since Molière held it up to ridicule, for no good reason.

I talked to her about Yfflasie. She sighed. I tried to take her hand in order to kiss it. She snatched it away.

"Oh, beautiful Fanny, you refuse your hand for Yfflasie's lieutenant to kiss! To the friend and confident of Dorate!"

At those words, Fanny looked at me, nonplussed. Then, suddenly surrendering her beautiful hand to me, she said: "Oh, a hundred times, Fontlhète, a hundred times, for Yfflasie and for Dorate."

I told her what had happened the previous night. She seemed amazed, and softened. I saw tears in her eyes...

My dream didn't finish there, but it changed object. I found myself in the Empyrean. Yfflasie and Clarendon did not say anything about Fanny; it seemed to me that we had never spoken about it. I saw two pretty incorporated women go by, not together but separately; then, suddenly, I saw them combined into one. Fanny appeared then, and the three were no longer more than one.

Surprised by that prodigy, I asked for an explanation. Clarendon replied: "It is indeed an extraordinary phenomenon that you see. Those four incorporated women are four friends: the Marquise de Chazu, Comtesse Fanny, the Marquise de Marigny and the Marquise Comarieu de Montalembert. They appear to you to be one, either because they all have the same

304

sentiments, the same dispositions, or because a very clever man, whom I have already mentioned to you, by the name of Duc Multipliandre, is presently making use of them, by the power of his sublime art, to make a single woman of them, endowed with all the talents and all the virtues. He takes the actions of each of them and composes therefrom the life and conduct of a single admirable and good Marquise, all of whose instants are marked by a service rendered, an assistance given.

"For example, it is to Marquise Marigny that is owed the feature of the gratitude of Saint Brieuc; it is to the Comtesse Fanny that the feature of Balcon belongs; it is Madame de Chazu who has helped so many unfortunate girls and women; it is to the beautiful Comarieu that the encouragement given to the Spectator is owed, and the good action attributed to a Dame Châtel."

That is why those four beauties are confused in one; it is by the power of the magician I named rather than that of the amity that links three of them.

Tomorrow, other news.

Response to Letter LXXVIII

4 May.

Oh, that is singular! A sorcerer who often makes a single person of my two friends and me! And as he does not find us perfect enough to compose a woman accomplished in all points he adds a fourth lady to give his Pandora what she lacks. It's true that she's charming. I've only seen her once, at supper in the home of Monsieur Le Peletier de Mortefontaine,[135] the Prevôt-des-Marchands, on 30 April 84, but the memory of her graces remains present to me.

Your magician must have his reasons, my love, for making all four of us a single individual in certain circumstances. We have all begun to conjecture, since reading your letter, in order to discover what each of us contributes...

It's necessary to agree that you sometimes write very strange things! But doubtless we shall have the explanation one day, already sketched in your letter.

While I was writing, the Marquise de Marigny came in, saying: "I've found it! I've found it! It's a prediction for our discorporate life..."

Neither the Comtesse, nor Filète, nor I believe that. We're counting on you to satisfy our curiosity.

---

[135] Louis Le Peletir de Mortefontaine, Marquis de Montmélan (1730-1799), not to be confused with the more famous politician Louis-Michel Le Peletier, Marquis de Saint-Fargeau (1760-1793), who cast the deciding vote for the execution of Louis XVI, and was assassinated..

Letter LXIX

F.m.T. 19 April.

On seeing Yfflasie and Clarendon again, I learned some great news. It's that there is such contentment among the souls for Yfflasie's genre of merit that she has just been elevated to royal dignity.

"She isn't yet crowned," Clarendon told me, "but soon will be. She hopes that you will attend the ceremony, even though your somewhat Republican character renders you an enemy of Royalty."

The husband of the Queen must be King, but devoid of authority, as our queens are here. Except that if the queen were to die by some accident, he would have the regency during the rest of his disengaged life, or only during the minority of his daughter...

"Of his daughter!" you cry. "Do souls have children?"

Yes, my beauty. I only discovered that at length, and gradually. The husband, seconded by his spouse, gives birth as women do here, to a child, but via the nose, after a sneeze, of an intellectual substance that is formed in the brain of the male, much as Minerva was crystallized in the cranium of Jupiter, as is proven by the theology of the Ancients...

It is even for that reason that the corporeal, by virtue of an obscure reminiscence, give themselves a compliment when they sneeze: "Bless you!" or something similar—which is equivalent to saying: *Fortunate childbirth*, or *Have a good idea*, etc.

It sometimes happens, when the nose is blocked, that the husband gives birth through the mouth, or even the ear, and it is also by virtue of reminiscence that one says that an author has given birth to a novel, a comedy, a tragedy or an epic poem, etc., and that one says to little children, for propriety's sake, that their mother has made them by the ear: an apparently puerile explanation that it true in the Empyrean.

A baby soul is at first only a concept; then another concept is combined with her and she becomes an idea. The masculine soul gives birth when there are enough ideas assembled to have meaning, for the ideas to be formed into thoughts and several thoughts have effectuated a desire. Then there is a new soul, which has never had a body, which lives the life of souls, and which, at the moment when the involuntary desire urges it to unite with a body, will throw itself into one procreated at the same instant by two corporate beings whom she sees commencing a copulation.

It is for that reason that souls can see bodies and bodies cannot see souls; souls, in order to go to animate them, need to see bodies, but bodies have no need to see souls in order to exist. Nature only gives us necessary knowledge and faculties.

The newborn soul fortifies herself by extending and corroborating her primitive ideas; she combines them in a hundred thousand different fashions, as far as making the most abstract reasoning. That is what is called growing, maturing and becoming reasonable for new souls, which older souls can assist with their enlightenment and experience. It is thus that everything is similar in Nature, and the individual who knows one link in the chain of beings knows, through that one, all the others. Whoever knows humans well knows all the inferior beings and all the superior beings: the planet, the Sun, and finally God, or the Being-Principle.

While we were talking, at the moment when someone came to look for the Queen elect, because the last Queen had died without posterity, Clarendon gave birth successfully, in six uninterrupted sneezes, in the presence of the Court, to a Princess.

I shall stop there, until tomorrow; I am obliged to give some care to the delivered parent.

Response to Letter LXXIX

5 May.

    Go on, witty husband, care for the recumbent. In truth, I like these imaginative follies, because they testify to the good humor of your soul in writing them. If my friends do not laugh as I do, it is because they do not have the same character and you are not their husband.

    But you compose these intellectual fetuses quite well and it is evident that you like to put as much plausibility into them as possible. We always await your letters with equal impatience, so don't neglect us...

PART TWO

We finally find, in the ninetieth letter, the beginning of the history of Duc Multipliandre, long delayed by the narrations of Yfflasie and Clarendon. It was on that marvelous history that Cazotte founded the hope of the success of his work. The reader will doubtless think the same.

Letter LXXX

F.m.T. 20 April.

Clarendon was quite well, and got up from his bed two hours later. The new-born was received with acclamations of joy, and her birth was regarded as the prognostication of the most fortunate reign. Everyone left within the hour for the coronation ceremony. The little princess was carried by one of the noblemen of the court, one of King Clarendon's gentle-men-in-waiting, and handed back to the father from time to time in order that he could aliment her with intellectual milk.

I shall now go into detail regarding the coronation cere-mony, which was preceded by the reading of *pacta conventa.*

Yfflasie emerged from her dwelling, followed by her husband, carrying her daughter and surrounded by the entire Court. She mounted a stallion-desire of the most beautiful color—which, in parentheses, had once been Bucephalus, then the horse Sejanus, then Bayard;[136] presently it is one of the horses sent from Spain to the First Consul; I don't know which.

The King, first subject of the Queen, was mounted on an all-white mare-desire. The nobles of the Court all had beauti-ful horse-desires, well caparisoned and very spirited. The Clergy followed the nobles, mounted on griffin-desires and chimera-desires; some priestly monads were riding donkey-desires; a larger number, especially those who were a little old, were doubled up on swine-desires, and I even saw two on

---

[136] Bucephalus was Alexander the Great's horse. The horse Sejanus is featured in one of Miguel de Cervantes' "exemplary novels," known in English as "The Conservation of Two Dogs." Bayard is Renaud's horse in the *chanson de geste* "Les Quatre Fils Aymon," eventually ceded to Charlemagne; other works in the same genre elaborated his imaginary history fur-ther.

tiger-desires. Certain courtiers had fox-desires, wolf-desires and serpent-desires for mounts, each according to his character.

Thy advanced to the Temple, known as the Pantheon, built of pious ideas, ostentation, superstition, bigotry and fanaticism—for all those intellectual materials entered into its construction. It is said that there was only ever one temple built purely and simply of pious ideas, and that was the one Confucius built at Tien three or four thousand years ago. Others, like Saint Peter's in Rome, the Cathedral of Madrid, etc., are only built of ostentation, oppression and fanaticism. There is one temple, Saint Paul's in London, which is only constructed of Jewish ideas. Of course, I am only talking here about the temples of souls.

The immaterial Cathedral of Paris, where Yfflasie was crowned, is a very irregular edifice, very Gothic and very sullen. The Archbishopess was waiting for the sovereign at the door. She welcomed her, complimented her, preceded her, and went to sit down on her episcopal seat. I looked at her attentively. She was young and beautiful, and I thought I recognized her as...La Lescombat?[137] I wasn't sure, though, having only seen the latter in the jar where a surgeon had conserved her until the time of Mirabeau père, who denounced him.

A approached an old woman in order to ask exactly who the Archbishopess had been in her last corporate life. A Sage, who assured me that she had been the physician Astruc,[138] told me that she had been...I recoiled in horror...that she had been...O great God, how incomprehensible you are! What she had been, I dare not say. I will make you a logogriph in prose: *The name of a partisan Saint; of a celebrated financier; of an immense capital; of a folly well known to the Academy (of gaming); of a famous Judge and a quarrel at least as famous...*

---

[137] The alleged murderess Marie Taperet (1728-1755) was also knows as "La veuve Lescombat."
[138] Jean Astruc (1684-1766) was Louis XV's physician.

Guess, my beautiful Hortense, by putting before the name the feminine article La, for I shall never write it.

Response to Letter LXXX

6 May.

So, discreet husband, not only do you make the souls of brutes immortal but you also conserve the memory of the corporate lives of horses famous in history! They will take you for their historiographer.

We would have like to have the entire coronation, but that will be for tomorrow. We are content with the god faith with which you admit that you were mistaken on the count of the crowning Archbishopess. That confession has a rare modesty as well as good faith. I know by word of mouth a certain Monsieur Arthaud who would not have wanted to let go and would rather have denied the evidence a hundred times...

There remains your logogriph. In truth, my love, you have not wanted it to require much intelligence to divine it. Saint Paris; Paris Montmartel; Paris; *paris* [wagers]; the shepherd Paris. Add a La before those five words.[139] That smacks slightly of impiety, my husband; one can see that you don't like the Church. Beware of the Holy Inquisition!

---

[139] "Madame Paris," sometimes known as Justine Paris, was the most famous brothel-keeper in mid-18th century Paris, particularly notorious—thanks to Giacomo Casanova's memoirs—for the establishment she opened at the Hôtel du Roule in 1850, celebrated in the anonymous collection of epigrams *La Constitution de l'Hôtel du Roule* (1755, the place of publication given as "Condom"). The pseudonym was appropriated by numerous members of the same profession in later eras

Letter LXXXI

F.m.T. 21 April.

I ended yesterday with a logogriph; today I shall continue the account of the sacred ceremony.

The Archbishopess, placed in the heart of the aerial cathedral, situated directly above the parvis of the visible Notre Dame, wanted to make the Monarchess kneel, but Queen Yfflasie refused flatly. She declared that she only recognized the authority that the discorporate French nation, and that she did not see why she should kneel before the Ministress of the Earth-Mother, who had no other employment than that of taking to Vesta the combined homage of all the intelligent beings emerged from her womb by virtue of the generative power of the Sun.

"You are arrogating another authority than your own; take our homages to Vesta; pray for us; consecrate us with a production of Vesta, since that is the custom, but do not attribute to yourself any authority over us."

"It is not before me," the Ministress replied, "but before the Sun-Father and the Earth-Mother that I tell you to kneel. As Ministress of the religion, I have the right to order you, because, in that regard, I am above all other souls; as a Frenchwoman, I recognize you as my sovereign."

"Go away, then, that I might kneel before the Earth-Mother, the Sun-Father and the Being-Principle, alone above me. You are hiding the Sun, the Earth and God from me!"

All the nobles applauded this speech; King Clarendon, especially, congratulated the Queen on her firmness. The Archishopess was obliged to withdraw. The Queen knelt before the Great Beings alone, having, in the quality of the Chief of the Soul-Nation, no superior intermediate between her and the Earth.

After having worshiped, she mounted her throne, and before sitting down she ordered the Archbishopess, via her

Chanceleress, to crown her. The entire nation cheered, and charged the King to command the Archbishopess. That he did,

"I order you, in the name of the Nation, to crown the Queen that she has chosen."

The Archbishopess was constrained to obey. She placed the crown on Yfflasie's head, and then knelt down, and made the oath of obedience.

The Queen set her foot on her head, saying: "Ministress of the Divinity, do not forget that you are only the deputy of the Nation, to present by one mouth her homage to the Being-Principle, and that you are, in yourself, only an individual; that I have the plenitude of the national power, and I can dispense with you if necessary. Go."

At those words the Archbishopess drew away, went up into the pulpit, and gave the customary sermon. Hers revolved around purity of heart, and was very fine.

Response to Letter LXXXI

7 May.

So there is Yfflasie crowned by the ludicrous Archbishopess, whom she treated less harshly than I would have done, especially knowing her. I am surprised that the souls made such a choice to fulfill august functions.

"You're scarcely a philosopher," the Marquise says to me, who is reading what I write. "What is august about the function of taking common homage to the Great Beings? It's only the spirit of the Nation that can give it value. Are you embracing, in Paris, the mores of the Cantor, whom you pay to sing a High Mass and Vigils, or the Irish priest to celebrate a mass?"

She is right, my love, I'm no longer scandalized. What do the mores matter of the lackey who goes to pay you my compliments, or the postilion who brings you my letter? The Marquise is right, and my friends are very content that I am adding that. Be brave, then, good husband, and continue to tell me everything that passes through your head.

Letter LXXXII

22 April.

"Queen," said the Archbishopess, "King and Nobles who are listening to me, and all you French souls who have given yourselves a sovereign, know that the first and the most beautiful of virtues is chastity. Do not think that, like a superstitious imbecile I am exalting celibacy. No—that is a crime. Celibacy is a crime, impure, contrary to the laws of Nature and the Divinity, which are always the same. What I am saying is that the holy act of propagation ought to be sacred. It is the exercise of the most beautiful of the faculties of the limited being, that in which one most resembles the Being-Principle. Anyone among you who abuses that respectable act for the sterile pleasure of libertinage, for brutal sensuality, is committing an unpardonable crime, not only in the present state of pure soul but also in that of corporeality. Conserve yourselves chaste, therefore, by acting like reasonable beings, who use and do not abuse. In the estate of marriage, let wives not prevail upon their natural superiority to outrage the modesty of their husbands, even though the latter are submissive by the laws of Nature and reason. Women, respect the modesty of men! They are tender flowers, which are damaged by small things, and wither forever.

"Do not excite the senses excessively by voluptuous titillations, incessantly presenting yourself with lubricous ideas, excessively tender thoughts or overly keen desires. The result will be that you will exhaust yourself too son, and instead of having beside you an active, amusing husband, you will have nothing but a dead, forlorn soul, a monad devoid of energy. Do not profane his charms by indifferent and overly curious gazes; they are more seductive, but also more fragile than those of the stronger sex, the female. Not that those of the female are not delightful, but they are more robust In the two lives, even the corporeal, in while the male is the stronger sex, it is always him who wearies first—all the more reason for him to be exhausted in discorporate life, where he is naturally more delicate. It is, therefore, necessary to be careful of him, and never lead him to exceed his means.

"I have little to say about your other duties, O Queen; you, and all the Frenchwomen who are listening to me, are too enlightened for me to have any obligation to remind you of their principles."

The continuation tomorrow.

Response to Letter LXXXII

8 May.

That is undoubtedly an edifying discourse. It nevertheless smacks of a woman who sees the inconveniences of her
métier in perfect consciousness of the causes. Very strange
things are said of her. She brought up very well those of her
daughters who had marked dispositions; she gave them a few
agreeable talents, doubtless to gain advantage, sometimes sell-
ing the appearance of honesty (for I cannot understand certain
men who go so far as to esteem that woman; it is necessary to
have a very false mind and to have scant self-esteem.)

A doorman had two very pretty daughters. The elder disappeared at the age of fifteen. The doorman searched everywhere for her, and had the police search for her. Finally he
discovered that she was at the Barrière Chaillot, in the house
of Madame the Archishopess. He ran there.

"What! You, my lady, are prostituting my daughter and
corrupting her with bad faith!"

"Me! I undoubtedly have your daughter, because she
came to give herself to me, but she is still as new as the day
she came here. I have only given her an education. She knows
how to sing, to dance, to do her hair. Look, this is what I
mean. Come and see her playing the harpsichord."

The doorman went into the next room. He saw his
daughter adorned like a demoiselle of quality, touching the
keys of the harpsichord gracefully. She played several tunes;
then she accompanied herself, with a delightful and trained
voice.

The delighted doorman withdrew toward the door,
backwards, and outside, said: "Don't disturb yourself, my lady. Keep her, keep her! Would you like me to send you the
younger one?"

That's how the naïve father's visit concluded, who would
indeed have sent his younger daughter if his mistress, the

Princess, had not forbidden it. She even had the elder released, who returned to her father and some time thereafter went to the Opéra.

Letter LXXXIII

F.m.T. 23 April.

The Archbishopess continued: "Queen, the people who have confided supreme authority to you, have only agreed to release it into your hands in the conviction that a single head governs better than a body composed of several, whose views can never be perfectly in accord. *Tot capita, tot sensus.*[140]

"It is in order to be happy, better governed, that souls are submissive. Do not, then, regard the true realm of France, of which the corporate realm that we see down there beneath our feet is only the vulgar image, as your property! Far from being its mistress, you are the glorious public slave of the Nation. You are the individual she has chosen, by reason of your superior merit, to renounce yourself in order only to exist for your nation. The People, who have raised you up above them, does not intend that you should have a particular happiness, but that you should only rejoice in general wellbeing. You are the head, of which the eyes, the ears, the senses of smell and taste, ought to see, hear, scent and discern for everyone. The honors that the generality renders you, your prerogatives and your preeminence, are merely a feeble compensation for your royal servitude—for that is the word.

"We hope that you will never forget these incontestable truths—for if you dared to do so, that Nation would, at that moment, recover her primitive rights.

"O Queen, it would have been better for you—finer, grander and more pious—only to want to take your authority from the Ministress of altars; you would then have had no other superior but the divinity. How much you would have gained from that! Reflect on it. Perhaps there is still time..."

---

[140] More usually *Quot capita, tot sensus*: as many opinions as heads.

The whole assembly was very surprised by that priestly doctrine, but I, who knew the *pelerine*,[141] found it quite natural. The Archbishopess added nothing more to the sermon but the usual peroration, thus conceived:

"After what you have just heard, you can see the route to happiness. It is in practicing these maxims that you give to the estate of good citizens, to your Queen, as a virtuous population, which responds to her sublime intentions, and which will acquire you the right to choose a body for the corporate life that must follow this one, an advantage that you desire. In the name of the Earth-Mother, the Sun-Father and the Being-Principle, producer of both of them, *Fiat! Fiat!*"

---

[141] This word is ambiguous, meaning both "pilgrim" and "peregrine" (as in falcon). In the latter meaning, it can also refer to a kind of shark.

Response to Letter LXXXIII

9 May.

We were not expecting what the Priestess of Venus, having become the priestess of the Being-Principle—which, says the Marquise, abuse aside, has more parity than one might think—had to say. We were not expecting the end of her sermon. And that proves that you do not like the Clergy, my dear husband. I hope that they do not do you a bad turn!

We have just been told more about our Archbishopess. She has done some very singular things in her life. A daughter rejected by Saint Cyr because she was not noble enough was put by her own father, on a whim of despair, and with a very scandalous outcry, in the house of the Abbess of the Porte Chaîllot. La Paris welcomed her. Intelligent as she was, however, she sensed that it was a good opportunity to obtain some relief for herself in society.

She had her brought up severely, while giving her the talents appropriate for a young woman destined for an honest establishment. At every visit from a noble lord—for she received several—she obtained a purse for the education of her pupil. If someone asked to see her she replied; "Gladly, but she won't see you and it will not be possible for you to see her; it's necessary that her soul be conserved as pure as her body. They gave; the Lady had a ledger, in which she made each lord write the amount of the sum himself. The title on the ledger was: *To Endow a Young Demoiselle.*

For ten years she gave her the best principles, until the age of twenty, when she decided to marry her. A husband was secretly sought, and the Priestess married them, not with a dowry of thousand écus, as to Saint Cyr, but with fifty thousand écus, which she had received for her and collected gradually, without any man other than her husband having seen her, she was sure, and talked to her of gallantry. The name of the husband was never revealed to anyone but the father, but he was a gentleman.

Letter LXXXIV

F.m.T. 24 April.

I cannot finish the story of Yfflasie's coronation for you, my beautiful Hortense; a god opposes it.

I semi-discorporated myself yesterday, in order to see the continuation of the souls, but alas, man proposes and God disposes; I found myself a winged man, not by means of the graundy invented by the English[142] but with artificial and mechanical wings having the rapid movement of those of the butterflies that one sees in summer sucking from flowers without ever resting or alighting. It was my foot that started the mechanism in motion and gave my wings a force of rotation while lifting me into the air that enabled me to fly very rapidly.

As soon as I knew that I was the possessor of that precious machine, I resolved to make use of it, for the wellbeing of the world. You will perhaps not suspect the idea that came into my head: it was to be a kind of anthropomorphic god, to make kings, ministers, noblemen and magistrates tremble by intimating my orders to them, and all the wicked, and showing

---

[142] The word "graundy" appears to have originated in the French translation of Robert Paltock's *The Life and Adventures of Peter Wilkins* (1751); it does not appear in the original. The French version, *Les Hommes volans*, first issued in 1763, was reprinted in Charles Garner's extensive collection of imaginary voyages in 1788. This abrupt change in the nature and direction of Fontlhète's story appears to be deliberately taking up a plot-thread that was broached but then abandoned in the *Découverte australe*, when Victorin contemplated using his power of flight to take a role on the stage of world politics, fighting tyranny, but never got around to it before isolating himself in the South Seas

them the assured punishment of their crimes suspended above their culpable heads.

That decision taken, I made my arrangements. I disposed an entire house. I lodged my servants in the lower parts, and reserved for myself the third to the sixth floor, above which was a platform invisible from the street. I had the staircase at the entrance to the third floor closed, first with a wooden door, and then one of iron. I transported my workers, who knew my secret, to a desert island, where I furnished them with food and the means of culture, and then the Parisian women they designated to me, for I wanted to render them happy. Then, seeing them provided with subsistence and pleasures, I left them there.

It was from my terrace that I was to rise up by night, to fulfill my projects. You see that it was impossible for anyone to come to surprise me without my being warned by the noise they would be obliged to make. I had also arranged things in such a manner that a paddle-mill, which was not on my terrace but another, which milled flour and drew water from a well by the same mechanism, would cover the sound that my wings made at the moment of my ascent. That mill, which only operated at night on that occasion, and which I gave orders to stop after my departure, spent the rest of the day milling the grains that I gave it to convert into flour, for one only succeeds by taking precautions that are often minute.

You will know tomorrow how I commenced the mission that I gave myself.

Response to Letter LXXXIV

10 May.

It appears, dear husband, that it is a new order of adventures that you are going to present to us. You astonish us with your fertile imagination, and my friends have had the cruelty to say to me that it is evidence that one will not live long! As I have nothing to say about your arrangements, which I believe to be marvelous and sure, I shall tell you another story about the Archbishopess.

One day, two Princes, Charolais and Conti,[143] came to her house at the moment when an unnatural mother brought her and sold her an eleven-year-old girl. La Paris hid her from the two roués, but, the unworthy mother having perceived them and having recognized them without seeming to, she went to them when the Abbess had her back turned and said to them: "Messieurs, there is a new fruit here for whose virginity I can vouch. The child is pretty, and only eleven years old."

"How do you know that?"

"I'm sure of it; I'm her mother and she hasn't been here two hours. There's only been time to bathe her, massage her and dress her."

The two roués replied "Well, shall we deflower her on her back or on her belly? Choose!"

"How much will you gave me?"

"A hundred strokes of the postilion's whip, after it's done."

The horrible woman, who knew that they were men of their word, swiftly made her escape.

Meanwhile, the two roués searched the house for the girl—but the Abbess was a cautious woman, and the child was

---

[143] Charles de Bourbon-Condé, Comte de Charolais (1700-1760) and Louis-François de Bourbon, Prince de Conti (1717-1776), both "princes of the blood."

no longer there. Finally, they demanded her, with horrible threats. She denied it. The roués cited the mother.

"The woman who was here? She's a slut, making fun of you. She's run away."

The Princes sent someone after her, but she had been careful to stay off the road. Their servants brought back another woman.

The Abbess, who knew that one, spoke to her in private. "Is it you?" the princes said to her.

"In person; I'll give you my daughter." And she went to fetch her.

It was, in fact, her daughter that she brought back, but it was a young unfortunate, without merit and without talent, who sold newspapers and lottery tickets in cafés, where she had been a libertine for six months; her mother, who complained about it, knew the princes and wanted to take away her daughter's taste for vice by means of their cruelties. She was pretty, and only fourteen.

The two ogres threw themselves on the child, whom they believed to be innocent, laid her on her mother, and after having whipped them both with juniper rods, possessed the little one with a cruel brutality. Exhausted by debauchery, they sent in their footmen to have them lacerate the naked daughter and mother with whiplashes. The latter, torn to shreds, covered her daughter with her body. No scene was ever so horrible.

Meanwhile, the Abbess, who had had the other victim hidden, sought to save those two. She had her valet, her concierge and her gardener fire pistol-shots through the windows of the isolated place of the torture, while uttering loud cries.

The cruel are all cowards. The princes demanded to know what was happening. The mistress replied that they were armed strangers who were coming up to their room, shouting. The torturers were afraid of being recognized by the strangers. They escaped, along with their valets, through a hidden door.

The young libertine of the cafés was, it is said corrected by that. As for the eleven-year-old girl, the Abbess having found dispositions, produced her covertly at the Opéra, an evil place almost as depraved as her own, but less scandalous.

That is all that I can tell you about your Archbishopess.

Letter LXXXV

F.m.T. 25 April.

When everything was done I fitted my wings, activated the mechanism with my foot and flew over France and the sea. I thought about the mortals who had the greatest need of my help. It seemed to me that it was the unfortunate Persians. Two fearsome competitors, one of whom was an old eunuch, were making war and devastating an unfortunate country, once civilized, the abode of arts and comfort, but which had become barbaric under Mohammedanism, even more odious than Christianity.

Having arrived over Ispahan, in the plain that faces the Diyarbekir, I saw the tents of the two armies ready to come to blows. I hovered above the tent of the old eunuch and cried out to him in Persian—for my disengaged soul knows all languages: "Yield, Barbarian, to the young and brave Khan, who is an entire man, able to have heirs, who will return order and peace to these desolate climes."

The old eunuch came out, looked at me, and ordered that a cannon should be aimed at me. I let the shot depart; then I repeated my injunction. He had a bomb thrown at me. Then, irritated by his temerity, I unleashed an American arrow made by a Carib. It fell on his skull and impaled him in the contrary direction. It remained fixed in the earth, with the body.

All the Persians, truck by astonishment, thought that the blow had departed from the hand of the prophet Mohammed, or else that of Ali. They prostrated themselves; then they all went over to the side of the old eunuch's young adversary.

Content with my success, I returned to France by night and descended to my terrace in darkness.

I started reflecting on what I had to do. I had been told, a few days before, that there was a strong and vigorous pastor in the Ardennes who abducted young girls, raped them and ate them when he was weary of them. I flew to that place and searched for the man. I discovered him by means of the fire he had lit. He was clad in the skin of a huge wolf of the Black Forest—wolves that we call, inappropriately, lynxes. He was holding a sixteen-year-old girl and was about to rape her. I descended quietly. The sound of my wings frightened him. He let go of the girl, who was already laid on the ground, and who was begging for her life. He stood up, and saw me.

"Wretch," I said to him, "what are you going to do?"

He made no reply but he took aim with his rifle. I transpierced him with a Carib arrow, which attached him to a tree. I left him there. I lifted the girl up and took her home, following her indications. I found out from her that she had believed the shepherd to be a huge wolf, and that she was about to be devoured, after having been raped. Her parents welcomed her with delight.

Response to Letter LXXXV

11 May.

Here we are in other adventures, which might take us a long way! But my friend, as you commence, I fear that you are going to resemble another work entitled *L'Enclos et les oiseaux*, which we finish reading recently, which displays an imagination as crazy as yours...anyway, yours will necessarily be different, as you are not him.

The story of the shepherd of the forest of Ardennes, or the Black Forest, made us tremble. But it is a pleasure ardently aspired by our sex to tremble at a distant peril. Madame de Beauchamois told us, in that regard, the story of the violator and eater of young women in Languedoc, and although we had read it in the public papers we listened to her avidly. He was condemned to be broken on the wheel by the Parlement de Toulouse. That was one occasion when that horrible torture did not appear to me to be excessive.

Letter LXXXVI

F.m.T. 26 April.

The fortunate trial I had made the previous night encouraged me. I went up to my terrace; I donned my winged jacket, such as I had read about in a work entitled *La Découverte australe*, and I set forth.

I went to Constantinople. The Captain-Pacha had just arrived from Egypt;[144] he was strolling in his gardens, followed by his lion—for he had been obliged to lock up his tiger, which had devoured the face of a slave, which it had the custom of licking, and had almost devoured the Captain himself the same day.

I shouted to him, with a loud-hailer: "Captain! Captain! The Grand Vizier is a madman! He has just made the Osmanlis two powerful enemies, Joseph II and the Empress of Russia, Catherine the Great. He has had the audacity to declare war on them. He's an insensate, a political infant! If you have any sense, you'll separate him from affairs. But don't have him strangled; let him feign an illness, and abstain from appearing at the Divan. Let him have the Mufti recalled, although I don't much like the rabble of priests, of all religions, for that one is a good politician."

The Captain Pacha was very surprised to hear me speaking in a loud voice without being able to see me. He searched with his eyes. I dropped petards at his feet. I had taken them from the Palais in the time of the riot of the law clerks and the apprentice jewelers in the Place Dauphine. Frightened, the captain went indoors, but he had the order taken to the Grand Vizier to be ill, and to the Mufti to come back and assist at the Divan.

---

[144] Presumably the Kapudan Pasha Hasan Pasha (1713-1790), who fought a campaign in Egypt in 1786 before taking part in the Russo-Turkish war that began in 1787.

And I, my dear wife, was coming back, satisfied to have that news to tell you, when I encountered a soul, which appeared to me to have quit its body temporarily by a particular privilege, and for reasons that I did not know. I tried to avoid being seen by it. I succeeded, and I saw the soul enter a house of poor appearance in the Rue des Bernardins, opposite the Église Saint-Nicolas-du-Chardonnet.[145]

---

[145] Author's note: "The soul that Fontlhète has just seen is that of Duc Multipliandre, going into the home of the beautiful Julie Labranque, his future wife."

Response to Letter LXXXVI

12 May.

Yes, we have heard mention of that lion brought from Egypt or Libya by the Captain-Pacha, as well as the tiger and the accident that befell the slave. It appears that these anecdotes are true. But we are surprised that people who are not mad should keep such animals, which can never be durably domesticated. They are like a Sultan who caresses in the morning and strangles in the evening... We think that Louis XIV, or Louis-Pierrot, had something of the tiger or lion about him when he caressed Fouquet and then had him arrested.

The short paragraph concluding your letter appears to announce a great story, an interesting story in which marvels will be heaped atop one another. We await it with impatience.

You give another swipe of the claw—for you too have something of the tiger about you for those poor priests—at the Turkish Mufti, at the same time as you take his side...but do you think priests useless, then? At least they amuse the devotees.

I knew one woman who went regularly to the masses of a handsome young priest of the Saint-Severin Church, and took pleasure in it. There was devotion in that! She came out of the church radiant, and yet she never spoke to him! It was, therefore, a pure pleasure and there was nothing carnal about it. For after all, she could have taken him for a confessor and accused herself to him for her sin of loving him...that would have been a new kind of declaration, and ingenious.

Letter LXXXVII

F.m.T. 27 April.

I was unable to frighten any sovereign or minister last night. I rose up with the intention of going to St. Petersburg to have a word with the Empress. I could not see her—because of a slight indisposition, I was told in a quarter of the city; but in another it was said in a whisper that the Princesse de Nassau no longer quit her, and in another that it was a young Frenchman named Gabriel de Meilhan that I had known well in Paris. It didn't matter to me who was keeping her busy, young Nassau, young Gabriel or Prince Potemkin.[146]

I directed my flight over Kinburn. I arrived at the moment when the fortress was attacked by the Ottoman fleet.[147] I took the side of the Russians, having always detested the Turks, although their enemies are scarcely more likeable—but it is as the brutalizers if the human species that I hate the Turks.

I launched petards at them, and blinded two or three of their commanders. The Vice Admiral was so frightened that he thought himself assailed by the Divinity himself. He gave the signal to retreat, and returned to lose his head in Constantinople, where he as punished for the blasphemous notion of having been able to imagine that the Divinity might favor Christian dogs full of courage against the pusillanimous true faithful. No one knew the true reason for the retreat of the excellent officer, who was unable to doubt the danger to which

---

[146] If the reference is to Gabriel Sénac de Meilhan (1736-1803) it seems doubly anachronistic, as he did not visit Russia, at Catherine's invitation, until 1792, when he was certainly not young—although the response to the letter suggests that he took two sons with him. It is not obvious which of the many Princesses of Nassau is the one slandered here.

[147] The Battle of Kinburn was fought on 1 October 1787.

he was exposed. In fact, I know by my prevision that he was to be exiled first, and that the Grand Vizier would then recall him, to interrogate him before having him strangled.

I then gave other assistance to the besieged on Kinburn. It was me who told them about the retreat of the fleet and the ground troops, but no one saw my wings. I only wanted to show them on a more important occasion, about which I shall tell you soon.

Response to Letter LXXXVII

13 May.

You give a singular idea there of the Empress of Russia with the Princesse de Nassau. Can all these tales about women who love other women thus be true? For myself, I've never been able to understand that. The same was said about the Queen, but I never believed any of it. As for the men, that's another matter. It is, in fact said, that de Meilhan, the former steward of Valenciennes, has gone to Russia with his two sons and that he is very close to the Sovereign. He's a man who has much brilliance in his intelligence, in addition to that which is solid. He is esteemed by all those who know him.

I feel sincerely sorry for that poor Turkish Vice-Admiral, exiled because he was unlucky, and recalled during the night and condemned to death by a Vizier, who will suffer that cruel fate himself in a matter of months, perhaps weeks. Someone could have said to him: "Vizier, come and see the man you have caused to perish; look carefully, and learn to die!" I shiver every time the appointment of a new Vizier is announced; the last one has been executed. The new one is led to the platform expecting the blow which is unavoidable, at the slightest mistake—for that omnipotent man cannot flee; he is under the eyes of the master and his satellites.

Letter LXXXVIII

F.m.T. 28 April.

I liked Frederick II, my beauty; he was my hero, although I have some difficulty forgiving him for his campaigns of 1756 and 1763. That's because I'm a good Frenchman. As for his successor, that's something else. I would have liked him to respect his uncle, Prince Henri, more.

Yesterday, I was angry with Frederick William, and I amused myself by planning against him in a terrible manner. Excited by that, like a lion whose flanks are beaten, I fitted my artificial wings I and flew over Berlin. There I shouted, with my loud-hailer:

"Frederick William! Frederick William! You who, on a vain pretext, are facing up to the French and oppressing the Dutch Republic, I declare that I, the Flying Man, arbiter of kings and the most powerful of humans, disapprove of your actions. I order you to withdraw your troops from the territory of the United Provinces, no longer to support a refractory subject against his legitimate sovereigns the states!

"If you do not obey me, I, the Flying Man, by virtue of my power, which only I hold, and my art, I declare that I will punish you. I forbid you to make an offensive and defensive alliance with England. I forbid you to attack Joseph. I order you to surrender Silesia, and the liberty of Holland, under pain of incurring my high indignation and exposing yourself to its deadly effects. For I can do as I wish, without any human power being able to prevent my terrible explosion.

"It is not kings I hate, Frederick William; I hate injustice, tyranny, a favorite without decency, and above all, an avid, self-interested master. I abhor those execrable monsters; I order you to distance them from you!

"Someone might tell me that this tone is not appropriate, that it is too despotic. I have been a slave for a long time, and

342

nothing is more despotic than a slave unshackled. Let those who have ears to hear heed me, for my words are pure verity."

Response to Letter LXXXVIII

14 May.

Indeed, my love, the tone that you have taken with Frederick William is very despotic, and I do not recognize your character in it. As for what you say, that you have been a slave, it is of the bigwigs of your Company rather than the Court. It is necessary to agree, also, that those petty Clements and other Jansenists were very imperious and very despotic to the stupid. It is true, dear husband, that you chide yourself for the one you have taken; that is a mark of conscience; but there is another in which you had a good deal of humor, when you wrote what preceded it.

Filète has told me about an adventure of a friend of hers named Julie, who has just experienced a horrible treason. A man of about forty, but who only admits to thirty-two, has fallen in love with her, because she is very pretty. As he has intelligence and his face is passable, he succeeded in making her love him, by promising her marriage. He never intended to keep his promise. He was a gentleman from elsewhere, and a marriage to a rich young woman whose source was not absolutely legal as being prepared for him. When one is in love one is weak. Julie undoubtedly was, for those men only become infidel after the final favor.

Scaturin's marriage, of which Julie was ignorant, was not yet ready; meanwhile, he told the young woman's relatives that he had to make a voyage to Lyon. He did not; he had seen a charming young woman in the Rue Jacques and had become desirous of her. He went to ask her mother for her hand, saying: "I'm not rich, but I adore your daughter, who was a natural daughter and only has an alimentary pension. I offer to make her one equal to the one she has from her father, to give her an estate and an honorable name, on one condition, which is that I marry her with the promise of a consented divorce in three months. I shall then go to make my rich marriage, and I shall ensure the promised pension by means of the dowry of the ugly heiress

How the wretch abused, by that infamy, the holy law of divorce! How he shamefully charged his future wife with the pension of La Pellèce!

The young woman's mother, who had never been married, thought that it was quite honorable for her daughter to be so genuinely for three months. She consented to the dishonest arrangement.

Scaturin thus trafficked with the life, the heart, the honor and the fortune of three women. All was set. Scaturin was seen. Julie was informed, and fell into despair. But the rich girl knew nothing, and she has married Scaturin, who has given the pension to his second victim...

Filète is very angry with Scaturin, and a little with Julie. "How," she said to her yesterday, "can you regret such a man?" She will to cure her by means of merited reproaches.

Well, the infamous Scaturin obtains places; he prevails over men of merit; it's true that he's a schemer.

This is a singular response! But I was dolorously affected by that infamous sharp practice.

Letter LXXXIX

F.m.T. 29 April.

Frederick William did not know who was speaking to him. Finally, he looked up and perceived a black dot above his head. He admired!

I did not want to do him any harm. I contented myself with letting a little bomb of five or six pounds fall at his feet. It exploded when it reached the ground, but without causing any damage, by reason of its composition.

The new King of Prussia shuddered in fright—and as he had already heard talk of my previous appearances, he was very intrigued. He had written in very large letters on a kind of white flag: *Who are you? What do you want?*

I responded, by means of a note written in mid-air, which I dropped: *Justice.*

An instant later, the orders were given to evacuate Holland.

I flew over the Batavian lands. I saw the sad Hollanders, bemoaning the fatal Revolution that had enslaved them. I strove to renew their courage, but they thought that I was a magician. They crossed themselves and did me the honor of believing that I was the Devil. In consequence, they didn't want to have anything to do with me.

I was sufficient myself. I chased the Stadtholder from The Hague; I ordered him to go to England and to await my orders. He was obliged to obey.

Then I returned to Louvain; I had the General Seminary of Belgium reestablished there,[148] and I threatened the Brabantines with the whip, if I saw them occupied with hose miserable quarrels again. I was very scornful of them because of their superstition and I frightened them pitilessly.

---

[148] The General Seminary in Louvain was reopened in January 1788.

"Tremble!" I said to them. "Nothing can stop the terrible explosion of my will, good or ill!"

The Seminary reestablished, by means of a few petards and a small bomb that I caused to explode near a group of guttersnipe students, I went to visit all the bishops. I threw a single petard at each one, but in such a fashion as to burn the tip of an ear. That was enough; none of them wanted to be martyred. That cooled the faith of the Brabantines considerably.

Response to Letter LXXXIX

15 May.

You've gone to a great deal of trouble, dear husband, to appease petty quarrels. I'm not talking about the affair of Holland, but that of the Seminary of Louvain and the Bishops. Anyway, in spite of the gazettes, the Batavians are pacified now and the Prussians have gone home. You have even deported the Stadtholder to England.

My friends, who are not great politicians and not great newsreaders, took these important facts to their Friday supper. People laughed and whispered in one another's ears. Finally, Rubiscée asked them whether they were being serious. The Marquise showed your letter, and I saw bewilderment on all the faces. There was more whispering, and then silence. I saw that people were looking at my friends like women of another world who did not know what was happening in this one. But I didn't want to say anything. That, however, is what you've exposed my friends to!

Julie, my Filète's friend, who has been so vilely deceived by Scaturin, has come to see us. She is really interesting. We talked to her in private, Filète and I, about her deceiver, and I made her a hideous portrait of him.

"My reason is cured, Madame," she replied, "so the heart soon will be."

"What! The heart..."

"Ah," exclaimed Filète, "that's what dies in love!"

However, Julie seemed to me to be well on the way to her cure.

Letter XC

F.m.T. 30 April.

Let us trace today, my beautiful Hortense, the most cheerful images. You know that yesterday was Sunday,[149] and that it was one of the most beautiful days of spring? I flew over the Tuileries with my wings. After having soared in the air, almost like Charles in his balloon, I suddenly landed on the statue of Boreas abducting Orithyia. There, I stood on one foot, flapping my wings. I shall allow you to imagine, my beauty how all Paris admired me, how, in an instant, the Tuileries were filled with people. They came from all directions.

As for me, who had a truly angelic appearance, I smiled graciously, searching with my eyes to see whether I could perceive you in the crowd. I was holding a golden apple to give to you. I did not discover you, which prompted me to sing a pretty ballad, then fashionable:

"I shall see you, charming Lise…," etc.

After I had deployed all the charms of a sweet, harmonious and strong voice, my gaze fell upon a charming young woman who was looking at me with astonishment. A handsome young man, who made an extraordinary impression on me, as holding his hand and appeared to admire her as much as he adored her. I flew toward her, and with an infinite skill, I lifted her is my arms. The young woman uttered a cry of fright, the young man a cry of dolor and despair.

I reassured the beauty. "Have no fear," I said to her. "You doubtless know Hortense, the most beautiful of beauties [or Filète, the delightful wife of the clockmaker of the Rue Honoré, who resembles her] and you understand that, beloved by her, I cannot love anyone else. My aim is to render you dearer to your lover, by the fear of losing you."

---

[149] 29 April fell on a Sunday in 1787.

"My lover!" replied the young woman. "He's my husband!"

"That's even better. I want him to tremble, and not to see you in his arms again without transports of delight."

"Oh, don't let him lose sight of me for a single second!"

"No, no. Will he be jealous?"

"I'm not, in his regard."

"What is his estate?"

"The most noble of all; he's a skillful maker of women's shoes." And she pronounced those words as if she were saying: *He's a Duc and peer of the realm*. I saw that she was very much in love. A mischievous person would have tormented her a little...

Until tomorrow.

Response to Letter XC

16 May.

Come on, my love, since you promise us more cheerful images, we're counting on it. You've always amused us, though. For myself, I refrain from competing with you in my responses. It's necessary, to interest you more, that there is only one interest. Besides which, if the four of us competed with you in imagination, it would be necessary to have adventures like yours, or of another genre, and our composition would give you an authorial jealousy, taking away the pleasure of admiring yours.

It appeared to us that the word you said about Filète was added afterwards; the ink is slightly different, and it's on the reverse. But it's all the dearer to us, because it reveals that you're only occupied with me while writing, and only added that flattering assurance as an afterthought. You come back with pleasure to the people I love! That reflection, which I've just made, appeared so just to my friends, who almost never quit me anymore, that all three of them kissed me.

I am really leading a happy life in your absence, and I sometimes reproach myself for it, for I ought to be sad more often. But a letter every day! How can one be sad in expectation of it, or after having received it?

Until tomorrow, my love.

Letter XCI

"A shoemaker, your husband!" I said. "Well, my beauty, calm down. I believe that fear is troubling your head."

"Why is that, Monsieur Sorcerer? For you must be one to fly like this and do all that you do. Know that the métier of shoemaker for women, in silk fabrics, is honorable, and that my husband never works in leather. He only makes masterpieces of delicacy. My father, who has exercised the profession for thirty years, is an esteemed man. He is a churchwarden at the Virgin, and that is leading him to make a masterpiece. My husband is a handsome man, as neat as a Marquis. He only makes distinguished footwear, and mine—see! Oh, every Saturday I have a pair, for he mirrors himself in me!"

"He has every reason—you're charming. But he's well-dressed! I would never have imagined that he was a shoemaker. I took him for a man of quality. As for you, more tastefully pretty than a Lady, I believed you his protégée..."

"You're right, Monsieur Sorcerer; I'm his protégée too, and a well-protected protégée, since he has married me in order to protect me better. When my amiable husband commenced to pay court to me five years ago, he had an income of eighteen hundred livres and nine thousand francs in cash. He always saved up until our marriage eight months ago and he had invested two days before for an income of six hundred francs, which gave him a hundred louis a year. A year ago he inherited from an aunt and invested the succession, which gave him another six hundred livres, and we have an income of three thousand francs as well as six thousand francs in cash, and a lovely room with a cabinet. That makes a little apartment, which is a jewel. But take me back to my husband, for he loves me so much that you're causing him a mortal chagrin...and me too."

352

"I'll do it, my beauty, but on one condition, which is that your husband tells me his story, without disguise, for I can see that he has one. So, let him not prevaricate, for I'll take you back and never return you!"

"Oh, just return me; I'm sure that my husband will content you as much as you wish..."

The continuation tomorrow, my dear Hortense. I only changed position, and went to the group of Arria and Petus, in order to continue enjoying the amazement of the Parisians.

Response to Letter XCI

17 May.

Oh, my love, this story is commencing in an interesting manner, and it seems to me in advance that its genre will please us greatly. We cannot foresee what it might become, but there is interest in it, and we are burning to know what you are going to do: what the husband of the young woman in silk footwear might be, and what his story will be...

It's necessary that the story should be true, for my Filète tells us that he has heard talk of a young woman of that estate, in the Rue de Hurepoix, who is small, very pretty and who has had a few adventures. You see how you are making us reason? But let's wait.

Letter XCII

F.m.T. 2 May.

I was, therefore, on the statue of Arria, holding the young beauty around the waist with one hand, like a doll, in the presence of a large crowd. She begged me again to return her. At the same moment, I saw her young husband at our feet. I told him aloud what I demanded of him, and on his promise, solemnly made, I rose into the air, capered over the crowd, and then flew horizontally, with dormant wings, almost skimming the heads, in order to replace the young wife in her husband's arms.

He received her delightedly. The crowd surrounded them, stifling them. I told them not to be afraid and I threw half a dozen petards, lit up in ardent glass, which I always carried in my aerial excursions. The petards scattered the crowd, by manifesting my determination, with the result that the young husband and his pretty wife were absolutely alone. I offered to take them home. They consented. I therefore lifted them up, to the great astonishment of the Parisians, and rose above the houses of the Quai des Quatre-Nations, passed over the Rues Mazarin, Saint-André, Galonde and Saint-Victor and set the spouses down at their door, at the entrance to the Rue des Bernardins, opposite the church.

I flew away thereafter, in order only to land on the terrace of my house in the dark.

Thus passed my adventure of the Tuileries about which there has been so much and such various talk.

Response to Letter XCII

18 May.

It appears, my love, that your heroine was not the young person that knows Filète. The dwelling is not the same. The one she mentioned to me, who has just been married, is a young beauty, as fresh as a rose, who dresses with good taste, which in Paris, people call "being a coquette." Two handsome men passed before her door, against which she was leaning. They seemed to be quarreling. They stopped in front of her, looked at her, and said to one another:

"It isn't worth the trouble of fighting. Mademoiselle, are you marriageable?"

"Yes, Monsieur."

"Have you a lover?"

"I don't know, Monsieur."

"What! You don't know whether you love anyone?"

"I don't love any of those who have paid court to me."

"Might you love me, one day, if I were one of our suitors?" asked the one who had not yet spoken.

"Yes, Monsieur."

"There!" said the latter. "This is mine. I find her at least as likeable as the other. Are your parents here, Mademoiselle?

"My mother is here, Monsieur."

They both went in to make themselves known. They were excellent matches, but in love, five minutes earlier, with the same woman, the young Mazurier, nicknamed Bellejambe, of the Rue de la Vieille-Bouclerie, and who had just ceased, at that moment, to be rivals at the sight of the pretty Nolentine. After negotiations, the suitor was accepted.

Letter XCIII

From my Tomb. 3 May.

My beauty, I'm sure that you're very curious to know who the young man was that I took back, with his wife, to the entrance to the Rue des Bernardins. For you've glimpsed that he's an extraordinary individual. Oh, I think so!—and a hundred times, a thousand times more extraordinary than you can imagine...

But I won't tell you that today.

I had landed on my terrace at the dead of night, having taken care to make the signal for my mill to start up as I landed. As soon as I had taken off my wings I left to go and see the two young spouses. I arrived in their quarter at eight o'clock and knocked on their door, with three groups of three raps.

The young man, who was holding his little wife on his knees at that moment, shivered and said to his father-in-law: "Open the door; someone's knocking; it's someone extraordinary. Mother, let's welcome him well." I was listening, with my ear to the door.

The father opened the door, looked at me and invited me in.

"Monsieur," I said to the young man, "are you not the husband whose charming wife was abducted by the Flying Man in the Tuileries?"

"Yes, Monsieur, that's me. Are you not, yourself, the Flying Man who stole from me a wife I adore?"

"Yes, Monsieur, I am. Monsieur, I desire to sup with you and present company, after you have given me your word of honor to keep secret all that I confide to you."

"Monsieur, I desire that you sup with my young wife, her father, her mother and me, on condition that you tell us how it comes about that you are the Flying Man, if you want to know how I am what I am. One secret for another—or we can sup together and each of us can keep his own."

"Monsieur, that will not be today. Let us sup merrily, you, your pretty companion, your father- and mother-in-law and me. We'll talk another day."

"So be it, Monsieur. Here is your place."

"Not a word before the maidservant, Monsieur!"

"Not a word will be said, Monsieur."

We sat down at table and supped cheerfully, on delicate fare that was usual to the house, since they were not expecting me: delicious wines, silver-plated cutlery and dishes, and gold-plated trays; at dessert, particularly magnificent, bonbons of the rarest quality, fine liqueurs served in flower-patterned crystal with gold rims, etc. All that came naturally; it was what they did every day. I had the opportunity to see how the young husband loved his little wife; he was her idolater.

I was, therefore, increasingly confirmed in the idea that I was in the home of a person who was at least my equal.

Response to Letter XCIII

19 May.

Oh, my friend, it is a perfidious trick to leave people for twenty-four hours in the position in which your latest letter has put us. To punish you, I shall only write these few words, and will not finish the story or adventure of young Nolentine.

Letter XCIV

F.m.T. 4 May.

Our conversation only concerned public affairs: the war against the Turks, the success of the Tsarina and Emperors; the glory with which the Grand Duke was covering himself; that, more flattering still, with which Joseph II was accumulating. I avoided any other subject, hoping to satisfy my curiosity fully by my own means.

The supper came to an end at eleven o'clock, when our conversations regarding the news were not yet exhausted. On leaving the table, we sat around the fire, and there I spoke, as if as a matter of form, about the state of souls, about Yfflasie and Clarendon, the coronation of the former and all that I had seen by their means.

They listened to me with a great deal of attention, but while I was speaking I perceived that the young man seemed embarrassed; he went almost violet. However, when the young wife said that I was telling incredible tales, he replied to her gravely that I was telling the truth, and that he had incontrovertible proofs of that.

He then said a few words to his father- and mother-in-law in a low voice. I was attentive, while talking, ready to escape if anyone had any hostile design—but I was far from imagining what was being plotted against me! The knowledge that I had of the estate of souls was what saved me from the greatest peril that a man can run.

I suddenly sensed a heaviness in my head, a pain in my eyes, ears, nose and palate, as well as over the entire surface of my body, from the tips of my fingers to the soles of my feet. I was astonished by it, not knowing what a singular man I was dealing with.

Response to Letter XCIV

20 May.

Again? You really are incorrigible! And me too—I shan't finish Nolentine.

Letter XCV

F.m.T. 5 May.

While I was surprised by what was happening, I darted a glance at the young man. He was leaning back in his mother-in-law's arms, unmoving. Surprised by what I saw, I wanted to penetrate the cause. I rendered my body motionless and I tried to emerge as a soul, to go to Yfflasie and Clarendon...

How surprised I was, however, when my soul had emerged from my body, to discover that of the handsome young man, similarly emerged from his own, which was trying to enter mine!

His soul began to laugh, as souls laugh, and said to me: "In, truth Comrade, we're both frozen stiff! And I sense that I can do nothing to you! I confess that your secret of flying corporeally has tempted me. I wanted to treat you as I have treated many others, but that isn't possible. So, let's be friends forever, since we're equals, for it's necessary to be equals to love one another, and since we can't do one another any harm, let's do one another good; we'll both be better off.

"Don't go any further; let's both go back into our bodies. I'll tell you my story as soon as possible. Only know that in my antecedent corporeal life I was Cromwell, that my dearly beloved wife was a natural descendant of Queen Anne Boleyn,[150] whom I violated because she hated me, and whom I stabbed to death. I'm compensating her today, without her knowledge."

My soul extended its hand to that of the young Cromwell as a sign of assent, and we each reentered our corporeal sheath. We made a semblance of nothing serious having happened, as if we had had a moment of torpor. They were doubt-

---

[150] It is not easy to see how Anne Boleyn could have had any descendants in Crowell's time, legitimate or otherwise, given that her only child, Elizabeth I, died without issue.

less used to it, as no one seemed astonished by the condition in which we had been.

Response to Letter XCV

21 May.

The two rivals, the lovers of young Mazurier with the Bellejambe and the pretty Nolentine, were not reconciled for long. They both fell in love with Nolentine, and fell out again. The one that had ceded before did so for a second time, and, finding himself in the company of Bellejambe, sensed that he was falling in love with her again. He told his friend, transported by joy; the latter was delighted for him, and they persuaded the parents to agree to the exchange.

Unfortunately, Chasublin, the other lover, saw Bellejambe again, and fell madly in love with her again. It was necessary to change back, because Stollin, the other friend, fell in love with Nolentine again when he saw her again.

The young women's parents did not know what to think, but before a further change had been proposed to them, Chasublin had encountered Nolentine in the Place du Pont Michel and had become smitten again, and Stollin was also easily resmitten with Bellejambe...

The mutations occurred ten times. Finally, the two rivals realized that they were always in love with the one they had seen most recently. It was agreed between them that they would draw lots, and that once fate had decided, they would forever avoid meeting the one that had fallen to the other.

When that was done, they were married, Stollin to Nolentine and Chasublin to Mazurier. But it is greatly feared that the singular versatility of the two young men might attract great misfortune to them, by rendering each of them the seducer of the other's wife.

You can see that I'm not sulking, my dear husband.

Letter XCVI

F.m.T. 6 May.

What our souls had just said to one another had not been heard by anyone, as you can imagine. I felt sharp pains on recovering consciousness. Astonished by my lethargy, which had not been anticipated, unlike that of the young man, they had pushed long pins into my flesh, and even an awl, in order to see whether I had any sensation. I complained bitterly to the maidservant, who had carried out that operation, and the young man's mother-in-law, who had permitted it. As for the young wife, she had not budged for as long as her husband was motionless, remaining lying on his bosom.

I had soon recovered from my pains, however, by means of a balm that the young man put on my wounds. Then he asked me to come and see his little apartment on the second floor.

It was necessary for the father and mother to be as good as they were not to see that their son-in-law's rather large room and its cabinet contained riches worth several millions. The three chests of drawers were gold, as were the recesses, the bracket-tables and the clocks. The chairs and the two sofas were garnished with diamonds, and the old frames of the mirrors were covered with them. The golden nails of the armchairs had diamond heads. The bedposts were garnished with rubies, and the awning with emeralds. Instead of wall-tapestries and a ceiling, there was a mosaic of precious stones forming various flowers and superb birds. There was a portrait of Anne Boleyn, entirely in precious stones, so nuanced that they expressed the natural colors of the face and skin. The parquet was scented wood. On the mantelpiece there were cups and saucers of rock crystal, with alternating circles of rubies and emeralds. In another cabinet taken from the house next door by a piercing, there was a gold bath, and superb linen in cupboards of precious wood, with golden nails and inlay.

Another cabinet on the floor above had a furnace for heating water, which fell into the bath via two golden taps, one hot and one cold—for everything was gold in the young man's rooms.

The good people who saw those marvels did not imagine that it was authentic, and regarded it all as gilt, and the diamonds as paste. I was amazed!

The young man and I took our leave of one another, proposing to meet again the following evening. Again he promised me his story, but after I had told him mine.

Response to Letter XCVI

22 May.

What was anticipated has happened. Chasublin has become madly enamored again of Stollin's wife, whom he met by chance in the Luxembourg. He showed his own to his friend, who was similarly resmitten. They resolved an exchange, but without communicating it to their wives. Everything was arranged for that. However, the turpitude was not achieved; in order to realize the exchange it was necessary for each to go to bed visibly with his wife. Now, the result of that was that each of them, finding himself next to a spouse of provocative cleanliness, having a tasteful nudity possessed of all the appetizing graces of a young woman, that at the moment when the switch was to be consummated, each of them fell in love with his own wife again, and stayed with her, with the result that they both remained, as if by common accord, with the one that belonged to him.

But the next day, it began all over again, and every evening the same thing happened. During the day, each of them fell in love with the other's wife and paid court to her. In the evening, they made all the arrangements for the exchange, but as it was then necessary for each to see his wife, and on seeing her, was necessarily recaptured by her, and all the projects of the day—closing the eyes, not looking—vanished.

The two young women were a little surprised each to have the husband of the other constantly with them during the day, but they did not have the final word, which Filète obtained from one of the husbands, who thought one day that he was in love with her.

Letter XCVII

F.m.T. 7 May.

You can well imagine that I did not miss the rendezvous at the home of the singular young man. We supped together as on the previous evening. I told my story, such as you know it, beautiful Hortense; I added to it all that I have detailed in these letters. My recitations gave the greatest pleasure, and I saw that the beautiful Julie esteemed me more for it. I concluded by promising the young man that I would lend him my wings when they became useless to me. That promise transported him with joy, and we were veritable friends.

Multipliandre—that is his name—then began to speak. "I have a double motive for recounting my adventures to you," he said, "because I love to talk about my happiness before my little wife, for whom I have such a vivid passion, because she is the mistress all my faculties, and because my Julie does not know me yet. I have never told her what I was.

The Marvelous History of Jean-Jacob,
Duc Multipliandre

"You know my anterior origin, by virtue of a word I said to you yesterday. As Cromwell was a privileged soul, he had the liberty to choose the body into which he would enter. He chose that of a fetus formed by the copulation of a young French Duc and a pretty demoiselle of quality, whom the young Duc had espoused that day.

"I was born to those two spouses. They brought me up with as much care as affection. My education was the object of the special attention of my father, who had no other child than me, and who cherished me beyond measure. He had me instructed by the cleverest men, and had me initiated, in particular into the secret sciences, in which other parents do not believe, and neglect for that reason.

"Among his acquaintances there was a Jew, a profound Rabbi, who possessed the whole of the Cabala, especially the art of Samuel, by which one evokes souls and separates them from the body without their experiencing anything other than a kind of lethargy. It was that Rabbi who gave me all the science I have. It is through him that I have the art, by means of absolutely physical efforts that have nothing supernatural about them, of extracting my soul from my body whenever I wish and putting it into another, from which I expel the soul as I enter it via the five senses.

"Possessor of all those secrets, and my own master by virtue of the decease of my father and mother, who let go of life voluntarily, I saw that I had no need to follow any of the rules of human prudence in order to be happy, opulent and honored. I resolved, therefore, to deliver myself to my appetites. I quit my name, the Duc de Mazarin,[151] in order simply to take that of Duc Multipliandre, and in order to present myself here I gave myself the name of Jean-Jacob Multipliandre.

I am now going to tell you the story of my marriage.

I was passing this street one evening. There was a light in the shop that you saw when you came in. I don't know what led me to look into it by raising myself up on tiptoe in order to see over the curtain. What was my surprise on seeing, beside her mother, a young beauty with whom there was nothing comparable in Nature. I remained delightedly motionless for several minutes. A charming face, beautiful eyes, a rosebud mouth, a ravishing bosom, a shapely figure. The more I looked at the young woman, the more worthy of love I found her. I wanted to know what she had been in her last corporeal life, and I found that she had formerly been Anne Boleyn, a natural descendant of Anne Boleyn, wife of Henry VIII.

I resolved to employ all the power that my admirable science gave me to render myself happy. I changed my exter-

---

[151] The title of Duc de Mazarin became extinct in 1738 when its last holder died.

nal existence and made myself an apprentice shoemaker for women."

"What!" cried Julie "You aren't?"

"Forgive me, my beauty; I am, but I was a Duc before: the young Duc de Mazarin, who has disappeared from the earth without anyone knowing how."

"And you work so well!" said the mother-in-law.

"I do all that I can, Mother, and when Monsieur Labranque, my honorable father-in-law, was so amazed by my work, that was the second pair of shoes that I had made."

"Ah!" said Père Labranque. "There's no masterpiece like the shoes of that pretty Comtesse with the dainty feet. You know? Or your wife's..." He turned to me. "Look at those, Monsieur Sleeper!"

I agreed that Julie's feet were charming.

"But my good friend, you're a Duc; how is it that you're not in your Duchy, like a Potentate?"

You shall only know his response tomorrow, my beautiful Hortense.

Response to Letter XCVII

23 May.

Your history of Duc Multipliandre becomes more and more interesting. I have nothing to tell you about my storiette, the denouement of which has not yet arrived. But the Comtesse also knows the story of Duc Multipliandre.

Letter XCVIII

F.m.T. 8 May.

"My Beauty, I am a Duc and a peer; consequently, you are a Duchesse."

"Duchesse and peeress?"

"Yes, Madame."

"Madame! He calls me Madame!" Julie exclaimed, bursting into laughter.

"Listen, Madame my daughter," said Mère Labranque, "you know that Monsieur Trudon the procurator never calls his wife anything but Madame. Now, a Duc is much more than a procurator."

"More than a President, Wife," said Père Labranque.

"Since you know that you're a Duchesse, Madame," Multipliandre said, gravely, "I am no longer able to speak to you otherwise."

The young person composed herself, and assumed a serious expression.

Her husband continued: "Dressed as an apprentice shoemaker, I presented myself in the shop of Monsieur Labranque, the father of the young woman I already idolized, even before having spoken to her. 'Master, do you need an apprentice?'

"Instead of replying, he took my hands and touched them, then looked t me. 'Yes, if he's a good worker.'

"'Yes, Master, and skillful, I can pride myself on that.'

"'That's not what your hands say.'

"'They're liars, Master.'

"'I'm a liar! That's not polite!'

"'No, Master, it's not you who are the liar, it's my hands.'

"'Oh, that's something else.'

"'Take me on trial, Master. If I don't work well, instead of receiving money from you, I'll give it to you.'

"'Well, all right—that puts me at my ease. Come tomorrow.'

"'Why not today?'

"'Although you seem to me to be a bad lot, I like you.'

"'Much obliged, Master. I'll go fetch my Saint-Crispin.'

"And I left.

"I came back about half an hour later, and although it was four o'clock I set to work. I made my pair, which was my second. The Master watched me. He took my work from me at ten o'clock, when I had finished. 'Let's see how they're stitched...' He examined them for a long time, and put on his spectacles. 'It seems that you don't want to give me money.'

"'Indeed, Master, if you wish.'

"'No, no...have supper here.'

"My resolution was to see whether I could seduce my lovable Julie..."

"Oh! Rascal!" interjected the young person.

"And that's what I would have done, if I had found a bad character..."

"Ho!" said the mother. "If..."

Her husband put his hand over her mouth. "Ducs," he said, "don't do otherwise when they fall in love with the daughters of folk like us.—and I even heard talk of one who seduced the daughter of an advocate! Ducs among people like us, Ducs among the birds,[152] they're all birds of prey...let's listen to Monseigneur my son-in-law."

"But from the first day, the sweetness, the grace, the amiability, the virtues and the qualities of the charming Julie suspended my evil dispositions. I studied her the next day, and he following days. There was naivety, candor...I wanted to see whether she was perfectly beautiful. I saw her in the bath. Then I was more smitten than ever. The beauty of her soul purified the amour that the beauty of her body excited. I finally became amorous in a manner worthy of the touching Julie.

---

[152] In French, an eagle-owl is a "*Grand Duc.*"

"I still waited for some time, but, my love only growing stronger, I sensed that in loving her honestly I had found happiness. I asked for her in marriage. As she was very young, I made my offers, which were that she would thus remain, with me, with her parents, and that I would conserve her as a maiden until she had completed eighteen years. She completed them yesterday, and today is her great day. That is why I took her to the Tuileries today, in order that everyone could admire her on the eve of ceasing to be a maid.

"I have tried to make myself loved before the marriage, and I have succeeded by means of delicate attentions..."

"Oh, yes, my love, you have succeeded, be sure of it."

"Madame la Duchesse, my daughter," said the shoemaker, taking off his cap, "it seems to me, saving better advice and your respect, that you ought not to address Monsieur le Duc de Mazarin my son-in-law as *tu*; and that, even more, you ought to say 'Monsieur' instead of 'my husband.' If you were Dauphine you would say Monseigneur."

"No, no, Father," replied the Duc, "let us still talk in the same way; let us live without ceremony for some time yet, for that I am passing with you, as one of the family, is the happiest of my life!"

And he became tender, to the point of shedding a few tears. He kissed his wife, Monsieur Labranque and Madame Labranque, and then he returned to Julie...

But that's enough for today.

Response to Letter XCVIII

24 May.

Courage, dear husband! These are interesting letters, and we await with impatience the continuation of Duc Multipliandre's story. He seems to us to be, fundamentally, a good person, in spite of the trick he wanted to play. His entrance to Père Labranque's shop is comical and natural, and the exposition of his sentiments has frankness. There is something of the Comtesse's story in that, and I can see that the adventure is true.

Letter XCIX

F.m.T. 9 May.

Multipliandre could not weary of caressing his little wife; he gave her more than a hundred kisses. Finally, he resumed his story.

"I occupied myself with forming the mind of the one that I wanted to make my wide. I have been her music master. I am teaching her Italian and English. I have given her a little history and geography. She has always learned with facility, applying herself with a docility that enchants me. At the fixed time, our marriage took place. On the evening of the wedding I returned her to her mother, who put her to bed in a pretty cabinet that I had arranged, but of which only Julie's mother had the key. I continued to work in the shop.

How can I express to you my happiness since that fortunate day? I see by my side, or I take to my little apartment, the person I adore and by whom I am loved. I find an inexpressible sweetness in observing the tenderness and regards of the honest father and mother. Since my marriage I have not once been for a walk without asking them to come too. I like to be with them, because they are good. We go along the Boulevard Neuf, near the Clos Payen, to a nice cabaret, for delightful snacks. We take care to sit by the window, in order to see the people outside, while we're admired by the people within—for we listen continually to what is said about my little wife.

"'Oh, how pretty she is!'

"'But,' say the women, 'he's as handsome a man as she's a pretty woman.'

"'They make a lovely couple.'

"'Look at the Father and Mother, how content they are!'

"'Well, he makes a good husband, and a good son-in-law.'

"'It's not difficult, when one has such a pretty wife' says a young fellow in quest of marriage, 'to be a good husband.'

"'But it is to be a good son-in-law,' an old woman says to him, 'for there aren't many of those.'

"Those remarks amuse us, and render out snack even more agreeable.

"And during the walk, how many compliments my beautiful Julie gets! Sometimes there are men who envy me; sometimes women touch me in passing, and cast a glance at me that makes me indignant.

"One day, a Lord stopped is carriage and called to Julie, to come and speak to him.

"I presented myself. 'What does Monsieur want with my wife?'

"'To offer you both a place in my carriage.'

"'We have a father and a mother there; we can't accept...'

"Sometimes kept women do me the honor of coveting me. Sometimes it's ladies of higher birth...but it's entirely in vain; I haven't ceased to be a Duc in order to go back to Duchesses."

Well, my beautiful Hortense, what do you think of the shoemaker Duc? For he doesn't yet merit his name of Multipliandre.

Response to Letter XCIX

25 May.

There's a husband very much in love with his wife, and that is good, on the part of a Duc. I admire the philosophy of that man who, sensing that he cannot be happy with the conduct he has formerly maintained—with which the Comtesse is familiar, for she has told us of a few very immoral adventures—has returned to virtue by way of Epicurianism. He has sensed that he could only he happy in amour by means of equality, and has descended to the estate of his future wife, although scantly honorable, humbling and even arduous. The details that he gives mark a grand passion!

But is she very pretty, then, the amiable Labranque? My chambermaid, before whom we were talking, knows a young woman living in the same place, who is indeed very pretty, but is it yours, dear husband?

Your son is well.

Letter C

F.m.T. 10 May.

"In order to render my pretty companion even more lovable," Multipliandre continued, "her parents will tell you, like me, that I have not flattered her in her little faults—for human beings cannot be perfect. In any case, without hers, my darling might perhaps be less lovable; they prevent her character becoming monotonous.

"One day, my little wife thought that, since her marriage, she ought to enjoy freedom of speech, to have the right to judge for herself, and not to give in to her mother—who was quite scandalized. They were upstairs; they came down and took me for an arbiter. My little idol was already triumphant.

"Her mother explained the subject of their dispute. 'It's my beloved who is wrong,' I replied. You should have seen my Julie's face! It was a picture! Her mother was almost sorry that I had agreed with her.

"However, I consoled Julie for her defeat by means of the most tender caresses, and she is of such good character that she did not hold it against me. She went out shortly thereafter, to see to the wedding arrangements.

"'Was I right, then, my son-in-law, to tell my daughter that a wife is only happy if her husband allows her absolute control?'

"'No, Mother.'

"'No! But you told her she was wrong!'

"'That's because an honest mother like you is always right so far as her daughter is concerned.'

"'Oh, my friend, that word makes me love you and esteem you even more that I already did! But I can't profit from it; I'll tell me dear daughter that she was right, and that a husband, especially one like you, should always command us.'

"Julie came back from the church. Her mother made her apologies. The little darling came to throw he arms around my

379

neck, saying: 'Oh, my love, how I thank you for having preserved me from the regret of a triumph over my mother!'"

It was at that point that Duc Multipliandre terminated his narration. I left immediately.

TO BE CONTINUED IN
VOLUME 2

SF & FANTASY

Adolphe Alhaiza. *Cybele*

Alphonse Allais. *The Adventures of Captain Cap*

Henri Allorge. *The Great Cataclysm*

Guy d'Armen. *Doc Ardan: The City of Gold and Lepers; The Troglodytes of Mount Everest/The Giants of Black Lake*

G.-J. Arnaud. *The Ice Company*

André Arnyvelde. *The Ark; The Mutilated Bacchus*

Charles Asselineau. *The Double Life*

Henri Austruy. *The Eupantophone; The Olotelepan; The Petitpaon Era*

Barillet-Lagargousse. *The Final War*

Cyprien Bérard. *The Vampire Lord Ruthwen*

S. Henry Berthoud. *Martyrs of Science*

Aloysius Bertrand. *Gaspard de la Nuit*

Richard Bessière. *The Gardens of the Apocalypse; The Masters of Silence*

Chevalier de Béthune. *The World of Mercury*

Albert Bleunard. *Ever Smaller*

Félix Bodin. *The Novel of the Future*

Louis Boussenard. *Monsieur Synthesis*

Alphonse Brown. *City of Glass; The Conquest of the Air*

Émile Calvet. *In a Thousand Years*

André Caroff. *The Terror of Madame Atomos; Miss Atomos; The Return of Madame Atomos; The Mistake of Madame Atomos; The Monsters of Madame Atomos; The Revenge of Madame Atomos; The Resurrection of Madame Atomos; The Mark of Madame Atomos; The Spheres of Madame Atomos; The Wrath of Madame Atomos* (w/M. & Sylvie Stéphan)

Félicien Champsaur. *Homo-Deus; The Human Arrow; Nora, The Ape-Woman; Ouha, King of the Apes; Pharaoh's Wife*

Didier de Chousy. *Ignis*

Jules Clarétie. *Obsession*

Jacques Collin de Plancy. *Voyage to the Center of the Earth*

Michel Corday. *The Eternal Flame*

André Couvreur. *Caresco, Superman; The Exploits of Professor Tornada* (3 vols.); *The Necessary Evil*
Camille Debans. *The Misfortunes of John Bull*
Captain Danrit. *Undersea Odyssey*
C. I. Defontenay. *Star (Psi Cassiopeia)*
Charles Derennes. *The People of the Pole*
Georges Dodds (anthologist). *The Missing Link*
Charles Dodeman. *The Silent Bomb*
Harry Dickson. *The Heir of Dracula; Harry Dickson vs. The Spider*
Jules Dornay. *Lord Ruthven Begins*
Alfred Driou. *The Adventures of a Parisian Aeronaut*
Sâr Dubnotal *vs. Jack the Ripper; The Astral Trail*
Odette Dulac. *The War of the Sexes*
Alexandre Dumas. *The Return of Lord Ruthven*
Renée Dunan. *Baal; The Ultimate Pleasure*
J.-C. Dunyach. *The Night Orchid; The Thieves of Silence*
Henri Duvernois. *The Man Who Found Himself*
Achille Eyraud. *Voyage to Venus*
Henri Falk. *The Age of Lead*
Paul Féval. *Anne of the Isles; Knightshade; Revenants; Vampire City; The Vampire Countess; The Wandering Jew's Daughter*
Paul Féval, *fils. Felifax, the Tiger-Man*
Charles de Fieux. *Lamékis*
Fernand Fleuret. *Jim Click*
Louis Forest. *Someone is Stealing Children in Paris*
Arnould Galopin. *Doctor Omega; Doctor Omega and the Shadowmen* (anthology)
Judith Gautier. *Isoline and the Serpent-Flower*
H. Gayar. *The Marvelous Adventures of Serge Myrandhal on Mars*
G.L. Gick. *Harry Dickson and the Werewolf of Rutherford Grange*
Raoul Gineste. *The Second Life of Doctor Albin*
Delphine de Girardin. *Balzac's Cane*
Léon Gozlan. *The Vampire of the Val-de-Grâce*

Jules Gros. *The Fossil Man*

Edmond Haraucourt. *Daah, the First Human; Illusions of Immortality*

Nathalie Henneberg. *The Green Gods*

Eugène Hennebert. *The Enchanted City*

Jules Hoche. *The Maker of Men and His Formula*

V. Hugo, P. Foucher & P. Meurice. *The Hunchback of Notre-Dame*

Romain d'Huissier. *Hexagon: Dark Matter*

Jules Janin. *The Magnetized Corpse*

Michel Jeury. *Chronolysis*

Gustave Kahn. *The Tale of Gold and Silence*

Gérard Klein. *The Mote in Time's Eye*

Fernand Kolney. *Love in 5000 Years*

Paul Lacroix. *Danse Macabre*

Louis-Guillaume de La Follie. *The Unpretentious Philosopher*

Jean de La Hire. *The Fiery Wheel; Enter the Nyctalope; The Nyctalope on Mars; The Nyctalope vs. Lucifer; The Nyctalope Steps In; Night of the Nyctalope; Return of the Nyctalope*

Etienne-Léon de Lamothe-Langon. *The Virgin Vampire*

André Laurie. *Spiridon*

Gabriel de Lautrec. *The Vengeance of the Oval Portrait*

Alain le Drimeur. *The Future City*

Georges Le Faure & Henri de Graffigny. *The Extraordinary Adventures of a Russian Scientist Across the Solar System* (2 vols.)

Gustave Le Rouge. *The Dominion of the World* (w/Gustave Guitton) (4 vols.); *The Mysterious Doctor Cornelius* (3 vols.); *The Vampires of Mars*

Jules Lermina. *The Battle of Strasbourg; Mysteryville; Panic in Paris; The Secret of Zippelius; To-Ho and the Gold Destroyers*

André Lichtenberger. *The Centaurs; The Children of the Crab*

Maurice Limat. *Mephista*

Listonai. *The Philosophical Voyager*

Jean-Marc & Randy Lofficier. *Edgar Allan Poe on Mars; The Katrina Protocol; Pacifica 1, 2; Robonocchio; Return of the*

Nyctalope; (anthologists) *Tales of the Shadowmen 1-12; The Vampire Almanac* (2 vols.)

Ch. Lomon & P.-B. Gheuzi. *The Last Days of Atlantis*

Camille Mauclair. *The Virgin Orient*

Xavier Mauméjean. *The League of Heroes*

Joseph Méry. *The Tower of Destiny*

Hippolyte Mettais. *Paris Before the Deluge; The Year 5865*

Louise Michel. *The Human Microbes; The New World*

Tony Moilin. *Paris in the Year 2000*

José Moselli. *Illa's End*

John-Antoine Nau. *Enemy Force*

Marie Nizet. *Captain Vampire*

Charles Nodier. *Trilby and The Crumb Fairy*

C. Nodier, A. Beraud & Toussaint-Merle. *Frankenstein*

Henri de Parville. *An Inhabitant of the Planet Mars*

Gaston de Pawlowski. *Journey to the Land of the 4th Dimension*

Georges Pellerin. *The World in 2000 Years*

Ernest Pérochon. *The Frenetic People*

Pierre Pelot. *The Child Who Walked on the Sky*

Jean Petithuguenin. *An International Mission to the Moon*

J. Polidori, C. Nodier, E. Scribe. *Lord Ruthven the Vampire*

P.-A. Ponson du Terrail. *The Immortal Woman; The Vampire and the Devil's Son*

Georges Price. *The Missing Men of the* Sirius

René Pujol. *The Chimerical Quest*

Edgar Quinet. *Ahasuerus; The Enchanter Merlin*

Henri de Régnier. *A Surfeit of Mirrors*

Maurice Renard. *The Blue Peril; Doctor Lerne; The Doctored Man; A Man Among the Microbes; The Master of Light*

Restif de la Bretonne. *The Discovery of the Austral Continent by a Flying Man*

Jean Richepin. *The Crazy Corner; The Wing*

Albert Robida. *The Adventures of Saturnin Farandoul; Chalet in the Sky; The Clock of the Centuries; The Electric Life; The Engineer Von Satanas*

J.-H. Rosny Aîné. *Helgvor of the Blue River; The Givreuse Enigma; The Mysterious Force; The Navigators of Space; Vamireh; The World of the Variants; The Young Vampire*
Marcel Rouff. *Journey to the Inverted World*
Marie-Anne de Roumier-Robert. *The Voyage of Lord Seaton to the Seven Planets*
Léonie Rouzade. *The World Turned Upside Down*
Han Ryner. *The Human Ant; The Superhumans*
Frank Schildiner. *The Quest of Frankenstein*
Pierre de Selenes: *An Unknown World*
Angelo de Sorr. *The Vampires of London*
Brian Stableford. *The Empire of the Necromancers (1. The Shadow of Frankenstein; 2. Frankenstein and the Vampire Countess; 3. Frankenstein in London); Eurydice's Lament; The New Faust at the Tragicomique; Sherlock Holmes and The Vampires of Eternity; The Stones of Camelot; The Wayward Muse.* (anthologist) *News from the Moon; The Germans on Venus; The Supreme Progress; The World Above the World; Nemoville; Investigations of the Future; The Conqueror of Death; The Revolt of the Machines; The Man With the Blue Face; The Aerial Valley; The New Moon; The Nickel Man; On the Brink of the World's End; The Mirror of Present Events*
Jacques Spitz. *The Eye of Purgatory*
Kurt Steiner. *Ortog*
Eugène Thébault. *Radio-Terror*
C.-F. Tiphaigne de La Roche. *Amilec*
Simon Tyssot de Patot. *The Strange Voyages of Jacques Massé and Pierre de Mésange*
Louis Ulbach. *Prince Bonifacio*
Théo Varlet. *The Castaways of Eros; The Golden Rock.; The Martian Epic* (w/Octave Joncquel); *Timeslip Troopers* (w/André Blandin); *The Xenobiotic Invasion*
Pierre Véron. *The Merchants of Health*
Paul Vibert. *The Mysterious Fluid*
Villiers de l'Isle-Adam. *The Scaffold; The Vampire Soul*
Gaston de Wailly. *The Murderer of the World*

Philippe Ward. *Artahe ; Manhattan Ghost* (w/Mickael Laguerre); *The Song of Montségur* (w/Sylvie Miller)

Victor Margueritte. *The Bacheloress; The Companion; The Couple*